For
Amy Wiener Sosnov
my sister and dear friend

Jo Joe

Jo Joe

a Black Bear, Pennsylvania Story
by Sally Wiener Grotta

PIXEL HALL PRESS
Newfoundland, PA USA
www.PixelHallPress.com

Jo Joe
by Sally Wiener Grotta

Published by Pixel Hall Press
Newfoundland, PA USA
www.PixelHallPress.com

ISBN: 978-0-9883871-1-9

Library of Congress Control Number: 2012922371

Publisher's Cataloging-In-Publication Data

Grotta, Sally Wiener, 1959-
    Jo Joe : a Black Bear, Pennsylvania story / by Sally Wiener Grotta. -- 1st ed.

        p. ; cm. -- ([Black Bear, Pennsylvania stories])

    Issued also as an ebook.
    ISBN: 978-0-9883871-4-0 (hardbound)
    ISBN: 978-0-9883871-1-9 (trade pbk.)

    1. Racially mixed women--Pennsylvania--Fiction. 2. Jewish women--
Pennsylvania--Fiction. 3. Grandparent and child--Pennsylvania--Fiction. 4.
Discrimination--Pennsylvania--Fiction. 5. Secrets--Pennsylvania--Fiction. 6.
American fiction--Women authors. I. Title.

PS3607.R688 J6 2013
813/.6   2012922371

TABLE OF CONTENTS

MONDAY

"Welcome to Black Bear, Pennsylvania." The carved wooden sign is new — dark forest green with gold-leaf lettering — the best that the firehouse cake sale could buy, no doubt. Little else seems changed as I drive down Main Street. I've been gone half my lifetime, and this tiny, insular mountain village appears just as threadbare as ever.

Seventeen years ago, I fled Black Bear, returning to Paris for university, vowing I'd never come back. If it hadn't been for that anonymous phone call, I never would have set foot in this town again. Does death nullify vows?

In the center of the village, at the crossroads where it all started over a hundred and fifty years ago, are the venerable steepled Moravian church and the modern single story Catholic Church across the street. For a Monday afternoon, the Chug-a-Lug beer distributor is busy, with two mud-splattered pickup trucks and an old beat-up Mustang in the lot. As usual, Cliff's True Value's inventory spills out onto its cracked asphalt parking lot, trying to convince lake tourists and returning snowbirds to stop and buy as they zoom past, routinely breaking the 25 miles per hour speed limit. Why Cliff doesn't close on Mondays had been a mystery to Grampa. "No one does yard work or barbecues or puttering on Monday," he would say. "Not when they have the weekend to rest up from, and the work-a-day week ahead of them."

And there, next to Engelhardt's sprawling Ford dealership, the vile old school is still a blot on the landscape, boarded up and falling down. How typical.

But no, not everything is the same. Some things — and people — are irretrievably lost. Next to Engelhardt's Auto Supply and across from the old school is Grampa's drug store, now a second-hand clothing shop. I wonder, what have they done with Gramp's soda fountain and snack counter? Are neatly folded recycled baby jumpers piled on the chrome and red leatherette stools where I used to love to twirl? Black Bear must have been one of the last places on earth where the local pharmacist would greet you by name and know how you liked your milkshake as well as what medicines you took, when and why. The Rite-Aid in Hamlin put an end to that about fifteen years ago, forcing Gramps out of business, but he had written me that he'd been thinking of retiring anyway. Or had he already known that he was dying and would be gone in a couple of years?

I pull into Dutch's service station, to top up the fuel tank. Ever since I first learned to drive, Gramps drilled into me that I should never, ever let the gas get below a half tank — just in case. Not that I was an overly obedient teenager; I would often drive until the car was almost empty. But I learned my lesson that horrid night after the homecoming game in my senior year, when I ran out of gas on Drumheller Lane. Fleeing for my life from that dark dirt road was a suitably wretched finish to the miserable day that changed everything. Now, back in Black Bear, where I vowed I'd never return, I'm determined to heed every precaution necessary to make it through this one week, including filling up my rental car at Dutch's before leaving town for the farm.

Just as I flip open the door to the car's gas cap, a big white man in his mid-thirties yells from the service bay, "Hey, I'll do that for you, miss!" and limps toward me as quickly as his bad right leg lets him.

I remember how Old Man Dutch used to rant at the alleged convenience store gas stations that had sprouted along the interstate. "Where the hell's the service in self-serve?" he'd ask.

This enormous man, with his unkempt, thinning, dark blonde hair and that beer belly protruding over his low jeans, isn't Dutch. Still, he must agree with Dutch because after he starts pumping the gas, he actually squeegees the car's windshield and rear window. All the while, staring at me.

Well, I knew that would be part of coming back. They never did get used to my dark skin, flat nose and kinky hair around here in Wonder White Bread territory. "You're like a one-two punch, for some folks," Gramma once tried to explain. "You're Schmoyer through and through, down to the family hazel eyes and high cheek bones, but in a very different package from anything they've ever known. You confuse them."

Confuse isn't the word I would use to describe how Black Bear reacts to anyone who's "different." From a young age, I learned to try to ignore the rude stares and cruel jibes.

So, why does the way this man's icy blue eyes bore into me make my skin crawl? Something about how his lop-sided grin seems to consume his entire face — it's all too disturbing — and familiar.

Even as he replaces the pump nozzle, caps the tank and wipes a spot where the gas splashed on the side panel, he doesn't take his eyes off me. "*Jo...?*" he finally asks, then, catches himself before saying anything else. Now, those pale, searing eyes that he couldn't keep off me just a moment ago are diverted everywhere but on my face. Mostly, he focuses on the oil splattered, cracked concrete around his feet.

Oh no! It can't be. Not this massive wreck of a man. His puffy face has that grizzled look of someone who's lived and worked hard. Wrinkles punctuate his eyes and mouth, like parentheses cut into his flesh. His nose has obviously been broken, perhaps more than once. And he's hunched over and soft, nothing like the wide-eyed, fair-haired, muscular football hero of our high school days. Once upon a time, nothing could have convinced me that a day would come when I wouldn't instantly recognize Joe Anderson, regardless of how long we'd been apart. Yet, it takes hearing his hesitant, hoarse voice, saying that damned nickname he gave me, before I can be sure he really is Joe Anderson.

Despite myself, I step back, hating that, after all these years, he can still make me flinch. "Hello, Joe," I say, determined to keep my tone even and unemotional.

He's standing so close that the smell of sweat and motor oil permeating his clothes wash over me. Stuffing his large, oil-rimmed hands into his scruffy jeans pockets, he mumbles. "Hell, you really did come back."

"Yes, well, Gramma's dead." To say it still doesn't give it any sense of reality.

"Yeah, I know."

I glance at the numbers on the pump. $37.50 for only a half tank of regular unleaded. A family of six in the Congo could live on that for a month, if they were lucky enough to have someone earning actual cash. When I hand my credit card out to Joe, he looks at it, starts to reach for it, then shakes his head. "Naw, don't bother. I own this place now." I guess he wants to show me that he's actually made something of himself.

Treating me to a few gallons of fuel is a meaningless gesture that isn't worth arguing over. I simply say "Thank you," as I concentrate on putting away my wallet, though gratitude is the furthest thing from my mind. All I want is to get away from him — fast. I force myself to not look in the rear view mirror, as I drive off.

Merde! Why did I have to run into that bastard the very second I return to Black Bear? *Damn him!* Even after so many years, just seeing Joe still twists me up inside. But then, for nearly two decades, my memories of Joe Anderson have been a scarred-over thorn that jabs painfully whenever anyone else tries to get close.

Hungry, and doubting that there'll be anything fresh to eat in the house, I stop at Buck's ShurSave. It hadn't been a franchise market seventeen years ago, and certainly not as bright and spacious. However, even if the new building is more antiseptic and anonymous, the prices and the produce look as good as ever.

I should know better than to walk into a supermarket only two days out of Africa; it usually takes me at least a week to decompress and readjust to the modern world. After spending even only a short time in one of my impoverished villages, I start to see things through the eyes of the women I work with. How amazed they would be at the variety and quantity of cheap, wholesome food available to everyone, including the poorest.

Buck's is so mannerly and clean, with none of Africa's pungent smells of overripe or rotting produce. But it's also bland, without the gem-like, almost riotous earthy colors of clothes, food and people under the scintillating African sun. The white noise Muzak punctuated with monotone announcements calling for *"Clean up in aisle three,"* and *"Don't miss our special on ground round, only $3.29 a pound"* is a far cry from the squeals and cackles of penned animals being bartered for the butcher's knife mixed with the ancient calls of the street sellers who don't hesitate to grab your sleeve to get you to stop and buy their wares. Long ago, I learned not to wear long sleeved light colored blouses when shopping in African open-air markets, because they end up grungy and grey from all the dirty hands pushing, pulling and grabbing. Even so, village market day still infuses me with a sense of exotic adventure, of the possibility of discovering a hidden treasure in the next stall, or the one behind it.

Shopping in Buck's, I feel as though I've been transported overnight to a sterile, futuristic, entirely predictable world, where everything is well organized, neatly packaged and sane. I can't deny the appeal of the safely refrigerated meat and dairy and the floral attractiveness of the cool-misted produce — with not one mosquito or fly in sight. My cart soon overflows with crisp baby spinach, plump vine-ripened red tomatoes, fat Vidalia onions, enormous strawberries, fresh asparagus stalks, a wedge of double Gloucester cheese, fresh whole milk, free range eggs, multigrain sourdough bread and other memory-laced delicacies. Even a locally baked cinnamon raisin cake. I haven't been in a western supermarket for more than three months; strange that the first one is Buck's.

While the store isn't crowded, no aisle is empty. As I would expect in Black Bear, not one shopper or employee is black or brown. Most people ignore me, as they concentrate on their shopping lists, on the labels and prices of food, or on their children riding in the baskets surrounded by cartons, cans and packages. A few stare at me, and two even nod. I don't recognize anyone, though several look vaguely familiar. Perhaps, it has to do with the limited gene pool, among the local mountain folk as opposed to the New York commuters. No, that's unfair of me to stereotype like that. But then, this is Black Bear, and fair is not a concept that has much traction here.

In the dairy department, a chubby twenty-something woman wearing a brown cable sweater and black Levis approaches me. "You're Judith Ormand, aren't you?" she asks hesitantly. She's too young for me to have known her.

"Yes," I respond, somewhat warily.

"I knew it! I saw your picture in *The Gazette.* People talked about it for weeks, about the important work you're doing." Then, she pauses. "Hey, sorry about your grandmother."

I say, "Thank you," as I roll my cart away.

The cashier is of a type that seems frozen in time. Dry, over-processed bleached hair with visible dark roots, pendulous breasts sagging to a waist that disappeared long ago, nicotine stains on her fissured fingers and cracked nails. She has the hardened look of a woman who has too many children and too little hope. I read the name tag under the faded artificial orchid. *Maybeth?* No, it couldn't be! This woman has to be years older than I. Still, the more I watch her ring up my overly large order, her arms moving with the speed of an automaton who has probably been performing these identical motions every day for years, the more I'm certain this is the same girl who was prom queen and head cheerleader. Maybeth. The most popular girl in town. Every boy's fantasy. And my personal nemesis from my first day in seventh grade until the day I graduated.

Gramma wouldn't be proud of me, not if she could read my mind, as I often felt she could. Seeing Maybeth the way she is now and remembering how she once was... well... how far the mighty have fallen.

Maybeth stops briefly in the middle of scanning the bag of Granny Smith apples and stares at me. "Hey, I know you," she says, not quite belligerent, but not friendly either.

I'm not sure how to respond, so I'm relieved when my cell phone chooses that moment to ring.

"Allo!" I answer in French, as I usually do.

"Hello, Judith." I instantly recognize Nigel's voice, calling from London. "How is everything?"

"Hello," I say, quickly switching to English.

Maybeth appears to have completely forgotten about me. Her head is down, following her hands from the food on the conveyer belt, to the scanner scale, then to the bags at her side. Such concentrated attention to details, focusing on accomplishing this one job that probably keeps her and her family going.

"Look, Judith, you don't have to go through this alone," Nigel repeats the same sentiment in different words that he said to me yesterday. "I can be on a plane to the States this evening. Let me do this for you."

I should know better by now than to get involved with an unmarried man. Not that Nigel isn't a dear person and a generous lover, but he's too readily available and wants more from me that I'm able to give. "That's sweet, Nigel. But no thank you. I've far too much to do this week to pay attention to anyone else." I hand Maybeth my credit card.

"I'm not asking for attention," Nigel insists. "Quite the opposite."

"I know Nigel." I sign the credit card screen. Then, I tuck the phone between my cheek and shoulder and start to put the bags into my shopping cart, but the damned device keeps slipping. Seeing my difficulty, Maybeth takes over loading the cart. "I'll see you in about a month," I promise Nigel. "After I return to Paris from Africa."

"Promise me you'll call, if you need anything. Or just to talk."

It's a kind, guileless offer, but I'm not about to make any promises to a man, especially not to a lover. "Good bye, Nigel." He really deserves better than me.

"Goodbye, Judith. I love you."

I slip the phone into my jeans pocket. With a nod, I say "Thank you" to Maybeth.

She holds out my credit card, but doesn't quite hand it back, staring intently at the name embossed on the plastic instead. After an awkward moment, she says, "I'm right. I *do* know you. You're Martha Schmoyer's girl."

"Yes," I admit. I really don't want to have this conversation with her.

Continuing to gawk, she smirks. "Well, I'll be... never thought I'd see you again. You actually came back. Guess folks were wrong. Welcome home, Judy."

"Judith," I correct her.

"Yeah. Sorry about your grandma."

"Thank you." I reach over and take my credit card from her unresisting hand.

The man in line behind me loudly clears his throat, reminding Maybeth to get back to work. I nod to him apologetically and wheel my cart out of Buck's, chagrined at the amount of food I've purchased, knowing what wealth and potential waste it represents. At least, none of it's rice or beans or cassava.

Everywhere else in the northern hemisphere, April reclaims the earth with colors and fragrances. But here in the Pennsylvanian Pocono Mountains, it's the season of mud, floods, and the usual surprise springtime snowstorms. Still, the stark, promising beauty around me is gentle and benign compared to Africa's exotic and often dangerous extremes of scorching red dust deserts, lush steamy rain forests and forever-sky savannahs.

When I turn onto Mountainview Road, each tree and bend pulls at yet another memory — of the weekend trips with Mom from Manhattan after we left *Papa* and Paris, the walks with Gramps when he'd try to teach me the names of the many different birds we saw and heard, Mom's funeral when Gramma told me I would have to return to Paris, to live with *Papa*. But I didn't get along with Bridget and the twins and the new life *Papa* had made with them. So, *Papa* shipped me back once more to Black Bear, to live with Gramma and Grampa and the birds whose names I never did get straight. I hadn't even had my *bat mitzvah* yet, and *Papa* had forsaken me to my white Moravian grandparents and their clannish village of sanctimonious, so-called Christians. How homeless I felt, leaving Paris for exile in Black Bear, not really believing I belonged in either place.

I pull into the driveway, turn off the engine and drink it all in. The generations-old stone house with its wraparound wood porch, slate roof and white shuttered windows. Gramma should be standing there at the door, looking at me, wondering why I didn't get out and get moving, waiting for her hug and kiss. Over to the left, the unpainted, weather-beaten barn, which hadn't been used as a barn since Grampa's father's time, had been Grampa's workshop and garage. I used to think he could make or repair anything, but that was before I learned how much hurt there was in this small village. Hurt that could break something inside a young girl that even Grampa couldn't fix.

The bare fruit trees and budding bushes seem much taller, but the evergreens surrounding the property are the same towering sentinels they always were, enclosing and protecting me from whatever lay beyond. How strange to be here at the farm once more — the one place that I once considered my only real home — the one place I solemnly vowed never to return.

I get out of the car, close my eyes and take a deep breath. Yes, there in the taste of clean, crisp mountain air are the deepest and sweetest memories, the ones that no words could describe or encompass, of loving refuge in

Gramma's kitchen or Grampa's workshop or my bedroom under the eaves. When I open my eyes again, however, everything is as cold and empty as before. Without the two of them, the farm is nothing more than a commodity, a piece of property, an unwanted responsibility that I need to dispose of before I can get on with my life.

I have never understood why I've carried the key to this house wherever I've traveled. What makes it even stranger is that I've never used it, not even when I lived here. Had this house ever been locked up before now?

Before turning the key, I gaze at the right doorpost. It's still there, the *mezuzah* Grampa installed that first day I came here to live with them.

"Why are you doing that?" I asked him as he bent down to screw it in at just the right angle, making sure it wasn't too high for me to reach. "You're not Jewish, Grampa."

"You are, Judith," he answered in his gentle voice. "And this is your home, too."

I press my fingertips to the *mezuzah*, not so much in ritual, but more to touch something that was Grampa's and mine. When I sell this place, I will take it with me, even though I have no doorpost where it could go. The apartment in Paris is nothing more than a rest stop, an oversized *pied à terre* that *Papa* and I both use but never share, with him in Brussels or London or wherever his politics take him, and me running around Africa, trying to stop the hurt, one woman at a time. It's been years since we were last in the same city at the same time. No, this *mezuzah* doesn't belong there. Besides, the Paris apartment has its own, placed by *Grand-père* when he purchased the building just after The War.

The farmhouse is almost completely silent, other than the usual floorboard creaks. If it weren't bereft of all who should be here and aren't, I might consider it peaceful. I head right for the kitchen. There, I put away the groceries, wash the fruit and vegetables, and busy myself with what needs to be done to settle in, trying not to see or feel too much. But the kitchen works its way into me despite my best efforts.

Gramma's kitchen, with its large windows over-looking her vegetable garden and the path to the barn. The old, handmade walnut cabinets are full of canned goods and the same spatterware china and assorted unmatched glass-ware that we used day in and day out. In the cupboard is what must be a five-year supply of homemade jams and preserves, though the fancy paper labels have a stranger's cursive handwriting very unlike the hurried scrawl of Gramma's usual black marker.

I boil a couple of eggs, tear a handful of lettuce and sliced up some strawberries along with all the other fixings for my salad. Gramma stored the numerous bottles of wine I'd sent them over the years, not in the aluminum wine rack we picked out together (which is nowhere to be found), but upright in the cabinet over the sink. I almost give up looking for the corkscrew, finally finding it buried deep in a jumbled bottom drawer among other seldom used utensils. I open a *Pinot noir*, putting a *Pouillez-Fuisse* in the fridge for later.

I take my usual place at the old plank table. Perhaps, out of habit, or simply because I can't bring myself to sit in Grampa's chair at the head of the table or Gramma's next to him, nearest the sink and oven. Fingering the unfamiliar blue and white linen placemat, I look for the telltale signs of Gramma's tiny, almost even stitches. No doubt the old yellow mats had frayed with use and age. Did Gramma sew these, too, or did she purchase them at one of the church craft sales?

Never one to pray before a meal, not since I left Black Bear, unless it's out of respect for local customs, the *Motzi* comes to my lips, for the first time in years. Some-how, here, at the farm, it's appropriate, where at every meal Grampa would say grace in the name of Jesus and then ask me to give the Jewish blessing over our bread.

"*Baruch atah Adonai Eloheinu Melech Haolam, hamotzi lechem min haaretz.*" How easily the Hebrew flows, dredged up from a time when I still believed, flavor-ing my meal in Gramma's kitchen with a sense of the sacredness of memory and the grace of their love.

After supper, I retreat outside to the porch swing that Grampa's dad had built. Wrapped in one of Gramma's colorful hand knit lap afghans, I watch the twilight fade to a moonless darkness that soon softens as my eyes adjust to the barely visible light. The trees and barn are deep feature-less shadows against the sky; only a handful of stars cut through the low clouds. Soon, the air chills, promising a typical April frost. On evenings such as this, Gramps would sometimes come out, bringing my parka and his pipe; Gramma wouldn't let him smoke inside the house. And we'd talk, or we'd just let the quiet seep into us.

I can't recall when I last allowed myself to sit silently, with no purpose other than to be fully where I am. As much as I fantasize about slowing down, taking time for myself, I never dreamed it would be here. Yet, here I am, where my body remembers the comfortable fit of the swing, the touch of the afghan's age-soft wool and the taste of the evergreen-laden air.

How bizarre life can be, turning around on itself in the blink of an eye. Forty-two hours ago, I was in Dakar, where every breath coated my mouth, throat and lungs with cloying dust. Three days ago, I was so deep in the Senegalese interior that nothing seemed to exist other than our overworked field facilitators, the bone-weary women who are our clients, and the ossified, obstructive all-male tribal bureaucracy.

Les Femmes has proven to be a better antidote for me than years of self-absorbed introspection. After all, what are my personal problems and private demons compared to those of our impoverished clients, who struggle daily to feed their families, and whose greatest dream is that some-day, somehow, they might be able to afford school fees for all their children? I can lose myself in my work in the bush; I like it that way. How much more alive — and relevant — it makes me feel than the Parisian social whirl of inane dinner parties and extravagant, profligate fundraisers. In the primitive isolation of our village outposts, I can almost forget that the outside world exists — that Black Bear ever had any power over me, or that Paris has so little.

That is, until that phone call.

The first thing I do whenever I emerge from one of our client villages into a town or city — or somewhere I can get a phone or Internet connection — is call Catherine, my admirably efficient secretary at *Les Femmes'* headquarters in Paris. Instead of rattling off the usual list of business messages, status reports, funding challenges, or requests for appointments and interviews, Catherine quickly told me about the anonymous phone call, alerting me, *"Break your promise. Return to Black Bear immediately. Your grandmother needs you."* The message had come through the international donations line rather than directly to our Paris headquarters, so it had probably passed through a multi-lingual whispering down the lane, before it reached my office. Catherine couldn't even say if it had been left by a man or a woman, or precisely when. All she knew for certain was that it had been routed to her desk three weeks ago. Since then, Catherine had been prepared with a schedule of flights to the States, anticipating my immediate return to Black Bear, before I could even conceive of such a thing. I had her book me on the first available flight out of Dakar. Then, I called the farm, and a stranger answered, a woman named Anita, who told me that Gramma had died that morning.

Although I left Africa that afternoon, it took me nearly two days and a tortuous series of connecting flights before I finally landed at JFK.

I shiver. Without Gramps and my parka, it's too cold and lonely to stay out on the porch. I retreat inside, grab my suitcase and head toward the stairs and my childhood bedroom on the second floor.

Before going upstairs to bed, I pause to stand in the doorway to Grampa and Gramma's room, as I so often did back when the three of us lived here. My night-adjusted eyes take everything in. The four-poster bed and highboy bureau, the windows with their ivory damask curtains drawn open, the mirrored vanity that Gramma seldom used. I say my usual "Good night," but it's a hollow gesture that I regret as soon as the words leave my lips. The room is dark and empty. More than that, it's sterile, with no life, no odors.

All my memories of Gramma and Grampa have smells. His cherry tobacco. Her rosewater and Pond's cream. And their other indefinable personal fragrances that told me they were in a room even if I didn't see them. Someone has scoured their bedroom thoroughly, erasing any hint of them. All that's left are cold artifacts and a disturbing hint of antiseptics.

Since the mid-1800s, the eldest in every generation of Schmoyers had moved into the master bedroom. It is by tradition and heritage my rightful place, as the last surviving member of the family.

Not tonight. Perhaps tomorrow.

Back when I moved in with Gramma and Grampa, I could have chosen any of the empty bedrooms. Certainly, Mom's in the new wing is more spacious and convenient. Uncle Robby's has that lovely view of the small garden pond. Or I could have settled into either of the guestrooms where Grampa's two spinster sisters had lived out their lives before I had a chance to know them. Instead, I claimed and fixed up the attic storage room in the old wing, attracted by its isolation from the rest of the house and the way the eaves carved all those interesting angles in the ceiling — and because it would be entirely mine, not Mom's or Robby's or Grampa's sisters'.

I don't need to switch on the lights to navigate the dark narrow stairs to my small bedroom. My feet know their way, know the shape and sensation of the worn wooden planks, even the creak of the step just before the halfway landing. A creak that I now welcome, remembering how it used to alert Gramma and Grampa that I was moving about. If it were in the middle of the night, Gramps would often come out from their bedroom just below the stairs to check on me, to make sure everything was all right. As I grew older, I learned to avoid that one step. Not now. I want Gramps to come and ask his questions that I once thought so intrusive.

Tonight, all the creak does is remind me how quiet everything else is. Quiet and dead. Not even a dog or cat underfoot. Is it the deep shadows of the stairway that bring that memory forward? The feeling of having to watch my step wherever I went, because Rascal, my foundling kitten, used to try to keep pace with me. And Maverick, Grampa's old mongrel hunting hound, considered it his personal duty to keep an eye on me, when he wasn't trailing Gramps. I'd come home from school, and there they'd be, side-by-side, sitting patiently on the porch, waiting for me — Rascal and Maverick. My constant companions, my two truest friends regardless of what happened in the outside world of school and village. Even when I tried to hide away in the woods, in the treehouse that Gramps had helped Joe and me build that first summer, Rascal would climb up after me, and Maverick would stand guard at the base of the tree.

Maverick died of old age the year after I left Black Bear. Rascal was run over by the heating oil delivery truck the following winter. Neither death felt very real to me, when Gramma wrote me about them. Whenever I pictured the farm, it was with Gramma in the kitchen, her garden or talking with me in her bedroom, Grampa in his workshop or study or sitting with me on the porch, and Maverick and Rascal nearby, playing or sleeping on top of each other, watching me, filling empty rooms and empty days with warmth and life.

Gramma and Grampa kept other pets since then. After Grampa died, they became even more central to Gramma, filling her letters and, in recent years, her emails, with their antics and personalities. The latest were Martin, Tedda and Acey. I assume that Gramma arranged good homes for them, before she died. I certainly can't take them with me, not the way I travel.

Here I am, back at my grandparents' home, and I'm still essentially homeless, no place where I belong, nowhere I can keep a pet and look forward to it greeting me whenever I return. But what was my sad fate as a child has become my choice as an adult. I prefer the constant rootless travel of my work, sometimes a different country every week, unencumbered by personal attachments, and free to achieve something meaningful.

When I get too old to travel, then I might find a place in the woods to live, tend a garden and have a dog and cat who would love me regardless of what the outside world thinks or does.

"Ouch!" I bang my shin on something just inside my bedroom, where there should be only empty space delineated by the old hook rug. Dropping my suitcase, I reach for the wall light switch, roll up my pants leg and gently touch a new red welt. No real damage, though it'll probably turn into an ugly purple bruise. Much more bothersome is the malformed chair that caused it. I threw that thing away years ago. And on my bureau and bookshelves, among my various school awards and family pictures, are photos that Gramma must have retrieved from the same rubbish heap.

Sitting on my old narrow bed, I stare at the relics of my life in Black Bear, wondering what it was that made Gramma restore the room to reflect my early years here rather than how I left it. But there he is, everywhere I look, even in that grotesque chair we made together in Grampa's workshop.

Joe Anderson.

It makes absolutely no sense. Gramma distrusted Joe and was clearly relieved when I decided to excise him from my life. After all her machinations to break us apart, why would she do this — find and save all the Joe-and-Judith crap that I tossed out, and put them back in place?

First thing tomorrow, I'm going to burn that mis-shapen chair and those stupid photos once and for all, just as I must dispose of so much in this house.

I throw my suitcase onto my old desk. Why bother unpacking? I'll live out of my suitcase, as I often do in other transitory abodes around the world.

As exhausted and jet-lagged as I am, when I huddle under the covers, my mind refuses to close down, and I replay the stories of each of those damned photos of Joe and me, and Joe and Gramps, and Joe and Gramma and me, and Joe.

Joe Anderson, my knight in shining armor. That's how I thought of him from that very first day at Wallenpau-pack Junior High. All the stares and taunts that had been mounting since Grampa had dropped me off that morning erupted after school, just outside the playground where everyone waited for the buses.

Maybeth Peters and Janice Wilson and Tracy Rauff sauntered over to the tall chain link fence and draped themselves on it. Miniskirted cheerleader decorations, meant to be admired and ogled. Only thirteen years old, and those girls already knew how to use sex to attract attention and instigate trouble. Especially pert, blonde, bosomy Maybeth.

I watched them. But then, everyone in the yard was watching them. That was the whole point and purpose of their performance, wasn't it? So why did my stare deserve that curled lip and daggered look from Maybeth?

All it took was Maybeth's sneer to ignite the boys.

Billy Thompson, Maybeth's current favorite, swag-gered toward me in a slow threatening manner that made my stomach knot. "*Hey, nigger,*" he snarled in his high-pitched voice, a lanky red-headed juggernaut. I didn't back away; something rooted my feet to the asphalt. Perhaps I was too dumbfounded or frightened to move. He stood so close to me, his scrawny freckled face only inches away from mine, I could smell the peanut butter cracker he'd just eaten. "Whatcha think you're looking at?" he demanded.

"Yeah, nigger," George Amack was at my right shoulder. "Whatcha looking at?"

And Jason Haupt on my left.

"*Nigger! Nigger! Nigger!*" they chanted over and over, in syncopated rhythms that sprayed my face and ears with their wet breaths.

I didn't know what to do, how to react. It was all so unreal, nothing that could ever happen to *me*. I clutched my books to my chest, clamping down on the tears that burned my throat, not letting them spill, not giving these boys and their silent cheerleaders the satisfaction of knowing how much they were hurting and frightening me.

Billy was the first to push my shoulder, with a flat-handed jab. The other two followed with progressively harder shoves and pokes. Not punches. Not yet. My center of balance tilted backward, forcing me to step away with each blow, until my back was against the chain link fence, and I could go no further.

Then Joe showed up.

Bigger in all dimensions than the largest of the boys who surrounded me, Joe didn't really have to say or do anything. Just "Hey!" which got their immediate attention. The mob of kids parted to either side of him, as he walked toward me, but they reassembled as soon as he passed, continuing to block my escape. The closer Joe approached, the smaller I felt. Small and vulnerable, knowing that this blonde giant could cream me without breaking into a sweat.

But Joe didn't lay a finger on me. Instead, he turned his back to me, blocking my view so I couldn't see the other kids' faces. He told them, "Leave her alone now. She's okay." Then, he looked over his shoulder at me and said, "Let's go."

The Black Bear bus — number 11 —rolled up, and Joe and I were the first to board. I sat against the window in the front row, while Joe wedged himself into the seat beside me. Everyone piled in after us, glaring at me or purposely averting their eyes as they walked past. However, because of Joe, no one dared say anything to me.

Those few horrifying moments in the school yard lasted no more than the time it took a bus to drive up the short, steep hill from Route 507 to its slot on the other side of the chain link fence. But they've echoed through the years, defining Black Bear for me. Until that day, I had thought of myself as half-American, half-French and thoroughly Jewish, with a proud, varied heritage that included African forebears. Those mean-spirited, bigoted bullies, especially Maybeth and Billy, showed me that none of that mattered in Black Bear. I looked different from everyone else and that was reason enough for them to behave like a pack of wild dogs.

I'll never know why Joe came to my rescue that afternoon, or how it was that he went against everyone he'd grown up with to become my protector and my friend, staying by my side in school, whenever possible. Unfortunately, we didn't share many classes, so Billy, Maybeth and their gang had plenty of opportunities to bait and threaten me when they knew Joe wouldn't be anywhere near. I quickly learned to avoid certain lunchroom tables, empty corners where I could be trapped, or being found alone in the girls' room.

About two months after that first playground encounter, Billy went too far. I was late for history class, and the halls were deserted. When I saw Billy leaning against the wall, I sped up, trying not to run, but needing to get past him as fast as possible. I thought I had made it free and clear, when he seized my arm with such force that my books sprayed across the floor. Twisting my hands behind me, he pushed me up against a locker, with a sickly sounding thwack. His full body pressed against me, pinning my chest and pelvis with his, crushing my hands between the metal of the locker and my body.

"You got no respect, nigger, treating me like... *ugh!*" Billy fell backward, clutching his crotch with both hands where I had kneed him.

I ran, stopping only to scoop up my books, but not looking back until I reached the door to my classroom. I took a couple of deep breaths, trying to slow down my racing heart, hoping I could walk into the room calmly, as though nothing had happened. When I opened the door, all eyes turned to stare at me, because I was late and disrupting the class. Then, Janie Yoder yelled, "*Eeyew! She's bleeding!*" I hadn't even realized that my left hand had been cut against the locker. I tried to wipe away the blood with a Kleenex, but Mrs. Gauger insisted on sending me to the nurse, which meant navigating the empty halls again, all alone. Luckily, this time they were truly empty.

Until I walked into the infirmary that afternoon, I had seen Ms. Ellert, the school nurse, only from afar, in the hallways or on the auditorium stage during Assembly. Up close, I realized that she was a lot younger than I had thought — probably in her late twenties or early thirties. But she seemed older, softer, with a gentle roundness that hasn't been fashionable since long before my great-grandparents were born. She was so very white — white skin, white uniform, and even a starched white nurse's cap; her skin had a slight blue tinge, and her eyes were an almost colorless blue. Her light brown hair was pinned into an impeccable bun under her cap. While she cleaned and wrapped the gash with a pressure bandage to stop the bleeding, she stared at me, as though, if she looked long and hard enough, she would burn the truth out of me.

"Who did this to you?" she demanded.

I shook my head and clamped my mouth tightly shut, afraid that if I opened it, even a tiny bit, only sobs would come out. I didn't want to cry in front of this stranger.

Ms. Ellert wouldn't leave it alone, and kept repeating, "Who did this?"

Eventually, I mumbled, "I fell."

She arched her left eyebrow in disbelief, but gave up trying to wrangle the story out of me.

Blood seeped through the bandage regardless of how much gauze she wrapped around it, so she insisted on calling Gramma.

I waited for Gramma in the tiny infirmary, the silence as palpable as the heavy ticking of the black second hand on the white-faced wall clock above the door. When-ever I looked up from the grey speckled linoleum floor, Ms. Ellert was staring at me, but I couldn't meet her gaze. I burned with shame, with the memory of Billy's body pressed against mine, the invasive, ruthless strength of him, making me feel so powerless, so humiliated.

Gramma stomped into the office, without knocking on the frosted glass-paned door. One glance at the bloody bandage on my hand, and she glared at Ms. Ellert. "What happened to my child?"

"Ask her," Ms. Ellert said, pointing at me.

"Well, Judith?" Gramma demanded in that tone that was more a command than a question.

"I fell and cut myself," I replied, forcing myself to look her right in the eyes when I said it.

"I'll get to the bottom of this, believe you me," Gramma said to Ms. Ellert, before rushing me off to old Doc Tallman, who closed up the gash with six stitches. I still bear that scar, a small crescent paler than the rest of my hand, a touchstone of violence permanently etched into my flesh.

What was strange was that Gramma never talked to me about the incident, never probed with her impossible-to-evade questions. Perhaps, she understood how mortified I was about it and, in her own stoic manner, was trying to help me forget.

Gramma kept me home the rest of the day.

Joe was at the Mountainview Road bus stop the next morning, waiting for me. "Hi Judy," he said as though it were normal for him to be standing there. But it wasn't. His stop was nearly two miles away, at Small Brook Road.

"Hi Joe," I replied. "What are you doing here?"

"I wanted to make sure you're okay. How's the hand?"

I showed him the bandage and flexed my fingers. "Everything still works. No permanent damage."

Joe's face burned beet red, but he didn't say anything. What was even queerer was that when the bus came, he didn't get on it with me. Instead, he waved goodbye, as it pulled away.

I didn't hear about the fight until later that morning. Though, given how much larger and stronger Joe was than Billy, it had to have been more a beating than a contest. The story, as I heard it, was that Billy stupidly bragged about cornering me against the locker and "feeling me up." When Joe found out later that afternoon about me being hurt, he became a raging terror, and it took several grown men to pull him off Billy. Both boys were suspended for a week for fighting on school grounds.

Joe was waiting for me at the bus stop again that afternoon. And the next morning, too. For the entire week that he was suspended, Joe was there at the bus stop every morning and afternoon. The other kids couldn't fail to understand the message he was sending them. "Hurt my girl, and I'll be here, waiting for you, too."

Joe made me feel safe. The biggest, strongest boy in school, and he was ready to go to any length to protect me. Not that I wasn't horrified by his quick brutality and afraid of the damage he was capable of inflicting, but I was naïve enough to believe that he would use it only to protect, never to harm.

I wanted to be as good a friend to Joe as he was to me. Academically, Joe couldn't afford to be suspended for an entire week; he was barely passing as it was. Not that he was dumb — far from it. He just couldn't function with the way school was structured; the logic behind test questions and homework simply didn't fit in with how his mind worked. So, I went to all his teachers and got the assignments for the week. When he met the bus in the afternoons, we'd go back to the farm, where we did our homework together.

Gramma didn't say anything about Joe coming home with me. I think she had heard from one of her friends what Joe had done, and why, and while she didn't approve of his fighting, she seemed satisfied that I had someone to stand up for me at school.

After Joe returned to school, he continued to come back to the farm with me.

A couple of weeks after the incident with Billy, Gramma took Joe aside for a talk. When they came out of her bedroom, Joe was subdued and solemn, but Gramma was smiling like a Cheshire cat. I tried to persuade Joe to tell me what she had said to him, but regardless of how much I wheedled and teased, he refused to answer and quickly changed the subject. All he said was, "She's something, your Gramma. One heck of a lady."

Soon, Joe was spending more time at our farm than at the rundown rented trailer he shared with his father. I didn't understand then that it was a refuge for him to be with people who liked kids, who would never think of hitting a boy, for any reason, regardless of how hard things got. He began calling me Jo, because he liked that the initials of my name — Judith Ormand — sounded the same as his name. And it felt good to have someone who had a special nickname for me, a special place for me in his life. We even had a secret name for the two of us — Jo Joe — as though it applied to a third person whom we created just by being together.

Gramma and Grampa made Joe welcome at the farm— for a while. Then we grew up, and things changed. Or, maybe nothing changed. His skin remained just as white as ever, and mine just as dark. Gramma had tried to warn me, how different he was from us, how his family was not our kind of people, but I wouldn't listen to her. After all, this was Joe, my best friend, my other self. Nothing she could say would convince me that wouldn't always be true.

Of course, she was right about him and his family, about their inborn brutality and treachery. The problem was I didn't understand who my kind of people were. When I had lived with *Papa* and Mom, all I knew was that I was a combination of the two of them. Cocoa brown like him with her long lithe body and her big hazel eyes. In Black Bear, all everyone ever saw when they looked at me was my dark skin. Everyone except Gramma and Grampa, and, for a few years, Joe.

TUESDAY

Traveling as much as I do, my body has become almost inured to jet lag. Maybe, I'm so used to pushing myself and getting right to work regardless of where I've landed, that I no longer recognize the disruption to my natural circadian rhythms, if I still have any natural rhythms. I often don't even know what country I'm in when I first wake up in the morning. I suppose it's that very sense of uncertainty and adventure, of exotic smells, sounds and sensations permeating my dreams, which keeps me alert even in my sleep. So, I usually awaken at dawn, wherever that dawn happens to alight.

Yet, in my old farmhouse bedroom under the eaves, I slept deeply, cradled by the long-ago familiar. Morning has come too soon. Now, I have to deal with all the lonely, hard responsibilities ahead of me. Curling on my side under the patchwork quilt, hoping for a few more moments of comfort and fond memories, the first thing I see is that ugly chair that I threw away years ago. Why did Gramma salvage it, along with all those photos of Joe?

I grab a mug of coffee and an apple for my breakfast and take it to Grampa's study, to eat at his desk, while I organize what I need to do over the next few days.

I love this room, where Gramps and I could talk about anything and everything. Or sometimes, in the evenings or on weekend days, I'd bring my homework or the book I was reading, curl up on the big brown corduroy armchair, and share a companionable silence with him, just the two of us.

Gramma took over the wood-paneled study after Grampa's death, but in her letters and emails to me, she still referred to it as his study, as though she were a temporary squatter.

And, yes, looking around, it's still indelibly Grampa's domain. The two walls of bookshelves are filled with his volumes and journals on pharmacology, history, philosophy and politics organized according to his own personal pattern approximating when and where he first read them.

Two of Mom's small wildlife bronzes retain their seats of honor. The hummingbirds are on the desk, the barn swallows on a slender marble pillar next to the window. Looking at them, I can almost hear the faint echo of Grampa whistling various bird calls, trying to teach me how different they were from each other.

Closing my eyes, I lightly trace the metal contours and textures of the hummingbirds with my fingertips. After Mom died, I'd often caress her sculptures, trying to recreate her touch on my skin. Needing to burn into my mind memories of her small smile of satisfaction or scrunched frown of frustration while she worked, and the way she shone sometimes, like when she would take my hands and dance around the room. As wonderful as it is to hold what she had created, as a child I quickly learned that the cold, hard bronzes are nothing more than chill reminders of how I will never again feel the warmth of her flesh against mine.

On the third wall are Grampa's diplomas, awards and commendations, surrounding the photo collage Mom had made for Gramma and Grampa's twentieth anniversary, two years before Uncle Robby was killed. The collage is a collection of pictures of my grandparents' wedding, honeymoon and married life. As long as I can remember, it has hung on the wall to the right of Grampa's big desk chair where he could gaze at it while he worked. I loved listening to his stories that went with the photos. Of him as a young man in uniform and his brand-new bride, both just out of high school and torn apart by The War. Of the baby, my mom, whose pictures sent to him in letters to the Pacific were his anchor through all the insanity he had witnessed but never would talk about. Of his graduation from the Philadelphia College of Pharmacy, where he had commuted weekly, so Gramma and Mom could live here at the farm with his parents, saving money and protecting his "two girls" and the baby from city life. Of his son, my Uncle Robby, a lively, mischievous boy, "bright as they come," but never about his death in Vietnam before I was born. So many other stories, including ones about people I never knew, whose names and relationship to me I can't really recall. Still, I will never forget the way he would tell them, how it once connected me to something larger than myself — my family.

Below Mom's collage is a much rougher one I made for their forty-seventh anniversary, the year I came to live here. I spent weeks poring through boxes and drawers, searching for just the right photos. Grampa claimed to love it as much as Mom's, though I knew it was crude compared to hers.

As much as the room remains indelibly Grampa's, Gramma made the study her own, too. I see it in the small touches that others might have missed. The black enameled fountain pen: she abhorred the inelegance and wastefulness of modern ballpoint pens. The small round *cloisonné* box I sent her from India: inside it is one carved coral earring. Gramma so seldom wore earrings. When she did, she'd inevitably take off the left one to talk on the phone. I wouldn't be surprised to find in their bedroom a box full of single earrings whose mates had been misplaced somewhere near a telephone. On the edge of the large green leather blotter is the magnifying glass with its ornate mother-of-pearl handle that Grampa gave her when she began to lose her eagle-eye vision, but hadn't yet accommodated herself to the fact. For the longest time, she refused to wear reading glasses other than Grampa's, which she frequently borrow-ed and often lost. The big, stylish magnifying glass was Grampa's attempt at getting Gramma to accept reality —

and to stop stealing his spectacles.

The biggest change is the computer on a small cart that now forms an L with the old mahogany desk. I was surprised at how enthusiastically Gramma adapted to the digital age. She even has a flatbed scanner and briefly tinkered with (then quickly abandoned) scrapbooking family pictures and mementos. Over the past few years, we emailed back and forth, almost weekly, whenever I was anywhere that had an Internet connection. Chatty, friendly emails or single line memos, usually about nothing of consequence, reassuring each other that we were fine. But she wasn't fine for a long time, and never told me. I blithely believed our emails were our way of remaining a part of each other's lives, staying connected between our periodic and progressively infrequent times together in Paris or London. Then, for the past year, the number of emails diminished, becoming shorter and shorter, with increasingly longer intervals between them, until there were none.

I powered up the computer. Gramma's password has never changed — MargBob, for the two children she buried. I know I will have to go through all her files, but right now, I simply need her contacts list, starting with Mr. Nichols of Black Bear Realty, to put the farm, store and hunting lodge up for sale.

I reach Mr. Nichols' voice mail, and ask him to call me back as soon as possible. Next, I order a mid-sized dumpster from Pocono Sanitation, for all the stuff I'll have to throw out. Not that I plan on trashing anything good, but this property has accumulated all kinds of junk over the generations, useless stuff that I can't imagine anyone wanting.

I'm going to forget something important, I'm sure of it; so, once more, I go over the To Do list I compiled on my iPad during the flight over the Atlantic:

Call Mrs. Denton (lawyer)
Call Mr. Nichols (realtor)
Arrange to have all mail forwarded to me in Paris
Arrange to turn off telephone starting next Tuesday

Arrange for property caretaker until sold
Review Gramma's accounts
    Bank
    Investments
    Insurance
    Bills
    Taxes
Put my name on her bank, investment accounts, etc.
Empty safe deposit box
Pack up everything I want to keep & send to Paris
    Need cardboard boxes, packing materials
    Need wooden crates & straw for Mom's
    sculptures
Pack up clothes and give away — where?
Call antiques dealer — who?
Decide what to do with other stuff

When I dial Mrs. Denton, I'm surprised that she, and not a secretary, answers after only two rings. "Hello, Mayfair and Denton, Meredith Denton speaking."

Denton became Gramma's attorney when Mr. Mayfair retired to Florida. I didn't know her when I lived here, but her voice has that familiar, unassuming mountain twang.

"Hello, Mrs. Denton. This is Judith Ormand. Martha Schmoyer's granddaughter."

"Oh, hello, Ms. Ormand. I'm glad you've called. Please accept my condolences. Martha was a grand lady; we'll all miss her. And, please call me Meredith." She has a well-rehearsed "just folks" manner that must keep her in good stead with her local clients.

"Thank you, Meredith. Call me Judith. I'm here in Black Bear, at my grandparents' farm."

"Welcome home. Sorry it has to be under these circumstances."

"Thank you." I repeat, because it seems to be the appropriate reply. "I called, because I want to settle the estate as soon as possible."

"I'll be happy to help you in any way I can, but you

don't have much to do legally, because I'm the…"

"Good." Okay, it isn't the best of form to interrupt, but how else am I going to break the relentless rhythm of pleasantries, so we can get down to business? "First of all, I'll be putting the farm, store and hunting lodge up for sale right away."

"Oh, but that's not possible, Judith… at least, not the lodge. It isn't yours to sell."

"What do you mean that it's not mine? Of course, it is." Is it possible I might be mistaken about Gramma being financially secure? "Or, did my grandmother sell it?"

"Well, no…. It's just that… well… your grandmother didn't… uh… leave the lodge and its land to you."

Of course, everything was left to me. Who else is there? I'm the last in the family. However, something in Denton's tone of voice — the awkward hesitation and the way she almost swallows her words — I better find out what I'm up against, before saying anything else. "Mrs. Denton, I think I need to see my grandmother's will. Where is it?"

"As the estate executrix, I have it. In fact, I was on my way to Honesdale this morning, to have it recorded and filed at the county courthouse. If you wish, I can drop a copy off on my way."

"Yes, please. When?"

"I could be there around ten. Does that work for you?"

I glance at my watch. "I'll see you in a half hour then. Thank you."

While I wait for her, I go through Grampa's desk. I find nothing related to the will or the estate, and end up with only a wastebasket full of out-of-date coupons, old Post-It notes with abbreviated, meaningless scrawls, and other irrelevant paper paraphernalia. I'm not really concerned. I assume that everything will make sense to me, once I read the will. Perhaps, Gramma left the lodge to one of her charities. But then, why didn't Denton say as much?

Meredith Denton arrives nearly on time, only twenty minutes after ten, which is considered downright prompt by Black Bear standards. A tall white woman of about forty-five, thick around the middle, she wears a nicely tailored navy blue pants suit and sensible shoes. Her dark auburn hair is cut too short and too blunt for her round face, but her makeup is understated and applied with a practiced hand.

"May I offer you coffee?" I ask, as I start to lead her to the kitchen.

"Thank you, but I have an appointment at eleven at the Wayne County courthouse, and it'll take me a half hour to get to Honesdale." Without any further preliminaries, she opens her brown leather briefcase, extracts a manila folder of papers and hands them to me. "I've made a photocopy of your grandmother's will for you. If you have any questions, my business card is in there, as well."

"Thank you, Mrs. Denton."

"Meredith, please," she reminds me.

"Thank you, Meredith."

Just as I'm about to close the door behind her, she turns and says, "I'm assuming that you'll want to take some of your grandmother's personal belongings with you when you leave the country. That should be fine, since, other than the hunting lodge and a few bequests, your grandmother left everything else to you. But I will have to take charge of her liquid assets for the time being."

"Liquid assets?"

"Bank accounts, investments, that sort of thing."

"Oh?"

"To pay off your grandmother's debts, funeral expenses and taxes, if any, and to generally settle the estate."

"Certainly, she didn't have any significant debts."

"Probably not, but we can't know for sure, until we look into her records and see what response I get from the ads."

"But…"

"I will, of course, provide you with a full accounting."

"How often?"

Her voice suddenly takes on a harder, less casual edge. Perhaps, she isn't used to being questioned about her professional dealings. "I will send you a verified inventory of the estate's current financial assets before any bills or bequests are paid. Of course, I will keep exact records with full documentation of how much is paid to whom, which you would have the right to inspect at any time. Does that suffice?"

"It sounds logical," I reluctantly acknowledge.

"Trust me, it's the way things are done. Ask your own attorney," she says rather dismissively.

"That's very sensible advice. I'll have them get in touch with you."

While she continues to smile benignly, her eyes widen, and the creases around her mouth become more pronounced. "As you wish." Before turning to leave, she says, "*Au revoir*," with vowels that are too rounded and long. I supposed she wants to show me that she's worldly, too, or am I being too cynical? After all, I should appreciate her courtesy of trying to say a couple of words in my native language.

Something about having to deal with matters I'd rather not face usually triggers my appetite. Retreating to the kitchen, I make a cheese and tomato sandwich on toasted sourdough bread, and pour a tall glass of milk. While I eat, I read the will.

I, Martha Hausman Schmoyer, a resident of Black Bear, Pennsylvania, being of sound and disposing mind and memory, do make, publish and declare this to be my last Will, hereby expressly revoking all Wills and Codicils previously made by me.

I appoint Meredith Denton, of Mayfair and Denton Associates of Black Bear, Pennsylvania, as Executrix of this my Last Will and Testament. Should Meredith Denton be unable or unwilling to act as Executrix, my granddaughter, Judith Roberta Ormand of Paris, France, shall appoint an Executor or Executrix of her choosing. The Executor or Executrix shall be authorized to carry out all provisions of this Will and pay my just debts, obligations and funeral expenses.

I leave my entire estate and all that I own, of whatever kind or character and wherever located, to my granddaughter Judith Roberta Ormand, with the exception of the following.

To Joseph Jacob Anderson of Black Bear, Pennsylvania, I leave the hunting lodge....

Joe?! Why in Heaven's name would Gramma leave Gramps' hunting lodge to *him*, of all people?

Suddenly no longer hungry, I push away the food, all my attention focused on trying to absorb and understand Gramma's will. Something is obviously terribly wrong.

To Joseph Jacob Anderson of Black Bear, Pennsylvania, I leave the hunting lodge in Greentown, Pennsylvania, all the furnishings, outbuildings, equipment and trappings attached to the lodge, plus the forty-two acres of land on which it sits. I direct the Executor or Executrix to pay any taxes owed on the hunting lodge and land for three years following my death, such funds to come from my estate. I also direct the Executor or Executrix to pay any debts up to $50,000 that Joseph Jacob Anderson owes at the time of my death. Should Joseph Jacob Anderson's debts at the time of my death be less than $50,000, the remaining funds of that sum should be divided into five equal portions, each of which will be turned over to Joseph Jacob Anderson annually for the following five years. Should Joseph Jacob Anderson predecease me, the hunting lodge, outbuildings, furnishings, equipment and land should go to his children, Anne Margaret Anderson, Henry Andrew Anderson and Martha Michelle Anderson.

His children, too? *Mon Dieu!* Had she become senile? Was it the medicines she was taking? I'd read about unscrupulous people targeting lonely, old women, but I couldn't imagine Gramma falling for any schemes that *salaud* could conjure. Not if she'd been in her right mind.

Break your promise. Return to Black Bear imme-diately. Your grandmother needs you. This must be what that anonymous caller was trying to warn me about.

That *connard!* How dare he take advantage of her like that?

Damn it! Why wasn't I here to protect her, to help her, to keep her from being so alone and vulnerable to jackals like Joe Anderson?

A bilious taste of acid burns my throat.

I ask that Judith Roberta Ormand distribute money from the estate, at her discretion, to those charities and organizations I have supported. She will find the list in my accounts records.

Any dogs or cats I have at the time of my death are to be placed in good, loving homes that are prepared to care for them as I have. They are not to be sent to a shelter or euthanized. I ask that Judith Roberta Ormand take on the responsibility of paying for any veterinary care or medicines they should need, for the lifetime of the animals, should it prove to be a hardship to the good-hearted people who adopt my pets.

Should Judith Roberta Ormand predecease me, then her share of my estate and her obligations to the estate should be distributed and shared equally among Judith Roberta Ormand's children, should she have any. If she dies without producing children, I direct the Executor or Executrix to distribute $50,000 to Les Femmes, Judith Roberta Ormand's non-profit organization based in Paris, France, plus $15,000 each to the Black Bear Volunteer Ambulance Association, the Black Bear Fire Department, the Wayne County Refuge for Women, the Black Bear Moravian Church and Temple Beth Shalom.

Now those three paragraphs sound more like Gramma, though I'm surprised to see a synagogue mentioned. However, Joe is no stray animal or charity.

Should Judith Roberta Ormand predecease me without having any children, I then leave the Mountainview farm in Black Bear, Pennsylvania, with all its buildings, furnishings, equipment and trappings to Joseph Jacob Anderson....

What!? I strike the table with my fist, hurting my knuckles and almost spilling the milk.

... I then leave the Mountainview farm in Black Bear, Pennsylvania, with all its buildings, furnishings, equipment, and trappings to Joseph Jacob Anderson, with all taxes paid, and direct the Executor or Executrix to create a trust fund for Joseph Jacob Anderson's children Anne Margaret Anderson, Henry Andrew Anderson and Martha Michelle Anderson from the remaining portion of my estate. The trust fund shall be used for their education, in conjunction with the zero coupon bonds that I purchased in their names, which are stored in my safe deposit box at the Black Bear branch of PNC Bank. Any funds remaining in the trust fund are to be handed over to Anne Margaret Anderson, Henry Andrew Anderson and Martha Michelle Anderson, in equal portions, when the youngest, Martha Michelle Anderson, reaches 30 years of age. Should Judith Roberta Ormand predecease me before having any children and should Joseph Jacob Anderson predecease me, then I leave the Mountainview farm, with all its furnishings, equipment and trappings to Anne Margaret Anderson, Henry Andrew Anderson and Martha Michelle Anderson.

The final two paragraphs are typical legalese about waiving the necessity of an estate inventory or appraisal, and issues regarding how the executor should serve and the court should interpret the will.

It was signed and notarized January 21st, 2012. I don't recognize the names of the witnesses.

Only this past January. Three months ago. How did he get her to do it? Was it that her illness was so advanced that she just didn't know what she was doing?

I sit at the kitchen table, staring at the document in my hand for some time. Rereading the paragraphs about Joe and his children, I can't believe my eyes. Why the hell would she leave anything to him, to his children?

I remember very clearly when I first began to understand how Gramma really felt about Joe. It wasn't easy to know what she thought about a person, certainly not by how she treated him, because she was outwardly courteous and welcoming to everyone she met.

Throughout junior high, and even my freshman and most of my sophomore high school years, whenever Joe came to the farm, she greeted him warmly, fed him, made him feel at home. Then, one day, near the end of our sophomore year in high school, when she and Grampa thought I wasn't around, I heard them argue about Joe. That, in itself, was unusual; they seldom argued, not where I could hear them. But what was remarkable was that Grampa was actually yelling. He hardly ever raised his voice, especially not to Gramma.

"For crying out loud, Martha!" Grampa's voice reverberated through the house. "Let the boy be. He's a good kid."

"Kid?" Gramma responded with her finely tuned sarcasm. "He's enormous, a monster, and his family is trash. Did you hear about his father and Hank Metcott's latest drunken escapade?"

"Village gossip." Grampa practically spat out the distasteful words.

"This isn't gossip; it's fact. The two of them tore up the Tavern last Saturday, and would have swiped the cash from behind the bar, if George hadn't pulled out his shotgun. The police are looking for them, but they've disappeared into the woods again."

"Joe isn't his father. You know that, Martha."

"The apple doesn't fall far from the tree. If you don't start paying attention, how can you protect your granddaughter from the likes of that boy?"

"And if you don't step back, you're going to drive her away."

"Like Maggie!?" Gramma actually screeched Mom's name. "Is that what you're trying to say?"

"This isn't about Maggie, Martha."

"Isn't it? Isn't it always about how I drove your precious daughter away?"

"No. It's about Judith and Joe."

"There is no Judith and Joe! Never will be, not if it's the last thing I do. Mark my word. Blood will out, and his is bad blood if I ever saw it."

"You're wrong, Martha. He's a good boy, and I won't have him chased away when we're the only thing standing between him and that father of his."

It was the only time that I know of that Gramma didn't get her way. True to her nature, however, she never showed any of her displeasure directly to Joe. He continued to come to the farm, practically living with us, going back to his father's trailer only to sleep. Gramma even helped him from time to time, when he needed to talk with a mother figure. As far as Joe was concerned, she was every-thing he could have ever hoped for in a grandmother, and he'd chastise me whenever I'd say anything negative about her. I could have almost forgotten that argument, if it hadn't been for the way she would slip in those pejoratives when it was just the two of us. Words like "brute" or "inbred" or "feckless," leaving no room for doubt that she would have used stronger language, if I hadn't been too loyal to sit still and listen to it — until it was too late.

Gramma would never have willingly signed over even a single *sou* to Joe. No way in hell that I'm going to let him get away with it.

What I need is a good attorney. Though I'm a partner in *Ormand et fils*, the company we inherited from *Grand-père*, my half-brother Antoine is the one who runs the business. We must have an attorney somewhere here in the States to handle this end of things for us. I grab the will and Denton's business card and go into Grampa's study where I left my cell phone. Damn, it's already 5 PM in Paris. But I try Antoine's office anyway. After all, he's the workaholic in the family and might still be there. When his secretary Geneviève answers, I don't bother asking to be put through to Antoine. He and I aren't exactly on chatting terms. Instead, I get the name and phone number of the lawyer who represents our interests in the States from her: Louise Abrams.

I'm put through to Ms. Abrams immediately, when I identify myself as Judith Ormand of *Ormand et fils*.

"*Bonjour*, Mademoiselle Ormand, "*Comment allez-vous?*" she answers in French after only one ring. A good accent for an American.

"Hello, Ms. Abrams." I reply in English, knowing that even individuals fluent in a foreign language are more comfortable conducting business in their native tongue.

She takes my hint. "How may I help you?"

Her directness is a relief.

"I'm here in Pennsylvania for my grandmother's funeral."

"My condolences."

"Thank you. I fear her will has some major irregularities, and that she might have been coerced to change it recently. I know your specialty is customs law, but could you recommend someone to help investigate and contest the will? An attorney licensed to practice in Pennsylvania?"

"Yes, of course. Where in Pennsylvania are you?"

"In Black Bear, a village in the Poconos. It's Wayne County. But I don't want anyone who is part of the community here, who might be influenced by connections and relationships."

"Certainly not. Still, it must be someone familiar with the local politics and personalities."

I can hear her typing on a keyboard as she speaks, no doubt looking up some names.

"Yes, here it is. Jerome Maeklin. That's spelled m... a... e... k... l... i... n. He's one of the best estate attorneys I know, and he happens to have a branch office in Stroudsburg, in Monroe County, not far from you, yet potentially far away enough to avoid local politics. Of course, I can't be sure, but I trust him to tell you if he has any conflicts of interest that would prohibit him from taking on your case."

After giving me his phone number and address, she adds, "If you have any difficulties or need anything else, please call me."

I don't get through to Mr. Maeklin quite as quickly as I had Louise Abrams. However, it appears that Abrams' name carries some clout, or that I happened to call when he's available, because I'm kept on hold for less than 15 seconds.

"Hello, this is Jerome Maeklin."

"Hello, Mr. Maeklin. My name is Judith Ormand. As I mentioned to your receptionist, Louise Abrams suggested I call you."

"Do you have dealings with Louise?"

"My family's business does; we're in import/export."

"Ah, yes, of course. How may I help you?"

"My grandmother's will has some irregularities. I fear she may have been coerced or unduly influenced to change it a few months before her death."

"What makes you think that?"

"She left a significant portion of her estate to someone who is no relation and whom I have reason to distrust. I fear that my grandmother was unduly influenced while she was ill and perhaps not fully herself."

"Before we proceed, I want you to consider this very carefully," he says. "Contesting a will is emotionally draining and time consuming. An uncontested will can take one and a half to two years to settle. Once we set the ball rolling on this, it could drag on for years and become quite expensive."

"Money isn't the issue," I assure him. "I can't stand to think of my grandmother being conned like this. He mustn't be allowed to get away with it."

"How much is the estate worth?"

I'm taken aback by the question. "I told you the money doesn't matter."

"In my experience, Ms. Ormand," he counters, almost condescendingly, "it is always about money, about who gets what from the estate. Plus, it costs quite a bit to contest any will... at least five figures... more, if it goes to litigation. You need to be sure it's worth it."

"If you're concerned about your fees..."

"That's part of it, Ms. Ormand, but to advise you what the best course of action might be, I need to understand the full extent of the case."

"I really don't know; I assume it's about a million, a million-five, perhaps more — there's a lot of land involved. However, even if the estate were worth only a few thousand dollars, it wouldn't matter; it's the principle involved. As for having the wherewithal to cover any legal costs and expenses, you can ask Louise Abrams about my family's financial status."

"That won't be necessary, Ms. Ormand. I just want you to understand what you're getting into. Now, if you are sure you want to proceed, I'll need to look at the will."

I turn on Gramma's flatbed scanner. "I can email it right now." I quickly scan and send the will to him. While we wait, I answer his questions, including my address, phone numbers and email, plus Denton's contact information. The will arrives in his inbox as we speak.

After a few seconds' silence, he says "I assume it's this Joseph Jacob Anderson whom you believe may have exerted undue influence."

"Yes."

"I need to know, Ms. Ormand, why you're so certain that the will is irregular?"

"I know him. So did my grandmother, and she didn't like him. Actually, it was more that she didn't trust him... vehemently so. Now, suddenly, he's a major benefactor in her will. It makes no sense, Mr. Maeklin. Deep inside me, I know something is terribly wrong. What can I do to stop him?"

"First, we need to notify the court and the executor that we're contesting the will. That will stop any distribution of property while we build our case. My fees are $350 an hour, plus costs; that's more or less the going rate up here. I'll need your signature on some papers to authorize me to proceed in your name, and a retainer of $4,000. One of my interns, Joyce Boyd, lives near you; she could bring the papers and pick up a check. Will you be at your grandmother's home this evening?"

"I'll make sure to be here." As if I have any other place I want to go in Black Bear.

"Good. Now, tell me, what do you know about Anderson?"

"I knew him as a child, when I lived here. I've not seen or heard from him since I left the States right after high school, about seventeen years ago."

"I'll be sending my investigator — Edward Felson — to find out what we can. He'll start by asking you to tell him everything you can about Anderson."

Despite myself, I picture *film noir* private eyes with their mysterious, sometimes violent manners. Of course, he'll most likely be a very ordinary person who's good at research. "I must return to Africa on Monday, and I'll be out of reach for some weeks."

"Then, I'll have Mr. Felson contact you as soon as possible."

"Excellent."

"In the meantime, I suggest that you search for another will, either a previous one that we might persuade the court to recognize, or a more recent one that might supersede this one."

"I've already started," I tell him. "I've been looking in my grandmother's files here at the house, and I plan to empty her safe deposit box."

"Oh, that won't be possible, Ms. Ormand, not until the estate is settled. When the primary safe deposit box owner dies, it's standard practice to search, inventory and seal the contents. You can, however, ask to be present when the search is conducted."

Dealing with the will and the estate is beginning to be almost as convoluted as navigating the labyrinth of African bureaucracy. Not that bribes are openly expected and required in Black Bear. Still, I'll have to handle the bank manager carefully, so he'll let me see the box. I don't like the prospect of letting a stranger root through Gramma's personal property, unsupervised and without constraints. It isn't so much a matter of security, of worrying about family heirlooms or important documents disappearing. Somehow, it seems like an invasion of Gramma's privacy, having a stranger pry into the very things that she cherished enough to lock away in the bank.

"I'll be in touch, Ms. Ormand," Mr. Maeklin says. "Please call me if you have any questions or think of anything else you feel I should know."

"Actually, there is one thing."

"Yes?"

"Is it usual for the executor to seize control over the estate's liquid assets?"

"It isn't always the way things are done, but it certainly isn't out of the question. Given your situation and how much you travel, it would probably be more efficient."

"What are the safeguards?"

"While there are laws and professional standards, usually it's a matter of the personal integrity and the experience of the executor. Do you have reason to be worried about Meredith Denton?"

"The thing is I know nothing about her."

"I know of her, though I haven't had any direct dealings with her or her firm. I believe she has a rather good reputation. If you wish, I can ask around."

"Thank you, Mr. Maeklin."

After I hang up, I feel better. Joe is in over his head; he's made a big mistake picking on the wrong woman's grandmother.

Unsettled by the business with the will, I wander the house aimlessly, my mind uncharacteristically scattered. I pace through the living room, study, foyer, dining room, kitchen, and back again, while my eyes and my memories are pulled this way and that. What things do I want to take with me? What am I willing to leave behind?

Without question, I have to save the family photos, so while I pace, I start by taking them off walls and shelves. I stack the pictures against the foyer stairway, passing the master bedroom each time. I still can't bring myself to go in there. To walk into their room, to take things away from it would mean that I finally and completely accept that Gramma and Grampa are truly gone.

Soon, the piles of pictures become completely unmanageable, spreading out around the stairway, almost blocking the door to their bedroom. I've got to stop being so harebrained and get organized. I need boxes, bubble wrap, labels, tape.

Settling back into Grampa's study, I call various shipping companies, truck renters and stationers. The one company that delivers packing materials to Black Bear won't be able to get anything to me until Friday. I order wooden crates and straw for Mom's bronzes from them, then I grab my purse and car keys and take off for the nearest Staples, just outside of Stroudsburg, about a thirty minute drive.

Driving along the one road out of Black Bear that leads south to Stroudsburg, I can't avoid passing Dutch's gas station. The sign is visible from a half-mile away — the same old blue and white marquee with the painted silhouette of the little Dutch girl, even though Joe claims to own it now. Despite the village speed limit of 25 mph, I stomp on the gas pedal, determined to zoom past. The closer I come to the gas station, the more my stomach churns and knots up. *Putain!* So innocent acting, when all along he was scheming to profit from Gramma's death.

When I see him pumping gas, I veer into the station so suddenly that I'm sure I left rubber on the road. Jumping out of the car, I yell, "*Joe Anderson!*"

He looks up from the gas nozzle, that damned face-wide grin of his forming before he realizes who's calling him. Just as quickly, he swallows the smile, and concentrates on removing the nozzle from the car, and latching it in place on the pump. After taking money from the driver, he folds the bills and puts them into his plaid flannel shirt pocket. Then he walks toward me, with that lumbering gimpy gait of his.

As much as I want to turn around and run away, I root myself in place. Damned if I'm going to retreat from him. I put my hand up, my index finger jabbing only inches from his mouth. "I'm on to you!"

"What's wrong, Jo?" I know that look on his face — so innocent and dumbfounded. I remember him using it on teachers when he couldn't answer their questions. Sometimes, it actually worked on the more gullible of his teachers.

"Judith! My name is Judith."

"Sorry. Judith." He shrugs sheepishly, as though it's all an embarrassing mistake.

If I didn't know better, I might have been taken in by it. "I'm telling you, Joe Anderson, you're not going to get away with it."

A small woman in her late twenties or early thirties rushes out of the station office. She has a chubby blonde baby on her hip and is buttoning up her wrinkled flowered yellow blouse, as though she was breast feeding. "Hey, stop that!" she screeches. "You leave my Joe alone!" She plants herself directly in front of him, blocking like a defensive tackle. With the type of chiseled features that once might have been quite attractive, the woman has that look I'd seen in villages all over the world — tired, worn out, with sallow skin and short stringy light brown hair that lost its shine years ago. The top of her head reaches no higher than Joe's shoulder.

"Betty," Joe says from above and behind her. "This is Jo… er… Judith." He places his hand on her free arm, but she shrugs it off.

Betty doesn't turn to respond to him. She's glaring

at me instead, her brown eyes wide and fiery. "I know who the fuck she is. That don't give her no right to act so high and mighty, like you was shit... Martha'd be ashamed of you, girl."

"Who do you think you are?" I demand.

"Uh..." Joe bends over her shoulder. "This is my wife, Betty."

She pivots her head, so their noses are only inches away. "Don't you dare being nice like that, Joseph Jacob, not after the way she's being, coming in here and treating you like shit. " He quickly retreats, and she refocuses her anger on me. "What the hell you want, anyway? Why you laying on at Joe like that?"

"He's a conniving bastard, that's why." I lock eyes with Joe. "Grampa's hunting lodge, indeed! When I'm finished with you, Joe Anderson, you'll be sorry you ever weaseled your way into the will. If you're counting on getting your hands on any of their property, forget it. I'll make sure that you never get a red cent!"

He stares at me, his mouth agape, no words coming out. Betty doesn't have a similar problem. "You don't know what the fuck you're talking about, missy. If I didn't have this baby here..." Her one free fist clenches and unclenches in rhythm to her words. "Just get the hell out of here."

I stomp away from them and slam the car door behind me, squealing the tires in my rush to get onto the road, not slowing down to a reasonable, responsible speed until the hairpin turn onto 191.

I keep picturing him, cowering behind that tiny woman and child, not man enough to deal with me himself. And that Betty, what a piece of work she is, classic trailer trash. Even so, she's got to be good in a fight, standing up like that for her no-account husband.

But the baby... was that the Martha Michelle Anderson in the will? A cute kid, like nearly any other healthy, well-fed infant. Named after Gramma. What great emotional ammunition for weaseling their way into the will. Joe doesn't have the smarts to figure that out.

Betty. I'll have to watch out for her.

❖

On my way back from Staples, Edward Felson calls to arrange to come by the farm within the hour. He arrives just as I finish unloading the car onto the front porch, and quickly volunteers to help me haul the flattened boxes, rolls of bubble wrap, bags of tape and labels inside.

Of course, Felson doesn't fit a *film noir* stereotype of a private investigator. At least forty pounds overweight on a frame that might be five foot nine if he stood very straight (which he doesn't), no way he could easily chase down a suspect or seduce a *femme fatale*. He's about fifty, maybe fifty-five years old; his pale white face is splotched with red spider webs of broken capillaries. His thinning hair has more salt than pepper. He's dressed informally, in pressed black chinos, oxford shirt, pullover grey V-neck sweater and black running shoes.

When he says yes to my offer of coffee, we go into the kitchen. I quickly throw the plate with the half-eaten sandwich from my aborted lunch into the sink, and start the coffee maker. Then, I sit down opposite him at the table.

"You've a nice house here, Ms. Ormand," he says, looking around the room.

"Thank you."

"Always wanted to move out this way myself, one day."

"Mr. Felson, I understand you're trying to put me at ease with small talk, but I'd be more comfortable getting directly down to business, if you don't mind."

"Of course." He takes a long, thin wired notebook out of his back pocket, pats his chest, reaches up to check his head, and finally finds his eyeglasses hooked onto the neck of his sweater. He puts them on, flips through a few pages of his notebook, and then pushes the glasses up onto his forehead. "Maeklin, Hawthorne & Yeager has asked me to investigate one Joseph Jacob Anderson, who I understand is a beneficiary in your grandmother's will, which you're contesting."

"Yes."

"At the county courthouse in Honesdale, I checked out everything that's a matter of public record — at least, within Wayne County. Anderson's mortgage and taxes on the gas station here in town, his work with the Black Bear Volunteer Ambulance Association, criminal record, that sort of thing. To compile a full profile, I'll need to know more about him personally... the kind of things that never make it into the records. What can you tell me about Anderson?"

"Criminal record? Joe has a criminal record?"

Pushing his glasses back down onto his nose to check the notebook, Mr. Felson skims over what looks like an illegible scrawl. "Public drunkenness. Disorderly conduct. DUI — that's driving under the influence. Several times. Alcohol. No indication of drugs. Lost his license for two years. Went to jail for felonious assault in '03." He flips a page. "Got out after a year. No other convictions involving jail time." He rattles off the offenses in staccato bursts like a ticker tape machine, devoid of emotion or judgment.

I knew Joe to be two-faced, bigoted, and cruel, but I never imagined him a felon. Gramma was right, again; the apple didn't fall far from the tree.

When the coffee maker beeps, I get up to pour two mugs. "Milk, Mr. Felson?"

"Black with sugar, please. Lots of sugar."

I hand him his mug and a spoon. "The sugar's there to your right," I say, pointing to the blue spatterware bowl on the table. "Would you like some cinnamon cake to go with that?"

"Just the coffee, thank you." He stirs three heaping spoonsful of sugar into his coffee, takes two gulps, then with a sigh of satisfaction, puts the mug down and picks up his notebook once more.

"Anderson's been clean for eight years, as far as I can see from the Wayne County records. I'll be checking state, federal and some neighboring counties tomorrow." He unclips a pen from the notebook's spiral binding, flips to an empty page, and looks at me over his aviator-type glasses which are perched on the tip of his nose. "Now, what can you tell me about him?"

"Not that much, really. We knew each other as children."

"'The child is the father of the man,' as they say. Please tell me what you remember."

"He was in my class in junior and senior high school, but older than I. He was never very good at studying and taking tests, so they held him back a year in fifth grade." I don't bother mentioning that I skipped a grade, which meant Joe was two years older. "We were friends for a while. Actually, for most of the time I lived here." I cup both of my hands around the warm mug, but don't drink.

"Which was when?"

"I moved here in the summer of '91 and left in '95, right after graduation."

"And you were friends with Joseph Anderson?"

"It's a small village, Mr. Felson." My flat statement of a former friendship is as far as I'm willing to go in that direction.

Instead of acknowledging my evasion, Ed Felson sips his coffee, then puts down the mug, his eyes never leaving my face. Obviously, he's waiting for me to fill the silence with information.

"Joe Anderson." The shape of his name on my tongue pulls me back through too many divergent memories. Where should I begin? Not that first day in the playground, nor that last time in the treehouse. Those are private demons that are none of his business. And, definitely, not that horrific run-in with Joe's brother Wayne. I've never told anyone about that.

"I guess I should start with his family," I finally decide. "His was the first I'd ever seen of the type. The abusive, angry father, who never kept a job for longer than a few months at a time. I can't tell you anything about his mother. She disappeared when Joe was still quite young. The brother... Wayne... was several years older, and ran away in his early teens, before I moved here, but showed up again for a short time in the autumn of '94." I shiver convulsively, only once, before clamping down on the memory. I gulp some coffee, then, continue. "So, for most of the time that I knew Joe, it was only the two of them... Joe and his father... in a series of rented houses or trailers."

"I found a bit about the father." Felson flips back a couple of pages in his notebook. "John Wayne Anderson. Seems to be one of those vets who never made the adjustment back into society when he came home from 'Nam. Was evicted by landlords several times over the years for non-payment of rent or destruction of property. Various arrests and convictions for drunk and disorderly behavior, spousal and child abuse, petty theft, firing a weapon within village limits. A long string of offenses, but nothing major. Longest incarceration was for two years, three months. No criminal records for him before 1976 and nothing since 2002, when he joined the Homeland Militia."

"Homeland Militia?"

"Self-proclaimed religious patriots... local misfits and troublemakers who formed up after 9/11; they've an encampment on the other side of Beaver Mountain. Indications are they're an offshoot of the Aryan Nations. The police haven't been able to pin anything on them as a group, only individuals. The hate crimes get the biggest play in the news." He pauses, then adds, "I'm surprised you haven't heard about them."

"I've been out of the country for a long time." The Aryan Nations, here in Black Bear? Why am I shocked? Hate and racism have always been barely under the skin of this picture-perfect village. "Joe's father is one of them?" It makes an ugly kind of sense.

"Apparently."

"What about Joe?"

"In my opinion, it's unlikely." Mr. Felson takes off his glasses, and polishes one lens with his napkin. "The fact that he's a volunteer EMT in the local ambulance company... it just doesn't gel with the Homeland's doctrine of self-reliance and seclusion."

"Still, you don't know for sure, do you?"

"I don't know much of anything yet; I've been on the case only a few hours." He stares at me. "Do you have reason to believe Joseph Anderson would be drawn to the Homeland Militia?"

"He is his father's son." Even as I say it, something deep inside rebels against the idea. What is it within me that I still want to disown everything that happened that last year? Do I really believe that pretending Joe and his brother hadn't been so damnably cruel and beastly to me would make it any less real? "Yes, I have reason to believe it possible, Mr. Felson."

"I'll check it out." He puts his glasses back on to scrawl in his notebook. "What else can you tell me about him? You said you were friends for most of the time you lived here. Does that mean something happened to change that?"

Mr. Felson has finally come to the one burning question I've never been able to answer. Why did Joe change so completely, literally overnight? One evening, we were in our treehouse, closer than ever. The next day...

"There was his injury," I say under my breath, testing out one of my hypotheses yet again. Not that I really believe that his being hurt was the whole story. But why should I break my silence and talk about the attack to this stranger?

"What injury?" he asks.

"Joe was the local football hero, the main reason Wallenpaupack was headed for the state championship in our senior year, but he was pushed too hard."

When I watched from the stands that Saturday, a hard knot of concern formed in the pit of my stomach. Joe had been dragging. I was sure that something was terribly wrong, and not just because the coach played him almost constantly that game, both offense and defense. He had that look that I had learned meant trouble. Probably his father had been on his case again. I doubted he'd slept much the night before. When Barrowsburg scored that last touch-down, tying the game, the crowd had started screaming for Joe, egged on by the cheerleaders, with Maybeth flouncing her curls in rhythm to his name.

"He was hurt rather badly in the last quarter of the final game against Barrowsburg High," I say.

"Tough luck."

"No, it was worse than that, Mr. Felson. Joe had dreamed of joining the Navy after school; he thought it would be his one chance to make something of himself. But with his mangled leg, there was no way the Navy would ever take him."

Mr. Felson scribbled while I spoke, but he must have heard something new in my voice, because he looks up at me, squints, then says, "I see."

"You have to understand Mr. Felson. I don't really know what he thought or felt about it. I'm just guessing."

How could I have known what Joe thought? When I tried to climb into the ambulance with him, he screamed *"Get out! Get out!"* making it crystal clear that he didn't want me there. He also refused to see me at the hospital. I didn't catch up with him until a week after he had been hurt. No one had told me he was home, or I would have picked him up. But there he was, in school, at his locker. I ran to him. "Joe!" I called, so happy that I could finally be near my best friend again.

He looked at me with a scowl that distorted his face into a grotesque mask I didn't recognize. "What d'ya want?" he growled at me.

I didn't know what to say to him, didn't understand what could have changed him so completely. "Joe, what's wrong?"

"Just leave me alone! Everything's different now. So ...so... just get lost and don't you go bothering me again. Hear me? I don't never want you to bother me again, ever. Now beat it!" It was almost the same tone as his brother Wayne. He slammed his locker shut, then, turned his back on me.

I watched as Joe hobbled away on his crutches, unable to move from where I stood, tears streaming down my face, barely able to breathe. From that day on, Joe turned into my worst nightmare. Whenever he would see me, he'd scowl and head in the opposite direction. Or, worse, he'd hang more fully on Maybeth, conspicuously ignoring me as I walked past. Eventually, he'd stand on the sidelines, watching when she and her gang sneered and cursed at me, using the same vile names that Wayne and his cohorts had screamed at me that horrific night in the old schoolhouse. When Billy and his gang cornered me against the schoolyard fence just before graduation, grabbing and groping me, even tearing my blouse, they no longer feared any reprisals from Joe. Why should they, when Joe had sicc'd his own brother on me?

Recognizing that this interview is at an end, Ed Felson stands. "If you think of anything else, Ms. Ormand, please call me." He hands me his business card.

"What will you do now, Mr. Felson?"

"Start asking around about Anderson. As you said, it's a small town. People tend to know a lot about their neighbors, and I've found they don't mind telling it to anyone who asks."

After Ed Felson leaves, the house feels both too large and too cramped. Every room is filled with memories, good and bad, all tied up together in a jumble of loneliness, pain and confusion.

Needing some air to clear my mind and give me space to think, I rifle through the hall closet and find my old rubber boots, Grampa's blue wool parka, and Gramma's gloves, scarf and hat. In my mind's ear, I hear myself calling, "Come on, Maverick. Let's go for a walk, boy."

Behind the barn, I cut through the swathe of trees and thick tangle of wild bushes that had sprouted over the generations around the crumbling stone wall that defined the perimeter of the original twenty-acre field. Schmoyers whose names I don't remember had cleared this field about 150 years ago. One by one, by hand and horse, the boulders and trees had been wrested out of the unyielding land, to create this farm, rooting Grampa's forebears to this place. The rocks had formed the wall; the trees went to building the first house and barn. And this field had fed and clothed them. Stubborn, strong, determined, they had made this land more than better, they had made it their home.

The fields haven't been planted or worked since Grampa's childhood, but they hadn't gone to waste. When I was young, old Mr. Matthews used to hay them for horse feed, paying Grampa a dollar a year for the right. One more item I should add to my To Do list — make sure someone who needs feed for their animals has access to the fields until the farm is sold.

The wet ground sucks at my boots with each step. The sky is filled with dark grey clouds, heavy with rain, or maybe snow, limned with sunlight that slowly turns pink.

Too early in the season for fireflies, I can still see them in my memory: millions of tiny lights that could cover this field at dusk. I couldn't have been more than five when I first saw them one summer evening, Mom and *Papa* by my side, the three of us running through the tall grass, laughing, surrounded by so much wildness, so many pin-points of light just above my head. I tried to catch them, but they were always inches beyond my reach. I don't believe *Papa* returned to the farm after that visit, not until Mom's funeral, when he came to get me — and then, briefly, for my *bat mitzvah*, which proved to be the disappointment to him that he expected. He insisted that I repeat the ritual at his synagogue during my summer visit to Paris.

A storm-brewing breeze rustles through the forest at the far side of the field. Why is it that the sweet smell of the damp evergreen woods feels so comforting, as though the trees themselves are watching, reaching out for me?

Gramps used to tease Gramma when she went into the woods on her own. "Off to hug a tree, again," he would say. I thought it was figurative, a joke, until one day, I saw her. The August before our senior year.

Joe and I had spent a typical summer day filled with chores around the farm — weeding the kitchen garden, mowing the lawn, repairing a shutter. It had been hot and humid, and the cool, shady woods had been beckoning to us all day. Finally, when even Joe, with his indefatigable strength, began wilting, Gramps said, "Why don't you kids get out of here." We didn't argue with him, even though there was more work yet to be done. There was always more work to be done those long summer days.

We grabbed our bathing suits and headed for the pond. We hadn't been skinny dipping since the spring after my *bat mitzvah*, when Gramma had blown a gasket after discovering that we had been swimming together in the nude.

"Joe, I expected better of you," she finally had said after she had calmed down a bit. "After all, you're older and have to be the responsible one."

"Yes, ma'am," he'd said, contritely. Joe never stood up to her, as much as I might have wanted him to.

"Now, promise me you'll always watch over our Judith, protect her, even from herself."

"Yes, ma'am." He had solemnly sworn.

Whenever they started talking about me like that, I'd inevitably storm out of the room. After all, if they were going to speak about me in the third person, as though I had no say in anything, why bother listening?

The problem was that Joe *did* listen to Gramma and obeyed her every command. After that, whenever I tried to convince him that we didn't need bathing suits, he'd simply stand there, all 210 pounds of him, refusing to move until I acquiesced. Not that I accepted the new status quo easily. However, the couple of times I stripped and jumped into the pond naked, he just turned his head and walked away, and I had to swim by myself. Well, not quite alone. Maverick loved splashing with me. But it wasn't as much fun without Joe.

So, of course, that summer day before our senior year, Joe insisted that we get our bathing suits before heading out to the pond. But I threw mine at him and started running.

"If you can catch me, maybe I'll wear it," I hollered.

I knew I couldn't outrun him, but it was fun teasing

him. And, maybe, just maybe, I could convince him that we should skinny dip. After all, it had been three years since I'd seen him naked. I often wondered what he looked like, now that he had a man's body. Of course, I knew how large his chest and arms had become, with smooth, strong muscles playing under his skin that was now covered with curly dark blonde hair. I loved the sensation of wonder and safety, of all that gentle strength, when he would lift me up to help me reach something high. I couldn't help being curious about how the rest of him had changed — especially, that mysterious bulge between his legs.

As I ran ahead, fantasizing about him, I veered off the path, to take a shortcut through the woods, and that was when I saw Gramma. Her arms spread as far as she could reach around the trunk of the biggest, oldest oak on the property, her cheek pressed against the rough bark, her eyes closed, her face calm, peaceful. I quickly crouched behind a boulder, hiding, feeling guilty for spying on her, but too curious to not look. Something stirred in the pit of my stomach, reaching down into my groin, with a pulsing sensation that both shamed and excited me.

Joe caught up with me, glanced at Gramma, and quickly pulled me away. But the sight of Gramma in private communion, melding her own spirit with that of the ancient tree, was burned indelibly into my mind. She had seemed so vulnerable, and yet fortified, as though the oak's own strength was seeping into her, buoying and healing her. Until that moment, I had never fully understood that Gramma could be anything other than the assured bulwark she was to us.

Joe and I never discussed what we had seen, the sacred sensuality that wasn't meant to be ours. It was Gramma's private moment that we had expropriated by spying on her.

Nor did I ever ask Gramma about it.

And Joe and I never did skinny dip again.

I've spent an entire day here and I've barely scratched the surface of all I have to do. Apparently, Gramma and Grampa never threw anything away, so there are generations and generations of trash and treasures all around the property. Am I foolhardy, thinking I can get everything organized and packed up within one week? What will I do if I don't finish before next Monday? No matter what, I simply can't face the prospect of staying longer or returning here ever again.

After my supper of omelet, salad and wine, I retreat to Grampa's study, to continue going through the desk. The room is denuded without the photos, stripped to the bare walls. In the bottom right desk drawer, where I knew it would be, is the large purple Louis Sherry candy tin box in which Gramma had organized their letters to each other from The War. Each year was bound together by a now frayed and faded red ribbon. Within each bundle, she had interspliced their letters chronologically, merging the two collections into one.

Grampa had called Gramma's letters his lifeline. They had kept him sane — and safe —amidst the horrors of jungle warfare. Sometimes, I would come into the study and I'd find him holding them, a faraway look in his eyes. He read a few of them to me over the years, shown me the pictures they had sent each other, of Mom as a baby, Gramma as a fresh-faced young woman, him as a skinny, uniformed soldier. Someday, I'll have to read them all, one by one, in the order they had been written.

I wrap the old scuffed tin carefully in bubble wrap and pack it into one of the cardboard boxes, along with other mementos from the desk: The magnifying glass. Gramma's black enameled fountain pen with the gold nib. Grampa's corncob pipe which still smells of his cherry tobacco. The corncob was his favorite, because he said it produced a sweeter taste. I think he also liked the simplicity of it, the connection to his forbearers of a pipe made from a corn husk they might have grown on this very property. The rest of his collection — the Meerschaums and calabashes that he had inherited, and others of fine-grained or gnarled woods that had been gifts or that had caught his attention from his store inventory — usually stayed in their racks, while he smoked this one pipe almost daily. I want only the corncob.

I uncover no other will, or anything that might reveal Gramma's state of mind when she wrote the one Denton gave me. If any such documents or notes exist, they aren't anywhere in the study. In the file cabinet next to the desk, I find Gramma's medical records. She had been ill for years without telling me. Blood tests. X-ray and CATscan reports. Urine analyses. Reams of paper filled with numbers and medical or insurance technobabble I can't possibly decipher, with not one simple statement of a diagnosis. Still, I can't bring myself to throw them out.

By 2:30 am, I'm so numb I can no longer discern what's junk and what's invaluable. At least, I have the desk and file cabinet sorted out, and most of the study's cabinets. I stumble upstairs to my bedroom, with only a moment's pause at the creaking step, the sound a sense memory that will always be connected to my grandparents sleeping nearby.

The last thing I see before falling fast asleep is that damned chair. Without fail, I remind myself, I'll get rid of it tomorrow.

WEDNESDAY

"Isn't she beautiful?"
"So peaceful."
"Martha's with God now."
The litany of comments washes over me, as what seems like the entire village files past Gramma's coffin. I want to scream, "No! She isn't beautiful. She's a plastic mannequin made up to look like Martha Schmoyer." That thing in the coffin is nothing like my Gramma, with her steely wise eyes that never let me get away with anything or her soft voice that could feel like honey on my heart when I pleased her. No, I don't see my Gramma lying there on the tufted white satin which would be more appropriate for a brothel boudoir than Martha Schmoyer's final resting place.

I don't scream, and I don't cry. I just stand here, at the head of the coffin, my arms at my side, like a soldier on review, or a child so hungry that she's dulled even to the rumble of her own stomach.

I hadn't really known what to expect when I arrived at the Black Bear Moravian Church. But certainly not this. Gramma lying in state in the entrance hall, so anyone arriving for the funeral would have to walk past her.

All I knew from Mr. Morton's email that was waiting for me when I landed at Kennedy was that I was expected at the church at 9:30 am, and that everything had been arranged and prepaid by Gramma, before she passed away. He offered to pick me up at the farm in the one Cadillac limo the funeral home kept for the bereaved. But I didn't respond to the suggestion, and he didn't pursue it.

When I arrived, Mr. Morton met me at the front

door, gently took me by the arm and planted me at the head of the glossy mahogany coffin. A wooden folding chair had been placed there, should I need or want it. But people started filing in almost immediately, and to sit would have meant that they would have towered over me, and I would have felt even more irrelevant than I already am. Just one more ornament among the profusion of mismatched flower arrangements with identical-looking small white enveloped cards.

So, here I stand, staring down into the coffin, at the figure with that waxy complexion. Gramma's wearing the grey Armani suit I bought her three years ago, during her last visit to Paris. It's too large now. This is probably the first time it's been off the hanger since our dinner together that night at *La Coquille*, the little bistro in the Latin Quarter she preferred, because she knew it and the waiters knew her and she had long ago deciphered the menu. Gramma had never been able to master French, as hard as she tried for my sake, but she got along just fine in Paris, nevertheless. Gramma got along wherever she went, as long as she had a chance to get used to things.

Soon, the vestibule fills with people. They wait patiently in line for their last goodbye to Martha Schmoyer, village matriarch and friend to all. People file past me, mumbling their "sorrys" and regrets, touching me on my shoulder or arm or reaching for my hand to grasp it. I acknowledge their presence with a nod to each, like one of those big-headed bobbing dolls. I recognize many of the faces. Most wear solemn expressions to match the dark funeral suits they've dug out from the backs of their closets. A few have tears in their eyes. Moving on, each is guided by an usher through the second set of doors to the sanctuary.

I had nearly forgotten what it was like to be a person of color in a sea of white faces. Mrs. Haus, Eileen Wilson, Mrs. Genters, Mr. and Mrs. Borger, Tiffany Jeffries, Gene Engelhardt, Alice Doughty, Mr. Wilcox, Bob Hayes and his son Brian and his father Bruce — nearly everyone I knew is here, even Maybeth Peters and Billy Thompson.

And Joe, wearing a dark suit that looks like it's been borrowed from someone twenty pounds lighter and two inches shorter. I see him the moment he enters the room, at the bend in the line, just before it snakes through the doors and presumably extends down the outside steps. Among all the people filling the vestibule, Joe looms. It isn't just his size, though he's larger than most, even more so now that he's developed a beer belly and his football-hero muscle has gone to flab. I feel his presence as a scorching resonance, discordant and warped, a mockery of the connection, the friendship we'd once shared. Betty walks by his side, wearing a dark blue belted dress, her light brown hair loose around her shoulders. Her right hand is hooked into Joe's arm, her head pressed against his upper arm. She holds a tissue to her face, making a show of drying her tears, though I see no actual dampness.

The line moves at a snail's pace, one person at a time; each one looks down at Gramma, with varying degrees of affection and solemnity, then greets me, the last remaining Schmoyer of the long line of Black Bear Schmoyers, even though my name is Ormand, and my skin the wrong color. One by one, the line diminishes between Joe and me. Though it undoubtedly continues behind him, I don't see past him, as he approaches closer and closer.

When Joe reaches the coffin, he gazes down at Gramma, while I nod to someone whom I don't really notice, not hearing the words being mouthed by the figure who then pats me on the shoulder and moves on. All I see is Joe tenderly brushing a curl of Gramma's white hair from her forehead, so it looks the way she liked it. He mumbles something to her under his breath. When he looks at me, his bloodshot eyes are brimming with fat tears that trickle freely down his cheeks. Damned if he doesn't seem to be holding himself tightly, trying not to reach out for me. This from the man who once couldn't stand to be near me, let alone touch me, perhaps afraid that my dark skin might rub off on him. He opens his mouth to speak, but no words come. Instead, he shakes his head slowly, deeply dejected. I never would have thought him so capable of putting on such a good show. Betty must have coached him. Now she's handing him a tissue while she pulls on his arm, coaxing him away from me and Gramma. I have to admit that's a nice touch.

Dozens of people follow after Joe. Did anyone in Black Bear stay away? Are any stores or schools or offices open? What should have been my private, personal farewell has become a public event, requiring my participation.

Eventually, I'm finally alone with Gramma. I search her composed face that's too still, and her neatly arranged body that has none of her poise, for some hint of the woman who taught me more about love and life than anyone, the woman who knew my heart even when I didn't, even when I struggled in vain against her unflinching sureness. No, nothing of her remains.

Then I see the ring. Mom's ring, with the two sapphires on either side of a small mine cut diamond. Gramma had taken it from Mom's lifeless hand at the hospital. I don't believe Gramma ever removed it from that day forward. Other than her plain gold wedding band that she still wears, it's the only ring I've ever seen on her. I reach across her body to take her right hand in mine. The touch of her cool, inert flesh is a shock of death made real. Mom's ring slips off her finger, with no friction or resistance. Like the Armani suit, it had become too large for her. I place the ring on my right index finger, vowing it will remain with me forever.

"*Adieu*, Gramma," I say to no one in particular, because Gramma isn't here, not in this lifeless body. Still, I need to say it, and this will be my last chance.

A small white woman, in her late thirties and attired in an understated tweed suit, approaches me. "Judith, I'm Rebecca. Rebecca Weis. May I?" she asks, as she holds up a small black grosgrain ribbon.

"Yes, please," I say, not sure what else I should do or say.

She pins the ribbon on my left lapel, over my heart, then snips it with a tiny brass scissor, symbolizing the traditional rending of garments by Jewish mourners. At the same time, she says a short prayer in Hebrew. *"Baruch atah Adonai Eloheinu melech ha'olam dayan ha'emet. Blessed art Thou, Adonai our God, Ruler of the universe, Judge of truth."* We say *"Amen"* together. Then, she gives me a small, sad smile. I thank her as she disappears through the doors to the sanctuary.

It happened so quickly, a brief moment of Jewish ritual. But I'm left with an indelible sense of her gentle, almost proprietary concern, the realization that, somehow, I'm not alone in this stronghold of Christianity.

I look down at the torn ribbon on my chest. I've worn a similar one only once before, at Mom's funeral. The first time I saw such a ribbon was at *Grand-père* David's funeral, on *Grand-mère* Amélie's tailored black lapel.

Two weeks after I turned seven, *Grand-père* David died — just as the two of us were beginning to know each other. Until I was six, he didn't have much to do with me, saying that children weren't interesting until they reached an age when you could reason with them. I think he didn't trust young children to be civil or fully toilet trained. Or, maybe, he really was a cold fish, with no instinct for nurturing the young. I'll never know.

Grand-père was so formal that Mom had to dress me in fine, "ladylike" dresses or skirts — never slacks — whenever we would visit them, even though they lived in the flat above us. And I had to obey all kinds of rules, like not speaking unless I was spoken to, not running around in their apartment, and saying *merci* and *s'il vous plait* for everything.

In my mind, when I picture *Grand-père*, I remember how he towered so high above me. I'd stare up at his ebony face and shaved shiny head, and wonder if he could touch the sun. When he frowned, I would hide in fear. But when he smiled, I felt blessed.

Once I was old enough for *Grand-père* to pay attention to me, the fun began. He'd take me aside and we'd invent games together — playing geography on his big library globe, or making up "what if" worlds in which everything would be changed because of a single scientific invention or one person doing something differently. Sometimes, he'd call to me from the stairwell, and with a wink of his eye, say, "Let's go have an adventure." And off we would wander, exploring the streets of *Montparnasse* or *Ste. Germain des Pres* or some other exciting, sometimes hectic neighborhood. He encouraged me to observe people and places, close my eyes, and then describe them to him. Pressing me to see more and more details, he challenged me to understand what those details meant. "Learn to read the hidden story behind the façade, *ma petite*, and you'll be formidable in any enterprise you pursue."

Grand-père promised me that when I was old enough, he'd take me to his office, where I could play the people game with him, watching silently during his meetings, then help him make decisions based on what I saw. However, it never happened. Suddenly, he was gone. Dead. I understood what that meant, because Polichinelle, the puppy *Papa* had given me, had been run over when he had darted from the playground into the street.

I don't remember much about *Grand-père's* funeral, except that my new black stockings itched and lots of strangers seemed to know me well enough to touch or kiss me. I was confused about how I was supposed to act, now that *Grand-père* was dead. What was the correct, ladylike behavior he would approve of?

The strongest memory I have of that week was the bustle of activity in their apartment, of people coming and going from morning to night, bringing and eating food, talking and praying and eating some more. And *Grand-mère* Amélie in the middle, seemingly untouched by it all. She sat on a low chair in their salon, dressed from head to toe in black, while everything else about her was red, from her tear-stained eyes to her flushed light cocoa face to her small hands that were constantly twisting one of her *lace mouchoirs* — hankies. What surprised me the most was that she wore no makeup or jewelry, not even her diamond wedding band; the only adornment was a small torn black ribbon on her chest.

She appeared almost as lost and perplexed as I was.

I went up to *Grand-mère*, soon after we returned home from the cemetery, and I stood by her side, waiting for her to notice me. Long minutes went by. As aloof as *Grand-père* had been until I turned six, *Grand-mère* had been the complete opposite, fussing over me with cuddles, gifts and special stories that only the two of us shared. Yet, here she was, not only ignoring me, but seeming to be vacant from herself, empty. It frightened me.

After what felt like forever, with her eyes not focusing on anything, especially not on me, I touched her hand lightly. She jerked, as though my fingers had given her an electric shock, then she looked at me with surprise. I wasn't sure if it was that she hadn't expected to find me there, or that she hadn't remembered until that moment that I even existed.

With a sigh, she gathered me onto her lap, and we stayed there, together, for the better part of the afternoon. Sometimes, we were silent. Other times, she was as she always was, chatty and conversational, brimming with the stories I loved hearing from her, about our family and people she had known in her own youth, and how *Grand-père* had swept her off her feet when he had been only fifteen, the darkest boy she'd ever seen, and so very handsome.

Grand-mère and I created a private cocoon for ourselves in that busy salon of well-wishers and mourners. Then, a certain friend of *Grand-père's*, a stunning white woman with flaming red hair came into the room, and *Grand-mère* stood suddenly, barely giving me a chance to scramble off her lap. *Papa* rushed to her, to find out what was wrong, and after a few whispers with *Grand-mère*, he went over to that strange woman, took her firmly by the elbow and quickly escorted her out of the flat.

Within a few weeks of *Grand-père's* funeral, *Grand-mère* took to her bed. When she died a couple of months later, I knew a bit better what was expected of me, but I didn't have *Grand-mère* to help me through it. Nor did I learn what the fuss was about that lady friend, until years later, when I overheard Mom and *Papa* arguing. Soon after, we left him, to live in New York.

Thank goodness, it's Jeff Smith who comes into the vestibule to escort me into the Black Bear Moravian Church sanctuary, and not one of the others. Still trim and fit, he looks much older, with thinning grey hair and deeper crinkles around his eyes and mouth. I don't know why it surprises me to look at him and see the passage of time. After all, he's easily twenty-five years my senior. Yet, somehow, I always imagined him as ageless.

As we walk through the crowded sanctuary, Jeff holds my elbow, gently guiding me. So many people fill the sanctuary that a few dozen of the younger folks have to stand along the side walls. The expanse of white faces is punctuated by far more dark shades — Mediterranean sallow to chocolate brown — than I have ever seen in Black Bear. Even so, people of color are only a small scattering among the scores of Caucasians. Exceptions that make the rule even more glaring.

Outside, the April day is chilly, but the sanctuary is overheated with the press of so many warm bodies. Paper funeral fans flutter throughout the room, waving as though they have wills of their own. Just seeing others cool themselves with the fans makes me feel hot and stifled.

One seat remains open, obviously reserved for me — all the way in the front, in the first pew, on the middle aisle. Everyone turns to watch, as Jeff and I walk forward. I feel their eyes on me as palpably as if their hands are still touching and prodding. I want to hide away, be anywhere in the world but here in Black Bear, in this church, at this funeral. Hoping to avoid meeting any of the stares, I look ahead at the geometric patterns of the carpet, the carved dark wood sides of the pews, the stained glass cross embedded in the high wall behind the pulpit. That huge gem-colored cross with the light streaming through it in almost heavenly rays still makes me feel so very small and out of place, as it used to when I was a child.

As I take my seat in the front pew, Mrs. Ringenhauer, the pastor's wife, scoots over to make more room for me. Our hips don't press against each other so much as abut, cloth to cloth. She hands me one of the paper fans; the front has "Morton Funeral Home" in black letters, while the other side has the twenty-third psalm against an idyllic, pastoral painting of a spring meadow. I drop the fan into my lap; it would take too much energy to use it.

Mrs. Ringenhauer has aged badly, but doesn't seem sickly. Just spent, with a gaunt face etched with a roadmap of lines, wispy grey hair and twisted arthritic hands. As a youngster, just a glance from her made me uneasy, certain that she was judging me and finding me wanting. What a relief that she doesn't try to talk to me or squeeze my forearm or make any other gestures of solace or solicitude. Instead, she looks straight ahead at the empty pulpit.

Mrs. Wallace plays a soft, gentle hymn on the organ. Hearing it up close, I realize that music had been playing the entire time I stood at the coffin, but I hadn't been aware of it as anything other than a subliminal buzz underlying all the greetings and condolences and hands touching me.

My earliest memories of this church are of music. How the Moravians love their hymns, and my Gramma and Grampa were no exception. Before I became too uncomfortable with the Jesus prayers and overt, seemingly disapproving stares, I enjoyed coming to services with them to hear all the voices raised in song. Grampa was a gruff baritone and went slightly off key on only the very low or high notes; Gramma was a warm, clear alto, with a wispy vibrato when she held a note longer than a half measure. When I would sit between them, I'd be buoyed up by their voices that blended so smoothly.

I stopped joining them at the church about a year after I came to live with them, even though they continued to take me to services at *Temple Hesed* in Scranton. Not that the three of us had been that religious. Friday evening or Saturday morning at synagogue, Sunday at church — neither was something we'd do every week. Only occasionally and of course for high holy days.

The one exception was that first year, when I was required to attend a certain number of *Shabbat* services, as I studied for my *bat mitzvah*. They'd sit on either side of me at temple, joining in the prayers, often discussing the *Torah* passage in the car on the way home, with the same joy I heard in their voices when singing their Moravian hymns. Sometimes, I would wonder if the temple services were more meaningful to them than they were to me. Not that I wasn't proud of being Jewish, but all that studying and being stuck inside on Saturday mornings was a hassle for a twelve-year old girl. And on top of the homework *Hesed's* Rabbi Cohen gave me, I had to complete the studies that *Papa* had his rabbi send me from Paris, not trusting an American Jewish education to be adequate for a proper *bat mitzvah*.

Gramma's and Grampa's delight in going to temple probably had a lot to do with wanting to share something special with me, but I sometimes wonder if it had also been their way of acknowledging and accepting my mother's choice to convert to Judaism, as they never could when she'd been alive.

Pastor Ringenhauer enters from a side door, steps up onto the raised chancel and takes his place behind the pulpit. Just as intimidating as ever with his meticulously trimmed Van Dyke beard and small black eyes, Pastor Ringenhauer isn't the tall, overpowering figure of my memories, nor does he fill his long black robe as fully. His dark brown beard is now completely white, while the thick head of neatly combed, Brylcreemed hair is nearly gone, except for a thin, close-cropped white fringe along the edge of his skull. He opens his black prayer book, leans heavily on the lectern and looks directly at me. Perhaps, he's acknowledging me as the deceased's kin, but it seems more like his usual disapproving stare. Then, he nods to someone in the back; I turn to see who.

The door in the back of the sanctuary opens and in rolls the closed casket, flanked by six pallbearers. I assume choosing them was another detail that Gramma took care of before she died. Jeff Smith, Dr. Nieffenegger, Al Marks, Jennifer Dougherty and Walt Bloch all make sense, for the affection, respect and friendship Gramma had long felt for each of them. But Joe? Why is he there?

As they push the coffin slowly down the aisle, the buzz of whispered comments and conversations quiet, row by row, until all is silent around me, except the rasping of the wheels of the coffin dolly gliding over the carpet and the fluttering of the paper fans. They position the casket parallel to the altar table, then sit down.

"Page 177," Pastor Ringenhauer announces in a conversational tone, which changes to the commanding power I remember the minute he starts to read. "*Lord,*" he calls out to God I am sure, but also to the assembly. "*Lord, our God, in whom we live, and move, and have our being.*"

After an initial shuffle of folks opening their prayer books, and, finding the right page, most people respond, "*Have mercy upon us.*"

"*Lord, our God,*" the pastor intones. "*You do not willingly bring affliction or grief to your children.*"

"*Leave your peace with us.*" The congregation builds up momentum, as they find their place in the service.

"*Lord, our God, you have raised Christ from death as the assurance that those who sleep in death will also be raised.*"

"*Bless and comfort us, we humbly pray.*"

And so it continues. Each time the pastor's stained-glass voice rings out, the reply comes back to him with even greater verve, with the power of scores of voices chanting in unison, feeding him more energy and sanctimony. It's a crescendo of prayer that I've seen replayed in churches, mosques, temples and spirit houses all over the world. What is it about faith, that it requires human reaction and interaction to make it real for us?

Yet, when it isn't your own faith, how like primitive incantations it sounds. I hear Jesus Christ this and redemption that, and none of it matters to me — just mouthed words that are appropriate only because Gramma was a Christian in the truest sense. But she'll never again hear any of it. Funerals are supposed to be a comfort and release for the family of the deceased; this is meaningless to me.

Then, the music begins.

When Mrs. Wallace plays the first few chords, the words of "*In the Garden*" fill my mind before anyone begins singing. It was one of Gramma's favorite hymns. She'd hum it or sing it out loud at any time of day or night, but especially when she was working in her kitchen garden or after attending Sunday services.

I come to the garden alone,
While the dew is still on the roses.
And the voice I hear, falling on my ear,
The Son of God discloses.

And He walks with me, and He talks with me,
And He tells me I am His own.
And the joy we share as we tarry there
None other has known.

Why can't I hear Gramma's voice in my mind's ear? Drowned out by the sound of so many other voices, I can't distinguish the tone and timbre that had been uniquely hers. I concentrate on the pauses between notes, where I can almost believe I hear her, but it's too distant and faint. A memory lost forever.

They sing all three stanzas, repeating the chorus each time.

And He walks with me, and He talks with me

And He tells me I am His own....

No, not in the silence between the notes, but in the exuberance of the congregation as they sway to the chorus, like an orthodox *rebbe* carried away by the words of the *Torah*, dovening to the harmonies that call to him within the ancient syllables. I still don't hear her voice, but her spirit, Gramma's joy in living and singing her faith, bubbling within her, consuming her, driving her forward through her days. I stop cringing when they sing of the *"Son of God,"* because though I could never believe in Jesus, I'll always believe in Gramma.

> *And the joy we share, as we tarry there*
> *None other has known.*

Pastor Ringenhauer waits several moments after the hymn ends, almost as though he's testing the sudden silence, or allowing us time to climb down from the heights of the last chord. Then, without saying a word, he nods to a man in the front pew on the other side of the center aisle from me. Rebecca, the woman who cut my mourner's ribbon, sits beside him, and he squeezes her hand as he stands.

A thoroughly average, undistinguished individual of medium height and medium build, with only a touch of early middle age spread, and slightly salted medium brown hair that's beginning to recede, I don't know the man and wouldn't have noticed him in a crowd, except for the fact that he wears a blue and white embroidered *yarmulke*. He walks with a certain sense of self, erect and much more comfortable than I would expect a religious Jew to be in a church, especially this church.

When he stands beside the pastor at the pulpit, the pastor says, "Welcome back, Rabbi Weis. Thank you for coming today to share our prayers for Martha Schmoyer."

As the pastor sits down on one of the chairs at the back of the chancel platform, the rabbi says, "Thank you, Pastor Ringenhauer." His voice is mellow, with a strange hint of southern lilt overlying the singsong tone of Brooklyn. About forty, forty-five years old, he wears gold-rimmed bifocals. When he looks at me, he cocks his head downward, focusing through the upper part of the lenses. His eyes on me are a brief, gentle touch. Then he glances at Rebecca; their connection is unmistakable, probably husband and wife. When she looks back at him, her face glows. I realize she's younger than I first assumed — probably no more than her early thirties, about my age.

"I'm honored to be here, to share this celebration of Martha Schmoyer's life," he begins. "We have a prayer that many Jewish men sing to their wives on *Shabbat*, the Sabbath, and I think you might know it also, since it comes from the Bible that is our common bond. From the Book of Proverbs, to be precise. Knowing Martha, how could we not feel it was written for her?" He opens his prayer book.

"*A Woman of Valor, who can find?*" The rabbi speaks with an emphatic tenderness. "*She is more precious than corals. Her husband places his trust in her and only profits thereby. She brings him good, not harm, all the days of her life....*"

I feel such pride that a rabbi would choose this paean to Jewish women written thousands of years ago to praise my Moravian Gramma. Even more than the tribute it is to Gramma, it's my heritage, of the many women who came before me, in my family and in my faith, over the centuries. Starting with the biblical Matriarchs, Sarah, Miriam, Judith, my namesake, and coming forward through the generations to Gramma Martha, *Grand-mere* Amélie and Mom. Women who worked, achieved, fought, lived. It roots me, to think of them, the women whose blood and spirit I carry.

"*... She opens her mouth with wisdom and the teaching of kindness is on her tongue. She looks after the conduct of her household and never tastes the bread of sloth. Her children rise up and make her happy; her husband praises her: 'Many women have excelled, but you outshine them all!' Grace is elusive and beauty is vain, but a woman who fears God, she shall be praised. Give her* *credit for the fruit of her labors and let her achievements praise her at the gates."*

The rabbi looks down at his prayer book and gently touches the open page with his fingertips. The gesture is almost a lover's caress. Then, he glances once more at his wife, before speaking.

"Yes, a woman of valor. Our Martha was that, and more. She was my friend, and a friend to *Beth Shalom*. From the very beginning, she made our small congregation welcome, giving us the keys to Henry's empty drugstore for our *Shabbat* services and *Torah* study, until we were able to build our own temple, and she refused to accept any rent. By choosing to see no difference between us and the rest of the community, she forced others to look beyond established prejudices and superstitions to understand how similar we all are.

"It wasn't easy for Martha. Bigots tried to drive us out of Black Bear, with their hateful graffiti of swastikas painted all over Henry's beautiful little store. However, she persevered. Not alone, of course. Pastor Ringenhauer soon stood up with her, as did so many of you who are here today. That was the force of righteousness within Martha; none of us could defy her." The rabbi smiled. "Not for long.

"I fully believe that Martha championed us, not because her own daughter had chosen our faith, nor because the granddaughter she raised and cherished is Jewish, but because it was in Martha's nature to be generous and open-hearted to all who came into her home. I'm not just referring to the farm on Mountainview Road, but to Black Bear, her home, which is now, thanks to Martha and many of you here today, our home as well.

"Martha Schmoyer. A woman of valor and righteousness. Of strength of will and power. A worthy matriarch for Black Bear and a founding mother of *Temple Beth Shalom. Adonai, God, we beseech you, give her credit for the fruit of her labors and let her achievements praise her at the gates."*

When he recites the *"el moley rachamim"* the Jewish Mourners' Prayer, for my Gramma Martha, here in her church, I don't know which surprises me more. That a rabbi should be praying in the Black Bear Moravian Church, in Hebrew, no less. Or that Gramma's funeral should include a Hebrew prayer naming her according to Jewish tradition, *"Martha bat Alfred v'Frieda,"* so that my great-grandparents are also part of a prayer that they might have considered tantamount to pagan.

When he finishes the Hebrew, he repeats it in English. *"Compassionate God, eternal Spirit of the universe, grant perfect rest in Your sheltering presence to Martha, daughter of Alfred and Frieda, who has entered eternity. O God of mercy, let her find refuge in Your eternal presence, in the shadow of Your wings, and let her soul be bound up in the bond of everlasting life. God is her inheritance. May she rest in peace, and let us say: Amen."*

Whispered, exclaimed, and choked *Amens* echo around the room.

The rabbi nods to the pastor, acknowledges me once more and then returns to his seat on the opposite pew beside his wife. As they settle into each other, she brushes her lips against his cheek.

I stare at them, at the rabbi and his wife, how anchored they seem to be within themselves and each other. Somehow, this rabbi was a friend of Gramma's. No, of Martha's — the woman who existed beyond her relationship to me, who was defined not by the blood and bonds we shared, but by who she was with people and events of which I knew nothing. A synagogue, here in Black Bear? Nazi graffiti on Grampa's drugstore? Struggles against anti-Semitism? All with her in the midst of the fray?

Gramma, what else didn't you tell me or let me see? And why didn't I ask you when I had the chance?

I realize that I haven't been listening to the pastor, assuming the droning sound of his words were just more Jesus prayers. When he laughs, I'm jolted out of my reveries.

"Oh yes," he says, "Martha was a stubborn woman."

My memories of Pastor Ringenhauer don't include

him ever laughing. Even his smiles once seemed somehow sinister or disapproving to me. Seeing him now makes me realize that he, too, loved my Gramma. In a different way than I did, or Grampa or her other friends. But real, nevertheless.

"Bullheaded even," he continues with a light, wry lilt to his deep baritone. "Any of us who ever crossed her, no matter how unintentionally, soon learned that lesson. However, it was a stubbornness borne of her innate sense of charity, justice and piety. Once Martha decided that someone wasn't behaving in a Christian manner, she'd let you know, in no uncertain terms, and set about fixing it, one way or another. Pity the poor fool who tried to thwart her."

Lowering his head, he prays, *"Gracious Lord, Martha Schmoyer has passed from this life and we will miss her, but we take comfort in knowing that she is with You, as You have promised. Glory be to Him who is the Resurrection and the Life. In Jesus's name, Amen."*

Once again the *Amens* echo.

Glancing around the sanctuary, the pastor says, "Now, it's your turn to share your memories of Martha with us. What do you celebrate and honor about her and her life? How was God visible through her?"

Though the room fills with the rustling of people moving uncomfortably in their seats, no one speaks up. This community has never been very effusive, clinging tightly to the stoic manners of their mostly Germanic ancestors. Whispered gossip rather than public tributes are more their way.

The pastor continues to glide his eyes along each row, patient and determined.

Finally, AH Engelhardt struggles to get to his feet, using first his two aluminum canes and then the back of the pew in front of him to pull himself up.

"AH, please, you can speak from your seat," the pastor says.

"No thank you, pastor." AH still speaks with authority, with none of the shake of his aged body in his voice. Dapper as ever, in a three-piece suit and his crimson college tie, he must be close to ninety years. "I may be old and infirm, but I was never one to sit when Martha or any woman I respected entered the room. I'll do no less for her now."

Leaning heavily on the forward pew, AH tilts his head towards Gramma's coffin. "Martha." He says her name quite tenderly, and I have the distinct impression he's speaking directly to her. Then, he straightens his shoulders, while still holding onto the pew, and addresses the congregation. "She was an Engelhardt, you know. Not by name, but my cousin nevertheless. You should have seen her as a girl. Beautiful, true, but more than that. Spirited and... well... sometimes intractable. But only when her back was up. And she got it up only over important matters that the rest of us might have ignored, if it weren't for Martha and her righteous indignation. Some might have called her sharp-tongued, but I never minded the way she would stick her nose into my business, because she was just as hard on herself." AH pauses. As he drifts back in his memories to a time before most of us were born or were even contemplated, his clean shaven parchment-thin skin takes on a soft, younger, luminous appearance.

"I fell in love with her the day she was born. My mama was the village midwife back then. At ten years old, I was suddenly her oldest and just learning all that meant, because my brother Eugene had died from the croup that winter. When Mama was called to Frieda's birthing bed, Pa had taken the truck to Scranton. So, it fell to me to drive the wagon to the Hausman's. Mama was great at handling the truck, but she and that horse never did get along.

"I'd never been to a birth before, and I didn't see it then. Instead, I took the Hausman kids to the barn to help me care for our horse, and kept them there until we were called back inside. There she was, Martha, red and wrinkly and bawling her head off. Mama put her in my arms; I was terrified, I can tell you. Such a tiny thing, making all that noise. Then, Martha looked up at me with those bright blue eyes of hers and stopped her crying, and I was hooked." AH chuckles softly. "From that day on, Martha could ask anything of me, and I would have done it. She knew it, too. Even then, as an infant, she knew. She was special that way, in her knowing and the way she could create a connection with another soul that could last a lifetime.

"Throughout her life, Martha was the angel on my shoulder, my conscience, my moral barometer. Anytime I wasn't sure what the right thing was, all I needed to do was think of Martha. That would settle matters, because when I listened carefully within me, I would hear her voice, telling me to be good. God had been with her the day she was born, and the Spirit of God remained with her until the day she died. I was blessed to be there at the beginning and be the first to know the truth of her. And I was there at her last breath, when she opened her heart to God and finally submitted to His will, as she would never submit to any living creature." He looks at the coffin once more. "I can hear what you'd be saying to me now, if you could, Martha. You'd be telling me I've rambled on long enough. But, no, young lady, it isn't nonsense. You were my angel, and always will be."

Taking the neatly folded handkerchief from his breast pocket to dab at his eyes, AH carefully lowers himself back to his seat.

After only a moment of silence, Bruce Hayes stands. About the same age as Gramma, Mr. Hayes hasn't changed much over the seventeen years I've been away. Still small and spry, almost elfin, with a mischievous grin that got him in trouble with the married men whose wives he attracted and, if rumors were to be believed, often bedded. His curly brown hair is now quite white and cropped in a severe crew cut. He wears faded jeans, which is what he usually wore. I doubt he ever owned any other kind of trousers. Instead of his usual denim flannel, he wears a white oxford shirt, a four inch wide mottled tie and a blue blazer with enormous lapels — no doubt purchased back in the seventies and taken out of the closet only on occasions such as this.

"Any of you old enough to remember the '55 flood, you might recall what it was like." His squeaky mountain twang is a bit muted today. I'm sure he still lays it on thick whenever he wants to remind folks that he's a true born-and-bred son of Black Bear. "The firehall siren blasted us into action. Henry and me, we drove the ambulance out to higher ground and got into gear, helping the firemen. Sorry gals, that was before women were full members of either company. You got to admit things were pretty good back then. You knew who was who just by seeing who wore pants or a skirt. Firemen and ambulance crews were men. The ladies were the auxiliary. That morning after the hurricane passed, when everybody woke up and saw just how bad the flood was, the ladies were at the mountain top outpost we'd set up, handing out coffee and sandwiches and taking care of the people we'd rescue, giving them blankets and finding high ground places for them to stay.

"Martha was nowhere to be seen. Henry didn't fret about it none. Not at first. Their farm was above the flood plain, so he figured she was sitting at home with their kids." Bruce slaps his thigh. "Not Martha. She'd been seen by lots of folks, chugging along in Henry's fishing boat, the one with the old tired Evinrude outboard motor he barely kept alive with all his tinkering. Damned if she wasn't as busy as any of the firemen, rescuing folks trapped by the flood waters. When Henry heard about it, he popped a cork. But when he finally found her, she got to talking before he could get a word in edgewise. You all know what I mean. Contrary as all get out, that woman could use words better than anyone. She could make you believe day was night. Nothing, not even her husband, was going to stop her from doing what she'd set her mind on. That's Martha. She was like that even in school. Darnedest woman I ever met for making her own rules and then getting you to think it was your idea. Never did understand her, but never respected any woman more. Yeah, pastor, God was in Martha's life, but she was a devil to control. Henry could tell you that."

One by one, others stand to speak, sharing their fond memories of my Gramma. Sometimes, I recognize her in what they have to say. Other times, it's as though they're talking about a stranger who seems familiar in her manners and values, but whom I never really knew. Once or twice, I could swear I hear undercurrents in the speakers' voices, especially when they mention how Gramma could be so sure of herself, regardless of what others wanted or believed. I'm probably imagining things, projecting my own memories onto theirs. After all, this is a funeral, a time for tribute — not old grievances — and for making Gramma come alive for us one last time.

Eventually, the pastor glances at me, with a question in his eyes. I realize he's giving me an opportunity to speak. What could I say that would be meaningful, that I haven't already said in my heart or will continue to feel for the rest of my life? Gramma is gone, and her death is a gaping hole within me.

It's a fleeting moment, a dip of the pastor's eyes as he looks around the room once more. When no one else stands to speak, the pastor takes firm control over the service again, announcing, "Hymn number 783."

At the end of the hymn, the pastor raises both hands in the air and bows his head, as I had seen him do many times as a child. "*Gracious God,*" the pastor prays in that deep baritone of his. "*We know Martha is now at Your side, and we rejoice for her. But our hearts are also heavy with our own grief to no longer have her with us. As a father has compassion on his children, have compassion on those who honor you. The Lord lifts up those who are bowed down, and sustains those who are bereaved. The steadfast love of the Lord lasts forever, and his goodness endures for all generations. Glory be to the Father, and to the Son, and to the Holy Spirit, as it was in the beginning, is now, and ever shall be, world without end. We ask this in Jesus' name, Amen.*"

Once more, the *Amens* ring out all around me.

Finally, the ordeal I have dreaded and endured has ended, and I'm sorry. Until this moment, I've known where I was supposed to be, what I needed to do. Now, I just sit here, watching as the pallbearers wheel my Gramma away through a side door. The rabbi and Rebecca come over to me and shake my hand. The pastor too, and so many others.

A throng of people come forward to say something to the one person left in Gramma's family, even though it's me, whom they never really wanted in their midst.

I don't really hear a word anyone says. They're a background buzz that fails to drown out my uncertainty about what happens next, wondering who I am now that I no longer have anyone, not here in Black Bear, and not really in Paris. Not anyone to whom I belong, to whom I matter more than life itself, as I had for Gramma, Grampa, my mom — and, for a short time, *Grand-mère* Amélie. *Papa* loves me; I know that. But in a somewhat distracted way, as though every time he sees me he's surprised to feel the bond we have. The twins — my half-brother and half-sister — were never really part of me, though in recent years we've learned to accommodate each other and share *Ormand et fils* equitably. Gramma was the last of the family who defined me as me. Who am I without her?

Eventually, Mr. Morton takes my arm and guides me through the crowd, out the same side door they took the coffin. He settles me into an awaiting limousine, just behind the flower-bedecked hearse. Behind me is a long line of vehicles, all with tiny purple funeral flags on their roofs. Alone, entombed in the limousine's leathery comfort, I don't really notice when we start to inch forward and slowly drive to the Black Bear Cemetery.

The Black Bear Cemetery is an open field of stone markers in the midst of a deep wood on the other side of Wallenpaupack Creek, down a narrow twisting dirt road with no name that I've ever heard. I don't know if the founders put it back there to conceal it, protect the village from dead spirits, or for its tranquil beauty.

The cemetery has grown considerably since the last time I was here — for Mom's funeral. Segregated by backgrounds and religions, the cemetery was actually the consolidation of several graveyards. The oldest markers are German, separated from the time-eroded stones of the

"English" by a grassy path everyone calls "the cemetery road." The Moravian area is the largest section, an extension of the old German graveyard. Similarly, other religions have their own areas — even, I'm surprised to see, a tiny new Jewish section.

When Mom was buried, the Black Bear Cemetery had no place for her, because no Jew had ever been interred there. The cemetery association decided she could be buried in the family plot, because it was at the far edge of the Moravian section, under the oldest of the tall evergreens. After all, they reasoned, she had been born a Moravian. We had only a graveside service, conducted by Rabbi Cohen, who traveled from Scranton. The simple dignity of Mom's funeral surprised her childhood friends, who were used to music and witnessing, public praying and reminiscing.

Mr. Morton opens the limousine door and gives me his hand. I follow Joe and the other pallbearers as they wheel Gramma's coffin up a slight rise to what once was the far edge of the cemetery. Behind me, the footsteps of scores of people crunch up the stony path, but no one approaches me. An invisible moat has formed around me. Inside it, I walk alone.

We reach the newly dug hole in the ground. Above it, a dark green canopy snaps in the brisk April breeze. Though the sun shines, dark ominous clouds loom to the west. The air is heavy with chill moisture and the earthy smell of newly turned soil.

Mr. Morton guides me to one of the few folding chairs. The other seats are given to the oldest and most infirm, some of them people I don't know or don't recognize. I feel awkward being the only young, able-bodied person sitting, but not enough to protest or make a fuss.

I recognize the spot, though I've been there only once before. To my right is Mom's grave. Beyond Mom is the new Jewish section, as though she's become the bridge between the two graveyards. And to my left is Robby's grave — the uncle I never knew, Mom's younger brother.

Robert Henry Schmoyer
Beloved Son and Brother
1947-1966
Hero and Patriot

That wasn't how Mom saw it, but I guess if she hadn't rebelled when he'd been killed in a war she couldn't believe in, I never would have been born — not the me who stands here now: French, Jewish and dark skinned.

Next to Robby's grave is the one I've never seen, but knew would be here — Grampa.

I should have been here for you, Grampa, for Gramma when she nursed you and buried you and mourned alone. Why hadn't you told me you were ill, Grampa? I never would have gone to the Congo when I did, where no one could reach me until it was far too late.

But Gramma knew what she was doing, keeping me ignorant about Grampa until weeks after it was over, regardless of what I — or he — might have wanted.

For my own good, Gramma told me when I was sixteen and just graduated from high school, "Never return to Black Bear."

Well, I'm here now, Gramma.

Hovering over a gaping hole, Gramma's mahogany coffin shines with reflected light; its glossy sheen flawless, dazzling. Another green canvas barely covers the mound of soil that will soon be shoveled over her, scratching that perfect wood, consigning whatever remains of Gramma to the deep, airless earth.

The pastor and rabbi stand side by side across the coffin from me. All the people who have accompanied Gramma to her final resting place pour out from under the canopy in every direction. When Pastor Ringenhauer opens his prayer book, I notice that some folks have their own copies. Somebody hands one to me, opened to the right page, but I put it down on my lap, without looking at it. Instead, I stare at Pastor Ringenhauer and Rabbi Weis. One tall and intimidating, the other smaller and compassionate, standing companionably in their solemnity, so similar in their pose of devotion that you might see them as brothers in faith. Why does the idea bother me, here in Black Bear, when I have fought for such tolerance in villages and towns in the Third World?

The Pastor raises his hand towards the coffin, in benediction, but also as a signal to the crowd to quiet down. It takes some time for the echoing "shushes" to reach those in the far back.

His voice echoes with quiet thunder, *"Lord, have mercy upon us."*

Most of the people around us respond, *"Christ, have mercy upon us."*

"Lord God, Father, hear us as we pray," the pastor says. Then, he intones the first line of the twenty-third psalm. *"The Lord is my Shepherd..."*

Nearly everyone, including the rabbi, adds their voices to the prayer. *"I shall not want. He maketh me to lie down in green pastures...."*

Everyone but me. The words reverberate around me, but I feel like I'm in a room by myself, with the doors and windows closed and locked, all sound dampened, all emotions muffled. Not that I don't hear every word that's said and every note that's sung, every rustle of clothing, every cough and sob. However, that's a separate part of me, the observer who isn't involved, not the granddaughter who should be crying but isn't. I promised myself years ago that these people would never again see my tears. I'm safe as long as I stay enclosed in that cocoon where nothing can reach me.

Someone touches my elbow, letting me know I'm supposed to stand. When I do, the prayer book falls from my lap, and another person picks it up. I hear the coffin being lowered, before I comprehend that it's happening. I realize the rabbi has been speaking for a few minutes, and now it's my turn, mine and any other Jew who's here. Hopefully, we have at least ten to make a *minyan* so the prayers will be said according to Jewish law, the voice of a community rather than a lone mourner.

The rabbi starts the mourner's *Kaddish*. *"Yit-ga-dal*

vyit-ka-dash ..." and I hear not ten, but dozens of voices joining with me, "*sh'mei ra-ba, b'al-ma di-v'ra chi-ru-tei, v'yam-lich mal-chu-tei b'chai-yei-chon uv'yo-mei-chon uv'chai-yei d'chol-beit Yis-ra-eil....*"

So many Jews stand with me as we pray together, that my mind reels with the implications. Gramma was ill long enough to make her own funeral arrangements, which included a rabbi and a *minyan* for me. But if I were to believe what Rabbi Weis said at the church, the people from his synagogue, a Black Bear synagogue, would have come out for her anytime without being asked.

When we finish, the rabbi translates the words of the ancient Aramaic prayer for the sake of all the Christians gathered around us. Not one word is of death, but of the debt of life we owe to the Glory of God. He concludes with the traditional benediction, "*May the Source of peace send peace to all who mourn and comfort to all who are bereaved. Amen.*"

The rabbi fills a small trowel with soil and throws it down the hole onto the coffin. He doesn't hand me the trowel, because that would be a passing of death from one person to the next. Instead, he pokes it into the pile of loose soil. I know I'm supposed to pick it up on my own. I stare at it, stuck in the mound of earth, knowing this is something I should do, I must do, not just for appearances but for Gramma and for me. Nothing I've done in my life has ever been more difficult, but I finally bend down and grasp the trowel. Whatever soil is sticking to the blade is enough; I can't bring myself to add more by digging into the mound. The phrase "*ashes to ashes*" reverberates in my mind, over and over again, as I swing the trowel in an arc toward the grave and watch those few grains of soil fly from the blade to fall with the sound of sleet on the wooden coffin below.

The rabbi whispers to me, "*Ha'makom yenahem etchem betoch she'ar avelei Tzion vi'Yerushalaim. May the Lord comfort you among the other mourners of Zion and Jerusalem.*"

I endure once more the multitude of handshakes and touches on my shoulders and even a few embraces. Then, I walk back to the limousine. At one point, Mr. Morton asks me for the keys to my rental car, so he can have it brought back to me at the farm. I see and hear and feel all these things through my protective cocoon, but I let nothing get through. Not even Joe, when he says something to me about being so very sorry and calling me Jo, yet again.

The limousine driver drops me off at the farm well before the rainstorm hits, but the winds are already whipping the treetops, and the temperature has plummeted. Out of habit and wanting to do something normal, something that Gramma and Grampa would do, I check the barn and the other outbuildings first, then I'll make sure all the windows in the house are secure.

By the time I head back to the house, several cars have already arrived, with more pulling round the driveway and jockeying for parking space. People swarm in the yard and up onto the wraparound porch. Not wanting to deal with all those people, I go in the back door. But I'm not safe here either. Several women bustle about the kitchen, unpacking coolers and boxes filled with casseroles, soups, salads and desserts, putting what needs to be heated on the stove or in the oven. Others arrange platters, which they hand off to still more people who carry them into the dining room.

One of them comes toward me — Rebecca, the woman who cut my black mourner's ribbon and said a gentle prayer over me before the funeral service. She doesn't presume to touch me, but her warm gaze is more of a caress than any of the handling I've endured all day. "Come," she beckons me, and I follow her outside to Gramma's bench in the garden.

Grampa had forged the bench for Gramma from scrap iron the year they were married. Nestled behind an enormous, gnarled cherry tree that is probably as old as the farm itself, it's a private refuge that can't be spied from the driveway or house. Rebecca and I sit side by side; she's small enough for both of us to fit on the bench without pressing against each other. When Gramma would sit here, she'd spread out so fully, that as I got older and larger, I'd often sit on the ground to talk with her, rather than wedge myself between her and the curved metal arm. However, whenever the world around me became too cold and confusing, I would sometimes seek out Gramma here on this bench, and squeeze in next to her, needing the physical comfort of her soft, round body.

I wonder if Rebecca knows what a special place this bench is. Did she sit here with Gramma, too?

The wind stirs through the trees, blowing old leaves from last autumn around Gramma's kitchen garden, which is still filled with dead plants. Only after the final snow of the season would Grampa plow under the twigs and debris of the previous summer. Then, Gramma would start her planting, beginning with green onions. I used to wonder how could Gramps know which snow would be the last snow, the onion snow?

As surprised as I was by all the people in the house, I understood the moment I saw them, though Rebecca's presence made it clearer: *shiva*. According to Jewish tradition, mourning isn't something you do alone, but surrounded by community. By Christian tradition, it is a time for friends and neighbors to express sympathy and find ways to help.

I hadn't expected it. Not just because this is Black Bear, where I had long been the only Jew in a Christian backwater village, but because I hadn't thought things through. *Shiva* was something others did. Others, not I.

When Mom died, I was too young to pay attention to anything other than my own pain and confusion. I spent the mourning period here on the farm, among people who didn't know me, hadn't really understood why Mom had left Black Bear, let alone converted to Judaism. Black Bear wasn't my home then, but neither was Manhattan, where I had lived with Mom for nearly two years before that cursed taxi ran a red light just when she happened to be crossing the street. Yet, I didn't belong in Paris anymore either, not since *Papa* had installed Bridget and then the twins into the only home I had ever had for the first ten years of my life.

Now, here I am once more, at the farm, trying to make sense, not only of death, but of my place within the death. *Shiva*.

"Mrs. Weis..."

"Please, call me Rebecca."

"Rebecca..." I acknowledge, but then I'm at a loss, uncertain what I'm supposed to say or do in this situation. The numbness I feel is more than an April chill.

She waits, silently, neither pressing nor questioning. Her small unadorned hands, save the one simple gold wedding band, rest on her tweed lap. Rebecca's round face, surrounded by neatly coifed, short brown curls, is calm and untroubled as she gazes peacefully at the land around us. Even when the air becomes damp, heavy with imminent rain, or perhaps snow, she doesn't stir. How did she know that this quietude is exactly what I need?

Despite the cold, I ache to stay out here on Gramma's bench for the rest of the afternoon, rather than face all the people milling about the farmhouse. At the first clap of thunder, I reluctantly follow Rebecca back to the house.

The porch wicker table has been moved near the front door, and on it are a bowl and a small pitcher of water. Like the *mezuzah* that Grampa had nailed to the doorpost, it's a sign that a Jew lives here — a Jew who has just returned from burying a loved one. I pour water over each hand three times, the ritual cleansing away of death before re-entering a place of life. I don't know why I do it, or what I believe, but it's something that I can choose to do, momentarily cutting through my damned passivity.

Rebecca hands me a linen towel to dry my hands. "No one expects anything of you today," she tries to assure me. "You can sit or walk wherever you want, say or not say whatever comes to mind, cry or be dry eyed. Your only role and responsibility is to be yourself, and let everyone else flow past you. If you want to stop someone within the flow, so they can sit with you or talk with you, or bring you food or drink, that is your right, too. However, do it only if it is something you want or need."

That's all well and good, but when I enter the house, conversations cease and all eyes focus on me as palpably as if they're touching me again. While Rebecca hangs my coat, I stand in the wide arch between the hall and the living room, looking everywhere but in the multitude of faces turned toward me. Somebody has covered the old oak mirror over the hall table with a black cloth. Like the water pitcher at the door, the severe black cloth is a comfort, a reminder that someone cared enough about who and what I am to put my home in order, according to the ancient traditions of Jewish mourning. I doubt I would have thought of any of it, or, if I had, that I would have bothered.

Rebecca leads me to the large armchair next to the living room window seat. She drapes one of Gramma's crocheted afghans on the ottoman, easily within my reach. On the side table next to me is Mom's life-sized sculpture of me as a sleeping infant. I lightly caress the head and back, feeling the texture and shape of the burnished bronze, seeking the warmth of Mom's touch within the cold metal. Looking around me, I realize that someone has squirreled away the pictures I piled against the stairway yesterday.

Disappearing briefly, Rebecca returns carrying a short, thick white candle in a clear glass. Gramma's memorial candle. "Do you want to light the *shiva* candle, or shall I?" she asks.

I stand, and take the candle and matches from her hand, place the candle on the slate mantle above the fireplace and start to light it. However, I haven't the foggiest idea of what I'm supposed to say. Did I ever know the appropriate prayer?

In a private whisper for my ears alone, Rebecca says, "*As it is written, the light of God is the soul of humankind. Baruch ata Adonai, asher b'yado nefesh kolchai, v'ruach kol b'sar ish. Blessed art Thou, Adonai of blessing, in Thy Hands are all souls and the spirits of all flesh. Amen.*"

The candle's small flame flickers at first, but soon burns steadily, as it will for the next seven days. However,

I'll be gone in five. Must I blow it out, cutting short the light of Gramma's spirit, or can I safely allow it to burn even after I close up the house and leave? And, why does it matter to me, when I don't really believe in God or the supernatural or everlasting life consigned to heaven or hell?

More people arrived while Rebecca and I sat quietly on Gramma's bench. Who among them might have left that anonymous message for me to return to Black Bear? Certainly, most of them couldn't have cared less if they never saw me again. Yet, someone felt or knew that something was dreadfully wrong, that Gramma needed me back here, right away. What's more, he or she knows about the promise, but not how to reach me at my office. A stranger then. One who is unsophisticated but cared about Gramma, enough to want to protect her, to reach out to me and drag me back here.

However, I've returned too late.

Among the many whites are nearly a dozen black and brown faces, a higher percentage than I had ever seen anywhere in or near Black Bear, far more than I would have ever expected to be here at the farm. They aren't segregated into cliques of their own, either, but scattered randomly throughout the various conversation groups.

Most of the chairs are filled; several have been moved out of place to form small clusters, disrupting and distorting the shape of the room. Other people stand together wherever they can find a niche. Through the arch, I see a throng surrounding the dining room table, filling plates with food, and pouring coffee, tea and soft drinks from the sideboard.

That's when I spot Joe, moving about proprietarily, helping serve the food, reaching for specific platters in the corner cupboard, with the easy assurance of one who knows where they would be. Even going into the sideboard silverware drawers for serving pieces. How dare he!

The storm lets loose outside with whistling winds, thunder and lightning; the voices inside grow steadily louder so they may be heard above the din. I curl up into the armchair and wrap Gramma's afghan around myself.

I'm mesmerized by the flickering candle on the mantle. When I gaze at the bare hearth beneath it, I whisper to myself, "I wish we had a fire," not expecting to be heard.

Jeff Smith pyramids kindling and logs into the fireplace and lights it. A woman I don't know hands me a mug of hot chicken vegetable soup. As I sip it, the fragrant steam plays over my face, and the hearty liquid warms me from within.

"Thank you," I say to both of them.

With a shiver of release, I uncurl, straightening my spine against the chair's cushioned back, my feet flat on the floor and the afghan draped only on my lap, more for comfort than warmth. I'm the center of attention here, and I'm not about to allow myself to appear so needful and supine in front of these people.

Features and names resolve out of the crowd. AH Engelhardt sits opposite me, in one of the Windsor chairs that have been moved from the dining room. His two aluminum canes are hooked on the table next to him. When he sees me looking at him, he nods, but doesn't say anything. Instead, he continues to listen to whatever Pastor Ringenhauer is telling him.

The pastor is ensconced in Grampa's favorite armchair, a plate of the scattered remnants of roast chicken and macaroni salad balanced precariously on his knee. Not having heard the beginning of the conversation, I can't quite follow what he's talking about, but it energizes him; his fork clanks as it bounces on the plate. His wife comes over, gently removes the plate from his knee, then brushes some crumbs from his jacket. He stops his narrative long enough to acknowledge her with a sheepish shrug.

Jeff Smith silently watches everyone from the window seat to my left. Not a very tall man, he'd never had much of a presence. As a child, I tried but failed to emulate his ability to fade into the background. When I first started babysitting Jeff's kids, Melanie and Bobby, I wasn't sure that I could handle them. Gramma tried to ease my mind by reminding me that they were my own family, cousins through their mother, Bonnie, AH's daughter. That wasn't much of a reassurance.

The handful of cousins left in Black Bear that I met my first autumn had the same range of reactions to my dark skin as everyone else — from two-faced, back-stabbing over-enthusiasm to mean, sometimes foul-mouthed snide remarks. Luckily, most of my grandparents' siblings had moved away or died off without progeny before I came to live here. The few who remained were much older than I, and, if they are still living in Black Bear, I certainly didn't recognize them among all the people who gave me their condolences at the church or hover about me here at the house.

Contrary to my fears, I enjoyed babysitting Melanie and Bobby. Perhaps, their easy acceptance of me was because their father was as much an outsider in Black Bear as I was. Jeff and I didn't talk much, usually only during the drives back from my babysitting stints with his kids. Jeff would ask me about my school work, or what I was reading, or my dreams for my future. And he'd really listen to my answers.

A few years ago, I heard from Melanie again, when she came to the University of Paris for graduate work in art history. I considered it my responsibility, my thank you to Jeff, to keep an eye on her. However, I found I was drawn to her, beyond a sense of responsibility. She's such a vivacious young woman, a fresh breeze of energy, interested in everyone and everything she discovers. I admire Melanie's knack for friendship, how she can be so strong and vulnerable at the same time. She was the first woman in many years whom I might be tempted to take a chance on as a friend, if our lives weren't so divergent. All I can do is call her every once in a while, whenever I'm in Paris. Sometimes, I take her to lunch, and play the role of an older, protective cousin.

"Have you heard from Melanie?" I ask Jeff.

"She emails me and her brother frequently, keeps us informed about her life, or as much as she's willing to share with a father." Jeff's grey eyes twinkle. "I don't suppose you'd care to tell me about the fellas she's seeing?"

"As far as I can tell, there's no one special... yet."
Though he recognizes my evasion for what it is,
Jeff doesn't press the issue. That's something else I remember about him, that he never indulged in Black Bear's
favorite blood sport: gossip. And he didn't pry whenever I'd
meet his questions with silence or oblique statements. His
respect for privacy apparently extends to his daughter, too.

He stands. "Can I get you anything, Judith?"

"No thank you, Jeff." I watch him as he heads
toward the foyer.

"Hello, Judith. Don't suppose you recollect me." A
woman stands over me, but not too close, as though she's
hesitant to encroach. About sixty-five, she's painfully thin,
with that strained scrawny appearance of one who's fought
her way through a hard life and survived. Her face is rough
and deeply lined; her nose and mouth twisted and papered
with small scars. Her dull, dark brown hair is streaked with
yellowing grey swathes but tightly groomed, not a strand
escaping the bun at her neck. Though decades out of
fashion, her flowered dress is starched and spotless. She
seems unquestionably familiar, but no name comes to mind.

"I'm Florence... Florence Wilson. Was Metcott
back then."

"Florence, *mon dieu!*" No, not sixty-five, probably
not even fifty yet, but she looked old and depleted even
when she came to live with us as a young woman. "How
have you been? Please sit, talk to me."

How could I have not recognized her? Toward the
end of my sophomore year in high school, Gramma, who
had always done everything for herself, suddenly announced that she needed a live-in housekeeper. Grampa didn't
argue. Not that he could have, not when Gramma had her
mind set. So, Florence became a member of our household,
though she remained skittish, never sitting at the table with
us or going on our family outings, though Gramma and
Grampa tried to coax her out of her shell. With the easy
self-involvement of adolescence, I quickly accepted her as a
convenient shadow who hovered nearby, but wasn't really
part of my life.

Florence is a living memory, the one person in this room who shared this home with me and my grandparents, and maybe knew them as I had.

"I know you're busy…"

"No, Florence, it's quite the opposite. I seem to have nothing to do at the moment." I gesture around the room. "Everyone else appears to have taken control. Please do sit with me."

I point to the ottoman, and she perches on the edge.

"I wanted to tell you. You got a right to know about your grandma. She wouldn't have me tell it when she was alive. But you should know. How she was when no one was looking, when no one cared about nothin'. She cared and she saw things that other folk turned blind to. She saved my life."

Florence's words come out in abrupt, halting rhythms. Her small, darting eyes meet mine only briefly, dropping to her hands in her lap, but glancing up during her pauses to make sure I'm listening. The storm outside has subsided, leaving in its wake a stillness that makes the din of conversation around us seem even louder, creating a private space for the two of us in the midst of it all.

"It was Hank, my first husband. Hank Metcott. He beat me. Bad. But I'd got no place else, no one else, and I guess I thought he was the best I'd ever get. So, I learned how to move so the punches don't break bones, most of the time." She says it with a strange pride in that one accomplishment. "But I couldn't duck all the way, or he'd get madder and hit harder. It was worst when he needed a drink, or just starting into a binge. When he drank hisself blind, I could count on some peace. So, I kept the trailer stocked with beer and whiskey. Spent money on drink before buying food or paying bills. That got him mad, too, when the electricity got shut off or he was hungry or any reason he could think of that he could make out my fault." She shrugs her bony shoulders.

I've seen and heard such stories often in my work with *Les Femmes*. But it doesn't make it any less horrific.

"One day," she continues. "I was outside Buck's, in

the pickup, trying to figure how much beer I can buy. That's when Martha showed up. Nearly jumped out of my skin, I can tell you. There I was, counting them coins, thinking so hard about how it wasn't enough to buy no peace that night, and there she was, all a sudden, at the window that was open 'cause it didn't close no more. 'Florence,' she says to me in that nice way she had that no one did when they talked to me. No one but your grandpa, that is, but I didn't know him yet. 'Florence,' she says, 'You been sitting in this here truck since I got here, and I done all my shopping. Is everythin' okay?' Sure, I say. I mean, what could I tell her that she'd understand? This was Martha Schmoyer. She's got a good house and a husband who treats her like a queen and enough money to fill that cart that was in front of her with all them bags of food and stuff, without worrying about nothin'. But your grandma, she was a bulldog. She saw somethin' was wrong, and she wasn't going to let me be 'til she found out what it was, even if it wasn't none of her business. And it wasn't. Any more than it was any business of any of the other folk who walked past and didn't see nothin'."

For the first time since she approached me, Florence meets my eyes, searching perhaps for some recognition that I failed to give her as a child.

I nod, not so much in agreement with any unspoken question, but because she seems to need that connection, that recognition.

"So, she got the story out of me, and got me out of that trailer. Pronto. Hank, he made an awful fuss, you can imagine. Came here when you all was gone. You at school, your grandpa at his store, Martha off somewhere. Hank came to get me. Beat me when I wouldn't move fast enough, and dragged me out to his truck. That's when your grandma come home, saw him, went inside to grab your grandpa's hunting rifle, jacked in a shell and aimed it right at him. I mean, right at him. '*Hank Metcott!*' she yelled like I never heard no lady like her yell. 'Take your goddamn hands off Florence and get the hell off my property!' He stared at her too long, I guess, 'cause she took a shot at the ground right in front of his toes. 'I'll put the next one between your legs,' she threatened, and jacked another bullet into the breech, keeping the gun aimed at his crotch the whole time. He threw me in the dirt, but I didn't care, 'cause that's the last time he ever lay a hand on me. Don't really know if she'd've shot him for real, but he believed it. That's all that mattered."

I'm floored. In my wildest nightmares, I never, ever would have imagined my Gramma shooting or even cursing at someone. But I can see the scene clearly in my mind's eye — her righteous fury, her resolve to face down that bloody bully, perhaps even a steely resolve to maim him if necessary.

"Your grandparents took care of things so's the police, they kept Hank away from me. Even got a lawyer to fix the divorce. But Hank smeared hisself on I-84 on a buddy's motorcycle, going over a hundred, the cops said, afore the divorce came final. Guess the bastard saved your grandma some ammo," she says with a single dry laugh that pops out of her unexpectedly, then is quickly gone.

"I never knew, Florence. I'm sorry."

"No child. You wasn't old enough to know. I wouldn't have you know back then how ugly the world is. But you got a right to know how good it can be, too, 'cause of people like your grandma. No question 'bout it, she saved my life. One night, Hank was sure to go too far, and I'd've been the dead one, not him. Instead, I got to live here with you, and learn that a woman can live good and have good, even with a man. When I met my Tom, Tom Wilson, I didn't get as good as your grandma had, but I was never again hit by nobody."

Standing to leave, Florence adds, "Well, I just wanted you to know."

"Florence, please don't go just yet. Tell me, how are things now? Are you well? Do you need anything?" I reach out my hand to her to keep her from leaving. She looks at it briefly, then clasps it and gives me a hearty handshake.

"I'm just fine these days, Judith. Thank you for

askin'. It were good ta' see you, child, and know you're fine too, or you will be when the hurt you feel 'bout your grandma becomes smaller compared to all them fine memories you got. You had yourself the best grandparents a soul could want. Hold onto that, and you'll be okay."

"Thank you Florence, and thank you for telling me your story."

As I watch Florence leave, I notice the rabbi give AH a cup of tea and the pastor a mug of coffee, though I hadn't seen him approach them earlier to find out what they wanted. It appears to be a gesture of longtime familiarity with their preferences. When he returns, with a glass of cola for himself, he pulls up a chair to sit with them, just across the fireplace from me.

"I remember that no-account Metcott," AH says, deliberately loud enough to bring me into their conversation. "Whenever he and his pal John Anderson got liquored up, no telling what trouble we'd have. The only part of that story that Florence got wrong was the motorcycle. The owner was no buddy of Hank's. He stole it for a joy ride, killing himself and the driver of the car he hit. A bad egg, if there ever were one. But," he adds with a mischievous chortle, "when I think of him having to face down a furious Martha with a rifle aimed at his crown jewels, damned if I'm not almost sorry for him."

Something passes between AH and the pastor, a recognition, I suppose, of both having been at the receiving end of Gramma's ire. Soon they're chortling, then laughing out loud. The rabbi snorts his laugh into the soda, which spills over the glass; he grabs a napkin from the side table to wipe his trouser leg and a spot on the carpet.

I can just picture Gramma's pudgy, capable hands chambering a round in the rifle, her short, solid legs spread as wide as her large hips, aiming her fierce gaze over the barrel at Hank Metcott. No wonder he ran off, probably stumbled over his own feet in his haste to get away. Before

I know it, I'm laughing as hard as the three men.

People look at us, curious, perhaps shocked; Bryan Hayes asks, "What's so funny?" When the rabbi tries to explain, the words come out in unintelligible spurts, and that sets off the four of us chortling uncontrollably. I can barely catch my breath; my eyes begin to water. As I dab my eyes, I suddenly realize where I am and why.

What the heck did I think I was doing? Laughing hysterically here, now, when we've just buried Gramma, and with all these people watching me.

The rabbi puts down his soda and pulls his chair closer to me. "Martha loved laughter," he says, almost as though he's continuing a conversation we started some time earlier.

"I know, but..."

"No buts about it, Ms. Ormand. It's a joy to remember her and laugh, just as it is to remember and cry. Your grandmother had a full, rich life, and we're here to celebrate it and honor how well she lived it. When you want, I can tell you more stories about her that you'll enjoy."

Of course, he's right. Why then does it feel like a betrayal to accept it? "Thank you, Rabbi."

"Please call me David."

"Thank you, David. Please call me Judith."

Standing, the rabbi retrieves what's left of his soda from the table behind us. "Please come by the temple before you leave Black Bear, Judith," he says. "There's something I'd like to show you that I believe you will want to see."

I watch the rabbi as he walks toward the dining room, wondering what he means by that last statement. It's the only answer I have for not noticing Joe approach from my left until he's planted himself in the seat the rabbi has just vacated. He offers me a plate. "It's your favorite... strawberry salad."

"No, Joe. That was *your* favorite, not mine." The only way Gramma could get Joe to eat vegetables, during those years he'd spent so much time with us, was to add something sweet or unexpected to them. Almonds in the green beans, sliced apples in the carrots, and strawberries in the salad. I'm not about to admit to him that I got so used to it that I now do the same.

He doesn't take the hint and continues to hold the plate out to me. So I take it and put it down on the side table. He still doesn't leave, but sits there, next to me, waiting for what? Suddenly, I see not Joe, but his father in that chair, large and threatening. I suppose it was AH's mention of John Anderson that makes the connection for me, of Florence coming to live with us at approximately the same time that Gramma became even more adamant about Joe not being the right kind of boy for me.

"Is there anything you want, Jo?" he asks.

"My name is Judith," I struggle to keep my voice flat, devoid of emotion and anger.

"Sorry... Judith."

He looks so flustered that I might be sorry for him, if he were anyone else, if I didn't know the truth about him, if I hadn't Gramma's will as concrete proof of his latest treachery. The fact is I don't want him anywhere near me. I hate his pretending that everything is as it used to be between us, using a childhood name that represents all that went wrong with my life here in Black Bear. Most of all, I resent him being in my grandparents' home, acting as though he belongs here as much as I do.

"I don't know what the hell you think you're doing here, Joseph Anderson." The words spill out of me, loud and sharp so anyone within earshot can hear every word. "But you've got another thing coming if you think I buy into any of it. Get the f... "

Just then numerous shrill pagers around the room go off, including the one on Joe's belt. "*Beep-Beep-Beep-Beep-Beep-Beep.*" Joe jumps up, nearly toppling the Windsor chair. At the same time, other people around the room freeze in midstride. All conversation and motion throughout the house ceases, as everyone waits for Wayne County CommCenter to announce what the emergency is. Just hearing the tones is a sense memory bringing back so much about Grampa, who continued as a volunteer EMT with the ambulance well into his seventies.

"Black Bear fire. Black Bear ambulance. Respond," pagers all around me announce in unison. *"To the fairgrounds. Structure fire fully engaged."*

As the tones and announcement are repeated one more time, Joe looks back at me, with that sad hangdog look that he's perfected. "Sorry, Jo...er... Judith," he says. Then, he takes off, as does Rabbi David, Jeff Smith and many of the other men and some of the women. Several call out to me.

"Gotta go, Judith."

"You understand."

"I'll call."

"Let me know if you need anything."

They coordinate their response even as they dart out the door. Someone near me says, "I hope it isn't that damned firebug again." Another answers, "Naw, probably lightning."

Through the window, I see flashing blue emergency lights revolving on the roofs of various cars, SUVs and pickups, plus the one red light of the fire chief. They speed away in an orderly single file out the driveway.

Many among my grandparents' friends volunteered with the fire department or the ambulance corps. Whatever any of them were doing, whenever a neighbor was in trouble, and the tones went off, they'd rush out the door to help. When crisis struck, they momentarily put everything else on hold, even their prejudices and feuds.

I forgot about that, just as I seemed to have forgotten how loudly the pastor could laugh or how the woods around this house could make me feel so safe and at peace. What other memories have I lost through the years, burned away by my anger and fear?

With all the fire and ambulance folk gone, not many people remain. AH and the pastor are still here, chatting companionably. Some women, mostly older men and a couple of kids hover about, several of them busy cleaning up all the plates, cups, mugs and glasses and putting away the food.

Rebecca dries her hands on a kitchen towel, before sitting next to me. "We still have a *minyan*, Judith. Shall I call them together?" she asks.

The mourner's *Kaddish*, here? It was one thing to do it at the cemetery, where the earth was freshly dug, and Gramma's coffin right in front of me. But to bring it home with me, this death that's more an absence than a thing in itself, to give it substance, make it part of this house.... Yet, it's something I'm expected to do, to honor Gramma.

Not wanting to express my misgivings, and hoping to get it over with as quickly as possible, I nod.

In a few minutes, I'm surrounded by about fifteen people, most of whom I don't know, in an impromptu circle of rearranged chairs, with a few sitting behind others. Most of the men and a few of the women take *yarmulkes* from the box that Rebecca placed on a table and put them on their heads, though some have their own embroidered skull caps, and others don't bother. I'm surprised to see the pastor claim two, for himself and for AH.

Retrieving a light blue *yarmulke* from a small dark blue velvet pouch, Rebecca clips it to her short curly hair. Then, she stands quietly in a corner of the dining room with her back to us, perhaps in meditation, or to give the rest of us time to settle down.

Taking the Windsor chair to my left, Rebecca looks around the circle, meeting everyone's gaze with an authoritative calm. She finally turns to me. "Judith, we are here to share with you, to support and help you, as you mourn your beloved grandmother, our friend Martha Schmoyer." Rebecca speaks in a quiet voice that nonetheless rebounds, like that of a trained actress who knows how to stage whisper. "In Judaism, traditions and laws tend to exist for a reason. The requirement that we have a *minyan* of ten Jews to share your prayers assures that in the midst of your great loss, you are not alone." She takes my left hand with her right; it's warm, small, though surprisingly rough. "However, as you can see, it's not just Jews who are here for you and for Martha." She releases my hand with a gentle squeeze. "Judith doesn't know all of us, so before we proceed, shall we introduce ourselves?" She turns to me once again and, with a slight smile, says, "I'm Rebecca Weis, the rabbi's wife." I've no doubt there's much more to her than that, but it's the role she has assumed for this occasion.

Rebecca looks toward the woman to her left. Rather obese, her large dark eyes sparkle with intelligence and vitality. She's about forty, with straight shoulder length brown hair. "I'm Jane Rosen, Judith, and I'm glad to meet you after hearing so much about you from Martha. We used to play bridge together. I can tell you, I much preferred her as a partner than an opponent."

I didn't know that Gramma knew how to play bridge. Scrabble had been her favorite game. She loved the challenge of manipulating words to make them fit together.

The man next to Jane Rosen sits with an exaggerated straight spine, as though he's used to standing at attention. Though his bald head shines like a polished apple, his lower face is covered by a thick, wiry grey beard that reaches nearly to his chest. His olive brown skin is crackled by age and weather. About seventy-five years old, he speaks with a slight Israeli accent softened by years in this country. "I'm Joseph Good. Don't know what to tell you about myself, except that I held your Grandmother in great respect and was honored to know her."

"I'm Eric Ringenhauer. As I suppose most of you know, I'm the pastor of the Black Bear Moravian Church. I'm honored to share your prayers for Martha." I don't know which surprises me more, to see him with a *yarmulke* on his balding grey head, or his humble demeanor.

"Well, I'm AH Engelhardt. Don't ask me what AH stands for. You won't like the answer. I certainly don't, which is why I haven't used my Christian names since The War. I've known this young lady since she was in diapers and crawling all over her grandfather. The first time she went fishing with him, out on Lake Wallenpaupack, I was in the boat, netting all the damn fish she caught. Didn't leave enough for me. Now, she's a grown woman, and both Henry and Martha are gone. But I see them in you, Judith, even if you might not right now. Trust me, they're alive as long as you remain true to who you are."

Though I continue to look at each person as they go around the circle, introducing themselves, I don't really pay attention to what they say, and their names slip my mind within seconds of hearing them. I'm thinking about what AH — Adolph Heinrich — said. Not about his names. I've known them since I was quite young, and knew how much he hated them, having fought the Nazis in Europe. Instead, I'm lost in that early memory of going fishing with Grampa and AH, in AH's speedboat that was much bigger, faster and shinier than Gramps' motorized rowboat. I was so very frightened of AH with his gravelly voice and piercing eyes. Especially when he yelled at me for stealing all the fish from the lake, and blamed me for his bad luck at not catching any. I was such a serious child that I cried, too young to recognize his jibes as the tease they were meant to be. Yet, when he retold the story just now, I saw the sparkling humor in those same eyes. How wrong I had been about him all those years. And about the pastor, too?

I sense rather than hear the woman to my right finish her introduction. The circle has been completed, and everyone's looking at me.

"I'm Judith Ormand." Of course, they know who I am, but it would be uncivil to not give them my name when they gave me theirs. "I thank you for being here and for your kind words about my grandmother."

Rebecca squeezes my hand briefly, and then says to the pudgy young man of about fifteen who sits opposite her, "Josh, please hand out the prayer books."

He reaches behind him, picks up the small booklets from the Adams console table and sends half in each direction around the circle.

While he does so, Rebecca explains, "The mourner's *Kaddish* is an ancient Aramaic poem. As we recite it, we turn our thoughts to those we have lost through death, but we do so by praising God, and praying for peace, not only for those who mourn, but for all humankind. You'll find it on page 39. Please stand."

Rebecca starts the prayer; we all join in, "*Yit-ga-dal v'yit-ka-dash sh'mei ra-ba, b'al-ma di-v'ra chi-ru-tei, v'yam-lich mal-chu-tei b'chai-yei-chon uv'yo-mei-chon uv'chai-yei d'chol-beit Yis-ra-eil, ba-a-ga-la u-viz-man ka-riv, v'im'ru: Amein.*"

My eyes wander around the circle as we recite the entire *Kaddish*, not really needing the book to guide me, because I know it by heart, though imperfectly. I notice that the pastor carefully sounds out the transliteration of the Aramaic, while AH, Mary Borger and Al Marks read silently. Others stumble occasionally over the beautifully rhythmic alliterations, as I do when I miss a word or syllable, but we all keep pace with each other, adding to the sense of being surrounded and enveloped by the echoes of tradition, the centuries of community and continuity.

"*Oseh shalom bim'romav, hu ya'aseh shalom aleinu v'al kol Yisraeil, v'im'ru: Amein,*" we conclude. Rebecca translates that last phrase, "*May the One who causes peace to reign in the high heavens, cause peace to reign among us, all Israel, and all the world, and let us say: Amen.*" When she reaches that last Amen, everyone says it in unison with her.

For a few brief moments, I no longer feel like a stranger, but part of something larger, grander than myself. We were brought together by death, but we're held together by the demands of life. That peace and comfort stays with me even as the circle breaks up. Everyone suddenly becomes quite busy, putting chairs back where they belong, picking up the last of the plates, cups, mugs and glasses, and making sure all the food is put away. Everyone except AH and me.

We sit opposite each other, in companionable silence. When he speaks, it's with a wistful edge that softens his usually tough baritone. "Judith, I am old, and I have outlived so many whom I have loved. I can tell you, no matter how often we bury someone, it doesn't get any easier." He pauses, and I have the distinct impression he's picturing each person he's loved and lost. "Though some are more difficult than others. No parent should bury a child."

His daughter Bonnie, Jeff Smith's wife and Melanie and Bobby's mother, died of cancer several years ago. That was one more thing AH had in common with Gramma and Grampa, the death of their children.

"I want you to understand something about this pain you feel right now," he continues. "It's a good thing. Don't try to hide from it, Judith. It's your love for your grandmother and, no doubt, your grandfather and mother, twisting inside you because you're so damned lonely for them. And, it's their love for you asserting itself, claiming you and reshaping you, so you can carry them with you for the rest of your days. That's what this wake... your *shiva*... all mourning is about. No, it doesn't get any easier, but it does help to know that you wouldn't hurt so much if you weren't loved so much. To deny the one would be to deny the other."

The pastor appears in the arch between the hallway and the living room. "AH, you ready?" he asks.

"Sure am." AH reaches for his two canes and, leaning on them, struggles out of his chair. I jump up to help him, giving him support at both forearms. Once he's stabilized on his two feet and two canes, he looks up at me with a warm smile. When did I become taller than he?

I walk with him to the hallway, find his coat and hat in the closet, and help him put on the coat.

"Thank you, Judith."

"No, AH, thank you."

"I want you to come visit me before you leave Black Bear. Will you?" AH asks. "We need to talk."

"Yes," I promise, knowing that I truly want, maybe even need to keep that promise. I think we're both surprised when I press my lips to his smooth cheek. Surprised and pleased.

The pastor shakes my hand. "If you need anything, please call me."

"Thank you," I say, doubting there would ever be

something I would want that he could give me, and certain he understands that.

One by one, the few remaining people leave, giving me their condolences, well wishes and, in many cases, phone numbers. Little by little, the comfort of the *Kaddish* slips away. The last to leave is Rebecca, but she doesn't appear to be in any hurry. I find her in the kitchen, sitting at the table.

"I've just put a pot up to boil. Would you like some tea?" she asks.

"Actually, I think I'd like some wine. Would you join me?"

"Yes, please." Rebecca turns off the light under the kettle and finds two wine glasses.

I take the *Pouilly-Fuissé* out of the ice box, uncork it and pour.

"*L'chaim!*" I say as I raise my glass to hers; Rebecca echoes the toast.

L'chaim. To life. Like *salut*, to health, it's an idiom I use frequently, but seldom contemplate. In these circumstances, in this kitchen, where Gramma should be — whipping together a meal at the drop of a hat for anyone who happens to come by — saying *l'chaim* feels awkward. I may drink to life, but I'm as empty and deadened as the too quiet kitchen.

And I understand why Rebecca is still here, why she chose not to leave me alone quite yet.

"Thank you," I say, trusting Rebecca to understand why I'm grateful, though we're strangers to each other. Or, perhaps, it's precisely because she's a stranger, that the two of us have no expectations or history to cloud the moment.

"You're welcome, Judith."

I sip the wine, enjoying its cool fruitiness. Then, I hold the stem of the glass, twirling it between my fingers, watching the golden liquid swirl. Rebecca's easy stillness helps fill the room. "I wasn't quite sure about the *Kaddish,*"

I say.

"Oh?" She pauses, and I have the feeling she's picturing our conversation in the living room, just before she gathered the *minyan*. "Yes, it's often difficult, especially the first time."

"But you handled it beautifully, and I'm glad I agreed to it." Thinking to compliment her, I add, "You should have been a rabbi yourself."

She smiles over her wine glass as she sips. "That's another story."

Curious about this women whom I've only just met, I ask, "Please, tell me."

She puts down the glass. "I was studying for the rabbinate when I met David; he was in the class ahead of me. When he graduated, he was immediately offered the job here at *Beth Shalom*. I had to make a choice. I could continue my studies, and become ordained in another year. Chances were that we would be able to conduct a long distance courtship, and that we would get married at the end of the year. However, how would we be changed by all the time we would spend apart? What we had right then, the way we were together, that was what I wanted to base our life upon, not who we might become in another year. So, we were married, and I came here to *Beth Shalom* with him."

"Isn't the seminary in Manhattan? I wouldn't exactly call that a long distance from Black Bear."

"Compared to the day-to-day friendship we were developing, seeing each other every morning and evening, sharing the same experiences down to the trivial influences? No, I wasn't willing to let go of that just yet. I knew the next year would be one in which we would both learn new things, meet new people, and that would alter who we were and how we viewed the world. I wanted us to change together, not apart. Besides, David is nine years older than I. If we're going to have the family we want, we need to start on it sooner rather than later."

"But to give up becoming a rabbi...."

"Oh, I haven't given up anything. I just wanted our bond to be stronger first. We've agreed that I'll return to school after this child..." she cradles her small stomach, "...is old enough to go to kindergarten."

"You're pregnant? That's wonderful." I look at her more closely, trying to see the signs. Her abdomen doesn't really show, though the tweed skirt is cut with a fullness that could conceal for a couple of months. "When are you due?"

"Not until November. Judith, I haven't announced it yet, so I'd appreciate it if you'd keep it just between us for right now. Around here, news flies quickly, and some of our friends would be insulted, if I didn't tell them myself."

"Of course. Believe me, I understand about Black Bear gossip."

Rebecca no doubt hears my bitterness — a sharp, sudden contrast to the fleeting joy of a moment ago — but she doesn't pry into its source. Her only recognition of it is a slight tilt of her head that reminds me of a small bird listening for danger or safety in a breeze.

"Are you hungry, Judith?" she asks. "I didn't notice you eating anything all afternoon. I'd venture to say you probably had nothing since this morning."

"No, not really." Eating is the last thing on my mind.

"Well, I'm hungry, even though I've been nibbling all afternoon." She goes to the ice box and looks inside. It's jam-packed with food that hadn't been there before the funeral. "I know what I want," she announces with glee, as she pulls out a glass baking dish covered with aluminum foil. "Esther's noodle *kugel*. Someday, I'm going to have to wheedle the recipe out of her."

Putting two generous portions onto a plate and into the microwave, she obviously has chosen to ignore my protest. She sets the table while waiting for the noodle pudding to warm up, opening drawers and cabinet doors with easy familiarity. I know that I should get up and help, but I'm limp, enervated, my body leaden.

"You seem to know your way around this kitchen."

"I've spent a great deal of time in it, especially the last few months, after the cancer metastasized." She pours some of the strawberry salad from a plastic bag into a serving bowl.

When the microwave dings, she put one of the portions onto a separate plate which she places in front of me, and sits down.

I ignore the food. "Cancer? What kind? How long?"

"Uterine. I found out about it only last year, but she'd had it for some time."

My flesh burns with anger and shame. Gramma had been terribly ill, and I had no inkling. "Someone should have told me. I had a right to know."

"It was Martha's choice. She didn't want to bother you, and we had to honor her request."

I study Rebecca. "Well, someone disagreed with you. At least, I think they did."

"What do you mean?"

"I received a phone message that I needed to return to Black Bear right away... an anonymous message." I pause, locking eyes with her. "Do you know anything about it?"

"No." She pauses, shaking her head while she thinks. "No, I don't believe I do."

It's a direct response to my question, but not the answer I was hoping for. Gramma was sick for a long time, apparently unable to protect herself from Joe's shenanigans, and the only person who thought I should know about it didn't leave his or her name. "Was it painful?" I ask, hating to think of Gramma suffering.

"Sometimes, but she had hospice care and the best pain management, when she allowed it. Still, you know what Martha was like. She hated the idea of relinquishing control to drugs or to other people, and she fought to keep her independence and her wits about her to the end." Rebecca reaches out to cover my hand with hers. "Your grandmother was a remarkable woman. I do regret that you weren't told in time; I know you would have liked to have helped her through her last days, to be able to say goodbye. But I don't think she wanted you to see her like that. She wanted you to remember her the way she was before the illness. Please forgive her… and me."

I nod. Though I resent being excluded and kept in ignorance, I don't want to discuss it further. I start to pull my hand away from hers, to reach for my fork, when Rebecca squeezes it firmly and begins the *Motzi* prayer, thanking God for the food we're about to eat. Only with her *"Amen,"* does she release my hand.

With my first mouthful of the noodle pudding, I realize that I am, indeed, quite ravenous. Rebecca's instinct for what to serve is, as Grampa used to say, right on the money — comforting and satisfying.

We chat while we eat, the way women just getting to know each other will. Mostly, we talk about my work, and politics, and philosophy, and what it's like for her to be a rabbi's wife instead of a rabbi. It's somewhat endearing that her conversation so often returns to David. He's her touchstone, her best friend.

However, unlike other happily married women I've known, she doesn't ask about my love life. I suppose she's already guessed, or Gramma told her, that there's no one special. At least, no one important enough that I would want him here with me for my grandmother's funeral. Then again, all I've ever had were short term sexual encounters or easily controlled long distance affairs that petered out without any real goodbyes. There's Nigel, of course, but I wouldn't call him special, as much as he wants to be. No, it's easier keeping him — and all men — on the periphery of my life where he can't do any real damage.

As we finish up the wine over our empty plates, Rebecca asks me, "What are your plans for the next week? Do you want a *minyan* each evening, so you can say *Kaddish?*"

"I haven't really thought about it. I've so much I need to do to settle the estate, and I'm flying to Dakkar on Monday."

"Please consider it. You've seen what a comfort it can be."

"Yes, but…."

"You don't have to decide right this moment. We

can get one together rather quickly whenever you wish. Just promise me you will call, if that's what you want."

"Yes, of course."

We both get up to clear the table. While I wash the dishes, she dries and puts them away.

As I walk her to the front door, she hands me a card. "Here's my phone number and email address. Please call me tomorrow or even tonight... whenever you want to talk. I know David invited you to visit the temple. Perhaps, you'd like to come for Sabbath services. Or, come over to our home for lunch or dinner or whenever you wish. We live in the small white frame house next to the synagogue. Just knock at the back door when you're in town."

I hug her goodbye, with deep felt warmth, thanking her once more, and knowing that Rebecca Weis is a woman whom I would like to call my friend, if I could ever learn Melanie's knack for friendship.

I watch Rebecca drive away; once her car is out of sight, I turn off the outside lights. Suddenly, the house is even emptier than before, and though it's rather early, just a bit past eight, I'm too wiped out to even think about all that I have to do. I consider sleeping in Gramma and Grampa's bedroom, just to feel them near. Instead, I end up climbing the stairs to my own room. As I drift off to sleep, I think about Rebecca and how much she has given up for the sake of love. Yet, she wouldn't see it that way. Why is it that I never had anyone I would have been willing to give my all to like that? No one other than Joe.

THURSDAY

At breakfast, I try to organize myself so that I can use my few remaining days in Black Bear more efficiently. I jot down thoughts as they come to me on empty pages of an old notebook.

The biggest problem is deciding what to do about all the many things I don't want or can't take. Of course, things like clothes and food I'll give away to the needy. But what of all the furniture, books, equipment, supplies — the sheer volume of stuff that fills every nook and cranny in the house, barn and outbuildings?

The easiest answer is to sell it off, probably an auction, with most of the proceeds going to the charities Gramma supported. So, I'll need to find a reliable, honest auctioneer. However, it will have to wait until the property is disposed of. I've heard that a home sells more quickly and for a better price, when it looks lived in and is comfortably furnished. This house is indeed beautifully furnished.

I stroke the rough, thickly varnished surface of the kitchen table. Somehow, I've always imagined that this large, old handmade plank table would one day grace my own kitchen, when I finally settle down and buy a home in the country, but I've nowhere to put it right now. Then again, I have no place for anything. Not the photographs. Not the candy tin of letters. Not even Gramma's recipe box over there on the shelf. I'll have to rent storage space or buy a small property rather soon, just to have somewhere to put everything until I find the time to make a real home for myself.

A real home? The idea is so nebulous, a far future

that never seems to come closer as the years pass. That means I can't take this table, or Grampa's desk, or the old corner cabinet in the dining room.

If only this house were anywhere but Black Bear, Pennsylvania.

The pages I scribble seem to generate more questions than answers. Where should I donate all the clothes and food? Will they pick up or do I have to arrange for that, too? Whom can I trust to act as caretaker until the property sells? How will the auction be arranged, and by whom?

I need assistance and advice, and my first thought is Rebecca. We met only yesterday, but she insisted that she wanted to help. What's more, we have no shared past that might make it difficult for me to ask. What I need from her, however, could be too much of an imposition. She has her own responsibilities and life, not to mention that she's expecting her first child.

Still, as Gramps used to say, "You'll never know 'til you ask."

The dumpster is delivered soon after breakfast. While I make sure they don't drop it on Gramma's flower-beds, the phone rings. It's Mr. Nichols, the realtor.

"Hello, Judith. Sorry I didn't return your call Tuesday. I was out of town. Did I understand your message correctly? You want to sell your grandparents' property?"

"Yes." I hadn't expected him to get right to business. Not after all the years of friendship with Grampa. Of course, he already expressed his respects and regrets for Gramma's passing at the funeral and then again afterwards, here at the house.

"The hunting lodge and drug store, as well as the farm?" he asks.

"All of it," I say. Regardless of how long it may take for the will to be overturned, I will eventually need him to sell off all property so I can completely sever my last links with Black Bear.

"Okay. May we come over tomorrow to take a look around?"

Considering the amount of the time he used to spend here, when Gramps was alive, I doubt he really needs to "take a look around." Still, I suppose it's the professional thing to do. But he used the plural pronoun. "We?" I ask.

"My grandnephew Matt works with me now."

Of course. Mr. Nichols is about Grampa's age. "You're still active in the business, aren't you?" I don't like the idea of a stranger handling the sale, someone who knows nothing about my grandparents and the history of this place.

"Only part-time these days. Don't worry, Judith, I'll supervise everything for you, for Martha and Henry. You'll like Matt; he's a good fella, smart, a real go-getter."

"What time would you want to come over?"

"Morning's best, I think."

How well I remember the irritating local propensity to be noncommittal. Appointments tend to be vague agreements to try to be in the same place at approximately the same time, give or take an hour or two. "Can you be more specific? I may need to go into town."

"Why don't I call you before we come?"

It's probably the best compromise I'll get out of Mr. Nichols.

Everywhere I look, I find things I don't want to leave behind. Gramma's knitted afghans. The handmade quilts on the various beds. The old family sterling silverware and serving pieces. The big brass school bell we could hear even in the fields and in the near edges of the woods, when Gramma would use it to call us for meals. I promised myself to not even consider taking any furniture, but it's hard walking past heirlooms like the grandfather clock or Gramma's garden bench, knowing they will be gone from my life forever, after Monday.

They're only *things*. A part of me rebels against

coveting them, the ache within me when I contemplate losing them. When I think of the spare, barely furnished huts and hovels where *Les Femmes'* African clients live, I'm ashamed that I'm being so materialistic. But these things are more than inanimate objects; they're artifacts of my life, milestones of my heritage. Nearly every piece is part of me and the people I loved, keepsakes of the many stories that they evoke.

One of my earliest memories was standing uncertainly on the top of a stepladder, reaching toward the face of the grandfather clock, while Grampa gently guided my hand, teaching me how to set and wind it. I must have been no more than four years old. I loved the solid heft of the enormous brass key in my tiny hand, Grampa's sure touch guiding me, and how grown-up I felt being entrusted to share this important ritual with him.

After I moved here, the year I turned twelve, it became my responsibility to maintain the clock, winding it every eight days, adjusting the time when necessary. If I hadn't, the chimes that paced our days would have fallen silent, as they are now.

While I sort, trash and pack, I can't get the grandfather clock song out of my mind. Most of the words elude me; however, the tune plays and replays, culminating each time with the fateful last line. *But it stopped short, never to go again, when the old man died.*

I hated that song as a child. Not that I was superstitious. I knew that if I allowed the clock to go silent, Gramps wouldn't die. Still, I was determined that I wouldn't tempt fate by ever forgetting to wind the clock.

Now, every time I walk past the clock, I glance at its stilled hands, its deadweight pendulum. Dead as Gramma and Grampa. At least, this is one thing I can restore to the way it was those many years ago. I check my watch, and, opening the face plate, guide the minute and hour hands clockwise, as Grampa taught me. I do it carefully, slowly, so as not to put pressure on the thin curlicued brass arrows. The engraved white metal face towers over me still, but is just within my reach without a step ladder, just as it was for Gramps. If Gramma kept it wound after Grampa passed away, she would have needed a step. Yes, there it is, half-hidden under the side table, one of those rolling kickstands. I wonder how long she was able to keep at it; I hope someone wound it for her when she became too infirmed. I don't want to think of Gramma having to live in a silent house, dying alone, without the grandfather clock ticking away and chiming on the hour as it always had.

I take the brass key from its hook inside the body of the clock, insert it into the hole in the face and wind until the springs resist my hand with just the right amount of tension. I nudge the big brass pendulum, and the clock comes alive. Just the sound of the gears clicking made the house seem a little bit less empty. As I put the key away, I realize that I will never again wind this beautiful old grandfather clock that has been in my grandfather's family for about a hundred and fifty years.

Mr. Nichols's mention of the hunting lodge makes me realize that I have to go there, too. I know I can't take anything from that property. Not until I get that part of the will set aside. But I need to be prepared with a list of what I want from there, so it can be sent to me when all the legal matters are settled.

If I arrange things well, I can make a single trip into town, stop at the bank, see Rebecca and the temple and ask for her help, and then swing around to the lodge. Afterwards, I should be able to stay at the farm taking care of things for the rest of my time in Black Bear.

I call Rebecca, to find out when would be a good time to come over.

"How about having lunch with me?" she asks.

"I'd love to, but I don't think I should take the time. I have so much to do."

"You have to eat, Judith. Might as well be with me. Trust me; I don't have time to dawdle either. But I'd enjoy the break and your company, if you could manage it."

I know I shouldn't stop for a social meal, but I need to ask her a few rather large favors, and it would be less awkward over a leisurely lunch. Besides, I can use the companionship. "I have more leftovers than I'll ever be able to eat. Why don't I bring the food?"

"That sounds great. By the way, I'm a vegetarian; both of us are. It's the modern kosher. What time do you want to eat?"

I check my watch. I can go to the bank and hunting lodge first, then to Rebecca's. "How about one o'clock?"

"Perfect. See you then."

Mr. Frank, who used to be a teller when I was a child, is now the PNC branch manager. Whenever I would come into the bank with Gramma or Grampa, Mr. Frank would have a nice greeting for me and, when I was very young, a lollipop. Because of him, the bank became one of my favorite places to go when I accompanied either of my grandparents on their errands. However, as I grew up, I realized that all his friendliness and special greetings for his customers' children were nothing personal. It was simply good business.

Mr. Frank's friendly demeanor hasn't changed over the years, though he has grown quite fat and bald, and wears a very good three-piece suit that he never could have afforded when he was just out of college and starting out at the bank. He invites me into his glass-walled office that overlooks the small bank floor from above. Below us, only one of the three teller windows is active, and the desk in the corner, where customers open new accounts and discuss loans, is unmanned.

Mr. Frank gives me his condolences again. (I'm pretty sure he was at the funeral and probably spoke to me there.) And we go through other social pleasantries, such as my congratulations on him becoming the manager, and his kind words about my work with *Les Femmes*.

After I've re-established something of a rapport with him, I gather my resources within myself, project as much goodwill as possible, and say, "I understand that you will have to search and inventory Gramma's safe deposit box. I'd really appreciate it if you would allow me to witness the process. I'm anxious to locate some personal papers that I haven't yet found at the farm."

He stares at me for a few breaths, just long enough for my stomach to tighten. "Judith, I'm sorry. Meredith Denton was here this morning. She showed me a short certificate, evidencing her right to act as the executrix for your grandmother's estate." He seems truly concerned, but it could be as much a business tactic as his overt friendliness. "Of course, I assisted her, according to the law. We inventoried and sealed the box, and closed out your grandmother's accounts. She then opened a new account for the estate under her name, transferring all the money your grandmother had with us into it."

I can't believe how quickly Denton has gone into action. What do I need to do now? "Ms. Denton... Meredith... told me that I have the right to an accounting of everything."

"Well, yes, of course." Mr. Frank turns to his computer, his fingers flying over the keyboard. "Your grandmother had several accounts with us. Let's see... Her money market account had $78,354.34 in it... The savings account contained $95,987.53. .... Several CDs totaling about $250,000. I'm pretty sure she had savings in other banks, but Meredith would be better suited to tell you about that." He presses the Page Down button and the monitor redraws the next screen. "Umm... that's interesting. Her checking account had more cash in it than usual... almost $25,000." He types a few keys. "Ahh... that makes sense. There was a lot of activity on the checking account in the past few months, related to her illness. Checks to hospitals, doctors... oh, my... even to Morton. I guess she paid for her own funeral."

"Wasn't Gramma somewhat limited in what she could do near the end?" I'm almost afraid to ask the next question. "Was someone helping her with her accounts, writing checks for her?"

He looks up from the screen. "Yes, of course, Joe Anderson was assisting her with everything."

"Joe!? He had access to her accounts?"

"Just the checking account."

Merde! He didn't even wait until she was dead; that ugly bastard's fingerprints are all over Gramma's private business. "How long did Joe have access?"

"About three or four months... since your grandmother took to her bed." He shrugs. "Someone had to do it, and Joe was closest to her. It was natural for her to ask him to take over that responsibility, too."

I clamp down on my anger, on the nausea climbing up my throat. I must stay outwardly calm and courteous, if I want to keep Mr. Frank in this helpful mood. But... damn it all... how the hell did Joe get so much influence over Gramma? "Mr. Frank, could I have copies of the accounts' activities and of the checks for the past few months, and the current status of the estate account? I'd really appreciate it."

"Of course." He keys in some data and then hits the print button. "It will take a few seconds."

"And, please take Joe's name off my grandmother's accounts immediately."

"Actually, Judith, no one has access to the new account, except the executrix, until the estate is settled, and she disperses whatever moneys are left to the heirs."

"What do you mean, whatever moneys are left?"

"The executrix will use the funds to pay off any financial liabilities and responsibilities the estate has."

"I see." So, everything depends on the honesty and abilities of Denton, a woman I don't know, but whom Gramma obviously trusted. Then again, for some reason, she trusted Joe, too — at least when she was too ill to know better. Hopefully, Mr. Maeklin and Edward Felson will find out more about Denton. "Thank you, Mr. Frank, you've been a big help. I'd like to ask you one more favor."

"Yes?"

"Would it be possible for me to have a copy of the box inventory?"

He pauses for several awkward seconds. Then stands and says, "Yes, of course. I'll be right back."

Mr. Frank returns after a few minutes, and hands me a photocopied form. I skim through the handwritten inventory list: Grampa's old coin silver pocket watch that he inherited from his father. The deeds to the three properties. Gramma's and Grampa's passports. Grampa's discharge papers from the Army. Four certificates: for their wedding, Robby's birth and death, and Grampa's death. Plus other odds and ends of their lives. And, yes, the zero coupon bonds for Joe's children that Gramma mentioned — for $100,000 each! And that's it. No will. I glance at the bottom of the sheet and see both Denton's and Mr. Frank's signatures. So, unless I'm willing to believe that he would risk censure and possible indictment, I have to accept the fact that the sealed box contains nothing that might have contradicted the travesty that Meredith Denton claims is the most recent will.

Mr. Frank gathers up a sheaf of papers from the output tray on his printer, puts them in a large manila envelope and hands them to me. "Here are those printouts from the accounts." I dread what I might find when I study them.

I thank Mr. Frank and leave for the lodge.

The hunting lodge is exactly thirteen miles from the farm. Not originally a Schmoyer property, it came from another branch of the family; I'm pretty sure it was Gramma's side.

As a kid, I didn't spend much time at the lodge, mostly because I didn't particularly like that it was dedicated to the killing of creatures whose only crimes were looking great as wall trophies. One family story was that Grampa used to hunt every season, and Gramma was willing to have him bring the carcasses home only if they ate everything he killed. After he shot a large black bear, she surprised him by insisting that it be butchered, frozen and eaten, though it took more than a year to consume. Despite the ghastly, gamey taste of bear meat, she served — and they ate — every steak and chop from that enormous creature.

Grampa didn't hunt after that. At least, he never brought a kill home with him again. But he allowed a handful of his best buddies to use the property during hunting season, and he sometimes would go with them, just for the walk, he said, shooting pictures instead of a gun.

I went on one hunt in my life, with Grampa, AH and Mr. Waters, that first winter I lived here. Though Grampa didn't carry a gun, I did. I even knew how to use it. In fact, I was a crack shot at target practice. So, I was excited when Gramps finally agreed to let me come along. Walking through the woods with the men was fun, even though AH intimidated me with his teasing, saying that I was so noisy that I was driving all the game away. I loved being with Grampa and the easygoing way he had with his friends, knowing how much everyone seemed to like him — and, by extension, me. I was still too new to Black Bear and too young to recognize or understand the subtle differences in the shadowy looks I'd get, compared to the open welcome neighbors had for my Grampa. I didn't yet realize that my problems weren't only with the kids, that they had to have learned bigotry and backbiting from somewhere.

While we trekked through the forest, Grampa chomped on a big, brown cigar, something I wasn't used to seeing. Gramps was a pipe smoker at home, refraining from cigars except when he went out with his buddies. But he didn't light the cigar during our hunt, because, he admitted, "The stink would scare away any game within miles."

I sighted the first deer, and without hesitation, chambered a round, aimed my rifle and pulled the trigger. A clean kill. However, shooting bottles and tin cans for target practice hadn't prepared me for the animal's death throes — the doe's look of surprise, the spindly legs that collapsed under her, the grace of motion that was suddenly and completely stilled. My blood rushed loudly in my ears, drowning out the men's praises and congratulations. I stood there for what seemed like forever though it was probably only a few heartbeats. Then, I threw down my gun and ran back to the car. It wasn't only that I was disgusted by the murder, but that I was fascinated by it, and that frightened me even more.

I seldom visited the lodge from that day to this.

From the road, all anyone can see of the hunting lodge property are the dense forest and a small dirt road with a heavy rusty chain across it. It could be deserted, or an isolated part of the nearby state park if it weren't for the NO TRESPASSING signs. As far as I know, the chain has never been locked. So, it's an easy matter to simply unhook it from one of the posts and drive over it. I get out of the car and put the chain back up behind me, just as I saw Grampa do the few times I came here with him.

The rough road winds behind the trees. In less than a minute, I'm deep in the woods, with no evidence of the outside world. I roll down the car windows to let in the cool, earthy smells that are different from those of the forest around the farm — heavier, muskier, layered with eons of decomposing woody detritus undisturbed by human civilization.

The lodge is an old-style log cabin, newer than it looks, rebuilt in the sixties on the foundations and in the style of an older structure that burnt down when it was struck by lightning. One concession to modernity is the added indoor plumbing.

Everything appears to be in excellent condition: no splintered wood, cracked glass or mildew odor. In fact, someone has recently swept the porch, and the windows even look clean. Inside, all the furniture is covered with sheets, the electricity is turned off, and the pipes are drained to avoid freeze damage.

I look under all the cloths. Nothing here calls to me

the way the things at the farm do. The furniture is utilitarian, comfortable, broken in just enough to fit Grampa's body, but not broken down. The three bedrooms have Hudson Bay wool blankets instead of family quilts, and the kitchen is a typical bachelor establishment, with only the bare essentials. I'm about to leave when I see Grampa's penknife on a shelf. The one with dozens of tools that I loved playing with as a youngster. Damned if I'm going to leave that here for Joe to claim. I put it in my pocket, lock the door behind me and drive away without a backward glance.

The synagogue is on the northern edge of town, at the corner of Main Street and Hoffstedter Road. When I was a kid, old Mrs. Hoffstedter lived there in the small white framed house that was tucked back from the road, in a glade of crabapple trees. It was the last remaining parcel of the original Hoffstedter homestead, most of which had been sold off by her deceased husband's father sometime before World War II. At Halloween, she gave out the most delicious candied apples for trick or treat. I'd see her most often at the Black Bear library, where she volunteered. With a crosshatching of wrinkles as deeply crevassed as the bark of a tree, even Grampa used to call her "old;" I thought she was the most ancient person in town.

When I met Mrs. Hoffstedter, she stared at me for long minutes, taking in my dark skin, flat nose and high cheekbones. Finally, she blurted out, "But this can't be Margaret's child." No one else in Black Bear had stated their surprise quite so directly, so honestly, not within my hearing, but she quickly recovered. Whenever she'd see me, she'd bend over backwards to try to make me feel as though I were the same as any of the other "ordinary" Black Bear kids she handled, encouraged and sometimes disciplined at the library. I doubt she ever realized how clearly she telegraphed her discomfort with me.

Mrs. Hoffstedter's house is still there, but now it's

hidden behind a new building and parking lot. Rather simple in design, *Temple Beth Shalom* is a single storey rectangle of about fifteen by twenty meters, with a dark green pitched roof, white vinyl siding and large windows. It sits comfortably on the land, as though it has always been there.

I pull up behind the temple, on the corner of the asphalt parking lot closest to the house. As I heft the cooler of food from the back seat, Rebecca comes out the back door of the old Hoffstedter house. "Hi, Judith," she calls, her voice a lilting welcome. When she sees the cooler, she suggests, "Why don't you leave that in the car for now? There's something I want to show you in the temple."

Inside, the synagogue's simplicity is almost austere. The high off-white walls and blonde wood trim convey a sense of lofty open space. The pews are dark wood, obviously well-worn hand-me-downs from another, much older congregation.

Rebecca leads me to the Wall of Remembrance, and I see the names among the various bronze plaques before she points them out. Margaret Schmoyer Ormand. Amélie Kohn Ormand. David Jawara Ormand. I'm speechless. Someone gave a donation to the temple so that my mother and paternal grandparents would be remembered in the congregation's prayers long after all of us are gone.

"Gramma." It isn't a question so much as an affirmation, and I don't need to see Rebecca's nod to know it.

Rebecca places her hand on the small of my back, and guides me to the front of the sanctuary. "There's something else you need to see."

The ark is made of the same blonde wood as the window frames, but the doors are a delicate mosaic of different grains and stains of wood, depicting the Tree of Life. Rebecca opens its doors, then pulls the curtain to the side, to reveal the congregation's single *Torah*. As she lifts it and puts it in my arms, the tiny bells in the ornate silver crown jingle musically.

I haven't held a *Torah* since the twin's *b'nai mitzvah*, when I stood next to our proud father and his newest wife, a part of the ceremony, and for that day, a member of the family once more. I had forgotten what a warm weight a *Torah* could be, the source of Jewish faith, history and laws cradled against my breast.

"Put it down here." She points to the *bimah* readers' table.

Gently, I lay the scroll down, almost sorry to let it go.

"For several years, we didn't have our own *Torah*," Rebecca explains. "Every spring, we would have to go begging, asking one of the large synagogues in Philadelphia or New York to lend us one of theirs for the year." She places her hand on the satin *Torah* covering, stroking it as affectionately as she would a child or lover. Then, with her index finger, she points to a string of tiny English words embroidered with gold thread at the bottom of the cover.

I read it silently, "*In honor of our granddaughter, Judith Roberta Ormand.*"

I start to speak, wanting to express my wonder and tender pleasure, but I choke on the words. Yet even now, I don't cry. I never cry, not since leaving Black Bear seventeen years ago.

"Do you need some time alone?" Rebecca asks.

I shake my head, determined to pull myself together. Taking a deep breath, I look around me, at the small, peaceful room where Jews gather to worship and celebrate and mourn. Here, in Black Bear, of all places. At the same time, my fingers trace the embroidered words, as though I'm a blind woman trying to read what's underneath. How is it that this *Torah* has been given to this synagogue by my Moravian grandmother?

Finally, I turn to Rebecca. "I'm okay. It just took me by surprise. I'm..." Struggling to find the right word, I glance down once more at the *Torah*. "I'm honored... truly."

I lift the *Torah*, hugging it to me, and gently put it back in the ark. Then, closing the curtain and doors, I say, "Thank you for showing me. I didn't know...." I gesture around me "... about any of this."

"If it weren't for your grandmother, we wouldn't be here."

"Please tell me…"

"I'm starved." She presses her hand against her abdomen. "Let's talk over lunch."

The kitchen hasn't changed much since old Mrs. Hoffstedter's time. Undoubtedly, the congregation spent all their funds on the synagogue rather than on modernizing the house for their rabbi and rebbetzin. Still, the 50s-style yellow cabinets, white enameled sink and linoleum counters are in good condition and pleasantly homey.

When we enter, I see a small streak of black and white fur scamper from the center of the room where the sun warms the floor. The cat crouches in a far corner, watching us warily. But within minutes, it's rubbing against my legs, and stretching up to my knees with its front paws, asking to be picked up.

"That's curious," Rebecca says. "Tedda hasn't done that since we brought her here."

"Tedda? Gramma's Tedda?" I ask, as I pick her up. She puts her front paws around my neck and rubs her face against my chin, purring with an audible vibration of pleasure.

"I think she recognizes you, Judith."

"How could she?" I ask, knowing how much I want to believe that something in me might be so much like Gramma that her pet would know me by sight or smell, even though she has never seen me before.

"Well, animals are sometimes smarter than people. If I can see Martha in you, why shouldn't her cat?"

After washing her hands, Rebecca starts unpacking the cooler; I put the cat down so I can wash up and help. Tedda stays by my side the entire time.

Like two old friends, we divide the chores of preparing our meal, without discussing it. Rebecca microwaves the manicotti and sets the table, while I combine and toss the salad. Bustling about the kitchen, with the April sun streaming in through the double window over the sink, and a cat purring underfoot, I'm actually lighthearted for the moment.

"Your grandmother was a bit of a fireball," Rebecca says, as she starts to set the table. "Am I correct in thinking it might run in the family?"

I nod. "On both sides. You should have known my mom. In *Papa*'s family, the women have typically been..." I search for an appropriate English word to describe a certain type of women the Ormand men tend to marry. "...adventurous... vivacious... sometimes notoriously so."

"And you?"

"I'm working on it. When I'm done, I plan to be that crazy old lady no one can do anything about." I slice the tomatoes. "Rebecca, I'd like to hear about my grandmother's involvement with your temple."

"David told much of the story the other day. She gave us a place to meet, supported us when we were attacked."

"Attacked?"

"Not physically, but the graffiti and vandalism... and, well, something of a whispering campaign... heavy-handed attempts to make us leave. Some locals didn't take kindly to having Jews in their midst, and they made certain we knew it."

"I'm not surprised. Black Bear doesn't easily tolerate strangers, especially if you're different in any way."

She turns from the silverware drawer, where she's gathering utensils, and studies me.

"Different?" I have the distinct impression that she's heard more than I meant to say. "I suppose, when you first moved here, you were as different as they come."

"That's putting it mildly."

"What about before you came to Black Bear? Weren't you a bit different wherever you were? Certainly, you're not a stereotypical Jew. At least, not what others think we should be."

I'm surprised that Rebecca would be so reticent

in stating the obvious. "You mean, because I don't have a hook nose?"

"Yes, that, too." She smiles. "No, really, Judith. Let's face facts. Not everyone is used to meeting a black Jew."

"True, many automatically assume I'm a convert or a descendent of an Ethiopian Falasha. However, before moving to Black Bear, I led a sheltered life. In Paris, I was so very young and innocent. Anyone I met knew who I was... or who my family was. After my parents divorced, my mother and I moved to Manhattan, where I could be as anonymous as anyone else. The people in Mom's circle prided themselves in being cosmopolitan, in not being seen to react to my dark skin."

"Do you mind me asking? I don't want to pry, if you feel it's inappropriate, but I am curious. What is your heritage, on your father's side?"

"No, I don't mind. The Ormands have been Jewish since the 18th century, though Adie, my half-sister, thinks she's found documentation of an even earlier ancestor. Our black roots stem from my great-great-grandmother Bouli, a Senegalese émigré, who married into the family in the 1920s. Each subsequent generation of Ormand men has been about equally divided in whether they married white or black; my father likes blondes. As far as I know, they've all remained Jewish, though Adie is currently flirting with Buddhism."

When the microwave dings, Rebecca stirs up the marinara sauce in the casserole and sets it for one more minute. Then, she licks the spoon. "Mmm. Jane makes a mean manicotti." She throws the spoon into the sink. "I think we're about ready. How's the salad?"

"Done," I say with a flourishing last toss.

When we sit down to eat, Tedda leaps onto my lap and makes herself at home. I put her on the seat next to me several times but she won't stay there. Eventually, I give up and let her sleep, curled up on my lap, under my napkin.

Rebecca takes my hand while we say the *Motzi* together, thanking God for the food we're about to enjoy.

She squeezes gently, just before letting go.

Watching Rebecca eat, I could almost believe she's French. She enjoys the food fully, savoring every bite, as do I. The manicotti melts on my tongue — sweet, pungent and spicy flavors playing against each other — and the salad is a fresh cool complement.

I glance down at Tedda, whose face peeks out from under my napkin, with her eyes closed, the most sensual expression of contentment on her face. "Who has Acey and Martin?" I ask.

"Acey ran away the day Martha died. Perhaps, he'll come back now that you're in the house. He's a small black cat, almost Burmese in shape, though I'm sure he's a mongrel."

I don't like the idea of a pampered cat, Gramma's beloved pet, having to fend for himself in the wild. "I'll keep an eye out for him. What about Martin?"

"Oh, Joe Anderson has him."

"Joe? Why the hell would Joe take him?" Tedda flinches at the acid in my voice and jumps down. I miss the soft warmth of her on my lap.

"Didn't you know? Joe was the one who found that scruffy dog and gave him to Martha. Ugly as sin, but he's a good dog. Joe's kids absolutely adore him, and it's mutual."

Damn. That man certainly knew how to wheedle his way into Gramma's life. A stray dog and kids. What an un-beatable combination, even with someone as smart as Gramma.

I realize I've taken several bites without paying attention to the food. Not a good sign when that man can interfere with my enjoyment of a tasty meal. I take a forkful of salad, and, chewing slowly, concentrate on the crisp, lively flavors, knowing from experience that it will excise him only as long as I focus on that simple pleasure.

"May I ask you another personal question, Judith?"

"You can ask…. I can only try to answer."

"It's your accent, or lack of it. Sometimes, it's as thick as any *Parisienne* I've ever known. Other times, you sound as native as your grandmother."

"Ya noticed?" I say, dampening the vowels like typical Black Bear trailer trash — like Joe's Betty. The dog was probably her idea.

With a twinkle in her eye, Rebecca replies, "*Mais oui.*" Her accent isn't bad, either.

"*Parles-tu français?*" I ask.

"*Non, seulement un peu.*" Rebecca holds her index finger close to her thumb, to show just how very little French she knows.

Tedda has climbed onto the chair next to me and is dozing once more. What's especially sweet is how her front leg reaches out for me so her paw presses lightly against my thigh.

"You haven't answered my question," Rebecca says. "Is it something you'd rather not talk about?"

"No, it isn't that." I pause, not because I don't know what to say, but because I have too many different answers. "My father is French, and, of course, my mother was American, from here in Black Bear." I swat my hand, dismissing my own words. "You already know that."

"Yes."

"I lived in Paris for most of my early years, until I was about ten. But my mother made sure I was bilingual."

"I understand your ability with the two languages... and admire it, by the way... but that's not quite what I was referring to." Rebecca stares at me, in her gentle probing manner, a glint of humor in her eyes. "You seem to purposely alter your accent the way other women might change the nature of their smiles, depending on whom they're with, or what they want."

How perceptive she is, but for some reason, it doesn't make me uncomfortable to be found out by her.

"Actually, Rebecca, it's very much the same thing. Being French is useful these days, certainly more welcomed in many places than Americans, especially in the Third World where my work takes me. Since I'm both..."

"You're not in the Third World right now."

"No, not officially, though there's a lot about Black Bear... still, you're right." I know exactly when it started, this easy fluidity of my public self, hiding behind whichever accent is most convenient, using it as protective coloring. "When I first moved here to live with my grandparents, I laid on the French accent rather thickly. You can imagine... the new kid on the block, needing to make a statement about who I was. But with my coloring, folks around here assumed I was Haitian, which, of course, would be an insult to any self-respecting adolescent *Parisienne*. I quickly reverted to my grandmother's Pennsylvanian accent to try to fit in. I shouldn't have bothered. It made no difference how I spoke as long as I look the way I do. The past few days, I've found myself slipping back and forth, with no real rhyme or reason, just because I can, or because a phrase sounds better one way or another, or maybe, because it's who I am, regardless of what Black Bear thinks or wants."

"You talk about Black Bear as though it's a monolithic entity, a single personality."

"To me, Black Bear has always been a single, monstrous being, small-minded, bigoted and treacherous."

"Don't you think you're exaggerating a bit, Judith?"

"Of course, I am. But you've seen what it's like yourself. If it weren't for my grandmother, your synagogue might have succumbed to it."

"Your grandmother and others... many others."

"Perhaps, but you weren't there."

"When you were a child?"

I nod, while biting my lip, not wanting to feel the same old bitter hurt, not wanting to let it affect me as deeply as it still does after all this time.

"You've been gone from Black Bear... how long?" Rebecca asks.

"Seventeen years."

"Seventeen years. Almost two decades. Have you noticed, Judith, how memories tend to be all black and white, like an old Frank Capra or Bela Lugosi movie? But life is much more nuanced. Most people are neither heroes nor villains, but ordinary individuals struggling to do right while dealing with their own everyday frustrations and personal needs."

Of course, she's right, but I keep picturing the long high school hallways, gauntlets of stares, jeers and physical danger. Only with Joe had I felt safe walking past the rows and rows of lockers and cliques, though that didn't last. Suddenly, Joe was gone. No, worse than gone. He became one of them. I'll never forget the look of revulsion on his face, distorted with his screaming to have me thrown off the ambulance. Then, Wayne and his buddies, following me that night, dragging me into the old deserted schoolhouse. In one day, my entire world collapsed, simply because Joe, the native son of a hate-filled village, reverted to type as soon as he was old enough to know better than to befriend — to love — someone who wasn't his own kind.

I sense Rebecca's warm stare again, and I look up from my plate. "Judith, to paint the entire village with the same wide-swathe brush…. Did no one show you kindness, friendship?" she asks.

"I'm not always a fool, Rebecca. I recognize my own prejudices as clearly as I can see those of the people around me. But mine are based on actual experience with this village. Not on ignorance, ingrained intolerance or fear."

"You didn't answer my question. Did no one show you kindness while you lived here?"

"A few," I acknowledge. "For a time."

"I'm glad to hear it."

My answer seems to satisfy her more than it does me.

Rebecca gets up, taking her plate with her. "I don't know about you, but I'm going to splurge and have more manicotti." She holds out her hand for my dish. "You, too?"

"Just a little."

While she spoons two generous portions of the manicotti onto our plates, she says, "Judith, you should know that your grandmother was very proud of you. She loved telling anyone who would listen about your work. I was fascinated by her stories, and often asked her to tell me more about you, which, of course, endeared me to her."

I'm certain it was more than Rebecca's willing ear

that made my grandmother like her. I can imagine the two of them together, Rebecca with her probing, questing mind, and Gramma's habit of making other people's concerns and worries her own. They must have made quite a pair. I wish I could have seen them together, shared their conversations and laughter.

Rebecca brings the plates back to the table, and immediately takes another bite, a look of pure pleasure spreading across her face. "I enjoyed hearing about your work last night, and I'd like to know more. How did *Les Femmes* come about?"

I put my fork on my plate and think for a few moments before speaking. "It's strange. Whenever you ask me a question, I find myself wondering how to respond... which of the various appropriate answers to give you. I suppose I could talk about how it all began when I was a young associate debt analyst on the Bourse, moving billions of dollars hourly from one anonymous entity to another. None of it seemed real to me... or satisfying."

I'm not about to name the international brokerage firm I worked for, because Rebecca would recognize it immediately from the news stories on the high profile indictments. The government failed to prove anything, but that was only because they didn't really look in the right places. I shiver at the memory of some of the things I was required to do in that position, and the lies I told to protect my bosses... and myself. I didn't even have the excuse of being too young to know better. If you don't know right from wrong by the time you're twenty-four, you'll never learn it. The problem was that, back then, I had my doubts that it mattered.

"I went to Africa for the first time, as my twenty-fifth birthday present from *Papa*," I tell Rebecca. Actually, he wanted to hustle me out of the country before the insider trading scandal broke wide open. "When I saw what it was like, especially for the women... their deprivation was beyond my darkest nightmare. What a contrast it was to my spoiled, privileged life in Paris. Then, I thought of my great-great-grandmother, Bouli, who had come from Africa with nothing but her brains, guts and lots of great luck. I realized all that the many destitute, often abused women needed was some luck of their own, a small boost to help them pull themselves out of the quicksand that was their lives. That's what *Les Femmes'* microloans are… a little bit of luck, a hand up, rather than a handout."

"Remarkable. What a wide world you live in, Judith. It makes everyday concerns seem so small, petty."

Of course, she's right again. I enjoy my work, not only because of the good I am able to do. I buried myself and my past long ago in *Les Femmes*, while trying to give some meaning to my life. However, ignoring my troubles, as small and petty as they may seem compared to the women of *Les Femmes*, hasn't reduced the power they still have over me. Now that I've returned to Black Bear, where it all began, everything, regardless of how deeply I repressed it, has come flooding back in spades. Leaving Black Bear far behind me is my only hope of regaining any equilibrium, or getting back to what I once thought could pass for normal.

Rebecca finally finishes her second plateful of manicotti. I don't know where she put it all; I gave up halfway through. As she takes our two dishes to the sink, she asks, "Green tea? We can pretend that it might have some effect on all those carbs we just ate."

While she prepares the tea, I wash the dishes. As soon as I get up, Tedda is on the floor again, staying within inches of my feet wherever I move. I'm not sure how to approach the questions I need to ask Rebecca, so I just start with the easiest one. "Rebecca, I need your advice."

"Yes?"

"There's quite a bit of clothing and food at the farm that I would like to give away, to people who need it."

"That's easy. The consignment shop in your grandfather's old drug store."

"I don't want to sell the stuff," I insist.

"Don't you know? The shop is run by a group of women from the two churches and our temple. Sales help to support it, but it's mostly a free food and clothing pantry for those in need. Martha allowed us to use the building, as long as we pay for the utilities and basic everyday maintenance. The agreement is if we make any profit, she gets a percentage, though we seldom break even." Rebecca turns around from the counter, where she's pouring boiled water into a flowered porcelain tea pot. "Oh my... I hadn't thought about that. I do hope you'll be willing to continue the arrangement. Our little pantry is nothing compared to *Les Femmes*, but it's an important stopgap for so many families, not just in Black Bear, but from communities all around us."

This estate's getting more complicated by the minute. However, in this instance, it sounds more like Gramma. "I'm sure we can work something out."

Sitting at the table once more, with Tedda back on my lap, Rebecca pours the tea into two delicate scalloped ivory and flower porcelain cups, reminiscent of *Grand-mère* Amélie's Rosenthal tea service. "Why don't you stop by the store this afternoon?" she suggests. "You can see what it's all about and, at the same time, arrange to have the food and clothing picked up."

First problem solved. I squeeze a wedge of lemon into my tea, and take a sip, trying to decide how to ask my other questions.

"Are you really planning to sell the farm?" Rebecca asks. "It's been in your family for so very long. It seems a shame."

"I don't belong here. It would be more of a shame to let the house just sit, unoccupied."

"I am sorry to hear it." Again, I have the distinct impression that Rebecca heard more than my words, more than I meant to say.

"The problem is that there's so much out there, in the house and barn," I say. "Things of value or interest that I won't be able to take. So, I thought, once the property is sold, I might arrange to have an auction. Do you know any auctioneers who are trustworthy and good?"

"Not off the top of my head. The only one I know is the fellow who used to run monthly sales at the firehouse, but he's disappeared. The rumor is that he's in jail for handling stolen goods. Of course, other auctioneers advertise around here; I just don't know anything about them. But then, I've lived here only a few years. We should talk to some of the old-timers. They'd know whom you can trust and who to avoid."

"I'd really appreciate it if you could help me with this." I hesitate. It really would be too much to ask any more of a woman I've just met, no matter how friendly I'm beginning to feel toward her.

"Happy to." Rebecca raises one eyebrow. "Judith, is something bothering you?"

"Why do you ask?"

"For the past several minutes, you've seemed to be on the verge of saying something, then veering away at the last instant."

I wonder if she's usually this perceptive, or if I'm being particularly transparent today. "Well... I... "

"Please, whatever it is, just say it."

"You know I have to leave Black Bear this coming Monday. I've appointments in Dakkar that I can't postpone." Nothing immediately imperative that I can't put off if I want, but I don't need to tell her that. "That means I'll have to leave some things undone, requiring attention."

"Such as?"

"I'm packing up a bunch of boxes that will have to be picked up and shipped to me in Paris." I look at her hopefully, not wanting to ask.

"So, you need someone to supervise the pickup and make sure they take the right boxes, they're addressed correctly, and so forth. Right? I can do that." She pauses as she studies me. "There's more, isn't there?"

"Yes." I decide to let it all out in a rush, and let matters fall as they will. "Until the property is sold, I'll need a caretaker to maintain it, and someone to keep an eye on the caretaker. Then, someone... probably that same person... will need to help me hire an auctioneer and deal with him. I just can't come back here... ever."

"I see." Rebecca stares at me, searching my face, as

she considers what I said. "I'm sorry to hear you won't ever return. I was looking forward to our friendship."

"Me too, but not here, not in Black Bear."

"I think I understand better now, but it doesn't make things any less sad."

Is Rebecca holding back something? Have I forced her into an uncomfortable corner, asking for her help?

"Judith, please do me a favor."

"What?"

"Be careful about making irrevocable decisions just now. It's a difficult time for you, and I don't want you to be sorry about selling your farm after you've thought things through."

"I know what I'm doing." Disturbed perhaps by the tension in my voice, Tedda stands up on my lap, looks at me curiously, then circling around a few times, settles back down. My napkin is now on the floor.

"Please, don't take offense where none was intended. I'm simply concerned for you."

"Thank you for your concern, but there are things you just don't know." I bite off my words, rather than let them crescendo into a shout.

"Undoubtedly." She shrugs her shoulders and nods in acknowledgment of her own limitations. How does she do that — defuse the tension with a simple, self-effacing gesture? She makes me want to laugh with her rather than yell. "By the way, yes, I'd be happy to help you with the property."

She changes the subject so quickly, I feel like I have whiplash. "Uh... thank you."

"I know the perfect person to ask to be caretaker."

"Who?"

"Let's talk before you leave Black Bear. We'll settle things then. Okay?"

"Yes... great." I've gotten everything I came here for. Then, why am I so off-balance, uncertain? I pet Tedda, then head for the door. "Thank you, Rebecca, for lunch and for all your help."

"And thank you, Judith, for bringing lunch with

you. By the way, do you think you'll be joining us for *Shabbat* services?"

"I don't know... I have so much to do."

"Friday evening at seven thirty. Saturday morning at ten. We'd enjoy having you with us either or both days. Please consider it."

When she hugs me, I return the embrace. So much of what I see in her I admire or enjoy, and I want to believe that I have indeed found a new friend. But what if she is just like everyone else in Black Bear? I've been wrong before in my judgment of someone I thought I could trust.

As I get into the car, I look back at the house. Tedda is sitting in the kitchen window, basking in the sun, perhaps watching me walk away. I don't like leaving her, but I can't possibly take her with me. At least, she seems to have found a good home.

On the door of Grampa's drug store, pasted against the inside of the glass, is a hand-lettered sign with curled edges and smudges from having been handled often. It says, *Back in 10 mins.* Knowing Black Bear, I judge it to really mean a minimum of 20, 25 minutes. Rather than go back to the farm, I decide to wait, since it would save me having to come into town later.

Remembering AH's invitation to come see him, I go next door to Engelhardt's Auto Supply. The shop hasn't changed much over the years, though some of the displays are shinier, with more electronics and digital devices. And those previously omnipresent posters of scantily clad girls have given way to ones showing men or women using the various automotive products.

When I was very young, visiting from Paris, I would come here with Gramps to get parts for his boat, truck, tractor or car. I used to stand tiptoe, leaning over the long counter with its cool hard stainless steel ribbed edge, to try to see into the mysterious back area. Jeff Smith, Gene Engelhardt or, sometimes, even AH himself, would disappear through the aisles of tall shelves, muttering a part name or number under his breath. Minutes later, he would return with a box that Gramps would take in hand, examine, and say, "That's it!" and pay for it. Or, he would shake his head. "Nope, not exactly." Then, he'd explain further what he needed, which would send Gene or Jeff or AH into the back again. It seemed a ritual reserved for men, to which I had been given a glimpse, even though I was a girl, just because I was Grampa's girl.

A stranger, a tall gangly clerk about twenty years old, is behind the counter today. He scrutinizes a complex gadget of oily metal in a customer's hand. "A '62 VW?" he asks uncertainly, as he rubs his open palm back and forth across the bristle of his buzz cut. "Don't know. Let me check." Taking the part with him, he disappears into the back.

The showroom is suddenly quite large, and yet too small, in that awkward claustrophobic sense of two strangers stuck in the same space, with nothing to do other than to try to avoid being seen staring at each other. The man nods self-consciously at me, then looks away, apparently fascinated with all the varieties and advantages among different wiper blades displayed on the opposite wall. I crane my neck, hoping to see a glimpse of someone in the back, maybe even AH himself. No one is within sight, not even the young clerk.

The front door opens and closes with a jolt of vibrating glass and metal. In walks Katie Wallerson, nearly dragging a short bald man I don't recognize, but whom I take to be the current browbeaten husband Gramma mentioned in one of her more gossipy emails. Damn, of all the people to run into, the firehouse auxiliary know-it-all who considers this village her personal fiefdom and is on a first name basis with everyone, whether they want to be or not. The years haven't been good to her; she looks over sixty, though I know she can't be much older than forty-five. Initially, she doesn't really look at me. It's more a survey of the room she has taken possession of, planting her considerable bulk in the far corner.

She bends her disarray of short henna curls close to the man's ear. "Speak of the devil. Look who's here," Katie says in a stage whisper I'm meant to hear. "Who the hell does she think she is, waltzing into town after all these years and making trouble? Like no one in Black Bear... not even her own grandmother... don't know enough to wipe our own butts."

Focusing intently on a rack of dangling car fresheners, I try to pretend I don't hear her, but my heart thumps in my throat, just like it used to, when I couldn't avoid going to the toilet in school, knowing the catcalls, or worse, that I'd get from the girls primping at the mirrors. Thank goodness, Jeff comes from the back just then. Apparently, the clerk has asked him for help finding the classic Volkswagen part. Jeff hands the gadget back to the customer. "Sorry, Hugh," he said. "We'll have to order it." Then, he sees me. "Judith, what a pleasant surprise." Jeff Smith has always been able to lighten my mood, even back in those bad old days. If I had to run into Katie Wallerson, at least Jeff is here, too.

"Hi, Jeff," I said. "Is AH in?"

"Sorry. He doesn't come into the shop that often anymore."

"Might he be at the dealership?" I gesture to the Ford showroom and sprawling lot across the street.

Jeff shakes his head. "Not today. Anything I can help you with?"

"No, thank you, Jeff." I scurry to the door. "I'll call him at home. Good to see you." I don't look back until I'm safely outside. Katie watches me through the window, a self-satisfied smirk planted on her round jowly face.

The *Back in 10 mins* sign is still on the drug store door. I go across the street, telling myself I simply want to avoid running into Katie when she leaves the Auto Supply, but knowing that I have no reason to head for Engelhardt's Ford. No, I have a very different purpose in mind, and veer to the left.

So, I come, at last, to the one place I have tried so hard to forget. The one place on earth I'll remember in excruciating detail for the rest of my life.

The old boarded up school.

Constructed of brick and concrete in the 1930s, it's an enormous rectangle that still dominates Main Street, dwarfing even the Ford dealership next door. During Mom's time, every kid in town went there from kindergarten until eighth grade. Then, the new schools were built, and it has remained empty ever since. Such is the lack of resourcefulness and new business in Black Bear that this solidly built structure, the largest in the village, is allowed to go to waste.

That first autumn I moved here, Joe warned me to stay away from the old school; it was where the really bad kids hung out. Of course, that made me even more curious about what went on behind the plywood-covered windows and shackled doors. But, in this, I obeyed, never daring to go inside, fearing the dangers inherent in following the likes of Maybeth and Billy into dark corners.

Then, came that day when everything changed.

One of the school's side door hinges is broken, making it easy to shimmy my way inside, where I never dared to go in my youth. Everything is in shadow, a twilight world of blacks and greys, punctuated by a few stripes of dusty daylight seeping through the boarded-up windows. Trash crushes under my feet. As my eyes adjust to the darkness, I work my way to the spot it happened. It looks no different than any other corner, covered with the same scatological graffiti and littered with cigarette butts, discarded condoms, broken liquor bottles, even a few used hypodermic needles. It's probably just as dangerous to be here now, as when I was young. But I have to see it, have to embrace it fully, just this once. Then, maybe, I'll finally be able to put it behind me.

It all happened in one 24-hour period.

The evening before the big homecoming game, Joe and I were up in our treehouse. And he kissed me, as he had never kissed me before. His body pressed against the full length of mine; I could feel the hard bulge of his erection straining against our clothes. I wanted it to be more, was ready to give everything to him. I had even stolen a package of condoms from Grampa's store, hoping for it. At the last moment, he pulled away. His features twisted with horror; he stared at my face, studying it, as though he had never seen it before. *"No!"* he gasped, and before I had a chance to ask him what was wrong, to assure him that it was okay, that I wanted him, he scrambled down the tree, jumping the last few feet, and ran away from me. Naïve, I ran after him. But Joe had always been faster than I. I was still in the woods, trying to catch up to him, when I heard his pickup's tires squealing, as he drove as fast as he could away from the farm, away from me.

I stood in the driveway, looking at the empty space where Joe should have been, waiting for me, laughing with me at the silliness of his tease. Pulsing waves of unrequited passion and shame flooded my body; I didn't know what to think.

I didn't sleep much that night, wondering what had gotten into Joe, why he had been so horrified about the idea of finally making love to me.

The next day was the championship game against our arch rival, Barrowsburg. Joe was distracted and playing badly, but the coach kept pushing him harder and harder. Suddenly, Barrowsburg's left guard and tackle came barreling down on him, from separate directions. He should have avoided them with a fast pivot and run, but he was too slow. They hit him. Hard. Crushing him between them. The sound of it, a sickly thwack of bodies colliding, catapulted me from my seat in the bleachers. He lay on the ground, broken, his leg bent all wrong. I had to fight my way through the crowd thronging around Joe, trying not to hear their comments rippling outward. "It's bad." "That kid will never play again." "Play? He won't walk again."

When I finally knelt by Joe's side, he had that same look of horror on his face that I had seen the night before in the treehouse. Something in me refused to recognize it for what it was. I convinced myself that the reason Joe screamed to keep me off the ambulance was because he was protecting me, not wanting me to see how severely injured he was. I didn't care what he looked like, or how much blood there was; all I knew was that I had to be by his side, helping him, taking care of him.

For the first time in my life, I drove far over the interstate speed limit, making it to Mercy Hospital in Scranton, 30 miles away, just as they were wheeling Joe through the double doors into the examining area of the emergency room. When I tried to follow, a guard stopped me. "Are you family?" he asked.

I should have said, "Yes, I'm the closest thing Joe has to a real family." However, in my stupor, I was honest. "No, but, I'm a good friend. He'll want me with him."

"I'll ask." The guard disappeared into the inner sanctum behind the swinging doors. "Sorry," he said when he came back. "You can't go in there."

I thought it was because some doctor didn't want me interfering with Joe's treatment. It hadn't yet dawned on me that Joe could possibly be refusing to see me.

So, I waited for hours among the other outcasts, seated in the rows of uncomfortable green vinyl and chrome chairs, with the TV high above our heads droning on and on. People came and went. An infant too quiet in his mother's arms, a man with a bloody head injury, a grey-haired woman crying silently, others infirmed or ill. All were dazed, looking up only when a nurse came out and called a name, hoping it would be their's, that someone, anyone would notice them and end their pain. A guy who looked like he had been knifed was rushed right inside, as was a very pregnant woman. The rest of us waited.

I lost track of time. No, that's not quite right. I lost sense of my place within time, within reality. All that existed was in that emergency room; the world outside faded away.

At some point, Joe's older brother Wayne showed up. I had never met him, but his resemblance to Joe was unmistakable. Big like Joe, over six feet tall, but with a more compact body, Wayne had the same sandy coloring, crinkling eyes and big smile. However, the effect was very different in Wayne's thinner, sharper face. His smile was sardonic, his eyes darting, checking out everything and everyone within his purview. On his right forearm was a large tattoo of two lightning bolts nested against each other, the Nazi SS insignia. One of his buddies pointed to me; I heard only a portion of what he said. "...Joe's nigger...." Wayne stared at me, but said nothing. All three of them were escorted right inside to Joe — the buddies, too. I was certain that they weren't family.

Had the guard stopped me because of the color of my skin?

I continued to wait, sure that Joe would tell them to come get me, that he needed me by his side.

What a fool I was.

Every once in a while, a receptionist behind a glass window gave me an update. Joe was waiting to be seen by the doctor. He was being taken to x-ray. But, she informed me, only family could be told the prognosis.

Wayne and his two friends came out. One of them glanced at me, and I stood, certain that they were about to tell me to go into Joe. Instead, they headed outside. I rushed after them and grabbed Wayne's arm to stop him. He looked at my hand, as though it were something dirty that had landed on his sleeve. I quickly removed it, realizing I was touching the Nazi tattoo, and he turned to leave.

"Wait!" I said. Then, when he glared at me, I added, "Please."

"What d'you want?"

"How is he? Can you help me get in to see him?" I pleaded.

"Leave him be. You don't belong here. Joe don't want to see you. Don't want you nowhere near." As he walked out the glass door, I heard him say to his friends, "Shit, can you believe the stupid cunt?"

Stunned, I collapsed into a nearby vinyl chair, identical to all the others in the room. I didn't know what to do. Surely Wayne had to be wrong. What could he know about Joe and me?

The shift changed, and a new receptionist sat at the desk behind the glass window. After she settled in, I went up and asked how Joe Anderson was.

She looked up his record. "He's been admitted."

"What room? I've got to see him."

"Sorry. Visiting hours are over."

No matter what I said, how hard I implored, she wouldn't budge. If I had managed to get his room number from her, I could have sneaked in, but she was a stone wall.

I sat in my car in the hospital parking lot, tears streaming down my face, every muscle in my body convulsing, sobbing. Joe was somewhere in that monolithic building, probably in pain, wondering where I was, why I wasn't there, holding his hand, talking to him. And there I sat, powerless; I couldn't get to him.

But what if what Wayne had said were true? Joe didn't want me near him. Not because he was protecting me, but because I didn't belong with him, not when it counted. Could it be possible that Gramma had been right about him all along?

No! Not Joe! He was my best friend. And more. Much more.

Wayne didn't know anything about us. After all, he'd been away for years, and now he was just making mischief. Or, maybe he was jealous of us.

I didn't pay much attention to anything on the drive home. Not my gas gauge and certainly not the fact that another vehicle was following me. Only when my car sputtered to a stop on Drumheller Lane did I realize that I was out of fuel. Even then, I wasn't too concerned. I got out and headed north. It would be an easy walk home to the farm, little more than a mile and a half, with a full moon lighting the way. Of course, the drug store was much closer; I could see the village street lights through the trees. But, if I went to the store, I'd have to call Grampa and explain that

I had run out of gas; I didn't want a lecture just then.

A dark car pulled up, with its rear door open. I could see Wayne in the back seat. His two buddies were in the front.

"Hey! Ya lost?" His voice was so like Joe's, that I instinctively started to move toward him. But I stopped in my tracks when I saw his leering grin.

"Look here, if it ain't the nigger girl," the guy in the front passenger seat said. "Wanna ride?"

"Yeah, let's ride, girlie," the driver called. The three of them laughed heartily, as though the *double entendre* was the wittiest thing they'd ever heard.

"No, thank you," I said, backing away from the car, telling myself that my imagination was working overtime. They were just good ole boys, harmless rubes. But my heart thumped in my throat. One step, then another, slowly I inched off the road.

"Hey, where ya going, babe?" Wayne asked. "We're just having some fun with ya."

"I know, but it's time for me to go. My grandfather is waiting for me at his store," I lied, and I knew they saw right through me, probably could smell my fear.

Wayne jumped out of the car, and lunged for me. But I bolted, so that his hand closed on air.

I ran faster than I ever had in my life, through the woods toward the village lights.

"Get her," one of the others yelled. I could hear them crashing through the woods behind me.

If I could get to Gramps' store, I would be safe. I felt for my keys in my skirt pocket, making sure they were there, practicing in my mind how I would unbutton the pocket, whip them out, open the door and lock it behind me. I better not drop them, or fumble or delay slamming the door. Otherwise, they'd get me.

I had one advantage. I knew these woods.

Maybe they did, too.

From the sound of it, they separated. One was directly behind me, shining a light toward me; the other two were fanned out. The guy to my left was gaining on me, but then he yelled, "Shit!" I hoped it was because he had tripped.

I broke through the trees to open field. I could see the drug store sign, just a little further. I was going to make it!

Suddenly, a pair of hands grabbed me and lifted me off my feet, pinning my arms to my chest.

"Got her!" Wayne said triumphantly.

I kicked and tried to wriggle free, but another seized my legs.

"Let me go," I screamed, praying someone might hear me, knowing no one would be around, not in the middle of the night. Black Bear was a ghost town after dark.

"Shut up bitch!" Wayne hissed into my neck, as he squeezed tighter, making my ribs hurt. "Hey, Jim, get over here, show this cunt what we do to noisy bitches."

Jim must have been the one who wasn't holding my legs. He pulled out a knife. The blade glinted in the moonlight, hovering just above my eyes.

"Now, shut up, or get cut up," Wayne said. "Got that?"

I was too terrified to say or do anything, though a silent scream burned in my throat.

They carried me away from the lights, into the old school.

It smelled putrid, old garbage and stale urine. I couldn't believe any of this was happening.

They dumped me on the floor, pushed up my skirt, and in short order, cut away my underpants, the sharp steel of the knife cold against my flesh. While the other two held me down, each holding an arm and a leg, Wayne took the flashlight from his back pocket and shined it on me. "Look at that. Never saw no nigger pussy before."

"Please," I begged. "Let me go."

"I told you to shut the fuck up!" Wayne hit me in the stomach. "That's for Joe, bitch. This too." He unzipped his jeans.

Dizzy and nauseous, I felt the world recede, or was I falling away from the world, from my own body? Not that

I wasn't aware of everything that was happening, of the tearing within me, something breaking that would never again be whole. Of Wayne's voice that sounded so like Joe's, saying Joe's name over and over again, in ways that made no sense to me. "... for Joe.... wouldn't touch this, not Joe... big brother'll take care of the nigger... just stay the fuck away from Joe." All punctuated with his grunts and thrusts.

But I wasn't fully here either, not in this hellhole, surrounded by those filthy beasts pawing me, laughing and cursing and taking turns pounding on top of me. I never again was fully anywhere, a part of me was lost somewhere far away, an observer, outside my body, outside my own life.

When they finished, Wayne spat on me, then hissed, "Tell anyone, cunt, and I'll chop off all your fingers and toes, cut out your eyeballs, and then slit your throat from ear to ear. I'll fuckin' kill your damned grandparents, too, real slow and painful."

They left me there, bruised and bleeding, in that dark corner, with no light to find my way out. I drifted away even further, oblivious to the passing time, until faint streaks of dawn cut through the blackness.

Coming out of the dark schoolhouse into the bright April sunlight is a momentary shock of disorientation, of reality only partially displacing the shadowy world of my memories. I half expect to walk out into the dull light of dawn of that dreadful November day from my past. I retrace my steps of that morning, crossing the street to Grampa's drug store, the one place of safety that I could depend on in the village.

In the here and now, Grampa's drug store is no more, replaced by a charity shop.

I brush my hands over my jeans, reminding myself that I'm not wearing the tartan skirt that I had worn for the big championship game eighteen years ago. The skirt with the key in the button-down pocket that saved my sanity that grey morning. In front of me is the same one-storey brick building, but I don't need to run inside, or lock the door securely behind me. No compulsion to wash, douche and cry, trying to scrub the violence from my flesh. As immediately real as it still feels, nearly two decades have passed. I have nothing to hide from anyone anymore; nobody ever found out what Wayne and his buddies did to me. I'm no longer a victim, but a woman in full control of her own life.

As I cross the street, I see a woman and child coming out of the shop. Both are very pale and rail thin, with lusterless brown hair pulled into tight ponytails. The woman is an old twenty-something, in faded, thread-worn blue jeans and a scruffy parka that's three sizes too large for her. Though she holds a large brown paper bag brimming with packaged food, and she grasps the child's small hand in her free hand, I don't believe the rounded hunch of her shoulders has anything to do with any physical burden or the need to hold onto her daughter. Her eyes are fixed on the goods in the bag, as though she fears they might disappear, if she turns away.

By contrast, the child, who is about five years old, and dressed in mismatched, slightly oversized hand-me-downs, is aglow with excitement, clutching a baby doll and chatting happily to it.

When I enter Grampa's drug store, the same old tin bell jingles as the top of the door hits it. Gramps should appear now, emerging from the back room to greet his customer or visitor, as he did whenever he heard that bell. But he isn't here, and neither are all his jars and boxes, magazines and candy, school supplies and cosmetics, tobacco and medicines. The fixtures are the same. The old dark wood and glass apothecary cabinets lining the walls. The racks and shelves dividing the room into three aisles. The back counter, blocking the way to where he used to keep the prescription drugs. Even the soda fountain, though the red-topped round stools that every kid in town loved to twirl on are gone. The magazine stand has been replaced with a clothes rack, where all manner of coats, dresses, shirts and suits hang. More clothes are folded or displayed wherever they fit, though it does appear that someone has tried valiantly to wrest some order out of it, despite the chaotic nature of browsing shoppers. Canned and packaged food are stored and sorted on the counters and in the apothecary cabinets, and toys are on lower shelves where children might reach them.

A woman straightens up from behind the soda fountain counter. "Hello, may I help you?" she says as she stands. Then, she recognizes me. "Oh, hello, Judith. Come to see what we've done with your grandfather's old store?"

I can't place her face. About sixty-five years old, with a swarthy complexion, she has the carriage of one as comfortable in a business suit as she is in the fitted denim shirt tucked into the belted jeans that she's wearing. Her short grey hair is both practical and feminine, and clearly maintained with frequent visits to the beauty parlor. She wears no makeup other than a muted rose lipstick.

She comes out from behind the counter, and offers me her hand. "Sorry, I should have introduced myself. I'm Anita... Anita Giacconi." Her handshake is firm and warm, and her dark eyes sparkle. "We met briefly at the church, but you saw so many people there."

"Hello Anita, nice to meet you... again." I don't recall seeing her at the funeral, but I know the name. She answered the phone when I'd called the farm from Senegal last week — the disembodied voice that told me Gramma had died. "I wanted to thank you for helping take care of my grandmother near the end."

She nods, with a small, quiet smile. "Martha was a special woman, and I was honored to know her." Then, in a more lively tone, she calls toward the back of the store, "Ellen, look who's come."

I hear an excited, happy woman respond from the back room, "Be right there." The voice becomes a bit louder through the walls as she comes closer. "Wasn't that child a handful? What a relief that she finally quieted down, Anita, when you gave her that doll. But wasn't it fun seeing her expression when she realized you didn't want the doll back, that it was hers to keep?" When she rounds the corner, I'm surprised to see Mrs. Ringenhauer, wiping her gnarled arthritic hands on a small brown terry towel. Wisps of her thin grey hair are uncharacteristically flying about, and this usually mousy woman is actually smiling broadly, a pinkish flush on her cheeks that's both attractive and much livelier than I ever imagined she could be.

Then, she sees me.

Mrs. Ringenhauer frowns, not so much with her mouth, but with her eyes that narrow to a squint, deepening the wrinkles on her brow. I remember that look from my youth and how her half lids never quite obscured her scornful disapproval. "Oh...Judith... hello," she says so softly that I almost don't hear her. In those few seconds, she has already begun to fade back to her usual drab protective coloring. How many people are fooled into believing she really is as passive as she pretends?

"Judith's come to see what we've done with the place," Anita says.

"Rebecca Weis told me what you're doing here..."

"Are you going to close us down?" Mrs. Ringenhauer interrupts me, still softly, but with a bite to the words that's as close to being aggressive and openly angry as I have ever seen her.

"I didn't even know about any of this..." I gesture around the room, "until today."

Anita moves closer to Mrs. Ringenhauer and puts her hand on the older woman's shoulder — to reassure her, show solidarity, or maybe, to remind her to be careful what she says to me.

"Ellen," Anita says. "Shall we show Judith around?" Moving down the middle aisle, she points to various piles of clothes and goods. "As you can see, we have clearly marked sizes and price tags on everything, and we make sure it's all in nice, clean condition."

"But I understand that you give things away," I say.

"Yes, to those who need it," Anita respond.

"How do you distinguish those who should pay and those who should have whatever they want for free?"

Mrs. Ringenhauer doesn't follow us, but answers with a huff from where she stands. "If someone is in need, who are we to question them? I'd rather give away a dozen dresses by mistake to someone who can afford to pay, than add to an unfortunate's shame by forcing them to prove their need."

I never would have imagined Mrs. Ringenhauer an idealist. Perhaps in a small village like Black Bear, with a tiny operation like this shop, it could work. I want to believe it could. My own idealism has been beaten into a more pragmatic form over the years. *Les Femmes* gives nothing away for free — not merely because the organization needs to be self-sustaining, but because we saw how out-and-out charity whittles away at the recipients' self-respect, until they've nothing left but shame and need.

Still, I'm not about to criticize any attempt to provide food and clothing to the many unemployed or underemployed of the Poconos, regardless of how temporary a solution it is.

Picturing the child chatting away happily to her new doll, I can't help but smile. It would indeed be pleasant to believe it could work.

"You've established a nice operation here," I tell them.

"Coming from you, considering the work you do, that's quite a compliment," Anita says.

"What I don't understand is why you would think I'd want to close you down."

"Well..." Anita starts to respond, but she's clearly uncomfortable, perhaps even a bit cornered by the question. For the first time since I entered the store, she doesn't meet my eyes, and her hands fidget among the clothes on the nearest shelf, not quite straightening anything, but busy and distracting nevertheless.

Mrs. Ringenhauer isn't so reticent. "Everyone knows how you're planning to sell off everything," she blurts out. "Grab the money and run out of here, without a backward glance for any of us, or anything that mattered to your own family." Her face is flushed once more, but this time with livid, unrestrained ire. "And look at what you're doing to poor Joe Anderson. Siccing that investigator on him, digging up all the old problems, accusing him of all sorts of bad things. And to top it off, trying to cut him out of your grandmother's will. As though you need any more money."

"Not that it's any of your business, Mrs. Ringenhauer, but Joe is no innocent," I dismiss her indignantly. "He wangled his way into the will of a sick and dying woman…."

"No missy, you don't know nothing….," she shakes her head and fist, and quickly corrects herself. "Anything. Joe was there for your grandmother when she needed him. Where, in heaven's name, were you? I don't care how much money and power you got, you don't hold no candle to Joe. Never did so far as I could see, not in what counts."

Anita puts her arm around Mrs. Ringenhauer's shoulders. "Ellen, please," she implores. "You mustn't get so upset."

"Why not?" Mrs. Ringenhauer insists. "This girl marches into town, from God knows where, just like she did years ago, looking down her nose at us ordinary folk, with her high falutin' New York ways. Now, she plans to destroy everything we've worked so hard to establish with this pantry, and she doesn't give a damn." She turns to glare at me, her face burning bright red. "Do you? No, not about this shop, or about what your grandmother went through while you gallivanted around the world, or about anything in Black Bear." Her entire body trembles with her anger, or is it fear?

Of course, I've heard the "New Yorker" label before. To the people of Black Bear, it's synonymous to being an outsider, someone who doesn't belong here (regardless of where you're really from), which is just about the worst thing they can say about a person. However, I never would have expected Mrs. Ringenhauer, of all people, to explode like that. How long had all that anger and jealousy been building in her? I can't help but be curious: has she become something of a tinderbox as she got older, after all those years of imperfectly hiding her true feelings behind that holier-than-thou façade of hers?

Anita appears genuinely concerned, perhaps because Mrs. Ringenhauer shouldn't be getting so excited at her age, or maybe because Anita is enough of a business-woman to know it isn't sensible to alienate the one person who controls the future of their pantry.

Anita guides Mrs. Ringenhauer to the door and helps her on with her coat. "Why don't you go rest, Ellen. You've been working so hard."

Mrs. Ringenhauer doesn't protest, but as she walks out, she scowls at me, with tears in her eyes. "Go back to where you came from and leave Joe… leave all of us alone. We all… your grandma, too… did fine without you all these years."

Then, turning to Anita, she says, "I'm sorry, dear." But I don't believe she's contrite about anything other than disrupting Anita's neat and orderly life.

The door bangs closed behind her, jingling the old bell.

"My apologies, Judith. Ellen's been worried, and it's wearing her thin."

"Worried that I'd shut the store down?"

Anita sighs deeply. "Yes, among other things. But now you've seen it…" she searches my face. "You won't, will you?"

"Actually, I'm here to make a contribution. We've a lot of food and clothing out at the farm that I'd like to donate. Could you arrange to have someone come pick it up on Saturday afternoon? You'll probably need a sensible man or two with good strong backs, a pickup and lots of empty boxes."

"Of course, but that wasn't really an answer to my question, was it?"

"No, I guess not." I look around the shop. How different it is from my memories, no longer a place of love and refuge, not for me, and that makes it feel somehow wrong. Just as the farm feels wrong, empty, bereft of the two people who should be there. Still, what's being done with the store is something Grampa would have appreciated and approved of heartily. "Frankly, Anita, I don't know exactly what I'm going to do, but I'll see if we can figure something out."

Anita doesn't respond. I guess she's hoping I'll say more, but is relieved that I haven't threatened to close them down. Before she can press me for a commitment that would give Black Bear any hold over me after Monday, I head for the door.

"Of course," she finally says. "I'll arrange for a pickup." Leaning on the soda fountain counter, she scribbles on a piece of paper and hands it to me. "Please call me, if there's anything else I can do, or if you have any further questions about our pantry." She holds onto the paper for a few seconds after I've taken it. "You know, Judith, Joe really *is* a good boy. But whatever you think about him, please don't let all our work here end just because you're piqued at him, or at Ellen, or even me. We're doing something good, something important. People need us."

The bell rings once more as I open the door. I can almost hear Gramps saying, "See you later," as he would whenever a customer left.

Only three days left to go through the entire farm.

I stand in the foyer, feeling the full weight of so many things demanding my attention, knowing every decision I make will be irrevocable. Whatever I don't take now will be gone forever.

On the long flight from Africa, I formed what I thought was a feasible plan. Sweep through the house. Quickly choose the few items I want. Then walk away and return to my own life, leaving Black Bear permanently behind me.

I must have been mad to think I could possibly do it

all in one short week. I've packed boxes upon boxes of photographs and heirlooms, papers and mementos, and I've barely scratched the surface.

Sitting in the living room window seat, I try to sort out my thoughts and organize the evening ahead. The first thing I need to do is look at the accounts records Mr. Frank gave me.

I empty the manila envelope and prioritize the papers on the cushion next to me. Back at university and, afterwards, when I worked on the Bourse, I used to love poring over numbers like these, losing myself in their orderly saneness, the sense of power I had when I'd manipulate them. So different from dealing with people, numbers were easy to understand, with no unpleasant surprises. I believed I had nothing to fear from them. But that was before the insider trading scandal broke, and the world of numbers proved to be as treacherous as any man.

As Mr. Frank said, lots of the checks were written in the last few months. I flip through the photostats, and the signature glares at me from every page. His penmanship has gotten even worse over the years, more a scribble than script, but the name is unmistakable. The vast majority of the checks from the past few months are signed "Joe Anderson."

Many of the checks are for normal things, such as payments for electric and phone bills, or for insurance. Quite a few are written to people and companies whose names I don't recognize. Surely, a good percentage of those must have been for medical expenses. But so many checks! Could some of them be instruments for getting the money into Joe and Betty's grubby hands? And what about all those that are written to "Cash?" None are for more than a few hundred dollars at a time, but they add up to thousands, all signed by Joe.

It was one thing when he betrayed me. At least, I was able to get away from him, to make my own life away from Black Bear. To prey upon my grandmother, when she was at her weakest with no defenses, when she should have been allowed to die in peace — that I'll never forgive.

Somehow, I will make him pay for that.

Before putting the papers away, I do a quick addition in my head of the totals from Gramma's various accounts and compare the figure to Denton's deposit into the new estate account. The amounts are the same, but I doubt that the funds transfers would be where any chicanery would be hidden. I'll have to keep an eye on the expenses she claims.

I put the papers back into the envelope and look around me. With so much to do, I find myself quite unable to focus on the one next thing I should tackle.

I've stripped this room of almost everything I want, except for Mom's bronzes. The crates I ordered for them should arrive tomorrow. Thank goodness, Mom seldom cast monument-sized pieces, wanting her art to become part of the everyday — something that would be intrinsic to the daily consciousness of people, in their own homes or offices. Besides, smaller bronzes were less expensive to cast and had proven to be quite sellable. To my eyes, the ones she gave Gramma and Grampa are among her most personal and most beautiful, precious far beyond their monetary value. I don't know where I'll keep them, but they will be among the first things I'll unpack, once I have a home of my own.

The study is pretty much done, too, except for the computer with all of Gramma's emails, letters and records. However, I plan to continue using it while I'm still here. I'll remove the hard drive and pack it at the last moment.

Two rooms down. Eight to go. Plus the attic, basement, barn and various outbuildings.

Impossible! Even if I ignore the attic, basement, barn and outbuildings, and pay attention only to those things I absolutely can't leave behind. So many shelves, drawers, closets and chests. Too many nooks and crannies where that one most treasured memory of Gramma, Grampa or Mom might be hiding.

I can ignore my room. I took everything important from it years ago, except for the down patchwork quilt Gramma and I had made together, and a couple of other odds and ends. But I certainly have no desire to ever again see any of those mementoes of Joe in my life that Gramma put back in there for some crazy reason. Okay, that leaves seven rooms to go.

I glance at the dining room across the way, picturing in my mind the old family serving pieces and silverware in the sideboard and china cabinet. Whenever I imagine settling down someday, having children, making a home for them and me, I picture my dining room furnished with those chairs, table, sideboard and corner cabinet. In my daydreams, we use the old ironstone platters to serve at family celebrations, the Adams pattern silverware and the Lenox plates at each place. I learned long ago that life seldom lives up to my dreams. At least I won't have to leave any of the silver, crystal or china behind.

I can't take what I want from the kitchen, because it's the kitchen itself, with its long plank table, hardwood cabinets and big windows. However, I absolutely must have Gramma's recipe boxes and cookbooks.

Knowing what I will pack up from those two rooms, I can deal with them later. But the two that I've have been deliberately avoiding — Gramma and Grampa's bedroom, and Mom's room — they're going to be the toughest. Taking a deep breath, to steel myself to the task, I walk straight to the master bedroom, and stand in the doorway once more, peering into the darkness. Then, changing my mind, I turn on my heels, and grabbing some of the flattened boxes, bubble wrap and tape, head to the "new" wing.

It hasn't been new for over a century, but the name stuck, though Gramps sometimes called it the children's wing, from the time when the four bedrooms had been filled with kids. However, his two brothers died in their youth, while his two sisters never married. The next-to-last generation consisted only of Mom and Uncle Robby. Now, it's just me.

When I lived here, the new wing was closed up

most of the time. Airing it out for the rare guest was a project that Gramma would attack with a cheerful vigor that made it great fun to help her. But it was the quiet, lonely times that drew me here, often to Robby's room, curious about the uncle I never knew. I seldom went into Mom's bedroom after she died.

In Uncle Robby's room, I sit on the bed and look around. No one has slept here since he went to Vietnam. Mom told me that Gramma and Grampa had kept it exactly the way he'd left it. It's an all-American boy's room, with definite allusions to the late sixties. Under the stuffed two-point deer head from Uncle Robby's first kill are various certificates and awards — from the Boy Scouts, church and school, for building his own tepee, winning a spelling bee, helping out with a food drive, being a member of a team that won the county championship relay race, and other honors that sketched the shape of a young life. Around the room are several trophies for other races, newspaper clippings and photographs. Uncle Robby had been a wiry kid, with an oval face, his sandy hair cropped short, often in a crew cut, his blue eyes crinkling with humor, as though he knew a joke that he'd love to share with you personally. His vinyl record collection is eclectic, with the Beatles and Bob Dylan alongside New Christie Minstrels, Loretta Lynn, Ella Fitzgerald and Gustav Mahler. His books are impressively varied, including well-worn translations of *Steppenwolf, Crime and Punishment* and *No Exit.* Above his bed is the one item Mom had torn down in her rage after the black sedan with the captain and chaplain had pulled up in front of the house — the Marines recruitment poster. The scotch tape that Gramps used to put it back together is now yellowed and crackled.

I often wonder if Robby would have liked me if he had lived. A part of him was Black Bear through and through, from the deer head to the merit badges. Did that mean he was like the other bigoted kids I knew? But then, I think about Mom, Gramma and Grampa. And I look at the books he read, the music he listened to, and I can't help but believe there was more to him than the typical Black Bear denizen.

I assemble one of the boxes and pack all the photos — of Robby with Mom, Gramps or Grampa, and a few of him alone. For long minutes, I look at his last photo, of him in his full dress uniform, debating whether it's something I want. Uncertain, but unwilling to be sorry later, I pad it carefully with the bubble wrap and put it in the box.

Everything else in this room are memories of a boy I never knew, whom I could only hope would have loved me, if he had been given a chance.

Down the hall from Robby's bedroom is Mom's old room. For several long breaths, I stand at the closed door with my hand on the cold brass knob, my eyes closed, my forehead resting against the painted wood, trying to gather strength.

I fling the door open and stomp into the room, before I can come up with an excuse to not go in.

Little has changed over the years. About the same size as Uncle Robby's room, Mom's is a study in contrasts. The matching ruffled curtains, bedspread and throw pillows are of a delicate spring flower pattern that she had picked out as a child, but which is far from childish in taste. I can imagine using them in a guestroom, if I ever have a home of my own. Or, perhaps, in my own daughter's bedroom, should I ever be lucky enough to have a child. I'd name her Margaret for my mom, and never call her Maggie. Mom hated that nickname. Then again, the way things are going with my life, I'll probably never have children. First, I'd have to find a man whose children I could want. And he would have to want me enough to stick around until I could trust him and let myself love him. Considering my history with men, I doubt that will ever happen.

As feminine as Mom's room is, it's filled with things that were once considered boyish — bird feathers, rocks and stones, strange shaped twigs, even a four foot-long gnarled tree limb with branches that looks like a giant twisted hand hanging from the ceiling. She used to have me close my eyes, while she'd guide my small fingers over the textures and shapes of her various finds. The game was to coax me to picture what was inside each item, that made it so craggy or smooth, sharp or soft — some inner being or purpose within each inanimate object that was the artist's responsibility to discover and disclose.

On the shelves, among her books and tennis trophies, are some of her earliest wood carvings — a robin in flight, a nest of newborn sparrows just emerging from their cracking eggshells, a bee on a hydrangea blossom, and a mountain lion cub. All were made in high school, when she had shocked her classmates and school officials by insisting that she had the right to choose woodworking and metalcraft classes with the boys rather than the home economics and typing that girls were supposed to have. "I'm never going to be anyone's secretary or maid," she had argued. Grampa used to joke how, after she won that fight, no one had ever doubted that she was Martha Schmoyer's daughter.

One by one, I take each sculpture down, holding it, feeling the warmth of the varnished wood. Mom made these out of raw logs that she carved and chiseled and stroked until they yielded up what she had known was inside them from the beginning. The knifework is coarse in places, as though she had been in a rush to capture the animals before they got away from her. As childish and amateurish as these early works are, I can see her in each and every one of them. The wild, gentle spirit that embodied her as well as the animals that she loved. Collectors of her wildlife bronzes would probably pay dearly for these early pieces. Not that they'll ever get a chance; I'll never put them on the market.

The metal abstract on the bureau is an entirely different matter. A hodgepodge of found items that had been her first attempt at welding, it has no grace or harmony. Even so, I pack it just as carefully as the delicate wood sculptures, padding both boxes with the bedspread, pillows and curtains, using bubble wrap to make sure the metal won't tear the cloth.

Mom's desk is an extended radiator cover that pro-
trudes a few feet into the room, set into the window over-
looking a pebbled path to the woods. Instead of the blotter,
pen box, set of pastels and other schoolgirl artifacts that
used to be there, Gramma has arranged lots of photos of
Mom, as a child, a young woman, a bride and, finally, a
mother, with me as an infant, toddler, and adolescent, in
Black Bear, Paris, and New York. On the walls surrounding
the desk are framed newspaper clippings, reviews of Mom's
work, starting with shows from her student days in Paris,
and ending with her final, retrospective exhibition in New
York, the year after she was killed.

I sit at the desk, imagining how Gramma might
have spent many hours, right here in this chair, holding each
photograph, arranging it carefully, so none obscured any
other, all facing her. In the middle of it all is a black book,
with no title or author on the cover, back or spine. Beside it
is a pair of Gramma's reading glasses. I open the book, and
it falls to a page near the end, as though it has been turned
to that one entry often. The white unlined paper is filled
with Mom's sprawling handwriting, though the letters are
more clearly formed than I remember.

After the divorce and our move to Manhattan, Mom
tried to get me to start a diary, telling me how she used to
keep journals when she had been a young girl, and that it
had helped her work her way through many problems and
quandaries. She bought me a beautiful red leather bound
book and a brass enameled pen at a small stationary store on
Madison Avenue. However, they remained untouched until
years later, when I used the journal during my first trip to
Africa, and then to sketch out my ideas and plans for *Les
Femmes*. I'm not sure what happened to the pen.

I've never before seen Mom's diary.

The entry that Gramma apparently read so often is
dated December 25, 1966. Only days after they were told
Uncle Robby had been killed. Mom would have been home
from college for the holidays. I pull the diary onto my lap
and read it.

I'm fucking freaked out!!!! Mother and Dad really expected me to go with them to church. Just because it's Christmas. No way I was going to sit still, while that sanctimonious bastard of a pastor droned on about the glory of this damned Christian nation of ours. Everyone in their Christmas best, crowding into the pews, cheek to cheek, like fat-assed sardines, all lined up and comforted in their self-righteousness, knowing they live in the best of all places, a God-blessed, God-fearing country that's willing to go anywhere, do anything, sacrifice however many of their own young, to fight the devil rampant.

I HATE THEM. I HATE THEM ALL!!!!!

Brainwashed, all of them. With their glorious flag-waving and Fourth of July parades and rousing, drum-beating speeches.

Rah, rah, sis boom ba! Kill the gooks, 'cause they aren't us, 'cause it's the only way we can save them from the yellow peril of godless communism.

Robby, why the hell did you listen to all that shit?

There's a blotch of black ink at that point, as though Mom put down her fountain pen, or, perhaps, rested the point on the paper, letting the ink spread, while she wracked her brain for an answer. After the blotch, her handwriting is tighter, smaller.

Al's home on leave. He finished his rotation in 'Nam, and he's now based at Quantico. He came over last night to see me, but I wouldn't budge and stayed right here in my room. I just couldn't see him, don't want to see him ever again.

Mother was really pissed at me. Told me, in that soft angry voice of hers that could chill an A-bomb, that I was being shameful, dishonoring your memory. God, I hate it when she twists things around like that, saying whatever's necessary, no matter how much it hurts, so you can see how wrong you are and how right she is. Shit! I wanted to scream at her, shake her, knock her off her damned high horse. She's so fucking sure of herself, even now, with you blown to pieces. How does she do that? Turn her mind off, and see only what she wants to see. Doesn't she get it? You're dead, and it's all because you believed in their fucking lies.

I've been trying to figure out where it all went so wrong. I've decided it started with Al. I was so damned proud that my boyfriend was the first in our class to enlist. Everyone at our senior prom was talking about it, how Al was a true son of Black Bear, a real American, an honest-to-goodness patriot. That evening, just before the prom, he told me his plans. Four years in the Marines, then college, then we'd get married. Or, maybe, we could be married while he went to school, just like Dad and so many other vets from the war ~ the other war ~ the one that had made sense.

I think I remember really loving Al. He was smart and funny and made me feel good. You really liked him, too. Well, I guess everyone did. Al had that about him, but I don't remember what he did or why everyone thought he was so cool, that they had to be like him.

Me, too.

And you, too, Robby.

I'll never forgive myself for buying into all that flag-waving bullshit ~ for getting you caught up in it ~ for not looking beyond our stupid, know-nothing backwater village, to see what's real.

Robby, why the hell did you listen to ME?!!!

It's all my own fucking fault that you're dead. I was supposed to be your big sister. All I did was walk lockstep with the rest of them, listening to the goddamn pastor, cheering for every boy who signed up and marched away to kill and be killed, bragging about Al, my big heroic boyfriend, making you think that it was the right thing to do, the only thing to do. From cub scout, to boy scout, to eagle scout, to Marine... to coffin.

If I live forever, I'll never forgive myself. I was just like everyone sitting in that stupid church right now ~ just like Mother and her god-damned self-righteous friends ~

believing everything I was told. And, damn it, a part of me wants to believe again. To put on a pretty dress, and squeeze my butt into a warm, crowded pew, pressing against Al, gluing my life to his once more. I guess that's why I can never see him again. It hurts too much to have nothing inside me where my belief once was. When they killed you, they killed that part of me, too.

I hate them, because I hate myself, knowing I'm just like all the rest of them. I listened to the lies, mouthed them too, then beamed with pride when you came home in your dress uniform, so tall and grown up, a true patriot, a hero, and cheered when you marched lockstep to your death.

Robby, I'm so terribly sorry. God, how empty and inane those words are. But that's all I'm left with ~ my guilt, my stupid words, and the knowledge that, no matter what I do, things can never again be right.

I slowly close the diary and put it back on the desk, in the same spot where I found it, embarrassed, as though I've intruded on a very private conversation. I stare at the photos for some time. Gramma sat here, reading that one entry so often that the book spine was broken there. Why?

I knew that Mom never got over her brother's death, and had turned her back on Black Bear and especially on Pastor Ringenhauer, who had preached rousing patriotism from the pulpit when other ministers were marching for peace. However, the way she wrote about it in this diary and the way she spoke about it to me were so very different.

In this diary entry, she was… I'm not sure who she was, or what. A young student, engaged to some Marine I've never heard of? A typical Black Bear youngster, who barely escaped being just like everyone else in this insular, irrelevant, bigoted village? Saved from that fate only by the tragedy of her brother's death? Is that what she meant, or am I missing something important here? Something that drew Gramma to read this one entry, over and over again.

Of all the things I've chosen to pack up, this diary is

one item I will take with me in my suitcase. I want to read it through, to understand whatever it is that nags me in the back of my mind.

I rummage through the drawers and cabinets of Mom's room, finding little else that I want to pack, other than the photos and news clippings. Then, at the bottom of the cedar chest, under the extra blankets and pillows, I uncover eight other journals, nearly identical to the one on the desk, from various times in Mom's life, the handwriting changing over the years, from the practiced artistic openness of a young adolescent, to the rushed scrawl of a graduate student. I arrange the nine books in chronological order, side by side on the bed, so they stretch almost the full length. Here, then, was a life. At least, the beginning of a life. The private thoughts of a girl, adolescent, young woman, growing up in this room, this house, which had once been the full scope of her entire world. Margaret Claire Schmoyer, before she became the woman who became my Mom.

I gather the diaries and hold the pile to my chest. Once the house is packed up, I'll have a lot of reading to do. Somewhere in these volumes are answers to questions I didn't even realize I had until now.

Sally Wiener Grotta

FRIDAY

I awake to the shrill clanking of the old Big Ben windup alarm clock. It's a sound from my school days, pulling me out of a vivid dream that disintegrates the minute I hear the hammering of the chrome bells. All I can recall of the dream is a vague sensation of comfort and security, and some great danger threatening to destroy it. Flicking the lever to turn off the alarm is so ingrained in me that I do it automatically, without fully waking up.

Then, I remember when and where I am, and why.

Last night, I set the alarm for 6:00 am, because I've been sleeping far too well in my old bed, and I have a lot to do in the short time I have left here at the farm. As I dress, I look around. It won't take me long to pack the few things I want from this room. Some of the photographs, the patchwork quilt, and, yes, that silly alarm clock I rescued from the discarded, no longer fashionable inventory in the drug store basement when I was fourteen. But none of the Joe garbage that's strewn around this room.

It's high time I get rid of that damned misshapen chair that Joe and I made together in Grampa's workshop. Tempted to just throw it down the stairs in front of me, I don't want to scratch the walls or bannister. So I carry it all the way down, and chuck it unceremoniously into the dumpster with the other trash.

After a quick breakfast, I go right to work in the dining room. I have almost all the good china, crystal and silverware packed up when I hear a car coming up the driveway. It's Mr. Nichols and his grandnephew Matt, who forgot to call first, as promised. What did I expect? In Black

164

Bear, appointments are ambiguous, and time is relative. 9:00 or 11:00, it's all before lunch.

Mr. Nichols hasn't changed much. Perhaps, a bit fatter and somewhat shorter, with not enough hair left to comb over the bald spot that now encompasses almost his entire globe-shaped skull. His pale, appraising eyes stare out through the same thick glass set in dark horn-rimmed frames. His thin-lipped smile exposes the same tobacco-stained teeth. Gramma used my horror of his yellow teeth and the sour stench of cigarette smoke that clung to his clothes as an object lesson, to warn me about the unpleasant consequences of smoking. It must have worked, because I never did pick up that disgusting habit. So, I suppose I owe Mr. Nichols a debt of some sort.

Matt is quite the opposite. About forty years old, with thick dark hair, he's tall, lean, and precisely groomed. His facile, well-practiced smile brims with cosmetically white teeth.

They wear similar clothes; dark trousers, tweedy sports jacket over a crew neck sweater, and no overcoat despite the chill breeze. However, Mr. Nichols looks as though he shops at the Salvation Army store in Honesdale, with pants that are too tight, a jacket that hasn't been *au courant* since the 1970s, and broken-down dirty sneakers that had once been white. Matt could have stepped off the pages of the *Sunday New York Times* Fashion section, with a carefully calculated air of pseudo-country squire about him.

As they approach the front door, I realize just how old Mr. Nichols must be. His gait is uneven, uncertain, and he leans heavily on Matt's arm. When he introduces me to Matt, it's with the assured, down home friendliness that was one of the keys to his success. Almost everyone in Black Bear who bought or sold real estate turned to Mr. Nichols at one time or another, because he was one of their own, someone they could depend upon to understand their needs and concerns, and who didn't have any big city affectations.

I invite them into the kitchen, serve them coffee, and we get right down to business. At first, Matt does most of the talking.

"Judy... may I call you Judy?" Matt asks, as he pulls a leather bound portfolio from his calfskin briefcase. His manner is thoroughly professional, his voice clear, with almost no discernible accent, which means he must have worked hard at excising whatever regional drawl he once might have had.

"I prefer Judith, please," I tell him.

"Sorry.... Judith," he acknowledges with a well-executed, slightly bemused, not quite dismissive shrug. "I checked the county records. You have 136 acres here."

I nod. I doubt if I've ever known the exact size of the farm.

He flips through his notes on the yellow legal pad that's inserted into the portfolio. "Local zoning requires a minimum of two acres per house in any subdivision. I esti-mate that we would need to devote about 15 to 20 acres to roads and public landscaping. Which means...."

"No!" I quickly interrupt him. "I won't subdivide the farm."

"But, Judith...."

"No, and that's final."

Matt studies me. "Why?" he asks. He sounds as though he might be honestly curious, but then I wouldn't be surprised if he's good at that, making people feel that he's interested in what they have to say. "Why do you care?"

I doubt someone like Matt would understand. "Because it would be wrong," I tell him.

"If you're selling anyway...."

"No!" I can't believe he's still pursuing the matter. I'm the client, and I won't consider raping the land that my grandparents cherished all their lives.

Just then, Mr. Nichols clears his throat, not loudly, but effectively. Once he's sure he has our attention, he takes another gulp of coffee before putting his cup down, then sits forward to lean on the table. "Judith," he asks. "Are you really sure you want to sell this place?" He forms each word slowly, with the round, open, only partially slurred drawl that is so distinctly Black Bear. "Why don't you think it over a while?"

"I don't need to think it over."

"There have been Schmoyers on this land for over 150 years. What are a few days, or even a few months compared to that? Judith, you really don't want to do anything in haste that you'll regret later."

"No, Mr. Nichols, I know my own mind, and no amount of time will change it. I want to get rid of this place. The sooner, the better."

"Then, listen to Matt. He's a smart kid, and he's only trying to do what's best for you, to help you realize the highest value for your property."

I don't bother retorting that Matt is no kid. Instead, I pick up my coffee cup, and stare at Matt through the steam that plays on my face. "Okay, I'll listen. However, you should know it will take a lot to convince me to allow this farm to be broken up into Levittown tracks."

"It wouldn't be anything like Levittown, Judith." Matt is the picture of sincerity, his brows knitted with concern, his voice smooth as synthetic velveteen. "Quite the contrary. Each lot would be two acres or more. Some may be as much as five acres. The idea would be to draw the boundaries esthetically, with full attention to the natural lay of the land. This parcel, here, with the house, barn and other original buildings, would probably be 15 acres or more."

"No." As I say it, I realize I've been shaking my head from side to side from the moment he started to describe how he intended to carve up the farm and merchandise it. "No. I can't allow it. Sorry. No."

"But, Judith," Matt insists. "It's the only thing that makes sense."

"There's nothing sensible or respectable about chopping up my grandparents' property."

"You don't understand. If you don't subdivide, then your buyer most probably will. Who do you think has the desire and ready cash to buy this much land?" Matt asks rhetorically, then answers before I can get a word in edgewise. "Developers and their backers. Within a week of putting it up for sale, I can assure you that we'd have bids from Dan Donleavy and Al Huff. I'd be tempted myself. A prime piece of land like this one... it's ripe and ready to make someone a lot of money."

"Can't I put something into the bill of sale, or the deed itself, to protect the land?" I'm not familiar with American law, but I have heard of such arrangements elsewhere.

Matt doesn't skip a beat. "A covenant is sometimes added to a deed, but I'm not sure how effective that would be. Of course, I'm not a lawyer, but the courts have been routinely overturning such impediments lately. Did you see the new development on Route 519? They're calling it Nottingham Woods. Donleavy bought the land about eight years ago, spent five years in legal hassles, but it was worth it. He got the covenant overturned and has made millions, with only half the lots sold." Matt shrugs. "Of course, if you wish to go that route, and try to tie up the land somehow, that's your decision. I suggest you talk to an attorney." He taps his notes on the yellow pad with his gold-plated Cross pen. "However, you need to understand that you would get far less in any sale, if you try to restrict the use of the land."

"The money isn't the point."

"What is the point, Judith?" Mr. Nichols asks.

"I don't think Grampa and Gramma would want it broken up."

"They wouldn't have wanted it sold, either, but that's what you're doing."

"It's not the same thing, Mr. Nichols. I don't want this property; that doesn't mean I no longer have any responsibility toward it."

"I see." Mr. Nichols sits back in the chair and temples his fingers together. "Judith, you're not ready to list the farm..."

"I'm leaving the country on Monday. I have to have everything decided and signed by then."

His wry smile exposes those nasty teeth of his again. "As old and old-fashioned as I am, even I know how much we can accomplish with email."

"But..." I start to protest.

"I know, you're in a hurry. However, we can't do the paperwork for this listing until we know if the deed is going to be amended or not. No realtor could. That doesn't mean any of us will be idle." He turns to his nephew. "Matt, while Judith looks into the covenant, why don't you consider how you'd subdivide the farm, if you had the go ahead from Judith." He holds the flat of his hand up toward his nephew, as if he's blocking a protest, though Matt's expression and posture hasn't changed one iota. In fact, he isn't even looking at Mr. Nichols, until he hears his name. "I know what you're going to say, Matt. No, I'm not going to charge this girl for any work you do on the possible sub-division. Not until she's made up her mind. You might not believe it to look at how grown up she is now, but I've known this young lady since she was in diapers. Hell, I knew her grandparents since the three of us were in diapers. I'll be damned if I'm going to nickel and dime her now, when we just buried Martha."

Having established his altruistic *bone fides*, Mr. Nichols now turns his gaze back to me. "And, Judith, you've some decisions to make before we can complete this listing." He ticks them off on his fingers. "First of all, you need to talk to your attorney about whether or not a coven-ant can be added to the deed, and if it would have any power. Then, you have to decide if it's something you really want. As Matt said, if you're really selling the farm, as you claim you have already decided, then you've got to under-stand the dollars and cents of it. With a covenant, you might get about a million, though few people, especially in this economy, have that kind of money to spend on a private farm that they can never do anything else with; we might have to go as low as $800,000. Subdividing, like Matt proposes, could easily triple or maybe even quadruple that figure. So, like it or not, you've got to sit back and do some thinking and planning, before we can list."

"Thank you, Mr. Nichols, for clarifying matters for me." I start to get up, assuming the meeting is at an end.

"What about the old drug store and the other prop-erty, the land with your grandfather's hunting lodge?" Matt asks.

I sit back down.

Matt flips to another page on his yellow pad. "The store may prove problematic. Commercial property in Black Bear can be difficult to sell these days. Especially something as small as the drug store. I don't know if you'll be able to get much for it. Maybe $80,000 tops, if we're lucky. The hunting land is another matter entirely."

"Have you seen the store lately?" Mr. Nichols asks me, his easy-going manner cutting through Matt's coldly professional *recitativ*.

"Yes, I was there yesterday."

"Then, you know about the good work the ladies are doing...."

"Yes...." I've an idea that I know where Mr. Nichols is going, and, for the first time since the two of them arrived, I'm comfortable with the shape of our conversation.

"Well, as Matt said, you won't realize much money from selling the store. So, why not just let things continue as they are?"

"The problem is I don't want to have anything holding me here after this week."

Mr. Nichols gives me that strange quizzical look again. "I see." He pauses a moment, then adds, "Normally, I'd suggest you consider signing the store over to the ladies running it, but I doubt they could afford to maintain it."

"Could the two churches and the synagogue afford the maintenance?" I ask.

Mr. Nichols grins wider than ever. "I don't see why not."

"Then, please draw up the papers to have the deed to the store transferred to *Beth Shalom*, Black Bear Moravian and St. Boniface, as equal partners. I'll pay all the fees."

He slaps his thigh. "Now, you're finally sounding like Martha and Henry's granddaughter."

Matt has been silent through our entire discussion about the store, concentrating on his notes and helping himself to a second cup of coffee. It's almost as though he's trying to distance himself from the proceedings, in which his uncle has taken over with his countrified sensibilities and folksy wisdom. Obviously, nothing has followed his carefully scripted plans. Instead of signing up a client for six percent of a potential multi-million dollar sale, he's now committed to handling the papers for a donation and preparing a subdivision that will never happen. "What about the hunting lodge?" he asks, not quite disguising his annoyance.

I shake my head. "I can't do anything with it at present."

"Matt, you really do need to pay more attention to what's happening in town, if you want to do business here," Mr. Nichols voice is stern, and his ears turn bright red, though I don't know if it's with anger or chagrin. "If you bothered to breakfast with me every morning at Good Taste, you'd be much better informed." Mr. Nichols shrugs his shoulders and looks over to me. "Sorry, Judith. Matt doesn't know about the contested will."

So, my personal business is now the talk of the village cafe. *Merde!* "It's just a formality. I'll be sure to contact you to handle the sale, when everything is cleared up."

"Will you consider subdividing that property?" Matt asks.

I have no feelings about the lodge, not like the farm. Still, it would be a shame to see it paved over and developed, disrupting all the wildlife that lives in those woods. How Grampa loved walking along the leaf covered paths, losing himself in the ancient woods. "We can talk about that when the time comes to sell." I stand once more. "I'll be contacting my attorney, to find some way to protect this farm. I will want to complete that listing as soon as possible. In the meantime, how quickly do you think you can have the papers drawn up for the transfer of the store?"

Matt folds his portfolio and puts it into his briefcase, as he answers. "It shouldn't take longer than a week."

"Any chance of having it done by Monday? I'd like

to have all the formalities completed before I leave the country."

"There's always a chance," Mr. Nichols retorts. "Right, Matt?"

"I don't mind working over the weekend, but it's more complex than a simple deed transfer. There may be some legal matters involved in giving one piece of real estate to three separate non-profits." Matt shakes his head. "No, it can't be done by Monday."

Mr. Nichols glares at him. "It shouldn't take more than a couple of hours, boy. You know better than that."

"Not if we have to have an attorney create a separate entity or trust, and confer with each of the parties involved."

"You're making it too complicated, Matt."

The two of them seem to be enjoying their argument, but it isn't getting me anywhere. "What if I gave it just to *Beth Shalom*? It would be a straightforward transfer then, right?"

"Well, I don't think you'd really want to do that, Judith," Mr. Nichols says. "It might cause some problems, after you've offered it to all three. You wouldn't want to make new trouble for the Jews, being as they're just starting to fit in."

"I haven't offered anything to anybody yet. So what kind of trouble could there be?" I lock eyes with Mr. Nichols. He's a long time member of the Moravian church and a devoted practitioner of the local gossip mill. He needs to understand that I don't want rumors about my personal business circulating around town — at least, none that I could trace back to him.

Mr. Nichols removes his eyeglasses and wipes them with a napkin. I doubt they had any smudge or dust, but it's an effective way of breaking my stare. "Of course, the ladies will be so relieved to know that they can continue as before," he seems to acquiesce. "They probably won't care who owns the deed."

"Then, you'll do the paperwork for me and have it ready by Monday?"

"I'll try," Matt says, in a manner that leaves no doubt how distasteful it is for him to be pushed and pressured like this.

"Thank you." I choose to ignore the fact that he has made no promise.

Matt picks up his briefcase with one hand, offers his other arm to his uncle, and the two of them follow me outside. Before they drive away, Mr. Nichols rolls down the car window and calls out to me, "Judith. All these legal concerns, they don't need to be so messy. I'm sure if you put your mind to things, you could simplify everything as easily as you did about the store. You've too much Martha in you to not realize most of your problems are ones that needn't be." Matt starts the car and drives away, before Mr. Nichols can roll the window back up.

After Mr. Nichols and Matt leave, I grab Grampa's parka from the front closet and go for a walk. I look around, at the house, the barn, the sheds, the gardens, all surrounded by the woods. Matt is correct about one thing. Carving out a 15-acre parcel around these buildings would retain the essence of the everyday experience of living here. But knowing that the other 121 acres of empty fields, ponds, creek, waterfall and forest are out there makes a difference, a cushion of greenery, wildlife and waters that surround and protect the farm.

This is Schmoyer land, where generations were born, struggled, lived, loved and died. Some are even buried out there in a tiny private cemetery. Grampa and Grandma were offered good money for sections over the years, and turned it down, even in their youth, when they could have used the extra cash. Financially, I'm set for life, by the lucky happenstance of being born into the right family. How could I do less than my grandparents? One way or another, I must find a way to preserve this small piece of the Poconos from becoming just another suburban tract.

I wander into the barn and sit down at Grampa's

workbench. Here, the odors — musky, with the dust of old wood and packed earth — are a sense memory of sitting here and watching Gramps fiddle with one contraption or another. Repairing the lawn mower. Tuning the outboard motor. Planing boards to make a table or bookshelf. Welding pieces of old iron into useful garden tools or ornamental trellises. I can imagine how Mom must have sat on this same old high stool, watching her Dad, learning much better than I ever did how to use the various gadgets and tools hanging on the pegboard. Is there anything here I want to take with me? No, nothing, other than the memories of both Grampa and Mom and the hours I spent with them, trying to be like them, but never able to get the objects I attempted to make look like anything worthwhile. Yet, neither of them let me feel like a failure, even when they laughed at the misshapen, useless creations that my hands and mind wrought.

Small critters have always been part of the barn, too. Field mice, chipmunks, nesting birds in the rafters, even raccoons and skunks occasionally seeking a warm haven in the winter, cool shade in the summer. So, I don't pay much attention to the various creaks, cracks and scurrying that I hear, even though some of it sounds like old wood responding to shifting footsteps. After all, I'm entirely alone on this property. It's probably my imagination.

Then, a small, plaintive *meow* breaks through my reveries, from somewhere nearby, to my right.

"Acey?" I call out, using a gentle tone and my best imitation of Gramma's accent. I've been worried about him, and hope he has found his way home.

Meow, he responds a bit louder.

I stare into the shadows, trying to spot Gramma's small black cat hiding under the piles of crates, tools, lumber and discarded furniture. Not wanting to scare him away, I stay as still as possible. I say his name once more, and lisp the *sspss, sspss, sspss* sound that Gramma used to call her cats. Suddenly, Acey bounds onto my lap, with a cry that's less plaintive and more an expression of righteous grievance. He kneads my thighs, until he settles down in a tight curl, laying claim to me as fully as if he had known me since kittenhood, in the same manner as Tedda had. But unlike Tedda, Acey is a scruffy mess, with tuffs of hair missing and bloody patches on his head, back, and front right leg.

I gather him into my arms, trying not to touch his wounds. While I gently carry him to the kitchen, he presses his face against my chin, places his front paws around my neck, and though he doesn't purr, he doesn't struggle or unsheathe his claws.

He allows me to bathe his wounds, with hardly any protest; I'm relieved that none of them appear to be septic, or severe enough to warrant calling the vet, especially since I know that Gramma would have kept his vaccinations up to date. When I put him down on the floor, he stays within inches of my feet, until I pour milk into a bowl, which he laps up hungrily, with an audible purr that I can hear even from nearly a meter away. I find the bag of Cat Chow in the mudroom closet and fill another bowl with kibbles. I watch him eat for a few minutes, taking pleasure in having him near, not only because I hate thinking of Gramma's pampered pet being lost in the wild, but because it feels so good to have another living creature in this home. His presence makes me even more aware of how barren the house was without him, without any pet, where animals and people have always been underfoot and in the way, filling the rooms with life and love.

But what am I to do with Acey? I can't possibly take him with me, nor can I leave him here. I pick up the phone and dial Rebecca. When their answering machine picks up, I leave a message thanking her for lunch and asking her to ring me back.

I put the bag of kibbles away in the mudroom. When I turn from the closet, to go back into the kitchen, standing right there, just inside the doorway to the outside and much closer to the kitchen than I,... *oh, my God!...* Wayne Anderson!

My stomach leaps up into my throat, choking off my scream of terror, making it sound more like a simpering wail.

He grins at me, with that same smirking leer that has chased me through my nightmares for too many years. Much older now, with some grey in his tightly trimmed sideburns and temples, he still has that Anderson sandy coloring, though his hair is darker, a muddy brown rather than dirty blonde. His sharp, thin face is crisscrossed with several scars, as though he's been cut more than once. Two long livid gashes on his cheeks look as though they had been sewn up hastily and purposely allowed to fester, proud manhood badges, like Heidelberg duelists. He wears a Nazi-type uniform — the Homeland Militia that Ed Felson mentioned? — brown shirt and brown jodhpurs, high black boots and a black leather Sam Browne belt across his chest. Unlike Joe with his flabby beer belly, Wayne's body bulges with barely sheathed muscular strength. His arms are raised, pressing each black gloved hand against either side of the door jam. On one sleeve is an American flag, and on the other is a strange insignia of a cross with twin lightning bolts. He looms there, all six feet of him, towering over me, taking possession of the mudroom, blocking any means of escape.

"Well, well, well, if it ain't the chocolate cunt, herself. Heard you came back, making all kinds of trouble for my kid brother... money-grubbing Jew. Miss me, nigger girl?"

"You better get out of here, Wayne. Jeff Smith is inside."

"No, sweet thing," he sneers. "You're here alone. All alone, 'cept me and my friends." He motions toward the woods behind the barn. "We've been watching you. Saw that old cocker and his fancy fag nephew leave. Saw you walking around back there and sitting in the barn looking so sad and lonely. Saw you carry that scrawny cat and treat him so nice and gentle, caring for his wounds like an expert." He lowers his arms and takes one step into the mudroom, moving with the deliberate slowness of a stalking hyena. "I got my own pain." He cups his crotch. "I know you can take care of it, like a real expert." Another step closer. "How about it, sweet chocolate, for old time's sake?"

I'm frozen in place, too terrified to move, lest it spur Wayne into action, while at the same time, my heart pounds in my ears and my eyes dart around me, searching for something, anything I could use as a weapon. I grab the snow shovel from the corner, and brandish the length of it between the two of us.

He looks down at the spade of the shovel pointed at his stomach, and he laughs, one short bark. We both know he could take it from me as easily as he might pluck a flower from the ground.

"That's okay, sweet cheeks. I learned a few things over the years, and one of them's that anticipation adds to the fun." Turning his back on me, Wayne clearly demonstrates his lack of concern over the shovel as a weapon — or my ability to harm him.

At the doorway, he pivots and glares at me. "And don't bother calling the cops. Won't do you no good. You know they won't listen to some yid nigger against an upstanding local." He raises his gloved hand. "Where's your proof that I was even ever here? Hell, we all know what liars your kind are." He gestures toward the woods once more. "We're watching you. Me and my boys. If you're a good little nigger, and don't bother the police about our private affair and stop all this trouble you're making for Joe, maybe we won't hurt you when we come back. Just some fun like we had in the old schoolhouse. See ya."

Then, he swaggers off.

I spring toward the mudroom's outside door, and try to lock it behind him, but the tumbler is rusted open. However, the kitchen door key turns smoothly with a reassuring click.

I run around the house, locking all the doors and windows, and looking out, to try to see where Wayne went. He appears to have completely disappeared; he could be hiding anywhere.

Acey scampers to follow me, and I nearly trip over him a couple of times. I double-check all the locks a second and then a third time, until I'm sure no one can get into the house, short of breaking a window.

Mon Dieu! What would I do if that happened?

I run into Grampa's study and rummage through the closet. In the back corner, I find his old hunting rifle standing upright, where he always kept it. On an upper shelf are two boxes of bullets.

Though I haven't handled a gun since killing that deer when I was twelve, the sleek heft of it is familiar and comforting. I load the rifle; the cartridges slide into place smoothly with reassuring clicks. Then, I stuff a box of bullets into my jeans pocket.

Now I'm ready for Wayne and anyone else who tries to break into the house, tries to get to me.

Cradling the gun under my left arm, I go into the living room and collapse on an armchair. I place the rifle on the floor next to me, within centimeters of my hand. Only then do I let it all wash over me: Wayne really was here, threatening me, so close I could smell him, a blend of soap and beer. My muscles begin to convulse in waves, until I'm shivering uncontrollably. *"Oh God! Oh God! Oh God!"* I sigh over and over again, not knowing what else to say or think.

Acey jumps onto my lap. Round and round he turns, rubbing against my abdomen or my hand, stretching up to press his face against mine, doing everything possible to maximize physical contact. No doubt he's reacting to my restless terror, needing comfort, or is he trying to give it? What it is about me that makes him so certain that we belong together? He never met me before today. Do I have a similar smell to Gramma? If such a thing as an aura actually exists, might mine have a familial color or vibration that a pet could recognize? Or is it simply that I'm a human being, living in the home where Acey has known only comfort and love?

I cradle him into my arms, cuddling him against my chest. "Oh, Acey, what am I to do?" He has no answer for me, other than a loud, warm purr.

Should I just grab my suitcase and run, leave Black Bear and everything now, tonight?

No. That would be giving Wayne and Joe victory over me, over me and Gramma. Damned if I'm going to let the two of them scare me out of town. Not again. I'll go when I'm bloody ready, and not one minute before.

But what will I do if they show up here?

I look down at the gun. It's been decades since I fired it, killing that deer, and the violence of that death sent me scurrying away. No, I remind myself, not just the violence, but the thrill and power of it.

Could I shoot a man? I never would have thought myself capable of it, but what if Wayne were about to attack me? And if I did shoot him, would I hit him? I might have been a crack shot when I was a kid, but can I even hit the broadside of a barn now?

If I'm going to stay in this house until Monday, I have to find out.

Before unlocking the back door, I look out the windows in all directions, to make sure no one is in the yard. I can't possibly know who might be hidden from sight, watching from the woods. With the gun still in my hands, I step outside. Sweat beads on my face and my neck, trickling down my body inside my clothes, though the day is pleasantly cool.

Acey starts to follow me, but I coax him back into the kitchen and lock the door, putting the key in my shirt pocket.

From the dumpster, I grab an old broken brass lamp I threw away, and I set it up on a wooden fence post. I chamber a round. Pressing my cheek against the stock, I aim at the lamp, and squeeze the trigger.

The explosion of the shot and the powerful kick of the recoil reverberates through my body, but the bullet misses the lamp entirely. Even so, if Wayne and his friends are hiding in the woods, watching me, I hope I've just given them pause for thought, that I'm serious about using Grampa's rifle to defend myself.

I work the bolt, loading another round, and follow Grampa's instructions from so long ago. "Hold the gun lightly, but with solid support." I ease my white-knuckle grip and brace my elbow against my chest. "Spread your feet shoulder wide, but keep your knees soft and slightly bent." Rocking my weight from one foot to the next, I loosen my legs and unlock my knees. "Close one eye and make sure you aim down the full length of the barrel and not just with the sight... now squeeeeze the trigger."

I hit the stump, just below the lamp, sending some splinters into the air. That near miss is my victory. My hands and mind are remembering; all I need now is some practice.

I keep at it for nearly an hour, filling the air around the farm with the booming *thwack, thwack* of gunshot, and using up nearly an entire box of bullets. Eventually, almost every shot hits the target, sending the brass lamp flying off the fence post. When it gets so dented and plugged with holes that I can't get it to stay upright any more, I replace it with a succession of cracked flowerpots, and, finally, that miserable misbegotten chair that Joe and I had made.

I hope Joe is in the woods with Wayne, watching me shred that rotten ugly thing from our past. Now they know I mean business, that no one will ever again lay a hand on me, unless they want that hand blown off.

Acey greets me at the kitchen door when I return, and with a *meow* demands to be picked up. I double-lock the door, put the gun down, leaning it against the jam, and gather the purring cat into my arms. As I walk toward the dining room, I feel suddenly naked and terribly vulnerable, leaving the rifle behind. I go back and exchange Acey for the gun, vowing I'll carry it with me wherever I go.

While I finish packing up the china, crystal and silver in the dining room, I try hard to avoid obsessing on Wayne and his threats, which means, of course, that I can't stop thinking about him.

When the phone rings, I'm in the middle of swathing the old turkey ironstone platter in bubble wrap, which isn't that easy, given that Acey considers the plastic one of the great toys of all time. It's remarkable how such innocent mischievousness can temporarily lighten even the gravest mood. I grab the gun and go into the kitchen to answer the phone, while I stare out the windows over the sink to make sure no one is out there. No one I can see.

"*Allô*," I answer in French automatically, before I remember it isn't the local language.

"Hello, Judith. It's Rebecca."

"Rebecca?" It takes a few seconds for my mind to focus away from the woods and Wayne. "Oh, hello, Rebecca." A little lightheaded, I sit down in the nearest chair.

"Are you okay, Judith?" she asks.

"Yes, I'm fine. I was just ..." I pause. I don't know what I was about to say. Wayne was right; what proof do I have that he was here, threatening me? Besides, I've never told anyone about the rape, how could I start now? Acey capers onto my lap, reminding me why I called Rebecca in the first place. "Acey's come home. He's here right now."

"That's wonderful."

"Yes, but I don't know what to do about him." I feel disloyal saying it like that. "I mean, I have to find a good home for him."

Rebecca doesn't hesitate one moment. "Please bring him to us. Tedda needs him. They belong together."

"That's great. Thank you."

"It will be our pleasure." She pauses. "You know, I had prepared a nice trumped up excuse for phoning... you left your cooler here. I wanted to ask if you'll join David and me for dinner this evening." Before I have a chance to reply, she quickly adds, "Please say yes. You don't have to stay for services, if you don't want to, though, of course, you would be welcome to join us at the temple."

An invitation to the rabbi's home for *Shabbat* dinner is an honor and a friendly gesture. Any other time or place.... "Rebecca, thank you so very much. I wish I could, but...."

"You have to eat, Judith. And now, you have to bring Acey over here sometime this weekend. Why not come this evening for dinner? It would be just the three of us, and I know how much David would enjoy spending time with you. I certainly would."

She's right about Acey, and if I don't go to services afterward, I can still put in several hours of packing before bedtime. Besides, Wayne has unnerved and terrified me; I need some gentle company just now. Maybe, I can even talk to them about Wayne. Just about him showing up here, not about the rape. Never about the rape. But what good will that do? Would they help me, someone they've just met, whom they have no reason to believe? And what could they do, when they're newcomers, and therefore relative strangers in Black Bear, too? Still... "If you're sure David wouldn't be insulted if I don't go to services, I'd be delighted. What time?"

"Insulted? No, not David." I can hear the smile in her voice. "We eat early on Fridays... 5:00... so David can prepare. I hope that isn't too American for you."

"5:00 it is." I haven't gotten around to eating lunch yet, so I'll be hungry by then. "May I bring something? I still have a fridge filled with food."

"If you wish, but it isn't necessary. I'm just delighted you'll be bringing yourself... and Acey, too, of course."

What a relief it will be to get away from this house — and from the eyes in the woods around me — for a couple of hours. Besides, I'm looking forward to seeing Rebecca again, and getting to know David. How unfortunate it is that they live in Black Bear. Will I ever see them again once I finally leave this horrid village for good?

I finish packing up the dining room and start on the kitchen. Besides being fascinated by the mischievous potential of bubble wrap, Acey considers it his personal duty to jump inside any box I assemble and check it out. I'm pleased that he's secure enough to be his old playful self that Gramma described in her emails. I wish I could say the same about myself.

Every creak, real or imagined, every branch swaying in the breeze and brushing against the house, even the silence when Acey is suddenly still makes me look around behind me. Is anyone there, just beyond my sight, right around the corner? Are they in the woods, watching me? When do they plan to attack? Will they attack?

The delivery truck arrives with the additional packing material I ordered, including the crates and straw for Mom's bronzes. While the delivery man is unloading, I keep the rifle out of sight, behind the study door, where I can reach it in seconds, if necessary. I spend the rest of the afternoon crating various sculptures.

Soon, it's time to leave for dinner. I quickly wash up, change from my jeans and sweatshirt to a pair of black wool pants and embroidered sweater, apply minimal makeup and generally make myself look more respectable. Among all the food left over from the *shiva*, I find a luscious looking chocolate cheesecake that, remarkably, is almost whole, with only a small wedge cut out of it. I locate another cooler in the broom closet, and since it's a large one, I also throw in a couple of casseroles. It would be a shame to see all that food go to waste.

Knowing that I'll be coming back after sundown, and not wanting to give Wayne and Joe any dark shadow advantage, I turn on all the outside lights before leaving. Thank goodness Gramma liked giving lawn parties, especially as charity fundraisers. She took her responsibilities as village matriarch very seriously. So, Grampa had to wire up the lawn and all the buildings with outdoor floodlights.

I carry the cooler outside, with my purse balanced carefully on top of it, and the rifle slung over my shoulder. In my mind, I've rehearsed how, if Wayne, Joe or any of their buddies show up, I would drop the cooler and unsling the gun. At first, I thought I would have to put the cooler in the car, then come back for Acey, but that isn't necessary.

He continues to follow me everywhere, including hopping readily into the car. He rides the entire trip draped over the back of my neck, purring quite contentedly. I've never before encountered a cat who actually likes being a passenger in a car.

As I drive up to Rebecca and David's, I realize that the problem isn't getting Acey into the car, but out of it and into a strange house. I certainly don't want him to run away again. I park as close to the back door as possible, pull him off my neck and hold him quietly for a few moments, speaking gently, trying to reassure him (and myself) that I'm not so much deserting him as reuniting him with his big sister. The more I talk, the louder he purrs and the guiltier I feel. I don't even see David approach the car, until he's standing right next to the car.

Damn, I shouldn't have allowed anyone to sneak up on me like that. What if Wayne followed me? The minute I have that thought, I try to push it away, knowing that I'm not on a dark, empty lane or an isolated farm. I'm as safe as I could be anywhere in Black Bear, with a rabbi right here, waiting to welcome me into his home. I gather Acey into a firmer hold, and get out of the car.

"*Bonjour*, Judith," David says as he pets Acey's head. "I see you have your hands full. Anything you need me to carry?"

"Hello, David." I nod toward the passenger seat. "Could you get the cooler and my purse, please?"

He notices the rifle wedged between the two front seats, but says nothing about it other than, "I suggest you lock the car, if you're going to leave that in there."

"Of course," I reply. I hadn't really thought things through — that I couldn't carry the gun into their house, or leave it casually in the car, without securing it.

Carrying the cooler, with my purse perched on top, David leads the way to the kitchen door. "I see you intend to give my wife another excuse to call you."

"I beg your pardon?"

"This cooler…"

"Oh, that. I don't really care about them," I start to

explain. But looking at his wry grin, I realize he's teasing me and, by extension, including me in on a joke he shares with Rebecca.

Rebecca is at the kitchen door, holding it open for us. Inside, the room is filled with the warm, yeasty odor of fresh baked bread. She wears simple, stylish navy wool pants, a pale yellow cashmere shell and matching cardigan and a short double strand of lustrous pearls. While David lifts the cooler onto the counter, Rebecca places her hands on my shoulders and leans forward to brush kisses on my cheeks — left, right and left again — in the continental manner. "*Gut Shabbos*," she says in Yiddish, then reaches to pet Acey. When she accidentally touches one of his wounds, he gives a short, shrill cry.

"*Oh!*" Rebecca draws back, looks closely at Acey, and frowns, not just with her mouth, but her entire face and body, her brows knitting tightly, and her torso slightly curved over her abdomen, as though in pain herself. "David! Acey's hurt!"

Almost in unison with Rebecca's exclamation, comes a questioning *meow* from another room, and Tedda is soon peeking out from behind the swinging kitchen door. Acey leaps from my arms, runs to Tedda, rubbing against her, while the two of them lick each other happily, proprietarily.

"The wounds aren't serious," I try to reassure Rebecca. "I cleaned them, and Acey doesn't even seem to notice them."

"We don't know what trouble might have found him." She stares at David, imploring him to do something.

David puts on his glasses, then reaches down to pet Tedda and Acey. Both cats go right to him. His hands are square and thick with short fingers, but his touch is gentle, even when he probes Acey's flesh and joints for internal injuries or areas that Acey might react to with discomfort. David's calm, assured manner, reminds me that he responded to the fire alarm the other day, with all the other volunteer fire and ambulance folk. If nothing else, he's probably at least a first responder, trained to evaluate wounds and medical conditions during emergencies.

Straightening up, he says, "Acey's fine, Rebecca. Look at him. I don't believe I've ever seen a happier cat. Just to be sure, I'll call Alice. She has a *Torah* reading in tomorrow's services. I'll ask her to come early to check him over. Okay?"

"Yes, please," Rebecca says, her expression brightening immediately.

While we take turns washing our hands at the kitchen sink, Rebecca explains, "Alice is a very skilled vet who's taken care of Acey ever since Martha found him. I wouldn't be surprised if she hasn't been just as worried about him as any of us." Rebecca hands me a fresh towel from a drawer, and opens the cooler. "You brought a feast!" she exclaims, as she unpacks the casseroles and cheesecake. "I hope you won't be insulted if I don't serve it all. It's just the three of us."

"No, of course not. I simply don't want all the good food that people brought me to go to waste. Do you have an *oneg* after services?"

"Can you imagine any Jewish gathering that doesn't end or start with food? However, some of our congregants are strictly kosher, so unfortunately, we can't serve any of this. If it's okay with you, I'll drop it off at the church tomorrow for their pantry dinner."

"Yes, of course."

Rebecca removes the just-baked challah bread out of the hot oven and wraps it in a linen napkin. "Let's go into the dining room. I'm starved!"

In the golden light of early evening that streams in through the bay window, the china, glassware and silver sparkle festively. A fine table, undoubtedly set with the best that Rebecca and David have, not in my honor, I'm certain, but to celebrate the Sabbath and set it apart from the everyday.

Rebecca places the challah in the middle of the

table, between two silver candlesticks. For several minutes, the three of us sit in silent meditation, separating the time of preparation from the time for celebration.

Rebecca strikes a match, lights both candles and waves her hands over the flames three times, as though she's gathering the light to bring it closer to her. Then, she covers her eyes with her palms and chants the ancient prayer, *"Baruch ata Adonai, Ehloheinu, mehlech haolam, asher kid'shanu b'mitz votav v'tzivanu l'hadlik ner shel Shabbat."* Her voice is melodious, warm, yet conversational.

As she sings, I silently translate the Hebrew, responding to the Sabbath prayer and rituals almost intuitively. *"Blessed are thou, our God, Ruler of the Universe, Who hallows us with Commandments, and commands us to kindle the lights of Sabbath."*

Rebecca looks at David, her eyes shining with the reflected candlelight, and the two of them say in unison, *"May God bless us with Sabbath joy. May God bless us with Sabbath holiness. May God bless us with Sabbath peace."*

David stands and holds up the silver *Kaddish* cup of wine. He begins the blessing of thanks for the "fruit of the vine," but soon Rebecca is reciting it with him. I find myself pulled into the rhythm of their shared prayer, saying the Hebrew for the first time in many years.

Then, David turns to me and asks, "Judith, would you care to do the *Motzi?*" Just the way Grampa would ask. First, Gramps would say grace, and then he would turn to me and ask me to give the Jewish blessing over the bread. How strange it feels and, yet, how natural. Here, at Rebecca and David's table, I'm more at home than I've been in a long time.

I reach forward to place my hand on the challah. David takes my other hand, and Rebecca holds his. As I lead the prayer, they join me, a soft, thrumming undercurrent of my own voice, buoying me upward. *"Baruch atah Adonai Eloheinu Melech Haolam, hamotzi lechem min haaretz,"* I recite the prayer for the second time within a single week. Yet this evening, it's something shared in joy and communion, rather than a haunting memory of love long gone.

The three of us break bite-sized chunks of the golden challah, and dip them in honey, to start our meal with the yeasty, sweet taste of Sabbath.

The dinner is delicious, not only because Rebecca is an excellent cook; I'm truly enjoying the conversation and company. What a relief to be here with them, in this temporary bubble of peace. If only it could last. But then, this lovely oasis is their life, and as far from my reality as a fairytale.

As David passes the braised asparagus to me for a second time, I decide I need to focus on some practical matters, instead of dwelling on my personal terrors. "Rebecca, I went to my grandfather's store, as you suggested."

"So I've heard. What did you think of it?" She looks up at me, but then returns to paying particular attention to the stuffed portabella mushroom on her plate.

"I've decided that the ladies should continue with the pantry."

With an audible sigh of relief, Rebecca puts her fork down and gives me her full attention. "I'm so glad; they've worked so hard and do such...."

"However, I've been told that the women can't really afford to maintain the building, or even fully support the shop. So, I can't sign the property over to them."

"Why do you need to sign it over?" David asks. "The status quo has been working quite well."

"The status quo was my grandmother's choice, not mine," I answer with more irritability than I want to reveal. "I will have nothing more to do with this village after the estate is settled."

David doesn't respond. Instead, he allows the silence between us to grow. I have the impression that he's studying me. Not that he is staring at me. In fact, his eyes are focused on the empty space between us, and his smile is more contemplative, reflective.

I feel the need to apologize, to explain that I'm not referring to the two of them but to a history of intolerance and pain, the revulsion I experience whenever I think about the years I endured in Black Bear. "You don't know what it was like to grow up here, David." I touch my cheek with my fingertips. "Being different, being stared at wherever I went, becoming the brunt of the kids' anger, the hate."

David arches his eyebrows, and his mouth twists into a smirk that seems turned inward rather than directed at me. "Children can be terribly cruel."

"Not just children," I remind him. "Their parents, too."

"Yes," he agrees. "It starts with the adults, doesn't it? Does that mean we should let that be the end of it? Be hurt, turn away and allow it to continue for the next child, and the next? Cruelty. Hatred. It exists in this world. What we do in response to it is what makes living on this earth worthwhile. But you know that, Judith. Isn't that an important part of the work you do?

"Then, there are the other people," he continues, a rabbi with an audience of two, preaching a theme that's obviously one he has thought about frequently. "The good folk, like your grandmother, who refuse to be quiet and who stand up against the hate. When you turn your back on the angry crowd that hurt you, you are also turning away from the good people who would work with you, fight by your side, if necessary." He pauses, then with an almost mischievous glint, he said, "When I was young, I met hate with hate, until I realized that it was letting the bastards win, turning me into a reflection of them. Now I try to answer hate with intelligence and strength of will, just as you do with your *Les Femmes*. What I wonder, Judith, is why you can do for strangers what you cannot... or will not... do for your hometown."

"Black Bear isn't my hometown!"

"If Black Bear isn't your hometown, where is?" David asks.

I have no answer. Ever since Mom and I left *Papa*,

I have had no home, not really.

"Give yourself time, Judith," David says. "You've just buried your grandmother, and you're angry. Not only at the village, but at her for leaving you alone."

He pats my hand. I want to think of it as an annoying, patronizing gesture, but his callused palm is warm, and his face is filled with what appears to be real concern. It reminds me of how he probed Acey's injuries, so gently, yet professionally. Unstinting.

Without warning, he suddenly changes the subject. "Judith, why do you have a rifle in your car?" he asks.

Rebecca stares first at David and then at me, her eyes wide with surprise, shock.

So, we come to it at last. Now, I have to decide just how much to say. Without finally telling these two friendly strangers the full truth, the story I have never, could never tell anyone, I would be seen as an over-reactive, hysterical woman, afraid of a man dressed up in a toy soldier uniform. "I don't feel safe here, David. I never did."

"Does the rifle make you feel safer?" David asks. "Or is it simply substituting one perceived danger for another more concrete one, albeit a danger you think you can control?"

I have no answer for him. At least, none that I can reveal to him.

"Just promise me you'll be careful, Judith. Once you have a weapon, it's remarkable how likely it is that you'll use it. I know you wouldn't want to hurt — to kill — anyone." David's voice breaks only slightly. Is he speaking from experience, perhaps from his days in the army?

"I promise," I say, though I don't mean it. If Wayne or Joe or any of their neo-Nazi friends attack me, I'm damned sure I'll shoot rather than let them touch me ever again. Would I shoot to kill? I don't know.

David stands abruptly and starts to clear the table. I begin to get up to help, but Rebecca catches my eye and shakes her head. "David's a terrible cook," she explains. "So he does the cleaning up after our meals."

It makes sense, but I had the idea that they had a

more traditional relationship. Perhaps, it's because they divvied the prayers according to the old ways: the woman lighting the candles, the man praying over the wine. Or, that David automatically took the seat at the head of the table. I remind myself that no matter how familiar they seem to me, I've only just met David and Rebecca. I don't really know them at all. Yet, it's hard to not wonder what it would have been like if they had been my childhood friends. How different everything would have been.

"Besides," Rebecca says. "I wanted to talk with you about something else. Just the two of us."

The way her manner changes, how her posture slants forward, the serious tone of her voice, her unflinching direct stare... perhaps I should have insisted on helping David in the kitchen.

"You know what it's like to live in a small village," she says. "Everyone believes they have the right to pry and spread stories about whatever anyone else is doing or supposedly thinking. I usually ignore the gossip and try to refuse to hear it. But you can't not hear some things." She sighs deeply, perhaps gathering her strength or, maybe, only her words. "Judith, there's a lot of talk about your legal action against Joe Anderson."

My stomach roils and I taste the bitterness of it on my tongue. "So, I've given the busybodies something new to talk about! Why should I care what they say?"

"You're correct. You shouldn't care what gossips say. Still, you need to understand..."

"Oh, I understand. Joe is a native son; I am and always have been an outsider. A troublemaker."

"That may be the reason some people are rallying to him, but there's more to it than that. I don't know why you're so angry at Joe. I can't believe it's the money or the property. You have more than enough of both, and he has so little. Yet, Joe is a good man, a...."

I stand, almost toppling the chair behind me. "It's none of your business what is or isn't between Joe and me!" My throat tightens on the words, as I try and fail to keep my voice level, unemotional. "You don't know what he's capable of doing. Sure, he can look all sweet and nice, in that bumbling, big bear way of his, but underneath, he's... he's... *merde!*... I don't know the words to describe what he is, but it isn't nice.... Yes, I do... He's an Anderson."

"What's that supposed to mean, Judith?" Rebecca's voice twists with her sarcasm.

"Have you seen his brother Wayne, strutting around in that damned Nazi uniform, pushing his weight around and threatening people so they know it's more than threats? And their father... I hear he's tied up with the local Aryan Nations, too. Andersons." I almost gag on the name. "Bigoted, violent hoodlums!"

"That's Joe's brother and father, not Joe."

"As my grandmother used to say, 'the apple doesn't fall far from the tree.' Just stay out of this, Rebecca. You've no idea how ugly the truth about Joe Anderson really is."

David flies in through the swinging door. "What's all the shouting about?"

"I'm afraid I upset Judith." Rebecca walks around the table and starts to put her hand out to me, then thinks better of it. "Judith, please accept my apology. You're correct that whatever it is between you and Joe is none of my business. I'm simply concerned and wanted to give you a chance to talk it out."

"Joe?" David asks. "Joe Anderson? He runs on the ambulance with me."

We both glare at him. "Not now, David," Rebecca insists in that tone that only wives can use with husbands. Somehow, the annoyance that we share at that moment, two women confronting a man who doesn't really get what's going on, defuses things. Besides, I don't want to be angry at Rebecca. I want to believe she really could be my friend. Not that we'll have the chance to find out. Maybe, I'm simply tired of being angry, and need to have this one evening of companionship. Damn it, why do I let Joe and Wayne poison everything?

I grasp the hand Rebecca offered earlier and squeeze it. "I accept your apology, but, please," I warn, "don't bring that subject up again."

At first, it's awkward sitting down with them for after-dinner tea in their tiny living room, but they quickly put me at ease with lively conversation spiced with gentle humor and their natural, easy grace.

David and Rebecca are surprised when I tell them about my plan to give the store to the temple, in trust for the community. When David continues to insist that I might change my mind, about the store, the farm, the village, it's not worth arguing any further. He knows me as little as I know him, and I have nothing to prove to either of them.

"Dinner was wonderful. Thank you for your kind hospitality," I tell them as I prepare to leave.

Rebecca asks, "Will you reconsider and join us for services?"

I don't appreciate that she makes me feel as though I should apologize, when I explained it all to her before. "I'd love it, Rebecca. I simply don't have the time, not with all I have to do to close up the farm. I have less than three days left." I hand a set of keys to the farmhouse to her. "Thank you for being willing to look after things until everything's sold."

David looks at me with those small piercing eyes of his again, but he doesn't disagree or pontificate. He simply says, "I understand." Then, taking my hand in both of his, he adds, "Please stay in touch with us. It would be very sad indeed if this were the last evening we would spend with you."

After hugging them goodbye, I walk alone through the cold blustery night to my car. Across the way, lights in the small temple beckon warmly, and I'm almost sorry that I decided to not go in. However, once I make a decision, I never like going back on it.

As I drive to the farm, I position the rifle closer to me, so it will be within immediate reach, should I need it. I'm relieved to see that all the floodlights are still on. I park the car as close to the front porch as possible. Before opening the car door, I make sure I have the key ready, grab the gun and, then, sprint toward the house. Suddenly, a loud shriek slices through the silence of the night, making me drop the key. An owl, perhaps? Or is it Wayne signaling his buddies? When I find my key, my hand is shaking so much that I have difficulty fitting it into the keyhole and turning the tumbler. I slam and lock the door behind me.

Leaning against the bolted front door, I clutch the rifle to my chest, knowing it's the only thing between me and another encounter with Wayne. No one will help me, because no one would believe me. Even Rebecca and David buy into Joe's good boy act. Then again, Joe was the one who sat things out, presenting himself as the bumbling innocent, while letting his big brother Wayne do his dirty work.

SATURDAY

I awake before the alarm clock rings at 6:00. The subtle transition from sleep to wakefulness is a noisy thing of lists churning through my dreams. The same words, ideas and events, replaying over and over again, until I realize I haven't been dreaming for some time. Lists of what I have forgotten to do, failed to do, or will never get done, no matter how hard I try. I'm sure I've overlooked something terribly important. I tick off my responsibilities to the estate, to my grandparents, to *Les Femmes*, to everyone and everything that depend on me. All are punctuated with memories of things I should have said or done to the people who had ridiculed, taunted or otherwise hurt me through the years, especially when I was a child here in Black Bear.

Then, I roll over and see the rifle on the floor right next to the bed, where I put it last night. Before falling asleep, I practiced reaching for it, repeatedly adjusting its position on the floor, until I was quite sure that I could grab it and load a round within seconds of hearing a noise.

Now, in the light of day, I feel a bit foolish. Yes, Wayne had shown up and made threats. But why did he leave so easily if he really intended violence? Why didn't he just attack me then and there? We both knew that I was virtually defenseless against him.

The only answer I can come up with is that his purpose in scaring the bejesus out of me has nothing to do with physical violence — not immediately. What he wants is to tyrannize me, and he has succeeded, in spades. Why? Obviously, so I'll drop the lawsuit.

Once again, Wayne is doing Joe's dirty work,

scaring me off. Why did I believe him so readily that he had any buddies in the woods, or that he would stay out there himself, through the chilly night? He probably delivered his message and went home, to get drunk and laugh at how easily I'm intimidated and unnerved, how much power he still has over me.

"You've got nothing to fear but fear itself," Grampa would often quote FDR to me, though I sometimes wondered if he really believed it himself. If that were truly so, why did Gramps refuse to talk about what he did and saw in the Pacific during The War?

No fear, no fear, I tell myself over and over again as I get up, get dressed, and go downstairs to continue packing. Just keep moving, get things done, and get out of here.

I carry the rifle with me wherever I go, an added appendage, as necessary to my comfort as my clothes.

I don't notice the snow until I go outside to throw some papers into the dumpster. Just a dusting of white, no more than a couple of centimeters at most. Still, it covers everything, transforming the April mud into a picture perfect winter wonderland. The classic Pocono postcard scene with confectioner's sugar on the evergreens and bushes, and a few grey clouds spilling flurries from an otherwise brilliant blue sky.

I don't dare linger outside, but I'm glad to have one last snow here, to burn the memory of it into my mind. Is this the onion snow? Will old-fashioned farmers, who trust their instincts and their almanacs more than The Weather Channel, look at the sky today and decide it's time to start planting next week? I should have asked Grampa how he knew the signs. Now, I'll never know.

So much of what I do today will be the last, something never again to be seen or experienced. This is probably the last snow I'll ever know here on the farm; I doubt it will continue through the weekend. So, I guess, in a way, it's my onion snow.

❖

I'm packing up things in the living room, when I hear Edward Felson's car pull up; he's actually a few minutes early. For the short time he'll be here, giving me his preliminary report from his investigation of Joe Anderson, I won't have to worry about Wayne. I hide the rifle in Grampa's study, not wanting to explain myself.

We sit in the kitchen as before, over two mugs of coffee and the leftover cinnamon raisin cake. Mr. Felson puts on his reading glasses, takes a notebook out of his back pants pocket, flips through a few pages, then puts it down in front of him. "This Anderson's an interesting character. His life breaks down into two very different periods... before 2004, and after. That's often the case with a recovering alcoholic."

"You mentioned that last time." It makes an ugly kind of sense. His father was a drunk. What children see they become. It's just that Joe always said how much he hated the stink of liquor. Of course, Joe used to say a lot of things to me.

"Apparently, he's been clean and sober since '04. That's saying something. To stay off the juice for eight years." Mr. Felson stirs three heaping spoonfuls of sugar into his coffee and takes a long gulp. "Where should I start... before or after '04?"

"Before." Despite myself, I'm curious what happened to Joe after graduation. Did he even realize that I was gone? I doubt it. Wayne did his dirty work, then disappeared. Ever after, Joe shunned and maligned me, calling me vile names behind my back, turning away whenever I was near, or laughing even louder with Maybeth, making sure I heard and saw what a good time he was having with her, despite the enormous cast covering his leg long into the winter. At first, I couldn't believe he could be so mean to me. It had to be a big mistake. Then, I realized I was the one who had made a mistake thinking he was any different from his violent, knife-wielding brother or his drunken, lawless father. Joe managed to graduate, so someone must have tutored him — certainly not Maybeth, who barely passed herself. Perhaps, the teachers felt sorry for him, the fallen football hero. Maybe, they just wanted to get him out of there, an embarrassment now that he was no longer useful to the school.

"You had it right about the Navy," Mr. Felson says. "They wouldn't take him with that busted leg of his. He tried the Army and Marines, too. Nobody wanted him." Referring again to his notes, Mr. Felson summarizes in that ticker tape-like reporter's voice of his. "Joe Anderson became an odd-job man, but couldn't keep any clients for long. First arrest was for brawling in a bar, in '95. He got out after ten days and disappeared for about six months. Then, turned up on a DUI... driving under the influence... alcohol again. In fact, I uncovered several DUIs, though only two ended up on his official record... the ones where he caused some pretty bad accidents. Luckily, no one was seriously hurt, except Anderson himself. One in '98 landed him in a hospital for a week." Mr. Felson removes his glasses, puts them down on the table and leans back in his chair. "There's something odd about that accident. He drove off that hairpin curve on Route 5, not too far from here. Would have gone all the way down to the bottom of the gully, if his wheel hadn't gotten caught in a big fallen oak. Do you know where I mean?"

"Yes." Of course, I know the spot. I'll never forget how much fun the two of us used to have sledding down that hill when we were kids.

"The thing is, there were no skid marks.... no brake marks ... and his blood alcohol levels barely measured. He was as close to sober as any drunk gets." Mr. Felson pauses and taps his right forefinger on the table. "Makes you wonder if he knew what he was doing."

"What do you mean?"

"Well, a couple of folks I talked to said he might have been trying to kill himself."

"Suicide? No, Mr. Felson. It doesn't fit. Joe Anderson doesn't have enough of an introspective, brooding nature for that."

"Well, what else is alcoholism, if not a form of suicide?" Mr. Felson shrugs. "In any case, he did nothing more about killing himself. That is, other than drinking and getting in trouble. The worst was when he fell in with his brother. That was no DUI."

Wayne. I knew Felson would come to him. "What did you find out about the brother?"

"Well, around '90 or '91, he disappeared. Stayed away for a few years. Rumors are that he went to Alaska. He came back around '94, then went missing again. The two of them hooked up sometime around '02 or '03." Mr. Felson reads aloud from his notebook. "Wayne Allen Anderson. Hunting without a license. Concealed weapon. Assault and battery. Small time drug dealer." He puts the notebook down. "It was that last one that got Joe Anderson in big trouble. Probably the best thing that could have happened to him. Hitting bottom like that, he had only one way to go."

Mr. Felson frowns, the creases around his mouth cutting deeply into his flesh, making me wonder if he's speaking from personal experience, that he knows what it's like to hit bottom.

"Joe was living in a trailer over on Beaver Mountain. Wayne moved in with him in '03, and probably got Joe involved in the drugs, though the police never could prove it. Cops figure there was a falling out. Joe went berserk, beat up Wayne and two of his pals...uh...," Mr. Felson checks his notes, "...Jim Allerton and Al Haas. Smashed them up pretty bad."

Could it possibly be the same Jim, the one with the knife?

"Wayne, Jim and Al were arrested for dealing, once they were released from the hospital. Joe was charged with attempted murder, but his attorney plea bargained him down to felonious assault. He got two to five for it, but was paroled after only 14 months." Mr. Felson shrugs, "That's unusual. For a first felony offense, a convict typically serves a minimum of two years. But Joe had a sponsor who signed for him and guaranteed that he'd go right into rehab at the Mountain Center... one of the tougher residency programs for alcoholics, and expensive, too, but they're good. Joe's sponsor ended up footing all the bills for his rehab that the state didn't cover... and supported him in lots of other ways, ever since."

The way Mr. Felson stares at me, almost as though he's trying to gauge my reaction, I have the sinking impression that I don't really want to know, don't want my fears to be confirmed, but I have to ask, "Who?"

Those dark jaundiced eyes bore into me. "Your grandmother."

I catch myself shaking my head slowly from side to side. Quickly tightening control over my body, I believe I cover up rather well by sipping my coffee and nibbling at the cake on my plate.

"That was the turning point," Mr. Felson says. "Joe Anderson's stayed clean and apparently sober ever since."

Why, in heaven's name, would Gramma take legal responsibility for Joe, pay his bills? It just doesn't make any sense. Not ready to talk about it, I ask, "What happened to Wayne?" Some cultures believe that saying the devil's name can invoke him, make him aware of you. Utter superstition, of course. Then, why do I glance behind me, to make sure he hasn't suddenly appeared?

"Wayne was released from prison two years ago, came back to Black Bear and got in with their father and the Homeland Militia. He's been arrested a few times for malicious mischief, on suspicion of vandalism, theft, arson, but nothing's stuck. No convictions."

"Any complaints of threats of violence, racial intimidation or sexual assault?"

"No...." Felson checks the list in his notebook. "Nothing I've uncovered. Have you heard anything about Wayne that I should look into?"

Now is the time to say something about Wayne, if I'm going to do it. But what help could Felson be? He isn't a Sam Spade or even a Jim Rockford-type hero who would brave all kinds of dangers to protect his leading lady client.

This is the real world, in which a private detective is an information gatherer and that's all. And it's information that I need. Verifiable, proven information.

"I have nothing to give you. Just gossip I've heard. Please check into it and see what you can find," I tell him.

"Will do." He jots down some notes, writing more than I thought I said.

"What about Joe? Did you find anything that links him to the Homeland Militia?"

"Not yet, though I'm waiting to hear back from the Southern Poverty Law Center — they track hate crimes and keep a sort of extremist *Who's Who*. To all intents and purposes, Joe appears to have become a model citizen. A volunteer EMT... emergency medical technician... with the ambulance. Little league coach. Seems to be the strong back and hands that people call for help with whatever needs to be done around town. Got married in '06 to..." Mr. Felson glanced down at his notebook again. "... a Betty Burkhoff. She was pregnant at the time. Likely not his kid. Their other two children appear to be his, and there's no indication of anything but a stable, steady marriage. In '08, he bought Dutch's gas station. Your grandmother co-signed the mortgage, probably gave him the down payment, too. He built a second floor apartment over the garage where they live. He's in debt up to his eyeballs, but, from what I can gather, he's a hard worker and not a big spender. As long as he doesn't hit any crisis, he should be able to keep up with his payments to the bank."

"How much money did she give him?" I manage to keep my voice level.

"Total? I can't say. With the rehab and down payment, and probably the initial mortgage payments... I'd guess... about forty, maybe fifty grand."

"Did you know about her checking account, that he had signing permission on it for the past few months?"

"I heard stories."

I shake the manila envelope of Gramma's bank records out on the kitchen table, more energetically than necessary, and they scatter across the wood. "This is no story." Sorting through the paper-clipped piles, I pull out the copies that I made, and hand him the photostats of the checks. "Lots of them were written to cash — over his signature. I don't know who the payees are on many of the others; I wouldn't be surprised if they're straw men that Joe used to siphon money from the account."

Felson glances through the papers. "May I have these copies? I'd like to look into them."

I nod, acknowledging his request, but I stare at the papers, lost in my own tumultuous thoughts. "Why? Why did she do it?" I didn't really mean to ask it aloud.

"I don't know. It doesn't appear to be blackmail."

"Blackmail!" How could he be so stupid? "My grandmother never did anything so shameful that she could be blackmailed."

"Please, don't be insulted, Ms. Ormand." He holds his pudgy hands in front of him, the palms facing me, as though I point a gun at him. Or is it the gesture of a man not knowing how to calm an angry woman? "My job is to look at all the possibilities. I don't think it's anything like black-mail. From what I've learned, your grandmother was one who got involved and took care of people."

"Fifty thousand dollars is beyond being a good neighbor. Far beyond." I stand abruptly. No way I'm going to sit here passively, listening to this idiocy. Looking down at Felsen, I see just how hairless the crown of his head really is. "I expect you to do your job. Fully. I want to know why and how Joe Anderson managed to take advantage of my grandmother. How he got her to pay his bills and put him and his kids in the will. How he ended up writing checks on her account. And what is Wayne Anderson's involvement in all this?" I spin around and walk out the room, not needing to look back to see if he follows. He scrapes his chair on the floor as he pushes away from the table, and his shoes make a clicking sound on the kitchen's wooden floor. Some detective. He walks far too heavily to be able to sneak up on anyone.

At the front door, I shake his hand, simply because he offers it, and I don't want to expend the energy to refuse.

"Good day, Mr. Felson. You have my email. Please be sure to get the information I need and send it to me."

"I'll do what I can, but I may not uncover what you want."

"Then, I'll find someone else who can."

"No one can invent information that doesn't exist, Ms. Ormand. I'll dig up everything there is to know." He holds up the copies of the bank records. "These might help."

When I close the door, I lean against it, feeling so very drained — and chagrinned for being irrational and unfair with Mr. Felson. It isn't his fault that Joe hoodwinked Gramma or that Wayne is terrorizing me. But, *merde!* He just doesn't know what he's talking about when he suggests that Joe could ever have anything on Gramma that he could blackmail her with. The very idea of it would be laughable, if the whole situation weren't so grotesque.

Retrieving the rifle from its hiding place, I throw myself into my work, trying to avoid thinking about Joe and Wayne. Not that I have ever been able to exorcize them completely, but I've nearly perfected the ability to bury them deeply, where they can't do any more physical damage.

As I continue to pack, other, more gentle memories flood through me with each room emptied of everything I can take — and all I must leave behind. The lights above the powder room mirror that I helped Gramps install. The dining room window that filled with the sight of apple blossoms in the spring. Grampa's favorite armchair in the living room, where he would read, pretending not to be staying awake just to make sure I got home safely, when I went out at night.

I decided from the beginning that it would be foolish and unnecessary to take any of the furniture. What would I do with it? Store everything for some time in the future when I might find a home where I could finally settle down? Besides, none of it would be the same anywhere else. This is where Grampa's grandparents' chestnut dining room set belongs. Where the grandfather clock fits so perfectly. Where every piece of furniture has a story and a history and a sense of rightness to it.

My fingertips trail over chairs, tables, cabinets, as I walk pass, needing to touch, to seal the memories into my flesh. I've never been materialistic, but this china cabinet, this hope chest, this rocking chair — none of them are mere possessions. They're all that I have left of Gramma and Grampa, of Mom and, even, Uncle Robby. And, yes, of me, when I was still innocent and loved and safe.

Whenever I walk past Gramma and Grampa's bedroom, I stop at the doorway, trying to get up the courage to go in. Each time, I allow myself to be pulled away to deal with something else. I can't avoid it any longer. So, after lunch, I stomp out of the kitchen and go directly into their bedroom, not giving myself a chance to think up yet another excuse.

I stand in the middle of the room for some time, letting it all wash over me. Sometimes, in the mornings, I used to come in here, ostensibly to help Gramma make the bed, but really to talk about whatever was on my mind. A blouse I wanted to buy, or a homework project that required going into Scranton for special supplies, or another party that I wasn't invited to. Or, I'd stop in the evenings, before going upstairs to bed, to kiss them good night and answer (or evade) their questions about my day. Other times Gramma would call me into the bedroom, her private sanctuary, when what she had to say was serious and meant only for my ears.

Of course, there were the sex talks and similar mother/daughter-type conversations. Gramma was pretty good with them, despite her discomfort with both the subject and the fact that she was only a stand-in for the one person who should have been sharing those rites of passage with me.

However, it was the first and the last of those bedroom heart-to-heart talks that made the deepest imprint on my memory and my life.

The first was seven days after Mom's funeral, when Gramma told me I would have to go back to Paris with *Papa*. I couldn't believe she would really send me away, to live with his new family who didn't want me.

I wielded my best logic. "But Gramma, Bridget has her own kids to raise now... I'd just be in the way... If Mom had wanted me in Paris, she wouldn't have brought me back to the States." I appealed to her maternal instinct and ego. "I want to be with you, Gramma." Then, guilt. "How can you send me away, when you know it isn't right? Don't you love me?" She wouldn't be moved by any of it.

I ran from the bedroom to Grampa, but he simply shook his head. "Sweetheart, a child belongs with her parent." He had nothing else to say to me about it.

When all else failed, I fled into the woods, feeling unwanted, unloved and angry at all the adults who controlled where and how I lived. Furious, especially at Mom, for dying and not being able to help me.

In the end, I did come back, because the family that *Papa* made with Bridget had no place for me.

Gramma's and my final private bedroom conversation was the day before I left for a summer internship in Geneva, followed by my first year at the University of Paris.

"How is the packing going?" Gramma asked from the front door, when she found me on the porch.

Maverick, Rascal and I had just come back from yet another walk around the farm. Over the past two weeks, we had spent more time wandering about the woods and fields, swimming in the pond, and splashing in the stream than we had the previous two months. That is, Maverick and I had swam and splashed, Rascal had watched from a safe, dry distance, busying himself with leaves and butterflies. The one thing that set this most recent walk apart was that this was my last full day here on the farm, and I had spent longer than usual, trying to burn the sights and smells into my memory.

I was sitting on the porch swing, sipping a Coke, with Rascal curled up next to me, and Maverick at my feet. Of course, I knew I should go upstairs and finish packing, but I wasn't yet ready to let go of the view, the swing, my companions.

When I saw Gramma at the front door, I knew it was her way of reminding me of all I had left to do before leaving tomorrow for Europe. However, instead of suggesting that I go upstairs and get back to work, she beckoned me into her bedroom.

Settling into our usual positions for these talks, I perched on the edge of the bed, and Gramma sat facing me in her armchair. Rascal jumped onto the bed next to me, and Maverick took up sentry duty by immediately falling asleep in the doorway, his nose pointed outward.

"I'll get it done," I said, with a slight whine of annoyance. I really didn't want to deal with her To Do lists at the moment.

"I know, dear. I've always been able to trust that you'll do what you say you will." Shifting her weight, so she spread out more fully into the deep chair, her thighs filling the wide space between the padded arms, she sighed deeply. "Judith, I'm going to miss you... terribly."

"Me, too, Gramma." The two of us seldom expressed these kinds of emotions. I guess it had something to do with her stoic Germanic heritage. Those few words were as close to being teary as we ever got with each other.

"I wonder if you realize how sorry I am that you've been so unhappy here," she said.

"I wasn't... not here, at the farm."

"No, not at the farm. But in Black Bear."

What could I say? It was true. I'd been miserable, especially over the past year.

"Do you think I didn't hear you crying at night, or see how difficult it's been for you to walk tall the way you used to? No matter how hard you tried, or what I said or did, the people in this village made it clear from the beginning that they didn't want you here, that they couldn't look beyond your dark skin." Gramma clenched her gnarled arthritic hands in her lap. "I'm ashamed of them," she said vehemently, her round face flushing almost as deep as the age spots on her creased forehead. "My lifelong friends and neighbors. I've seen them be thoroughly good and charitable... to those they consider their own kind. But they've shown their true selves... bigoted, prejudiced and cruel to my own grandchild." She spat out the words of that last sentence in a halting hiss.

All the times we had talked about this, about the stares and cold shoulders, the mean-spirited slights and vicious insults, this was the first time she allowed me to see the full extent of her fury. Of course, I had never told her about Wayne and his buddies, or how Billy's gang had torn my blouse. Or, about Joe. I couldn't imagine how she would have reacted if she had known the full truth.

"I'm so very sorry, Judith." She stared into the space between us, seeing, I supposed, what might have been, or what never could be. Her rage drained from her, as suddenly as it had appeared, and she seemed smaller, deflated. "You shouldn't have had to go through anything so wretched."

I hated seeing her dejected. Not my Gramma, who had been a tower of strength and comfort to me, the one person who had tried to convince me that, with enough hard work and good deeds, any hardship or obstruction could be overcome. Not that I had appreciated being prodded to "rise above" and "take the higher ground," when all I wanted to do was either ignore or flee, to pretend that the people who ostracized me didn't really exist, or didn't matter. Still, it had helped that I could depend on Gramma to be my personal cheerleader, encouraging me to seek ways to make things work out, to, as she liked to say, "make lemonade from lemons." If she could be defeated, what hope could I have? I said the first thing I could think of, to try to make her feel better. "But it's over now, Gramma." I guess I was thinking about never again having to run the gauntlet of the high school hallways.

She nodded. "I'm glad you agree with me."

"Agree about what?" I asked.

"That we can now put an end to your unhappiness. We couldn't do much about it while you were so young and had nowhere else to go. Besides, I couldn't stand the idea of someone else raising you, of not being as close to you as Grampa and I have been these past years." She sat forward in her chair, her steel grey eyes locking onto mine. "Now, Judith, it can finally end, but it depends on you."

"What do you mean?"

"You mustn't come back here, ever." She said it flatly, a fact that wasn't to be argued.

"Not come back? Not ever?" I repeated, sure that I had heard wrong, hoping that she would contradict me and herself.

"You must promise me, Judith."

I looked around me at the room, out the window with its view of the garden in its late spring glory, at Maverick sleeping in the doorway, and finally at Gramma ensconced in her chair, where she sat whenever it was just the two of us, solving whatever problems life threw at us. "Never come home? Don't you want me with you?" I didn't dare ask the one question on the tip of my tongue — don't you love me?

"Almost more than anything, but not more than I want you to be happy, to feel wanted and needed."

"But, Gramma…"

"I know, it's hard to bear. For me, too. But hear me out, and I know you'll agree it's for the best."

I reached for Rascal, pulling him onto my lap, needing the physical contact and comfort.

"You must escape from all the abuse and pain this village has inflicted on you. To return here, even for short visits, would be like picking at a scab. Did you know that when you keep re-injuring a wound, cancer can develop, because your body has to keep growing new flesh until it no longer can differentiate between needed and unhealthy cells? It's the same with emotional hurts. You must leave

Black Bear behind once and for all, so you can become whole again, become a healthy woman with no fears and lots of friends."

"Why can't I come home to the farm, to you and Grampa, at least for vacations?"

"Because this farm, as wonderful as it is, mustn't continue to be your hiding place. Life awaits you outside this small, hate-filled village. A rich, full life, but only if you turn your back on the people who would try to tear you down just because they don't like the color of your skin."

"What about you, Gramma? You and Grampa? When would I ever see you?" I asked, tears brimming in my eyes.

"We'll come to you, wherever you are." She smiled for the first time since I had entered the room, her eyes sparkling. "What an adventure that will be, Judith, for Grandpa and me, to finally travel the world, and to share it with you!" Then, just as quickly, the smile was gone. "You see it, don't you, dear? How necessary it is for you to make a complete, clean break?"

As usual, Gramma's logic was compelling; did that make it right?

"Will you promise me you won't return to Black Bear, ever?" she asked.

"I don't know." I felt cornered to make a decision right away, but it seemed that it had already been made for me, by Gramma.

"Trust me, dear, this is for your best."

"Yeah, I know." As much as I had rebelled against her throughout high school, I recognized that she lived and breathed for my well-being and happiness. I might not always agree with her, but I trusted her completely. She was just about the smartest person I knew. Besides, everything she said about Black Bear being vile and hateful was true, even more than she realized.

"So, please, promise me."

"Okay."

"No, Judith," she insisted. "I need to hear you say it."

"I promise, Gramma," I gathered Rascal into my arms, holding him to my chest. "I won't come back to Black Bear... ever."

Gramma stood, and I knew she considered the conversation ended, the decision made.

She had my promise.

Going through the drawers and closets in their bedroom feels like an invasion of my grandparents' privacy, a betrayal of my promise, but I have no more time to waste. I start in Gramma's closet, flicking through the hangers, my hands brushing the various textures of her dresses and suits, blouses and pants. Although most are dated from after I left Black Bear, they are familiar in style and, especially, in smell, a hint of her rose water wafting from each one. Boxes are filled with purses, scarves, hats and all the other accessories that she had chosen one by one, over the years. Nothing here that I want.

I start to turn away from the closet to tackle the rest of the room, when I spot Grampa's sweater in her closet, the brown cable cardigan that I had helped her knit when I was about thirteen. Despite the tiny burn hole on the chest from a stray pipe ember, and the leather patches Gramma had to finally sew onto the frayed elbows, Grampa had worn it more than any other sweater or jacket, especially around the house. Pulling off my old sweatshirt, I slip on the cardigan, wrapping it around me, enclosing myself in her smell and his warmth.

"I'm a creature of comfort," Grampa told me. "Comfort and sentiment. I prefer the familiar. I live in the house where I was born, where my forebears lived and died for generations. My best friends are people I've known most of my life. "

We were sitting in his study, him at his desk,

wearing the brown cable cardigan Gramma and I had knitted for him almost a year ago, and me sprawled on my favorite chair, my legs draped over one of the deep upholstered arms. I had asked him why he so seldom got new clothes. In fact, he resisted coming with Gramma and me whenever we tried to take him shopping with us, knowing we'd want to buy something for him.

"Don't you ever just want to wear something new, Grampa? Do something different?"

"No, not really. I had enough of that during The War and when I went away to school. My life and my clothes suit me fine."

"Well, I couldn't wear the same old sweater every day for years."

He laughed, that deep throated chuckle of his. "Until recently, I doubt anything could have fit you for years." His bright hazel eyes twinkled at me over his bifocals. "Do you think you could manage to stop growing now? It would save us lots of money."

It was an old joke of his that rolled easily off my back. Whatever his personal aversion to change, he took special pleasure in the private fashion shows I'd give him whenever Gramma and I came back from a shopping spree.

I kicked my heels up from the side of the armchair, to show off my long, gangly legs. "Nope, I intend to keep growing until I'm ten feet tall."

"Ten feet, heh?" Laughing, he picked up his corncob pipe, cleaned the bowl and pressed in some fresh cherry tobacco." Well, I don't know about that, but if anyone could do it, you could." Chomping on the pipe for only a moment, he put it down again, knowing that he shouldn't light up inside the house. "You know, Judith, lots of people are like me. Comfortable with what and who they know, doing things the same way they ever have. Some folks don't really know how to react when faced with something... or somebody... new."

"You mean like me." I hadn't yet learned to hide my emotions from Grampa, and I was sure he heard the bitterness in my voice.

"Unfortunately, yes." He nodded, and I felt it was in agreement with something on his mind, in addition to what I had said. "People here in Black Bear are basically good men and women, but you're different from anything they've ever encountered, so they react by raising their hackles and going on the defensive. Those who feel most threatened might go even further."

I wondered if he had guessed, or maybe had heard about some of the things that happened in school. "It's stupid. I haven't done anything to them. What are they scared of? It isn't fair."

"No, dear, it isn't fair, logical or right. However, I'm not talking about the injustice of it all, right now. Learning to live in this world, peacefully, among people who sometimes aren't smart or fair... that's important, too."

I didn't like the idea that Gramps was trying to get me to accept the way things were, just because that was the way they had always been. "But Grampa.... isn't that... like... becoming part of the... uh... system? I mean... if I don't fight it... the injustice and meanness... aren't I saying it's okay?"

"No, it's fighting it with the best ammunition you have... yourself. Give folks a chance to know you."

"How long am I supposed to wait, Grampa?!"

"If I had my say, you wouldn't have to wait at all. But I can't control what other people think or do, and neither can you." Realizing that he had crossed his arms and clenched hands tightly over his chest, he dropped his hands to his trousers. "The thing is to not let them change you, sweetheart."

"Well, I don't have forever."

"No, that's true. Life goes by so darn fast, and before you know it, your chance to make a difference has passed."

Again, I had the impression he was referring to something else, beyond me and him, that made him wistful and reflective. I felt awkward, as though I were seeing him naked. No, worse than naked — uncertain, melancholy. So, I tried to make a joke, hoping to get him to chuckle again.

"Besides, Gramma says it doesn't matter, because I'm destined to go places and do things."

"Do things? Like what?"

"I don't know." I shrugged. "It's just what she says to me."

"Sometimes, I think I made a mistake. I should have taken your grandmother with me, when I went to Philly for school. Gotten her away from here for a while. Then, maybe, she could have been the one to grow to be ten feet tall." He smiled, but he didn't laugh.

One more glance through Gramma's closet, but I find nothing else I want take back to Paris. I'm about to deal with Grampa's closet, when Mr. Nichols and Matt return, without calling first. Signing the paperwork to transfer Grampa's store to *Beth Shalom* takes less than five minutes. My Grampa's lifetime of work and devotion in that wonderful pharmacy, erased by a few scrawls of my signature. However, I'm certain he would have approved.

After they leave, I retrieve the rifle from the study. I start to head back toward the master bedroom, when someone bangs loudly on the front door. Clutching the gun, I hide behind the heavy living room damask curtains and look out onto the front porch. I don't have a very wide field of view of the front door, but what I can see makes my heart thump and my mouth dry up. Two men stand there, staring intently at the door. The one closest to my inside window perch has his fist raised, ready to pound the door again. About thirty-five, his left ear is scrunched against his head, and held there by livid scars that stretch down to his neck. The other is taller and slightly younger-looking; his oblong shaved head sports tattooed twin lightning bolts. Both have that thickset appearance of men who have earned their strength through hard labor, rather than health club weight training. If I saw them on a dark country road, I would probably quickly backpedal to avoid getting too close. As it is, they're at my front door, demanding entry.

Are they pals of Wayne's? They certainly look the part, though they're wearing ordinary jeans and dark rumpled T-shirts (with no jackets) instead of Wayne's brown shirt uniform. But I can't imagine Wayne or any of his group knocking on my door, asking for entry. They would just barge in, when given the opportunity.

I can't take my eyes off those SS-type lightning bolts on the bald one's scalp. So like Wayne's tattoo. These men can't possibly be up to any good.

What should I do? If I call the police, what could I say? Two men I don't know are knocking at my door? Not exactly an indictment of their intentions.

Besides, the nearest cops to Black Bear are at the state police barracks 40 minutes away, outside of Honesdale. By the time they could get to the farm, whatever damage or violence these men planned would be done.

While I cringe behind the curtains, a woman walks up to the porch, says something to the two men, then reaches toward the door, knocking on it much more gently. When the man with the cauliflower ear shifts his weight backward, I see her face. It's Anita Giacconi.

"Judith, are you home?" she calls. "We're here for the pickup."

My muscles are so taut, my nerves so acutely strung, that it takes me about a half-minute to realize that I'm not in immediate danger. Those two fearsome-looking men have come with Anita to help pack up things for the thrift shop. After returning the rifle to the study, I go to the front door. But I can't bring myself to open it all the way, keeping the thick solid wood between my body and these strangers as I look out at them.

"Hi, Anita." My hands are still shaking, but I think I manage to keep my voice from quivering.

"Hello, Judith. Is this a good time? You did say Saturday afternoon, didn't you?"

"Uh... yes... that's right." I can't stop staring at the two men flanking her.

Anita looks at each of them in turn, and smiles, probably realizing just how frightful they appear. "This is

Nick." She indicates the man with the deformed ear. "And Eddie." The one with the tattooed head. "They offered to help with the packing and lifting."

"Please come in," I say as cordially as I can manage.

I lead them to the kitchen, where I open a few cabinet doors. "You're welcome to take any food, dishes or utensils for the thrift shop. Please leave me a few plates, cups, silverware and such to use for the next couple of days." When I open the wine cupboard, I realize that I had sent Gramma and Grampa some of my favorite vintages. Not that it would be worth it to ship them back to France, still... "I think it would be best to not take the wine."

"We couldn't sell it anyway," Anita said, somewhat wistfully. I think she may have recognized some of the labels. "Only the state stores can handle liquor in Pennsylvania." I make a mental note to give her one or two of the bottles before I leave Black Bear. I'll split the rest among Jeff, AH and Rebecca.

"When you're finished in here, I'll show you where the clothing is. If you have any questions, please come looking for me. I'll probably be in my grandparents' bedroom near the front door. Okay?"

"Okay," Eddie and Nick say, overlapping Anita's "Thank you, Judith."

I retreat quickly, needing some privacy to regain my equilibrium after the fright they gave me. Damn, I hate that Wayne and Joe have me so on edge that they needn't do anything to make me afraid of my own shadow. I'm doing it to myself.

I'm surprised at how much of Grampa's stuff still fills his closet. After all, he died more than a decade ago. On closer examination, I realize that his good suit, dress shirts and other seldom worn clothes are gone. Only those things that he favored remain, such as his red plaid flannel lumberjacket or his denim workshirt, his old, broken down sheepskin slippers and faded college sweatshirt — the clothes that he sported in my memories of him. If I weren't selling this house, I'd leave everything in his closet, just as Gramma had. But I am, so it's better to give all of Grampa's clothes to those who need them.

At the bottom of Grampa's closet are three shoe-boxes. Faded pencil labels in Grampa's scrawl identify them only as *Family*. On top of that is a darker, more recent black marker *Send to Judith* in Gramma's distinctive hand-writing. I open one, and see that it's filled with old photos, letters and postcards. I don't want to take the time to go through them, so I put the boxes on the stairs to my bed-room, to remind myself to sort through them before going to sleep.

I'm about to walk away from Grampa's closet when I impulsively turn and grab his lumberjacket. Besides being very comfortable and warm, it was Gramps' favorite jacket, so much so that whenever it finally wore out, Gramma had to buy him the exact same one to replace it. It won't take up that much room in my suitcase.

Gramma's jewelry is exactly where she used to keep it, in a small needlepoint box in the box drawer of her mirrored vanity. She was never one to wear anything flashy, but she did like her pearls. She felt that a nice pearl neck-lace could make almost anyone look like a lady. In the same box, I find Gramps' school ring, and a few pins. The antique jewelry I inherited from *Grand-mère* Amélie is certainly finer and more valuable, but I can't leave these few pieces behind, even if I never wear them.

Eddie's light tap on the bedroom door doesn't fit the tough guy persona he's fostered. Nor does his tentative, "Mz. Ormand?"

I turn toward him. "Yes, Eddie."

"Anita said I was to come to ya… see what's to do. Her and Nick can handle the kitchen stuff. She said ya got some clothes for packing."

I show him the linen closet in the hallway and the foyer coat closet. I tell him to pack everything except Grampa's parka and my old boots (just in case I need them over the weekend), then I go back to work in the master bedroom.

When Eddie returns, I glance at the clock, surprised to see that almost an hour has passed since he started on the linen and foyer closets.

"I'm done out there. Do ya want to check it out?" he asks.

"No, thank you." I have the notion that Eddie is used to people checking up on him, making sure he's done as he's been told, that he's generally kept on a tight leash by someone or by life in general. While a part of me is curious why he is so hesitant or tentative — in a manner that I usually associate with a very young child who has been abused — my empathy hits a roadblock when I look at his skinhead Nazi tattoo. I wouldn't leave Eddie alone in any room that might contain easily pocketed valuables. And I'm embarrassed that he not only probably realizes it, but that he seems to see nothing out of the ordinary in being treated that way.

I point toward Gramma's and Grampa's closets. "Everything in there can go. I'm sure I'll have some things for you from this bureau, too, but I'm not finished going through it yet."

"Okay." He brings in a stack of boxes from their truck and starts filling them from Gramma's closet. Moving slowly, deliberately, he removes each item from its hanger, then focuses on doing his best to try to fold it neatly, though he doesn't quite know how to handle women's dresses.

As he works, I concentrate on going through the drawers of the highboy. However, Eddie's brutal appearance grates on my nerves. Anywhere else in the world, I'm rather good at handling all kinds of people. Heck, in Africa, I have to face down ruffians and corrupt village headmen almost daily. But here, in Black Bear, where I've been the prey of boys like him, I feel claustrophobic and cornered just being in the same room as Eddie.

I desperately need to get outside and breathe some unencumbered fresh air. If Eddie notices when I leave the bedroom, he doesn't say anything or even look up from what he's doing.

    I consider ducking into Grampa's study to grab the rifle before going out the front door. But I don't want to answer the questions that Anita would invariably ask if she sees me with it. Besides, I doubt Wayne would try anything as long as Anita, Nick and Eddie are within shouting distance.

    Snow still blankets everything, no deeper than a few centimeters, but enough to make a difference. Just to see the clean, sparkling whiteness, almost iridescent under the bright blue sky is a relief and a release. The wind gusts briefly, swirling the snow around me; I turn around and around in it with my arms fully extended, as I used to when I was a child.

    Just as suddenly, the wind stops, and I feel terribly foolish, realizing that I'm not alone on the farm and could be seen by Anita, Eddie or Nick — or by Wayne and his friends. I start walking toward the barn. However, that would be too far from the safety of the house, without the rifle. So, I veer the other way, circling around the house, just past Gramma's kitchen garden. Once again, the wind blows gusts of dry snow across the ground. That's when I see the tiny green tips poking up through the snow. Our crocuses. Grampa was right about them, after all.

    Mom and I had come to the farm for our annual summer visit from Paris. I guess I was about eight or nine. While Gramma and Mom never let me hear them argue, they often bristled when they shared the same room; it seemed to be worse that year. But between the sniping, I remember seeing them laughing or putting their heads together, whispering happily, conspiratorially. It was very confusing for me, not knowing what to think of it all, never quite understanding how they really felt about each other. Was it love, or anger, or something else that was a combination of the two?

What made it more confusing is that it seemed a lot of it that year had to do with Gramma's litany of complaints about *Papa*. That forced Mom to defend him, even though, at home, I had heard Mom say similar things to *Papa* in anger.

One morning in June, the atmosphere at the breakfast table was particularly tense. Neither had said anything out of sorts. Actually, they were quite courteous to each other, with that jaw-clenching determined politeness they both had.

I tried to ignore it by focusing on my cereal, even though I didn't really have much of an appetite. Then, when I glanced up, Gramps winked at me, cleared his throat and said, "Who's going to help me put in that flower bed your Grandmother's been asking for?"

"Me!" I squealed, knowing from his mischievous twinkle that he had a plan up his sleeve.

At the same time, Mom said, "Sorry, Dad, I've got to go to the foundry today. They've finished casting the *Mother's Hands* bronzes, and I need to pick the patinas."

Gramma sat there, listening intently, though the muscles in her body seemed to have relaxed a bit, and she was leaning forward, toward us.

"Come on, Maggie, you don't really have to go right now," Grampa said. "Knowing you, I bet you already have a pretty good idea what colors you want for those pieces."

Mom seemed to want to agree. All year, she would talk about what it would be like in the summer at the farm, and part of it was how much she enjoyed helping Gramps in the workshop and on the land. She glanced at Gramma, gauging which one of them would back down first. Of course, it was almost never Gramma.

"Besides," Grampa continued, "you can help me this morning, have lunch, and still get to the foundry in plenty of time. How far it is? An hour and a half at the most?"

"I must be there by early afternoon, Dad."

"Fine, so you can pack your lunch." Obviously, Mom was ready to acquiesce; all Grampa needed was to give her a graceful way out. "What do you say, hon? We'd really like your help."

"Okay." She matched his grin, the big teethy one that we both inherited from him.

"Martha?" he asked. "Will you show us where you want it?"

All three of us looked at Gramma hopefully. Would she join in and let us have fun as a family, or would she hold onto whatever resentment had built up between the two of them this time? "What a nice idea, Henry," she replied, as though it were the most natural thing in the world, and that no other option was possible. "Thank you, dear, for thinking of it."

Once again, Gramps had managed to make peace between them — or, at least, a temporary truce.

Gramma showed us where she wanted the flower beds: on either side of the path from her kitchen garden to the woods. Gramps and Mom drove stakes into the ground, and I tied string at the base of the sticks, creating two long rectangles.

Gramma stood back to look at the result. "I don't know. It's not quite right; maybe, they should be wider." She turned to Mom. "What do you think, Maggie?"

The two of them studied the layout in companionable silence. Then Mom said, "They're too angular and regular. We need soft curves to match the path and the way the land slopes."

"Yes!" Gramma's face shone. What I realized at that moment was that as much as Mom and Gramma fought, no two people were closer and more needful for each other's opinions and good will. It added to my confusion, and yet made me feel — I guess the word would be safer — as a child should feel when surrounded by her family.

Grampa used a pickax to break up the ground that Mom and Gramma outlined, pulling out all the rocks and putting them to the side for a possible border. Then the four of us knelt in the dark moist soil, with Gramma on her gardening cushion. That day, we planted purple and yellow crocuses. The irises, daffodils, day lilies and bordering bayberry bushes came later, though Gramma and Mom designed it all that day.

With the four of us working together, we finished well before lunch.

Mom stood, brushing the dirt from her clothes and said, "Well, that was fun, but I've got to get cleaned up and leave, or I'll never get to the foundry in time."

"Wait, Maggie," Gramma said, as Gramps helped her up. "I'll pack you a lunch to take."

Gramps watched the two of them walk toward the house, arm and arm, and he shook his head. "I'll never really understand either of them, you know. It's something to do with the female constitution, I think. I guess they're like the crocuses we just planted. Such tiny flowers, but sturdy, unbeatable, always the first to come up, fighting through all kinds of weather, even snow, to show us spring is on its way. I wouldn't be surprised if it weren't the fight that makes them so strong." He turned toward me. "Yep, those two women are like beautiful, feisty crocuses, but I wish they didn't have to perpetually compete over the same ground."

I didn't get to see our crocuses in bloom until years later, after I moved to the farm. Grampa did send me pictures the spring after we had planted them, the small purple and yellow flowers poking through a light snow. "You know, if we tend them carefully," he wrote me, "and if we're very lucky, they'll outlive us all. That's a comforting thought to me, to think that something the four of us created together will be part of this earth, of this farm of ours for a long time to come."

Instead of returning to the master bedroom, where Eddie is too large a presence for my peace of mind, I pick up the three boxes of photos and letters from the stairs and take them into Grampa's study. I suppose Eddie heard me return, because he comes to the study, just as I'm settling behind the desk.

"Um... Mz. Ormand," he says from the doorway. He doesn't quite look at me, his eyes skimming, instead, over the entire room.

His survey of the study makes me feel vulnerable, naked, especially when he stares momentarily at the rifle leaning against the wall, near where he stood. "Yes, Eddie," I respond, trying to sound as if I'm in total control.

"I found this on a jacket." He opens his hand, and in the middle of his large, callused palm is Gramma's antique cameo pin. "Ya don't mean the thrift store to have it, do ya? Looks kinda nice."

I'm dumbfounded. Every bone in my body had reacted to him so negatively, I could have sworn he'd be the kind of sleazy character who couldn't be trusted. But here he is, bringing me a valuable piece of jewelry that he could have easily pocketed, and no one would have been the wiser. How wrong I've been about him! I judged him solely on his coarse manners and the tattoo that remind me of Wayne, and I hadn't bothered to delve any further, to see the man rather than his appearance. Is this what being in Black Bear has reduced me to — a caricature of everything I hate about this place? A bigot as bad as the worst of them?

I get up from the desk and approach him. "Thank you, Eddie," I say, as he gives me the cameo. "It was my grandmother's favorite pin; I would have been sad indeed to lose it." I want to say something else to him, to make up for how I treated him. However, I hadn't actually said or done anything to him that might have been considered insulting. To apologize for what existed only in my mind and was never expressed might assuage my guilt, but what good would it do him? If anything, it would be hurtful, and he doesn't deserve that from me.

He starts to leave.

"Eddie," I say, and he turns back toward me. "I do appreciate all your help. Thank you."

"I ain't done nothin'… ya got nothin' to thank me for." He looks down at his feet and mutters, "Ya doing the good thing, not me… givin' all this stuff to the thrift store." He ambles away, a clunking man with a fearful presence, but apparently, also a gentle, good heart. Of course, that might be just as false and prejudiced an impression as my first. I really don't know anything about him, except that in this one case, he has proven himself to be honest and courteous.

The three boxes I found in Grampa's closet would easily fit in the bottom of one of the shipping cartons, allowing me to deal with whatever they contain sometime later. But once everything goes into storage, I have no idea when I'll have the opportunity to go through them again. It might be years before I have a place to unpack it all.

Gramma wrote "Send to Judith" on them; she wanted me to have the things in these boxes for a reason. Maybe, because she knew I would want family pictures and mementos. Perhaps, they contain clues, or even answers to the questions I have about the will and her thinking when she had signed it. Or, just possibly, I might uncover another will that makes more sense.

The first box is filled with photos from my childhood before I came to live in Black Bear, plus postcards and letters Mom and I sent the two of them. Pictures of me as an infant, with Mom and *Papa*, with both sets of grandparents, and with other people, both children and adults, most of whom I don't recognize. Others instantly remind me of specific moments or occasions in my life, of a school teacher or a bosom friend, my cat Fidelio or my rag doll Musette. In almost all of the pictures, I was a happy child. I didn't smile in every one, but even in contemplative moments, I appeared comfortable with my surroundings and myself. At least, that's true of the younger pictures, not of those taken during the last year or so in Paris, when Mom and *Papa* argued so much.

I don't read the letters or postcards, though I'm tempted as I browse through them. I don't have the time right now.

The second box has more papers than pictures. Buried in the bottom is a letter in Mom's handwriting, with no envelope. It's dated just a couple of days before she died, and addressed only to Grampa, not to Grampa and Gramma, which is strange in itself. But it's the first paragraph that catches my eye. I won't find out anything about the will in it; however, maybe I will finally understand what it was between Gramma and Mom that made them bristle, careening into each other with soul-wrenching anger one moment and heart-smiling love the other.

July 6, 1988

Dear Dad,

Now, you know as much as I do. I'm so very sorry you got caught in the crossfire between Mother and me. I never meant to hurt you, for you to find out all that I've learned ~ about how very much she has destroyed in my life, in all our lives. I wish I could put the genie back in the bottle, and never have blurted it out like that. I wish I had never found out about it myself, when there's nothing I can do now.

It was the damned Independence Day parade that got to me. Seeing Al and the other ex-soldiers who made it back whole and safe, and all those other poor saps who were broken in body and soul. But not Robby, never again seeing Robby.

Then, hearing her prattle about how wonderful all those heroes were and demanding that the three of us go to the cemetery to lay a wreath, to celebrate Robby's fine sacrifice.

I couldn't go through it all again, that damned charade she plays.

It was Al who told me the truth, about how Robby had been asking questions, feeling conflicted about the righteousness of the war, that maybe the ethical choice would be to go to college that fall, take the student deferment and hope he pulled a low draft lottery number. You know how important leading a moral life was to Robby. For him, ethics wasn't just a word, but something he struggled with, trying to understand what's right and wrong. He was so young and so idealistic.

Mother got hold of him, and twisted everything around like she always does. It must have been during one of those private bedroom discussions. Her summoning him into her lair, where it would be just the two of them, and she could spin her web of words with no interference from either of us.

All this time, I've thought I was to blame for his foolish patriotic gesture, for his being killed. Okay, I was his big sister, and I should have listened to him. But she was the one who did more than not listen. I can picture it now, just like the times I sat there in your bedroom with her, called in for one of her special conversations, when all they really are is her talking and talking, until things get so warped inside, making whatever you thought to be good and right all wrong.

She's done it to me so many times, that I can't see straight any more. I don't really know what are my own beliefs and actions and what she indoctrinated into me. I'm sure that's what happened to Robby. He probably went right from their 'talk' to the recruiting office.

When I realized what she had done and that so much of my own life has been based on that kind of muddled, deluded thinking, I couldn't take it anymore. That's why I left in such a frenzy, grabbing Judith and running away from her. And that's why I have to stay away for a while, until I can finally figure out what and who I am without her telling me.

I love you, Dad. I guess I still love her. But I need some breathing space. I'm sorry.

It was signed with Mom's usual scrawly Margaret that she had perfected for her art, and used on just about everything. It had no fully formed, easily recognizable letters, but was distinctly her signature.

I'm not quite sure what I should make of Mom's letter; it's all such ancient history, about a boy I never knew, a mother I never really got a chance to know. However, I recognize the scene she described. The bedroom summons and "just us" talks.

How much of Mom's perspective was distorted by her anger and shame? How much of it was true?

I fold the letter and put it in my shirt pocket. Quickly leafing through the remaining pictures, cards and letters in the boxes, I find nothing I need to deal with right away, and no hints about the will. But I'm not about to send them into storage where I might not see them again for years. I put the boxes back on the stairs, intending to take them with me when I leave on Monday, even if I have to pack an extra suitcase.

The early April twilight makes the house seem even more isolated than it is, a dark curtain descending that pushes the rest of the world into the distant backstage. Anita, Eddie and Nick have to leave before they can finish. Filling their pickup with as much as it can hold, they leave a few boxes in the kitchen, two of which are only half full, and others in the master bedroom. They promise to return Sunday, to pack up and cart away the rest of the stuff.

I turn on all the floodlights, ostensibly to give them more illumination, though the night hasn't yet fully fallen. After they leave, I retrieve the rifle and go around the house to make sure that all the windows and doors are locked.

The house is suddenly so very quiet, hollow. I turn on the radio in my grandparents' bedroom. It's already tuned to WVIA, and I hike up the volume so I can hear NPR's *All Things Considered* throughout the old part of the house. Not that I really listen to the news stories, but it's soothing to hear friendly, familiar voices following me around as I work. Then, I begin to worry that the comforting white noise might mask the muffled footsteps of intruders. Could someone already be in the house, stalking me, and I hadn't heard the break-in? I run back to their bedroom and switch off the radio.

I stand in the silence, sending out tendrils of my senses to all corners, gripping the rifle too tightly to really feel it. Every creak and sigh of the old building plays on my imagination. I don't sense that anyone is near, but I never have truly trusted my instincts. I walk through the house once again, re-checking all the windows and doors.

I am safely locked in. Hopefully, Wayne is locked out. Hopefully.

With all the people coming and going during the day, Wayne hadn't shown his face. What could I expect now? Perhaps, nothing. After all, Wayne didn't come back last night, why should he tonight?

The answer is as clear as the nightmares I've never been able to escape. Because he can.

But why? What does he really want from me?

I consider Ed Felson's surprising revelations (and ridiculous accusation) about Joe and Gramma. How does it all add up to that travesty of a will? Where does Wayne fit in? Has he been part of it from the beginning, helping Joe and Betty concoct their scam? Or is he a late comer to their party, planning on cutting out a hefty piece of the pie for himself?

I'm washing my supper dishes when I hear a god-awful crash outside; I drop the spatterware plate on the floor, as I spin on my heels and grab the rifle. Chambering a round as I run, I dash to the living room window seat to look outside, making certain I stay behind the heavy curtains.

I'm not sure what I expect to see. All I know is that

the loud, splintering thud hadn't been natural to the farm, had to be manmade.

Is Wayne making his move?

Under the floodlights, everything within view is as bright and clear as day. But when I look toward the circular driveway, I'm blinded by two new lights blazing right at me. Nor can I see the full porch, because the window is on the porch itself, and the wall occludes my view. Someone could be lurking within meters of me, and I wouldn't know it.

I run to the new wing, to get a better angle, moving as in a nightmare. Too slow in relation to my surroundings, too fast to think. Blood thumps through my veins and heart, nerves fire throughout my body, and my rapid shallow breaths leave me breathless.

The front bow window in the corner guest room gives me an excellent view of the entire driveway and both the front and side yards, all the way to the barn and beyond. The side window looks out onto the left field and the woods.

A blue pickup truck's front end is crumpled against the large cherry tree in the center of the driveway circle. Its headlights on high beam silhouette an incredibly large man staggering toward the house. I see no one else near or approaching the house. Not merely tall, he's almost as thick as the oak tree he barely misses walking right into. When he comes out from under the branches, the flood lights from the house illuminate his face.

Blood flows from a cut on his head and streaks down the left side of his face. Obviously dazed and unable to walk straight, he stumbles and falls onto all fours. I react without thinking, rushing out the side door. Then, I realize what I've done, and raise my gun at him.

"Joe Anderson!" I yell. "What the hell are you doing?"

He gets up and staggers toward me. "Jo... er... Jude... I gotta... ya don'..." His speech is slurred, stopping and starting erratically, but he seems proud of himself that he remembered not to call me "Jo."

The stench of alcohol reaches me from four meters away. "You're drunk!" I exclaim.

He holds up his right index finger. "Yep... drunk." Then he grimaces, childlike, as though he's been caught with a half-eaten stolen cookie, rather than a grown man who has just smashed his truck. He looks around him, making a cockeyed circle. "Sorry... didn' mean... gotta tell ya...." He swats at the air. "No, can' do that." Then, he starts back toward the truck. "Gotta go fore say too..."

As disgusted and angry as I am, I can't let him drive in that condition. I sprint past him, keeping my rifle trained on him the whole time. I throw the truck's gear shift into park, pull the keys out of the ignition and make sure he sees me chuck them into the dense shrubbery.

"Hey! Why'd ya do that, Jo?" It's more a whine of exasperation than a question. I choose to ignore him.

"Wayne!" I call out to the woods. "Come and get your brother. He's getting blood all over the yard." I back up, toward the new wing side door, not lowering my rifle at any time. I feel only a little safer with my spine pressed against the door, knowing Wayne can't rush me from behind.

"Wayne? Why ya' yelling for Wayne?" Even drunk, Joe keeps up the act. Just a slow-witted good ole boy. "He get an'where near ya', I... " He swats the air in front of his face. "Shuttup, Joe," He tells himself.

"Why should I believe you?"

"Don' know. Guess you can't. Not no more... guess truth don' matt'r no more."

I don't know if Wayne is out there or not. However, even standing still, Joe sways like a sapling in a strong breeze. Is his slurred speech entirely from being soused? Blood continues to flow from his head wound, dripping over his chin and staining his old frayed denim jacket. He takes several uncertain steps toward me.

"You're bleeding Joe. I'm going inside to call for an ambulance. Sit." I point to the porch steps with the gun barrel. "Don't move from this spot." I know enough first aid to realize an accident victim is supposed to be kept still, until medical help arrives. Besides, it's a good excuse to keep the *salaud* as far from me as possible.

"Naw." He shakes his head which makes him almost lose his balance again. "Can' do that. Sat'day's mine... can' drive myself." Giggling, he seems to lose track of what he's trying to say.

"I'm sure you're not the only ambulance driver around. Now, sit." Reaching behind me for the door knob, I have to lower the rifle.

"Wow! ya sound jus' like her... your gram."

My face burns, hearing him refer to Gramma with such familiarity. "Damn it, Joe! Just sit down." I start to close the door.

"Yes, M'am," he says with a sloppy salute of his hand nearly reaching his temple.

He doesn't actually force the door; he simply keeps walking until he's through it, standing in the hallway.

I raise the gun in his face. "I told you to wait on the porch."

"Yep." He grins idiotically, at some joke that only he knows.

If the big lug wants to follow me, I can do nothing to stop him, unless I'm prepared to shoot him. "Well, don't get blood on the carpet," I say as I lock the door behind him.

"Nope."

In the kitchen, I point to one of the chairs. "Now, sit!" I put the rifle on the counter and pick up the phone to dial 911.

He takes the phone from my hand and hangs it up. "Nah, I'm okay. Don' bother 'em."

In the bright kitchen, I see that all the blood is coming from what looks like a small cut. He's probably right. After all, he couldn't have been driving very fast, given that the damage to the truck looked minor. Still, Gramps taught us to be wary of all injuries to the head.

"Sit down. Let me wash that off to see how bad it is."

He gives me another grinning "Yep," but this time

he complies, collapsing into a chair at the table and staying there.

I soap up a cloth, and start to wipe the blood from his face. He takes my hand from his head and holds it in both of his, squeezing so water drips from the cloth.

"Beautiful...always... most beautiful I ever seen..."

I jerk my hand away, annoyed with the bastard's drunken display, the crafty lies that come so easily to his lips, but more so at myself, for the lump in my throat when he looks at me with those big puppy dog eyes of his.

"Aw, Jo... I didn' mean nothin'."

I rub away the blood, more brusquely than necessary, and dab at the cut just below his temple. As I suspected, it isn't very large or deep. I doubt that it needs anything more than a thorough cleaning and a butterfly bandage. Can I help it that I take some pleasure at his yelp, when I swab alcohol on his open wound, knowing how much it stings?

Now what do I do with the lug? I have to get him out of here, out of this house, away from me.

"Like ole time... heh?" he says, looking around the kitchen where the two of us spent so many hours, snacking, talking, sharing our lives.

"No, Joe, it's nothing like then." So many things come to mind that made this scene a travesty, a horrible parody.

"I'm taking you home, Joe."

"Na... I'm okay." He pats his pockets. "Jus' have ta find my keys." Remembering, his eyes twinkle, with that same sense of a private joke. "They gone, ain't they? You chucked 'em, Jo. Darn silly. Why'd ya have ta do that?"

"You're drunk, and in no condition to drive."

"Then, I'll walk." He stands, rocking back and forth until he achieves a tentative equilibrium.

He fumbles at the back door lock, manages to accidentally unlock it, then he lurches headlong outside, tumbling over his feet and landing in a pile of fallen leaves that had blown against the house. He stares at the ground, surprised that it's so close to his nose. He crawls to the wall, then continues, climbing it, one hand after another, until he pulls himself upright. With a nod of satisfaction, pleased that he has accomplished that much, he staggers toward the road, every other step yanking him in the wrong direction.

If he were a little closer to sober, the walk into town would probably do him some good, clearing his head with fresh cold mountain air. However, I doubt he could make it very far without falling down or passing out, in which case the chilly night could end up being dangerous or deadly. In his state, he might even get lost in the woods, despite knowing the paths as well as I.

I want to just let him go. Whatever happens to him would serve him right.

But I can't.

Cursing myself for being a fool, but unable to do anything else, I grab my purse, parka, keys and rifle and follow him outside, making sure I lock up the house behind me. "Don't argue with me, Joe. Just get in the car."

"Yep, jus' like 'er," he mutters once more as he collapses into the passenger seat, then doesn't say another word.

Before getting into the driver's seat, I glance into the back to make sure no one is hiding there. I put the gun between me and the door, acutely aware that it wouldn't do any good at this close range if Joe gets out of hand. Still, it makes me feel better having it nearby.

Joe snores for the entire eight-minute drive into the village.

Once I get to the gas station, I'm not sure what to do with Joe. I can't just push him out of the car onto the asphalt, and I doubt that he can get inside on his own steam — that is, if I can awaken him from his drunken stupor.

I don't really want to deal with yet another confrontation, especially not with Betty. But I have no choice. After all, Joe is Betty's problem, not mine.

I ring the bell to the upstairs apartment.

She comes down in a pink velour robe and old sneakers, "What the fuck!? What do you want now?" she demands when she sees me.

"Joe's in my car," I tell her, keeping my voice flat and emotionless, determined to not plummet down to her level.

Betty pushes past me, the broken backs of her sneakers flopping with each step. Opening the passenger door, she leans in toward him, then recoils at the smell of alcohol. "Oh, no, Joe." It's more a sigh of disappointment and sadness than an exclamation. I expected her to react like a fishwife. Instead, she slowly shakes her head; tears pool in her eyes. "Why Joe? After all these years with no drink? Why now?" Then she turns on me. "What the hell did you do to him now?" The words seethe through her clenched jaw.

"Me?!" I point at Joe. "That... that drunk showed up at my farm. Crashed his truck into a tree..."

"Damn!" Betty shakes him gently. "Joe, are you hurt?" Cupping his chin with her hand, she very gently turns his head to look at the bandage and sees the blood on his clothes.

He mumbles incoherently in his sleep, and shifts to lean on his side, but doesn't wake up.

Straightening up, she glowers at me, making a point of looking me over from head to foot and back again. "I used to be scared of you. I shouldn't've worried. You're poison. Everything bad ever happened to Joe was 'cause of you."

I almost laugh her in face. The idea of her judging me. "I didn't turn him into a drunk or send him to prison."

"Oh yeah?"

"What is that supposed to mean?" I ask, curious what lies he has told her.

"Why don't you ask him?" She's actually sneering at me. "Joe's got a lot to say; he just don't shout it like some people."

"No, you're right about that. He whispers, goes behind your back and connives, and he steals from an old woman when she's too sick to do anything about it."

"Thief!? You calling Joe a goddam thief?" She screams, and she starts to raise her fist to strike me. At the last moment, she spins on her heels, turning her back on me.

"I found the checks, the ones he wrote to cash," I yell, and I hate the sound of it, the loss of control, that this woman could break my resolve to remain outwardly calm.

She glares at me over her shoulder. "Shit, you really are a dumb bitch." She leans into the car, and nudges Joe's arm. At first, he resists, snuggling deeper into his sleep. She ruffles his hair and whispers something in his ear, and he opens his eyes.

He grins at her. "Hi, babe."

"Come on, Joe, let's go inside." She tugs at his arm, and he slowly unfolds from the seat. When he stands, he sways uncertainly. Betty fits her full body under his arm, to help balance him. Then, the two of them shuffle toward the building.

When Joe stumbles, I rush forward to help, but Betty's dagger stare warns me away. She jostles him, until he takes more of his weight on his own two feet, and the two of them slowly work their way toward the apartment door.

As I drive home, I keep picturing them tottering together, Joe towering over Betty, so much larger than she, though she shouldered the burden with stubborn loyalty. She isn't much to look at or listen to, but he's no bargain either — a drunk and a scoundrel. Yet, the lasting impression I had was of them as a unit, a whole, supporting each other, being stronger because the other was there.

In the dark of my car, in my deepest thoughts, I'm surprised to realize that a part of me is jealous, not of either of those very sorry people, but of what they have.

SUNDAY

All night, I toss and turn, not quite sleeping, but not awake enough to go downstairs and resume working. I know I doze, because the green radiant arms on the Big Ben alarm clock jump the hours from one glance to the next. Asleep or awake, the same scenes play in my mind, over and over, a jumble of my various encounters of the past week, mixed up with incidents and conversations from so many years ago, returning always to Joe. Of course, it isn't just one person that my mind sees, but the many people he has been, as he's changed through the years.

My childhood playmate and protector.

The boy I'd once believed was my second self.

My love.

My betrayer.

Wayne's brother and co-conspirator.

Maybeth's plaything and cohort.

My personal tormentor.

And, now, a thieving drunk, swindling my Gramma, stealing from her checking account and wheedling his way into her will when she was at her weakest.

Of course, it isn't Joe who has changed through the years, but my ability to see him more clearly, as I've learned the truth of him. Joe has ever been true to his nature, just as Gramma knew he would be, growing into his birthright as the shabby son of a worthless father.

I accepted all that long ago. Then, why does it still hurt so much?

Around 4:00 am, the snow begins again, thick, heavy flakes, turning the farm into a snow globe wonderland. How many times in my life have I lain here, watching the snow, dreaming or crying or simply enjoying the beauty of it all?

I see the beginning of dawn, a slight lightening of the sky, making everything grey and indistinct. The next thing I know, the sun is streaming in through my window; I've overslept. Not believing my eyes when I look at the Big Ben, I count the muffled chiming of the grandfather clock. Ten o'clock! Only one day left, and I've wasted hours already.

Nick and Eddie show up around eleven. I recognize the loud banging at the front door from yesterday. Obviously, Nick isn't one who does anything halfway, throwing all his considerable weight at the door. As before, I put the rifle in the study, check the view outside to be sure it's safe to go outside, and then open up for them.

"Mornin', Mz. Ormand," Nick says. I didn't really talk with him yesterday, and I'm surprised at how gruff his voice is, grating on my nerves with its guttural resonance.

"Good morning." Scanning the driveway behind them, I ask, "Isn't Anita with you?"

"She's at church." Nick doesn't hide his disgust at the idea. "Told us to come along and finish the job."

Apparently, Eddie is content to let Nick do all the talking. However, he's staring at me in a strange, almost apologetic way. When I return his gaze, he averts his eyes.

Dismissing my misgivings as an overactive imagination, fed by my terror of Wayne and memories of Joe, I thank them for returning, take them into the new wing, and show them the closets, cupboards, bureaus and chests that need to be cleaned out. "When you're done, please don't forget the boxes you left yesterday, in the kitchen and my grandparent's bedroom," I remind them.

Then I return to the old part of the house and begin going through whatever closets and cabinets I haven't yet tackled. So many nooks and crannies! Whenever I think I'm nearly finished, I rediscover somewhere else that needs to be checked, just in case it holds a memento I don't want to leave behind. Or perhaps, another will.

In the early afternoon, I realize how hungry I am, and that Eddie and Nick need to be fed, too. I put together a couple of plates with two turkey sandwiches each, plus potato salad and coleslaw. I also cut two large slices of a chocolate layer cake from the *shiva*. Then I go into the new wing, to tell them it's time to break for lunch.

I hear them arguing about something as I approach Robby's bedroom. I call out, "Lunchtime, guys," and both abruptly stop speaking before I open the door.

Eddie is at the closet, carefully removing and folding clothes, while Nick is pulling out a drawer from the bureau, and upending it over a box.

"I've put together a lunch for you," I say from the doorway. "It's on the kitchen table. Help yourself to some milk or soda from the ice box."

"That's awful nice, Mz. Ormand," Eddie says, though he still doesn't look directly at me.

"Yeah, nice." Nick pushes the drawer back into the bureau, with an audible scraping of wood being forced against wood. I hope he isn't doing any permanent damage to that lovely old piece.

Before they get to the kitchen, I take my own lunch into the study, closing the door behind me. I really don't want to spend more time in the same room with them than is necessary. When I finish, I wait until I hear them heading back to the new wing before taking my plate and glass into the kitchen to wash up. That's when I see the newly emptied cans of beer in the trash. But what do I expect from such men? I only hope that they aren't too inebriated to get their work done.

I hate that my fear of Wayne has kept me trapped in the house. I simply must get to the barn and other outbuildings and see what's out there. If not now, when people are on the farm with me, when?

Of course, I take the rifle with me. I can depend on nothing — and nobody — else. When I pass Joe's pickup, with its front end crumpled against the old tree, I'm surprised that no one has come to get it. If Joe is too hung over, Betty or Wayne could have easily come for it.

Climbing the rickety wooden ladder to the barn's hayloft, with the rifle balanced in the crook of my arm, is a slow, precarious process. In one corner is Grampa's hoard — the things that Gramma didn't want in the house, and would sometimes throw away, but which he would rescue and put up here. I wonder, was it Grampa, not Gramma, who saved that ugly chair and photos in my room? That would make more sense. Despite Gramma's private sharp-tongued disapproval of Joe, Gramps had a soft spot for him.

What was strange was that I never saw Grampa looking at these boxes. Once he put something away in his hayloft corner, it seemed as though he forgot it had ever existed.

I lean the rifle against the wall. Then, one by one, I open his boxes, but find nothing other than broken pieces of pottery and china, chipped crystal, ragged clothes, brittle yellowed documents and such. No doubt, each broken or torn piece had been important to him. Holding a cracked, faded sepia photo that must have been from the 19th century, I can almost hear his voice, lilting with his contagious humor, catching on his sense of loss for people I never knew. The woman is standing behind the seated man, her hand draped on his shoulder; they were so rigidly posed that I can barely discern any humanity in the picture. Looking more closely, I see a sparkle in their eyes, perhaps a shared joke, so like Gramps that I ache to know who they were. But, without his stories to make them alive for me, they're nothing more than two long dead strangers.

Why didn't I record his stories when I had a chance?

As I go through the other piles in the hayloft, that photo keeps nagging at me, until I retrieve it and put in it my pocket. Maybe, someday, I'll learn who they were. Until then, I'll let my curiosity about them be my link to Gramps' memories.

Just as I uncover an old, beautifully carved cradle, I hear a car. Looking out one of the filmy grey windows, I see Jeff Smith helping his father-in-law AH Engelhardt out of a big American car. Undoubtedly something expensive like a Lincoln or Cadillac. I've never been able to tell the difference among makes or models. When he stands, AH leans heavily on Jeff for a few moments, until he's balanced squarely on his feet. Then, Jeff hands him his two aluminum canes and takes a step back, respectfully giving AH the space to walk slowly but resolutely toward the house on his own steam. Jeff keeps pace with him, an arm's distance away. They stop briefly to look at Joe's pickup. AH says something to Jeff, then the two of them move on.

I'm slowed by my tentative climb down the ancient ladder that feels like it's about to splinter at any minute. By the time I'm out of the barn, they've already reached the front porch. "AH! Jeff!" I call. "Hello!"

They turn and wave. At least, Jeff does, while AH partially lifts his right cane and shakes it slightly in greeting. Their dear faces are so familiar to me, part and parcel of all that was good about living here on the farm with my grandparents. Seeing them standing at the front door and recognizing how their smiles become broader as I approach make me feel lighter, the weight of the world momentarily slips from my shoulders.

"What a nice surprise," I say as I brush my lips against AH's cheek, then Jeff's. Both clean shaven, Jeff's flesh is rougher, with a slight bristle, while AH's is silky smooth and more pliant.

"Well, if Mohammed won't come to the mountain," AH quips in a gruff manner that I once would have taken as a reprimand for not having found the time to visit him. How I used to fear his jibes when I'd been a child. Now, I see the sparkle in his eyes and know that he's teasing me, as he always had.

In the way they dress, they are as different as two men could be. Jeff wears faded blue jeans and a navy blue pea jacket over a denim shirt. When I take AH's full-length wool coat, Homburg hat and kidskin gloves to put in the hall closet, I see that he wears a beautifully tailored double-breasted blue blazer, grey flannel trousers and his ubiquitous crimson school tie. How like AH to dress according to some outmoded yet appealing concept of respect for a house of mourning.

Jeff hangs up his own jacket, then walks around looking at the empty walls and bare shelves in the foyer and living room, the sealed and half-packed boxes and crates scattered about. "You've been busy," he says.

It isn't a criticism or complement. Just a statement of fact. Even so, I feel as though I should explain myself. My grandparents' home is a shambles, devoid of all the small details that Jeff and AH are accustomed to seeing. But what can I say that won't sound like a child defending herself? I decide to not respond at all and change the subject.

"You wouldn't believe what I just found in the hayloft," I say. "A fabulous baby cradle. Hand carved cherry, I think, with the most delicate floral designs. I wonder how old it is."

"Floral, you say?" AH asks. "Does it have a face on the back piece, like an angel watching over the baby?"

"Yes."

"Well, I'll be! If it's the cradle I think it is, you've stumbled on a valuable piece of your family's history. For over 100 years, nearly every baby in our family was rocked in that cradle, including your mother and uncle." AH turns to Jeff. "Son, why don't you climb up into the hayloft and bring it down here. I want to see that cradle."

Jeff takes his jacket from the closet and while he's buttoning it back up, AH adds. "When you're done with that, make yourself useful or go for a walk. This young lady and I have some things to talk about."

Jeff nods. "Judith, AH obviously wants me out of the way. Is there anything I can do, to help?"

Not wanting to take advantage of him, but realizing how much help I really could use, I hesitate. "If it isn't an imposition..." I start to say, until I see the look Jeff is giving me. He was never one to voice annoyance or anger, but whenever he would lift one eyebrow and cock his head like that, I had learned to take another tack. "I do need a count of the boxes I've already packed. They're all over the place, including the new wing. And..." I pause, uncertain if what I was about to ask would be too much of a strain for him. After all, Jeff might look fit and trim, but he's about sixty years old.

"Yes?" he asks.

"Well, if it isn't too much for you, I really should get all the boxes together in one place. I don't know where.... I guess piled up in the living room and foyer, as long as we have a path to get through them. Not the boxes in the kitchen or master bedroom... they're for the thrift store... or the ones that Eddie and Nick are packing in the new wing."

"Done," he says.

"But, Jeff, some of them are quite heavy."

"Don't worry; I'll get help. Bobby's home; I'm pretty sure he has nothing special planned for today. My son has almost as strong a back as AH did in his prime." He pulls his phone from his pocket, and thumbs a speed dial. "I'm assuming there's a hand truck in the barn?" he asks.

"Used to be."

Jeff starts talking on the phone as he walks out the door. "Bobby, can you get over here to the Schmoyer farm? Judith has some boxes...."

In the kitchen, AH sits at the table while I warm up some apple strudel and put the kettle on to boil. He belongs here, in Gramma's kitchen, as much as that old plank table, the walnut cabinets, and the view through the big windows. Fixtures that can't be conveniently packed away. However, the room is a ghost of what it once was; so much has been carted away to the thrift store or into my own boxes. Undoubtedly, AH notices, but he makes no comment about it. I find the canister of AH's favorite tea — Earl Grey — next to the stove, where Gramma used to keep it for when he would visit.

AH stares at me in silence while I set the table. Then, with a wide grin, he says, "You know, you're the spitting image of Martha. Don't look anything like her, of course, but I've never known two women more alike. It is good to be in this kitchen with you, child, and see how much of Martha is still here with us."

"Thank you."

"Yes, indeed. And you've a right to be pleased about it. Still, your grandmother was no saint, I can tell you." He pauses, his face darkening for a moment, an unspoken unease just below the surface, but then he continues in the same jovial manner. "Stubbornest woman I've ever known, and you've got that, too. Haven't you?"

I don't really think he's asking me a question so much as making a point. So, I don't bother answering with more than a small smile.

For the next few minutes, AH chatters away without saying very much about anything while I get the strudel out of the oven and prepare the tea. Once the tea is poured and the cake served, he continues spouting inconsequential nothings about different people in Black Bear, most of whom died long ago. Then he abruptly returns to the same train of thought about Gramma.

"As I was saying, you've a lot of Martha in you, young lady, and you know how much I loved that woman. From the day she was born...." He pauses. "But you've heard that story, probably more times than you care to count."

"I've never tired of it." I'm not being merely courteous; I have learned to appreciate those kinds of stories. Something about the way old folks weave their memories into tales that grow with each telling is enchanting and enthralling. Or, maybe, it's simply because Gramps and Gramma's voices are forever stilled, and AH is my only tenuous link to them.

"You're flattering an old man." His eyes twinkle

with pleasure. "Not that I don't enjoy it. Your grandmother wasn't averse to employing the same tactics when they were useful, and they often worked on me. But she sometimes got herself in trouble, setting her mind on a goal, before she thought things through. Sound familiar?" AH takes a sip of tea and watches me over the rim of the mug.

"AH, I'm not sure what you're trying to say, but whatever it is, I'd rather you'd come right out with it."

"Fair enough." He takes one more sip, pats his mouth with a corner of his napkin, then folds it neatly on the table. "Judith, I fear you may have backed yourself into a corner. And being Martha's granddaughter, you might end up being stuck there, because you don't know how to turn around once you've set your feet on a particular path."

"Please," I insist. "I understand that you like your folksy metaphors, but we both know you're a Harvard man and can say things quite clearly and directly when you want."

AH leans forward, his arms crossed in front of him on the table. "Judith, you're moving too damn fast for your own good. Selling this farm like it's no more than a sack of potatoes, when I know you love this place. Henry and Martha are probably rolling over in their graves. Not to mention all of your other ancestors who worked and lived on this land, gave their lives to it, and were given life in return by it. You mustn't sell it. It's not yours to sell, but a trust you've been given, to hold onto and treasure and pass on to your children when you have them."

"I have no desire to live in Black Bear…" I start to explain.

He quickly cuts me off. "It's not about what you want or don't want, Judith." His words are clipped, the consonants forced through a tightening jaw. "This is about what you owe your family and yourself. A home like this isn't simply a piece of real estate you can own one day and not the next. It's the earth that made you who and what you are, and, if you sell it, years from now, when you look back on your life, you'll find that something essential, something vital, is missing within you." The veins in his temples bulge

purple against his pale parchment-like flesh. "I can't sit by
and let you do this to yourself, Judith. It's not too late to
change your mind and save yourself a whole parcel of
heartache. All you have to do is get off your high horse and
break out of this damned stubborn trap you set for
yourself."

"I don't belong here."

"Nonsense, girl!" AH's hands ball up into white-
knuckled fists that shake with his passion. Deliberately flat-
tening his palms on the table, he takes a deep breath. "While
we're talking about mistakes that you're making but still
have time to correct," he continues. "What is this foolishness about contesting Martha's will?"

"With all due respects, that's my private business."

"No, child. It's Martha's business... and executing
her will as she wanted is the last thing we'll ever be able to
do for her."

"AH, I know you think you're trying to help..."

"No, I'm not going to help you one iota. You need
to start doing it for yourself. All I can do is remind you of
your obligation to Martha... and to yourself."

"Do you know what the will says? Somehow Joe
Anderson conned Gramma and got her to leave a chunk of
money and Grampa's hunting lodge to him."

"Martha? Conned? Now, that's simply hogwash."

"It must have been while she was sick. Perhaps, she
didn't know..."

"Don't be daff. Martha may have been bull-headed,
but she never lost control of her senses. I was there at the
end. She was as lucid as anyone I've seen under similar
circumstances."

"You don't know...."

"No, Judith. *You* don't know what you're doing.
Not only to Joe, but to yourself. Selling this farm. Contra-
vening Martha's last wishes..." AH shakes his head slowly,
his eyes downcast. "It's so very wrong. How can I get you
to understand, that some things once done can never be
undone? Those are the mistakes that will haunt you to your
dying day. When you're old as I am, your regrets will keep

you up at night, rob you of peace and pleasure, make you realize how much life you squandered. Don't do it, Judith. Please. Turn around, pull yourself out of this mess while you still can. It's not too late for you." He unfolds the napkin and dabs at the corners of his eyes, where tears threaten to pool. Then, he busies himself with the piece of strudel on his plate, concentrating on calmly cutting a small piece with his fork and then chewing it resolutely. I recognize the ploy; I use it myself often. Focusing on the trivial to divert attention, including your own, from much larger and more emotional issues.

If you had told me when I was a teenager that I would ever see AH teary, and that I would be the cause of it, I would have laughed. Not this tough old geezer, with his understated sense of humor that made me certain he was testing me. I was so frightened of him and what he might say to and about me. Now, I'm filled with remorse that I've upset him. It doesn't really matter that he has the facts all wrong and doesn't fully understand the situation. He loved my Gramma, and with her gone, all he has left of her are her stated last wishes — and me. Regardless of how misguided he is, I can't hurt him any further. So, I lie to him.

"Thank you for your concern. I'll consider what you've said."

He looks up from his plate, his eyes now dry and clear, the way they were in my youth, when I thought he could see right through me. "Don't coddle me, young woman. I know your tricks as well as I knew Martha's. It's going to take a heck of a lot more than a blabbering old codger like me to get you to change your mind." He pats his lips with the napkin once more, folds it again, and leans forward. His dark eyes bore into me, the air between us bristles with his dogged determination. "All Martha's life, I watched over her, tried to protect her, mostly from her own damned foolishness. She knew I'd never betray her trust, but some things…" AH pauses and sighs deeply. "You have a right to know, child. Martha wasn't …"

"Mz. Ormand." I hadn't heard Eddie come into the kitchen, and from the way AH flinches, it's evident that he hadn't either. "Sorry to interrupt, but me and Nick got some questions about some stuff. Well, I got the questions, and Nick sez ta stop botherin' him with 'em, and ask you."

"Yes, Eddie?"

"It's a closet ya didn' show us. Lots of clothes, but other stuff, too. I don't know what ya want us to do with that other stuff."

"Okay, Eddie, give me a moment, I'll come see what you're talking about."

With a nod of satisfaction, Eddie leaves.

As I stand to follow him, I say, "AH, please excuse me."

With the tension of the moment broken, AH seems to collapse into himself, in relief perhaps. But relief from what? Leaning heavily on the table, he gets up onto his feet. "It's time for me to leave, and for you to do some thinking."

I rush over to help him, but he shoos me away; he needs to do as much for himself as possible. Too much has already been taken from him by time and illness. I hover in the background, while he fights for balance.

When I follow AH into the living room, a young man I've never seen before is putting a box onto a new stack near the window seat. About sixteen or seventeen years old, with light brown hair pulled back into a short pony tail, he towers well over six feet and is sinewy thin. His face is open and friendly, though scarred with the pockmarks of poorly managed adolescent acne.

"Hello Mr. Engelhardt, Miss Schmoyer," he says in a high tenor voice.

"Hello," I respond. "Actually, it's Ormand, not Schmoyer. And you are....?"

He wipes his palms on his jeans, before offering his hand to me. "I'm Johnny. Johnny Peters."

Just then Bobby, Jeff's son, walks into the room, followed by another boy, both carrying a box. "Hi Judith. See you met Johnny. This is Tony."

I watch, astounded, as the boys put down their loads and leave again, presumably, to get more boxes.

AH grins at me. "Guess Bobby got the word out

that you needed help."

I stare at him. At least, my mouth hasn't dropped wide open. "Who are they?"

"Johnny is Maybeth Peter's oldest boy. Tony's folks moved here from The Bronx, a few years back, after 9/11. Good solid Irish Italians, who hit some hard times."

Maybeth's son? He doesn't look anything like her, except for his coloring. His face is much broader than hers, with a large nose and square jaw. She had to have had him right out of high school. But, no, he doesn't look like Joe, either. So, they must have broken up soon after I left, or she continued in her old free and easy ways even while the two of them were a "couple." What I don't understand is why her son is here, helping me.

The boys have been busy. The living room is nearly filled with neatly stacked piles, about shoulder high, dozens of boxes, each numbered with thick, black felt pen strokes.

The boys return, carrying still more cartons, with Jeff behind them, wheeling in two of Mom's crated sculptures on the old hand truck.

"I found the cradle," Jeff says.

AH and I follow him through the maze of stacks to the arch between the living room and foyer.

"Is this the one you remembered?" Jeff asks, as he picks it up and hefts it onto a nearby pile of boxes, so AH can reach it.

Larger than the box it rests on, it rocks slightly at first, then is still. The wood is bleached dry by time and neglect, but the grace of its curved silhouette and the artistry of the fine woodwork still shine through.

AH hooks his right cane on his left wrist, and lovingly strokes the cradle's smooth, worn wood, his fingertips tracing the delicate floral carvings along the sides, then reaching to caress the angel's face on the headboard. "The first time I saw this cradle," he says softly, "was the night your grandmother was born." His voice is tender and low, as if he doesn't want to disturb the sleeping child his memories see.

I imagine AH as a young boy, gazing down on a

newborn child — my Gramma. So many years ago. Even so, the time must seem compressed to AH. A short moment, a lifetime. How lonely he must be, to find himself so old, all his childhood friends gone. Yet, the cradle is still here, spanning the generations.

"Look closely at this cradle, Judith," AH says, his voice still soft, but with an adamant edge. "If you sell this farm, this..." He points his knobby forefinger at the cherub in the headboard. "... this is exactly what you'd be walking away from, this sense of belonging, of a connection to something much larger and deeper than any one person's memories. Sell this farm, and you'll never again feel the way you do right now, looking at this tired, old piece of carved wood."

He then places his hand on my shoulder. I expect it to be a heavy weight, as he leans on me. Instead, it's warm and gentle, similar to how he touched the cradle, as though I'm an extension of it, a living remnant of those he loved and lost.

"You're young, Judith. You think you have all the time in the world ahead of you, but now is all you'll get in this life. A long string of nows. How you use each day, the decisions you make along the way, what and who you choose to keep with you from one moment to the next... these are the things that matter in the end, that define who you are and the shape your life takes. Think carefully, child. What you are planning to do today is downright wrong, and you won't get a second chance to correct it. In this one thing, don't be like Martha." His eyes cloud for a brief moment. I have the impression he is about to say something else. Instead, he gently squeezes my shoulder, takes his right cane from his wrist, and leaning on the two canes, navigates around the boxes to the hallway.

After helping him with his coat, and handing him his hat and gloves, I kiss him on each cheek. I will probably never again see AH Engelhardt. I walk with Jeff and AH to the car, and hug Jeff, with a heartfelt "Thank you."

Then, I turn to AH. Bracketed by those aluminum canes, he is physically unapproachable. He grins, hooks the two canes on the open car door, and, leaning his back against the car frame, raises his arms toward me. When we embrace, I sigh deeply, inhaling the aroma of old tobacco and wintergreen liniment, but also of the woods where we once hunted and the lake where we used to fish, of jokes I never understood and an ageless love I never before recognized.

He reclaims his canes and slowly maneuvers into the passenger seat. Through the open window, he pats my hand. "Goodbye, Judith."

"Goodbye, AH" I respond. It's so inadequate, but all that is left to be said. He will never understand why I have to sell the farm and leave Black Bear, forever.

I watch them drive out past the bend to the road before returning to the house and all the work I still have to do.

In the foyer, I stand by the cradle, my hand draped on it, absentmindedly tracing the floral carvings. The boys wander in and out of the room, stacking more boxes.

As Bobby walks past me, headed back to the new wing, he glances at the cradle and says, "Neat old piece."

"Yes," I reply. "I'll be sorry to leave it."

"Well, then, don't." Bobby's enthusiasm and directness make me feel old, defeated.

"I've no choice."

"Pop says you've always got choices."

How do I explain to this boy that I promised myself I wouldn't take any furniture? If I start with this one small heirloom, it would be like letting the camel's nose inside the tent. "Look at it, Bobby. It's too big. How in heaven's name do you expect me to pack it?"

He carefully examines it from several sides. "Shouldn't be much of a problem." Johnny returns, carrying a box; Tony has two more on the hand truck. "Hey, Johnny, come here," Bobby says.

Johnny puts down his box. "What's up?"

"We gotta figure out how to pack this thing." Bobby taps the cradle. "Any ideas?"

"Got any wood?" Johnny asks.

"Lots," I reply. "In the barn."

"Okay" is all Johnny says as he grabs a roll of bubble wrap under one long arm and the cradle in the other.

Bobby opens the front door for him, and he's gone, before I can react with anything other than the sense that somehow I've lost control over the situation.

"Don't worry, Judith," Bobby tries to reassure me. "Johnny's real handy. You should see some of the stuff he's built."

"Uh, sure, thanks, Bobby. For all this, too." I gesture at the room full of boxes. "It's a big help."

"No problem. We're happy to do it." When Bobby shrugs and gives me a small smile, he looks more like his father than I realized. He has the same slight, tight build, and the same gentle grey eyes that focus completely on me, fully interested and involved in being with me for that moment. Then, it's gone, and he's once again just a kid with a job to do and no time to chat. He lopes off to the new wing.

I wander through the maze of boxes. Part of me — the rational, highly organized business woman me — is aghast at the volume of things that all these boxes represent. But that doesn't really matter. For once in my life, I'm content being purely sentimental. Each carton contains items that evoke tender memories, mementos of the people who loved me, created me. Then, why do I feel suddenly paralyzed, uncertain what of the many things still remaining I should tackle next? Then, I remember that Eddie is waiting for me.

Eddie seems relieved to see me. He doesn't appear to be comfortable with uncertainty, with not knowing what he should or shouldn't do.

Nick is in the corner guest room, tossing linens from an old hope chest into a carton. He looks up and stares at us through the open doorway, an apprising, leering squint that sends a chill down my spine. I suppose he's annoyed that Eddie has asked me to check on things.

Eddie shows me the storage closet hidden in the eaves behind the hall bathroom. I had completely forgotten it was there. Quickly flipping through the hangers of old clothes, I see nothing of value. On the shelves above the hanging clothes is a jumble of hats, gloves, scarves, sweaters, swim suits, and even ice skates — things Gramma kept in case a guest forgot to bring along one or the other. Then I push my way through the clothes to the back of the closet, which is filled with large plastic containers. Years ago, I helped Gramma organize all their Christmas ornaments, lights, wrapping and bows in them.

"You can take everything in there, Eddie. Thanks for asking."

"The Christmas stuff, too? Looks kinda nice."

"Yes, the Christmas stuff, too."

The first Christmas I remember spending at the farm was the year I came to live with Gramma and Grampa. I had spent winter holidays here before, but that was when I was too young to understand anything. All I have are vague happy sense memories of the pungent smells of evergreens and cookies baking and piles of wrapped gifts that I was handed to tear open — many of them especially for me. However, Mom and *Papa* didn't think it was appropriate for me to celebrate Christmas. So, by the time I was six, they made certain that we always had other plans for our winter holidays, far from Pennsylvania.

It wasn't until I was twelve and studying for my *bat mitzvah*, that I had a real Christmas. I wasn't sure how I should behave, what was expected of me. After all, I knew that Jews don't celebrate Christmas. Still, a part of me loved the spectacle, all the jingling joyous music, bright colors and twinkling lights, just when winter's dark short days were taking hold.

When Grampa invited me to go into the woods and pick out our Christmas tree, I was as happy as any child, riding in the pickup deeper into the hunting lodge's forest than I had ever been. I carefully inspected every tree Gramps suggested, rejecting each, for one reason or another. Just as the snow began, we found the perfect tree, a lush, green spruce that towered even over Grampa, whose heavy branches spread out around it symmetrically. It wasn't too tall for the living room, however, and it wasn't too large for the two of us to pull onto the truck bed, though we were both sweating when we finished.

Gramma ooh'd and aah'd over the tree. "The most wonderful, most beautiful, I've ever seen." She made me feel as though I were personally responsible for making her so happy, for picking out the very best Christmas tree there ever could be.

Then the three of us decorated it together, draping the lights and tinsel carefully on each branch. One by one, Gramma gently removed the ornaments from their cotton swaddling and gave them to me to hang where they caught the light just so. Grampa seemed to have stories about each glass, porcelain or cloth ornament, about the people who first made or bought it, and about the Christmases of his childhood.

That was my first real Christmas, and it was wondrous. But, in the quiet times, I couldn't help pondering if I weren't being disloyal to Mom by letting myself become a part of what was the ultimate non-Jewish, perhaps even anti-Jewish, celebration. Not that Gramma and Grampa didn't make an effort to acknowledge my Jewishness whenever they could. For instance, even though *Chanukah* came early that year and had already ended, Gramma kept Mom's simple silver menorah on the fireplace mantle during the entire season, just above the red stockings we hung.

In early January, when we finally took everything down, and Grampa carted the tree out to the woods to dry up and rot away, I felt sorry that we had ever cut it down. If we had left well enough alone, it would still be alive, reaching to the sky, further and further with each passing year.

After that first magical Christmas, I never again went out with Grampa to select and cut down a tree. Nor did I ever again feel comfortable with all the fuss and fun of that particular holiday. But I wish I could remember his stories about the ornaments.

With Johnny Peters working in the barn, building a crate for the cradle, and with so many other people in the house, I feel that I'm safe in going out to inspect the various outbuildings.

I find nothing that I want to keep in the garage, the sheds, or the old cold house where Grampa's forebears stored perishable food and Gramma kept her garden tools.

The first thing I notice when I walk into the barn is the cradle on Grampa's workbench, swathed in a thick cocoon of bubble wrap. Johnny is squatting, his long, lanky figure folded in on itself to fit under the tool overhang, so he can reach into the piles of lumber scraps. Between him and the workbench are several planks he has already laid aside. He finds another, tests its strength by flexing it across his knee, shakes his head and puts it back.

How often I saw Gramps do the same thing, bending a piece of wood or knocking on it, sometimes even sniffing it, gauging its wholeness and suitability by sound, smell or heft. Mom probably had the same instincts, but no matter how much I've tried, that innate knowing doesn't flow in my veins as it had in theirs.

Johnny is so involved in what he's doing that I'm not sure he knows I'm there, watching him. That makes me uncomfortable, as though I'm a peeping Tom, an interloper in my own barn.

My own barn???

Never before have I thought of it as mine, as opposed to my grandparents' property. I quickly shove that unwanted thought aside, dismissing it as an unwarranted emotional reaction — my annoyance at Maybeth's son usurping Gramps' workshop, seemingly belonging here more than I ever did — at his ability to confound and confuse me by being so ready to help me.

I clear my throat, to announce my presence. Johnny starts at the sound, nearly banging his head on the overhang, but he quickly recovers when he sees me.

"Have you found what you need?" I ask.

"Sure thing." He stands, telescoping slowly to his full height, wood planks clasped in both hands. "But most of this stuff is too good to use for a crate."

"Don't worry about that. Use whatever works."

"But you've got some fine lumber here, Miss Ormand. It'd be a pity to waste it."

"It's all going to waste anyway, Johnny. Might as well put some of it to good use." Now that he's brought up the subject, I remember how Gramps prided himself in using only the finest quality lumber. "I'll tell you what, Johnny. Build me the strongest, most secure crate you can imagine, and you can take as much of the other wood as you can carry, as my thank you."

Johnny stares at me wide-eyed, like a kid given *carte blanche* in a candy store, afraid to believe it could possibly be true. "Seriously?" he asks.

"Seriously."

He looks at the planks in his hands, then at all the wood around us, apparently speechless, or maybe he's calculating its considerable value, and determining how he'll transport and store it.

"Only if the crate you build for me is so strong and secure that nothing could possibly happen to that cradle, regardless of how rough the shipping handlers are."

"Yes, M'am." His voice is almost a soldier's snap of a parade salute.

I wander around the barn while he assembles lumber, nails and tools. Ostensibly, I'm looking around to see what I might want to take with me, but to be perfectly honest, I want to keep an eye on Maybeth's son, who's about the same age I was when I left Black Bear.

Hearing Johnny power up Gramps' table saw, the grinding of the wood against the saw's sharp spinning teeth, sends a chill up my spine. I've never gotten over my fearful fascination of that machine. As a youngster, I tried to learn to use it, under Grampa's expert guidance; however, my hand shook so much that we both decided it would be safer if I'd let him or Joe do any wood cutting I needed.

Johnny handles that fearsome machine with assured competence and familiarity. I eventually dispense with the pretense of being busy, and watch him. Bobby was correct about Johnny's skill. I watch as he measures a plank, marks where he needs to cut, and then feeds it steadily into the saw.

"You're a carpenter?" I ask, during a lull when his hands aren't near the saw blade. It would be a rather good trade for a boy like him to pursue.

"I like to build things," he responds. "Mr. Hendricks says that means I'm supposed to be an architect or engineer."

"Mr. Hendricks?"

"My guidance counselor at school. He's been great. Helped me get a full scholarship to Penn State."

I hadn't imagined Maybeth's son as the type to go to college; she barely graduated high school. "Architecture and engineering both require years of hard study," I tell him.

"That's okay. I'm pretty good at that."

"I'll say." I hadn't heard Bobby and Tony come into the barn. "Johnny gets straight A's."

Johnny looks up from measuring another plank, a slight blush reddening his ears. "Not really, Bobby."

"Yeah, right," Tony retorts. "You got a B once, didn't you? What was it in? Gym?"

"You know it isn't that way, Tony." Johnny acts as though being set apart as an honors student is embarrassing for him.

After an awkward moment of silence, Bobby says, "We're done with the boxes. Anything else you want us to do?"

"I can't think of anything." I shake my head, hesitant to turn down his generous offer, but unable to picture how they could assist me at this point. "You've been a big help, guys. Thank you."

"Well, I could use your help," Johnny pipes up. "See these two piles of wood? I need all the pieces in this pile marked off to the length of this one. Those there need to be four inches shorter. That way, I could just keep cutting. Okay?"

"Sure."

"Okay."

I'm uncomfortable standing by and watching while the three of them work. So, I find another thick pencil and help with the measuring. Johnny continues to feed the planks to the saw, one at a time. I'm impressed with his ability to quickly break down the job into tasks that can be easily delegated. Even more interesting is how readily the other boys accept his sure, easy-going direction. Johnny is a natural leader. Can this bright, intelligent, helpful boy really be Maybeth's son, the girl whose only skills had been sex and being a world-class bitch?

Once the measuring is done, the three of us relax and watch Johnny work. I perch on one of the old high stools, while Bobby stands at the workbench, leaning forward on his arms, and Tony lounges against the wall. We're all mesmerized watching Johnny handle the wood, his large hands feeding each piece to the blur of steel teeth, the clean cut that slowly, steadily forms where the blade bites. When Johnny finally finishes and turns off the motor, the sudden quiet is like the snapping fingers of a hypnotist, a release from the intensity of our shared fascination.

Without a word passing between them, Tony moves forward to lend a hand, holding the pieces in place, while Johnny hammers them together.

I pick up the conversation from where we left off. "So, which will it be, Johnny, architect or engineer?"

Johnny shrugs. "Don't know. Ma says I don't have to decide right away. Just study and find out what's out there."

"Good advice." From Maybeth, of all people. Perhaps, over the years, she finally discovered one useful skill she could do well — being a mother.

"What about the two of you?" I ask Bobby and Tony. "What are your plans?"

Tony looks up at me, but doesn't say anything.

"I'm headed for U of P. I want to be a writer." No longer leaning on the workbench, Bobby becomes animated, his face shining, his manner earnest and energized. "Grandpa says I've got to study business, because writing's no way to earn a living. Besides, he keeps telling me that in a few years, I'll have to take over the business, since Uncle Eugene's sons don't want any part of it. I guess he's right. I mean, heck, if I make it as a writer, then I'll need to know how to handle contracts and money and stuff. If I don't, well, I'll have the skills and smarts to take over Engelhardt Auto."

With the crate starting to take shape, Johnny no longer needs Tony's help holding the pieces in place. So, Tony returns to lounging against the wall. I look at him fully for the first time since we met. He has a mop of thick, black curls over a square, light caramel face. Though his six-foot frame curves in on itself, nothing about him is relaxed. Yet, his tension has no spring to it, no sense of impending action.

"What about you, Tony?" I ask him. "What are your plans?"

He crosses his arms over his chest. "Don't know. No more school, that's for sure. The recruiter says I should sign up. Go into the Army."

"You can't, Tony," Bobby protests, in a manner that makes me think they've been arguing about this for a while. "You'd end up in Afghanistan or some other hellhole."

"What choice do I have? It'd be a job with benefits. And Sarge Murtoy says they'll give me training, teach me a useful skill."

"Benefits? Are you kidding?" Bobby's voice cracks with emotion. "They'll teach you, all right… to kill or be killed, or both."

Tony straightens his back against the wall. "What

d'you want me to do, Bobby? Sit around here, hire out as a part time handyman for the summer folk, when they think to call me? You know there ain't no decent work around here for someone like me. And don't give me that crap about your pop saying there's always a choice."

"But there is," Bobby insists, though with less conviction than before.

"Only when your family has money, or you've got brains and good grades, like Johnny. All I've got are my two hands, and the only people interested in helping me do something useful with them is the Army."

It's the old story about the Poconos: not enough jobs, and too few skilled workers to attract new industry. Tony isn't the first kid from the area to look to the military when nothing else offers him a decent future. Just as Joe had once dreamed of the Navy giving him his one chance. How different it had been for Uncle Robby, who had plenty of opportunities ahead of him and had joined up anyway, out of patriotism. Of course, Mom had seen it as misplaced patriotism that had killed her brother — a casualty of faith— or of Gramma's interference.

"It's done!" Johnny exclaims proudly. Suddenly and without any warning, he picks up the sealed crate, with the cradle inside, and drops it.

"Stop!" I yelp, too late.

It crashes onto the rough-hewn plank floor, bounces, but doesn't break open.

"See?" Johnny picks it up and puts it onto the workbench near me. "It's solid, and with all that bubble wrap, the cradle's safe."

"Couldn't you have proven it without scaring me?"

Johnny grins. "Yeah, but it wouldn't have been as much fun."

"I told you Johnny would do a great job," Bobby quips. "I forgot to mention that he's got a strange sense of humor."

When Johnny takes the crated cradle into the house, I go in for my purse. Then, I walk with the boys to Bobby's car. I pull out six twenties. At first, the boys refuse payment for their help, though not wholeheartedly. When I press them to take the money, they accept it quite graciously.

As we say our goodbyes, I realize I have one more favor I need to ask them. "If the offer is still open, I could use your help with something else," I say.

"Of course. What?" Bobby asks.

"I'm sure you noticed Joe Anderson's pickup over there."

"Yeah, heard he got drunk and totaled it," Tony comments.

How quickly stories travel in Black Bear! The gossip mill has probably worked out how I'm somehow at fault for his self-destruction. Maybe they think I poured the drink down his throat, then forced him off the road.

"Doesn't look totaled to me," Johnny says.

"No, I believe it is quite drivable," I reply. "I was wondering if you could stop at Dutch's, get the keys and come back for it."

"Sure, no problem," Bobby says.

"Johnny, that might be a good way for you to get your lumber… using Joe's truck," I suggest.

"Gee, thanks, Miss Ormand." Johnny practically glows with his delight.

Dusk is already darkening the sky as I watch them drive off. They're good boys, pleasant companions and hard workers — Maybeth's son included.

After turning on all the outside floodlights, I wander the house, not certain what task to tackle next. Nick and Eddie have been rather quiet for some time; I decide to find out what they're doing, when they might be finished and leave. The minute I open the door from the foyer to the new wing, I can hear their voices, though not their words.

Nick is clearly annoyed at something Eddie has said or done, and Eddie sounds as though he's trying to get back onto Nick's good side. Then, I hear a third voice, rougher and more distinct, and much more sinister. "Ed boy, the brotherhood don' brook no deserters. Ya either with us or agin' us."

Wayne!

I freeze in mid-step, too terrified to move, fearful of making any sound that would alert him that I'm within meters of them. Is it possible that my ragged breathing might be as audible to him as it is within my own skull? I clamp down on the gorge climbing up my throat; I refuse to give into the rubbery feeling of futility. I need to get away from them, from *him*, fast. Away from the house that was my only refuge, but no longer.

I creep backwards, toward the side door, thankful that I'm wearing sneakers, trying to remember which floor planks squeak. When the loud creak of the door's old hinges shoot up my spine, I stand stock still, listening to the house with my entire body. Did the men within hear it? Are they moving toward me?

What am I to do now? With the floodlights on full blast, wherever I run, they will see me, will be able to chase me down.

I glance at the barn. My only chance is to get to the hayloft and retrieve the rifle where I left it when I saw AH and Jeff drive up. But can I make it to the barn before they realize that I'm trying to get away?

Throwing caution to the winds, I dash across the driveway and yard, unable to mask the sound of my movement, desperately praying that it's muffled by the old farmhouse's thick walls and the thin coating of snow over the dry fallen leaves.

"*There she is!*" Wayne yells from behind me. "*Get her!*"

I can hear their heavy boot stomps and rasping breaths closing in on me. One is coming up on my right side, another to the left, and the third on my heels. Just like it happened on that terrible night eighteen years ago. This time, I'm damned and determined to fight tooth and nail. I'd rather die than be raped by them again.

I scream when someone grabs me from behind. No, I screech, a wild animal sound torn from the flesh in my throat. My assailant lifts me off my feet, throws me to the ground, and falls on me. It's Wayne. His entire body smothers mine, his full weight compress my lungs so I can barely breathe. I try to kick, but Wayne has pinned both my legs and hands. At least my head is free, so I bite him hard, on his cheek, drawing blood. I thrill at the taste of salty iron flowing from his flesh over my teeth and tongue, knowing I can inflict pain on him, even when he thinks he has me entirely helpless.

"*Fucking bitch!*" He spits in my face, then he butts his forehead against mine, so hard and painful that I almost lose consciousness. "Get the fuck over here and help me teach this cunt a fuckin' lesson she'll never fuckin' forget!" he yells.

I hear people running toward us, but it sounds like more than two. Wayne's buddies who'd been hiding in the woods, watching me? Instead of the other two coming to help Wayne rape me, I hear a surprised "*ooph,!*" followed by the thumping sound of bodies colliding and falling to the ground. From the left, I hear what sounds like fists hitting flesh, and grunts of pain. Suddenly Wayne is off me, so I quickly scramble away on all fours, get to my feet, then run toward the barn and Grampa's rifle.

While running, I glance back, to see what's happening. Tony has his arms and legs wrapped around Nick's back. Eddie is shaking himself and getting up off the ground. Johnny and Bobby are desperately trying to hold Wayne by his arms, but he spins, ripping himself out of their grip, then turns on them, punching like a prizefighter. It's two against one, but the boys are hopelessly outmatched by the much bigger, more experienced bully. Wayne's fist solidly connects with Bobby's head, and he instantly falls with a sick thump against a tree. Johnny's reach is longer than Wayne's, so he manages to keep just out of range of Wayne's fists, but he doesn't seem to know what to do with that advantage.

Eddie catches me before I can get through the barn door, his two hands grabbing my arm, yanking me around. "*No!!*" I shriek, kicking him in the groin with all my might.

Doubling over in pain, he releases me. I resume running for the rifle.

I make it up to the hayloft without being stopped or pulled off the ladder. Thank God, the rifle is exactly where I left it, fully loaded. I'm so shaky, and focused only on getting back to the boys before they're beaten to a pulp, that I slip on one of the high crosspieces of the ladder, but I hold onto the rifle even as my feet dangle below me, swinging in air. Somehow, I manage to plant my feet back onto the rickety rungs and get down the ladder in one piece.

Back on solid ground, I cock the rifle as I rush outside, ignoring Grampa's voice in my head, "Never run with a loaded gun; you'll never know what you might blow off."

Bobby is unconscious, with blood streaming from a nasty-looking head wound into an expanding pool on the ground-cover snow. Wayne and Johnny are wrestling and bashing each other, until Wayne pulls a knife from his boot and slices Johnny across the chest. Johnny collapses into a tight ball, with his knees bent and arms crossed protectively over this chest. Off to the side, almost up against a cherry tree, Nick has Tony in a chokehold, with a stiletto at his throat. Eddie is about to rush me, but stops dead when I swivel the rifle at him and fire off a round just in front of his feet.

Then I point the gun at Wayne. "The next one goes right between your legs, Wayne, if Nick doesn't release Tony." I'm surprised at how calm I am. A buzzing white noise fills my ears, almost like a tantric chant, a reverberating *om*. Everything before me is sharply delineated, with no ambiguities or soft edges. Tony, Bobby and Johnny. Nick, Eddie and Wayne. I see them all, almost motionless, each in his own perfectly staged position, as in a still life tableau. And me, holding the gun, ready to shoot to wound or maim, to kill, if I have to.

"No, girlie," Nick sneers. "Put down the gun, or I cut the kid."

I lock eyes with Wayne, and he finally understands just how far I'm ready to go. Though the floodlights still burn, the entire world seems to recede, swallowed by the night. Only Wayne and I exist, with Nick and Tony somewhere on the periphery.

"Nick, she's not bluffing," Wayne says, his voice as steady and unwavering as his steely stare. Blood streams from my bite on his face, but he doesn't move a muscle.

"Ya think I am? I'll slit this motherfucker's throat from ear to ear if you don't drop that rifle *NOW!*" Nick's sneering tone jars my focus, forcing a slight shift in my tunneled field of view to include not Nick himself, but the blade pressing against Tony's throat, hard enough to create a red pencil-thin dot of blood, then a trickle, then....

Suddenly, two sets of hands grab Nick's arms from behind, twisting the blade out of his hand, violently pulling him off Tony. Jeff Smith and David Weiss throw Nick to the ground, while Eddie runs off into the woods.

I see it all, even recognize Jeff and David, without being surprised that they should be there, but none of it registers. All I know is the solid heft of cold, loaded metal in my hands, pointed at Wayne, aimed not at his groin, but at his chest, where his heart would be, if he had one. The slightest pull of my index finger on the trigger would finally and forever finish all the terror and nightmares, the sordid memories, the filth that never quite washed away.

Then David is at my side, whispering into my ear, with one hand on my shoulder, the other wrapped around the barrel of the rifle, pushing it down towards the ground. "It's over now, Judith."

I'm aware of hearing his voice through the white noise, as though it's someone else hearing it, a person I once dreamed myself to be. He repeats it, a bit louder, and I can no longer deny his presence. I let David take the gun from my hands, and I turn away from Wayne.

I start shaking uncontrollably. My legs begin giving out from under me. Damn, not here, not now!

David yells "*Halt!*" I spin around to see Wayne and Nick run away towards the woods. David lifts the rifle, starts to aim, then he shrugs and lowers the gun.

"*Shoot them! Stop them! They're getting away!*" I scream at David. When he ignores me, I try to yank the rifle from him, but I'm unable to get it out of his tight grip.

"No more killing," David mutters to himself. Then he looks at me, his dark eyes burning with pain and anger. "They're not worth it, Judith. The police will pick them up."

"Police?" The only cops in the area are at the State Police barracks, forty-five minutes away. "Wayne will be long gone by the time they get here. We've got to stop them, now!"

David walks away from me. "No, Judith, our job is to take care of these boys. We radioed for the police when Bobby called us. They'll be here soon enough." He bends down to look at Johnny.

What could I do? Run into the dark woods, where Wayne, Nick and Eddie could jump me again? I don't even have the rifle anymore.

Johnny moans when David gently helps him uncurl so David can look at his wound.

"Thank God, you're wearing such a heavy coat, Johnny," David tells him.

David stands up and walks briskly toward the darkened ambulance parked in the driveway.

"Judith, check Tony," David calls to me, but the words don't really register, not as something requiring a response from me. Just an acknowledgment that I'm still here.

But yes, I now see Tony. He's standing, looking at Bobby on the ground, and at Jeff kneeling beside his son, talking to him, trying to get Bobby to respond. Bobby opens his eyes slowly. "Hi Dad," he says, and at that, Jeff sighs deeply.

David returns, dragging a stretcher with an oxygen tank and two medkits on it. I hear him say to Jeff, "I radioed for the second rig." Then he leaves everything but one kit with Jeff and comes back to Johnny. Johnny is shivering, as he clutches his bleeding chest.

Tony staggers when he tries to pick up the kit from the stretcher to give it to Jeff.

"*Judith!*" David's urgent voice cuts through the fog around me, like a slap on the face. "Tony needs you."

"Tony?" I ask stupidly. What can I do? What can I ever do again? Everything is out of my hands, beyond my control. Has anything ever been within my ability to do, to fix?

"*Judith!*" David is standing next to me again, though I hadn't seen him leave Johnny's side. "You've got to snap out of it right now! I know you've had a fright." He speaks softly, insistently, allowing for no disagreement. "Right now, we need your help." He reaches out and holds both my hands in his, with a pressure that cannot be denied or ignored. "You said you were trained in first aid. Tony's been cut." He continues to squeeze my hands and stare at me, until I allow my eyes to drift to his, to connect with his. "Are you with us?" he asks, and I nod. "Good. Now, go look after Tony. Tell me how bad it is."

In the recesses of my mind, somewhere between conscious and unconscious thought, I understand what David is doing, trying to pull me back into reality. But it's more than that. We have three injured boys, and David and Jeff must take care of the two who seem the most severely hurt — Bobby and Johnny. If I don't pull myself together, there's no one here to help Tony.

I can hear Grampa's voice instructing me exactly what to do. I take Tony by the elbow and guide him to sit on the big boulder under the cherry tree. Fortunately, his wound is more a nick than a cut, the flow of blood is minimal, and it has already begun to scab over. I relay all this to David.

"Excellent. Clean and bandage it, then examine him for any other problems... contusions, abrasions, breaks, internal injuries... you know the drill."

I probe Tony's abdomen for any swelling that might indicate internal problems. "David, when will the police get here?" I ask.

"They're on their way."

"Be sure to tell them that there are four of them, not three." I tell him.

"Who's the fourth?"

"Joe Anderson."

"What?!" David exclaims.

"Naw," Tony mumbles. "Joe's at his garage with a splitting hangover. Saw him when we got the keys to his pickup. Looked green to me. Betty says it serves him right."

Only then, do I look at Tony fully, his blanched face, quivering chin, hunched shoulders, and I see his terror, the horror of helplessness. Tears flow down Tony's slightly grizzled cheeks, and a sob bursts from my lungs, before I can clamp down on it. It took his pain to force me to feel mine, but I can't give into it. Not now, not in public. I concentrate once more on examining his body, retreating behind the armor I've girded around myself. I'm certain about one thing; I am going to make Wayne and Joe pay for this, not just for my own peace of mind, but for Tony, and for Bobby, and for Johnny.

Soon the yard is filled with strobing red lights from Black Bear's second ambulance and, a couple minutes later, three state police cars. A few blue lights as well of village volunteer firemen, who heard the call on their beepers and have come to see what's happening. Grampa often quipped that the local firemen were motivated by about 40% altruism and 60% gawking curiosity. At least, they make themselves useful fending off the reporters and TV crews until the police string up the crime scene tape.

An attractive white woman with raven black hair wearing a Black Bear Ambulance jacket kneels next to me. "What do we have?" she asks me.

"Knife slash to the neck. Nothing major cut. I've found no breaks or other injuries," I respond. Then I stand and let her take over.

Her partner, a man wearing the same red and yellow jacket, concentrates on me. "How are you, Judith? Did they hurt you?"

I don't know him or her, but they obviously know who I am. Staring glassy-eyed at all the people who now swarm around the property, I shake my head in answer to his question. Then I realize that he needs a verbal response, if I don't want to be taken into the hospital for shock. "No, I'm okay…" I look at the metal name tag on his chest.

"...Jack. Please just take care of the boys. They're pretty bad, even Tony, though his wounds are beyond the physical."

A pair of Advanced Life Support vans arrive just as the boys are being loaded onto the two ambulances; paramedics climb into both rigs. Before they take off for Scranton, Jack has me sign a Refusal of Treatment form. "Please let me know how they are," I ask, my voice much calmer than I feel. Inside, I'm crying silently for them, for Bobby, Johnny and Tony, youngsters who jumped head first into danger for my sake. I hadn't even thanked them. I ache to still believe in the power of prayer, to be able to do something, anything for them.

The young, buxom policewoman assigned to question me has a smooth, old-ivory kind of light brown complexion. Was she chosen for the task because she's a woman, or because she's the furthest they have from a pale-skinned redneck? Handing me her card, she introduces herself as Dawn, rather than Officer Evans. She tries her best to turn the official interrogation into a facsimile of an informal conversation, for my sake. It isn't her fault that every word she says, every question she asks cuts too close to the quick.

Officer Evans — Dawn — fills me in on how such a swarm of people came to my rescue so quickly. Bobby, Johnny and Tony heard me screaming when they returned for Joe's truck and the lumber I promised Johnny. Bobby called his father, before quixotically darting off to try to rescue me. Luckily, Jeff and David were just returning from an ambulance call, so they came directly to the farm, after radioing the police and paramedics.

Dawn shakes her head, in a rather good impression of a disapproving school marm. "Jeff and David forgot all their training and rushed headlong into an unsafe situation. Those darn fools know better to wait for the police in these kinds of situations."

What a stupid thing to say. If they had waited for the cops, Wayne would certainly have raped, maybe killed me. Instead, I'm whole and safe, all because Bobby, Tony and Johnny were irresponsible, because David and Jeff ignored all protocols and didn't wait for the cops.

Eventually, one by one, individuals, then groups separate out from the milling crowd, and cars, vans and trucks drive off down the driveway and away from the farm. Joe's pickup too; I suppose one of the firemen got the keys from the boys. As Dawn turns to leave, I clutch her sleeve. "You're not going, are you?" I beg her. "They're still out there."

She places her hand over mine, the warmth of her flesh a sharp contrast to the chill that has taken hold of me. "Don't worry, Judith. We're posting a trooper right here, at your front door," she reassures me. "No one will get past him. In the meantime, we have people combing the woods and the roads back to the Homeland Militia compound. If they're true to form, they'll head there; those bozos think their camp is beyond the reach of the law. Don't worry Judith, they were stupid to attack you, and they'll be stupid enough to get caught."

Before leaving, Dawn introduces me to Officer Alfred Warman, a huge white man in his mid-forties who dwarfs even Joe or Eddie. As he settles into one of the cushioned porch armchairs, I tell him to come in whenever he wants to get warm, needs the bathroom or something to drink or eat.

I should feel safer with him here, but I can't help wondering if he might not fall asleep in that comfortable chair.

The TV crews finally leave. Then, the last of the firemen and police drive off. Only three vehicles remain: my rental, Officer Warman's unmarked car and a great big American sedan. Only AH has a car like that in Black Bear, but I haven't seen him anywhere around.

I find AH sitting at the kitchen table, preparing two mugs of tea. For several moments, I watch him from the doorway, taking pleasure in seeing that dear man once more, in knowing he's here because I need him, and he knew it.

He pours some amber liquid from a silver hip flask into one mug, then looks up at me with a half smile. "Hello, Judith." Holding up the flask, he asks, "How about some Irish in Earl Gray? Best thing for whatever ails you."

He's right. I need something to calm my nerves, if I'm going to hold myself together and not let everything churning in me, all the terror, anger and despondency, boil to the surface. "Thanks, AH. Don't mind if I do."

I sit next to him, in Grampa's chair at the head of the table, and we sip our tea in silence. The heat from both the whiskey and the Earl Grey seep into me, easing some of the knots in my muscles.

"Is Gene with you? Did he bring you?" I'm surprised how calm my voice sounds.

"I'm not so senile that I can't manage to drive my own car when I want to, whatever my son or son-in-law may think." The old fire that used to intimidate me as a child flares in his eyes, and though I'm concerned about him navigating dark roads at night, I say nothing.

Instead, I ask, "How's Bobby?" sure that AH would have the latest update from Jeff at the hospital.

"The boy's got a hard skull. Looks like a mild concussion; they're keeping him overnight for observation."

"What about Johnny and Tony?"

"Johnny's a very lucky young man. He was sliced open from chest to abdomen, but it missed the arteries and organs."

I picture Maybeth, not as the bitchy, busty cheerleader she was in school, but as the weary, hard-working mother I saw at Buck's, pushing groceries down the conveyer belt, day in and day out. "Does Maybeth even have health insurance?" I wonder aloud. "AH, can you help me contact the hospital, so all of Johnny and Tony's medical bills are sent to me and not their folks?" I assume AH will take care of Bobby and would be insulted if I offer to help. But the other boys' families don't have the same resources that Bobby's does.

AH nods solemnly, but he doesn't meet my gaze. Instead, he stares into the steaming mug, holding it so tightly that his hands shake. A greyish yellow pallor leaches the blood from his parchment thin skin. "I've been a god-damned sentimental fool. A hellbent coward!"

Shocked by his outburst, at how dejected he seems, I don't know how to react. Just now, I need AH to be his indomitable self. "A coward, AH? Not you. You stormed the beaches at Normandy."

He appears to not hear me. "I started to tell you the truth this afternoon, Judith, but I stopped short and, I'm ashamed to say, I was relieved to shirk my responsibility. I was going to let you leave without telling you. Now, after all you've been through, to add to your pain.... But if I don't, you'll leave tomorrow, never knowing what really happened." AH locks eyes with me. Then, squaring his shoulders, he pushes onward, a steely edge to his voice. "I can't protect her anymore."

"Gramma? Are you talking about Gramma, AH?"

"She was no angel, but she was my angel. And I spent her entire life protecting her," he declares. Is he ever going to get to the point, if there's any point to get to? "From the moment Mama put her into my arms, a red-faced wailing newborn, to the day she died, I watched over her, and cleaned up whatever messes she got herself into. So many messes! I would have kept her secrets forever, into my own grave. But I can't. Not this one, not when it's cost you so much. If I have to destroy what you think and feel about your grandmother, so be it."

"Please, AH!" I'm trembling in fear, dreading but needing to hear whatever revelation he's about to divulge. "What are you trying to say?"

Swallowing a long gulp of the Irish-laced tea, he then puts his mug solidly on the table and leans forward. "Perhaps I should start when you were born," he rambles on. "A cocoa-brown baby. It was a slap in your grandmother's face, proof of your mother's open hostility and rebellion." AH covers my hand with his. "Don't get me wrong, Judith. Martha loved you. You were flesh of her flesh, even if your flesh were the wrong color, and that confused her."

I pull my hand out from under his. Mustering what little strength I have left, I bite my tongue and promise myself that I will not argue, will not interrupt. I need to be silent and learn the full truth, or at least, AH's version of it.

With a deep breath, he gathers his resources within himself. "When you came here to live, Martha was determined that you would know only her love and not her consternation, that she would do everything possible to make sure your life would be what it could be, should be. To her, it was obvious that you had greatness in you, and you've proven her right in that, Judith, I'm proud to say. However, in her mind, Joe Anderson was a threat. The damned woman believed that he would bring you down to his level, trap you in this village that she herself had never escaped."

Was that what Grampa tried to tell me, about Gramma and why she never grew to be ten feet tall?

"Poor Joe. He didn't have a chance. You know how your Grandmother was; she could sell ice to an Eskimo, if she put her mind to it. Whenever she got Joe alone, she harped on how special you were, how it was his responsibility to protect you, to keep you safe and pure."

Safe and pure? How archaic and absurd those words sound, even coming from the elegant old man himself. And wrong, too, given what really happened, how Wayne and his pals shredded whatever sense of security or purity I might have once had. Of course, AH couldn't know about that, and I suppose, to his mind, the innocence of a young teenage girl was one of those ideals, like Mom and apple pie, sacrosanct and inviolable.

"After Florence came to live with you," AH continues, "Martha became even more of a bulldog. She was damned determined you'd never end up living in a trailer with a gaggle of brats and a mean drunk of a husband. No one would ever lay a hand on you, the way

Hank Metcott beat poor Florence.

"Martha harangued and browbeat Joe until she convinced him that you were far too good for the likes of him. She brainwashed that boy into believing that his one and only mission in this life was to protect you against anything and everything, including and especially himself. Martha didn't give a second thought to Joe, how all this was twisting him inside out. She kept at him, working at his guilt at being an Anderson, the son of a drunken, abusive father and a mother who deserted her own children. Martha told him that if he really loved you, he had to reject you, with no ambiguity or regret."

A sudden, sharp chill slices through me, down to my bones.

"To Joe's credit, he resisted Martha." AH sighs so deeply that it becomes a kind of silence hanging between us for a moment or so. "As long as the boy could dream of getting into the Navy, he could fight her off. But when he was injured... you saw it, how bad it was, folks were saying he'd be lucky if he ever walked again. Lying there on the ground, in all that pain, Joe knew everything was over. Martha's poison was all that was left. He lost all hope, all he had ever dreamed. He had nothing to offer you." AH lifts the mug to his lips, but puts it down untasted.

"Even without Martha, did the two of you ever have a chance of a happy life together? I don't know." AH shrugs, a shiver of his frail shoulders that seems more a resignation to time irretrievably gone than a gesture of uncertainty. "What I do know is Martha schemed and manipulated, until both of you were broken. You left here, believing Joe never loved you, when rejecting you as cruelly as he did was the greatest expression of love I've ever seen."

Love? Calling me those horrid names, laughing at my pleas, my tears? But AH's tale makes a twisted kind of sense. Could Gramma really have orchestrated it all? Did she truly believe such viciousness could be for my own good?

"Martha lived on pins and needles your last year

here, fearing Joe would break down and tell you the truth, or you would figure it out on your own. She had to send you away, permanently, before Joe and you could have a chance to get back together. That is why she extracted that god-awful promise from you to never return here. Henry never knew; me neither, not then. Martha was too damned good at what she did, pulling the wool over everyone's eyes, including sometimes her own. Can you believe it, when she finally confided in me years later, she still believed she had sacrificed her own happiness for yours?

"Martha got a rude awakening, a few years back, when Joe was arrested for attempted murder. He had gone berserk, nearly killing his brother Wayne and two of Wayne's friends. But he refused to say anything about it, even when the police offered him a plea bargain. Then, word got around. Wayne boasted in the prison hospital, about how he and his friends had raped you back in high school. The idiot probably had bragged to Joe, too. No wonder Joe beat the shit out them when he found out."

AH is talking about the rape! He knows about it, and Gramma probably did, too. But Joe didn't — not until years after?! I gulp the whiskey tea, without tasting it, without feeling its heat. Not when I'm burning up inside, charring all that remains of everything I believed true.

"When the story reached Martha, she went to visit Joe in jail. She found a broken shell of a man, whose only real crime had been loving you... and yes, loving her.

"It was horrific," AH continues. "However, out of the horror, Martha now had a new purpose in life, to make up for all that she had done to poor Joe, to atone for all her failures... with Robby and your Mom, too... the mistakes that had haunted and deflated her. In her mind, Joe was her very last chance to make right what she had done so very wrong."

"But he had become everything she had predicted," I protest. "A drunk, a dead end."

AH shakes his head. "We'll never know who or what Joe might have become, if your Grandmother hadn't screwed up his life. All I can say is that once she owned up to her part in his destruction, once she turned the full force of her love and determination to restoring Joe's spirit, he became a solid man, an outstanding citizen, and a good son to her. It was Joe who helped Martha the most through her illness and her death; he was holding her hand when she passed away. With Joe's love and devotion, I do believe that Martha finally found solace and the hope that she just might be allowed to enter the holy gates, to see Henry, Robby and your Mom again."

AH drains his mug in one long gulp. "Judith, I hope you can forgive this foolish old man. In my need to protect Martha's memory, I almost let you leave here tomorrow not knowing the truth. It's the curse of love, that it can do harm in its own name. Does the fact that my silence... and Martha's machinations... grew out of love, does that mitigate the harm we've done? All I can hope is that, when tonight's pain and disillusionment fades, you'll remember how very much you were and are loved."

I sense AH's searching my face, trying to gauge the impact of his words and how I'm taking them. But I can't look at him.

"Judith? How can I help you?"

I don't want to hear him anymore.

"Judith?"

He reaches over to touch my shoulder, but I fend him off, with both my hands in front of me, to ward off any physical contact.

A short, hard rap on the back door jolts through me. Then, the door opens a few inches and Officer Warman peers into the room. When he sees us, he walks in. "I hope I'm not disturbing you, Ms. Ormand... Mr. Engelhardt. I thought you'd want to know that we've caught all four men. Joseph Anderson has an air-tight alibi. He was working at the time. Several people saw him and will swear he never left his garage. So, we released him. We booked the other three on attempted rape, attempted murder, and a half-dozen other charges. With their history, no way the judge'll let them make bail. So, you're safe now, Ms. Ormand, and I'll be going."

I nod. If I speak, would it be in shrieks or sobs?
"Do you want me to stay, Judith?" AH asks.
I shake my head, silently.
"I'm sure you have questions…"
Through my clenched jaw, I rasp, "Not now, AH Maybe later."

I hear AH stand slowly, pushing himself up from the table that creaks slightly under his weight. Though he's behind me, where I can't see him, I have the sensation that he's leaning toward me. It's a magnetic pull on my body that I cannot, will not respond to or acknowledge. Instead, I sit rigidly transfixed, staring at the wood grain pattern of the old plank table.

"Judith, I hate leaving you like this, but I will respect your wishes. Please call me, any time, day or night. I don't usually sleep much these days, and I certainly won't tonight. Let me help you. Please."

His need to touch me is a palpable pressure of the air between us. When I don't move, he sighs and hobbles away.

I hear the officer escort AH off the porch, the tips of his two aluminum canes tapping on the wooden planks, further and further away, until I'm alone. Completely and fully alone.

I don't know how long I sat at the table. Nor do I remember getting up to pace back and forth. I'm disconnected from anything around me. I'm jolted from my stupor, when I stumble against one of the half-filled boxes that Nick and Eddie left yesterday and never got around to taking today.

Damn! I kick the box. Never got around to it? No, raping and killing me was higher on their To Do list!

My head is buzzing. The very air around me is charged with unrelenting, feral energy.

"*J'ai été une maudite imbécile!*" I want to scream, but it comes out as a whine, impotent and defeated.

"Salope!" I kick the box again, with all my might, hearing the satisfying rattle of chipping and cracking glass and china.

"Foute-le!" I reach into the box, grab the first thing my hand touches and throw it with all my might against the counter. Before the shattered pieces of china fall to the floor, I hurl another then another and another, cursing up a storm like a *Parisienne* street *gamine*, not stopping until the box is empty and the floor littered with shards.

Only then, do I see the green dragon tail handle, peeking out from under a large fragment of yellow china. *"Mon Dieu! Non!"* I cry, as I crawl on the floor, among the wreckage, shifting through the rubble with no thought to the splintery cuts I'm getting on my hands. If I do nothing else, I simply must find the rest of the pieces of the mug Mom made for me after we moved to Manhattan.

Mom explained, "Dragons are magical, only because we can believe in them being magical. I want you to hold that within you always."

I didn't really understand what she meant, except that she was trying to make me feel better about all the changes in our lives since leaving *Papa.* "I will, Mama," I promised, because I wanted to make her feel better, too.

After she was killed, I used to take great comfort in holding that mug, filled with hot cocoa, soup or tea, cupping my hands around the warm texture of the dragon's scaly body and head, playing with the curving tail that made up the handle. It would help me remember — so many things — about Mom, about our life together, and about how she'd smile when she dreamed of things that no one else could see until she gave them shape.

Now I've destroyed the dragon.

On my hands and knees, I frantically pick through the broken china and glass, sorting out and scattering away everything but the few pieces of green pottery. Then I sit at the table and attempt to reassemble the mug, moving the fragments around like a jigsaw puzzle. At least they're all sizable chunks; none shattered. Whatever Mom made was usually tough to destroy. I find the Elmer's and carefully fit each piece, holding it in place until the glue dries. It's meticulous, heartbreaking work. When I'm finished, with no more pieces to put in place, part the dragon's head is still missing.

I wish I had enough of Mom inside me that I could believe in magic. I would go back to the moment before I blindly flung the mug. Instead, I would have cradled it against my bosom, then put it somewhere safe.

Or better yet, I would go back eighteen years, to just before that awful homecoming game, and somehow, I would have kept Joe from playing, from being hurt, from giving up everything we could have been together.

And further back, to that moment before Mom stepped off the curb just as that damned taxi ran the red light. I'd catch her hand, pulling her to safety, to live, to teach me how she could see magic and wonder all around her, how she knew where to look for hidden treasures. Then, Gramma would have never gotten her claws into me. Into me and Joe.

Damn her!

I grab the broom, and with a single brisk sweep under the counter, bring out all kinds of cobwebs and crumbs, and more glass and china from my rampage. No green fragments.

I rummage through the trash, to no avail. That last piece of the mug is gone forever, and it's my fault for losing control, for letting Gramma get to me, for being a god-damned idiot.

I stare at the table, where AH sat. How can any of this be real? Everything I believed to be true, the solid "facts" that I based everything on, had been lies. Half my lifetime, my entire adulthood, twisted by Gramma's poisonous maneuverings. How can I even begin to understand who and what I'm supposed to be when all I've been is her marionette, her invention?

Who the hell did she think she was!? *Garce!* She had no right!

And what have I become that I could let her destroy Joe so easily? How could I have allowed myself to believe that he could have changed so drastically overnight? Poor Joe. All his hopes and dreams had centered on me, on us, and I stood by while she trampled them to death. He gave up everything for me, even his pride and self-respect, pretending to be like the kids he most despised, because she convinced him it was all for the best, for my best. That lying bitch! And what did I do for him? Abandoned him, when he needed me the most, when all he could see in front of him were endless empty years, adrift and unloved. No wonder he tried to kill himself the one way he knew best — as his father had before him — in a bottle.

"Oh, Joe! I'm so sorry!"

If only he had never met me. If only I had never been born.

At some point, I find myself at the sink, gulping down a glass of water, staring out into the empty floodlit night, though I have no memory of willing myself to stand, to walk, to reach for the glass or fill it with water. No matter how much I drink, my mouth remains parched and my throat burns with the bitter taste of bile. I try to wash away the nausea with another deep drink of cool spring water. But my stomach won't hold it, rejects it, and with painful convulsions jettisons it back up my esophagus. I clutch the edge of the sink in rhythm with the spasms of sour vomit.

In the master bathroom, I gargle away the foulness from my mouth and throat with mint Listerine. Then I soak a washcloth with icy water and scrub my face and neck. My flesh responds to the chill, wet cloth, awakening to itself, to myself. I feel battered and bruised and so very drained, soiled to my depths, the way I had that ugly grey dawn in Grampa's store, after Wayne raped me.

Kicking off my shoes, I drop my clothes and underwear on the floor. I stand under the shower, letting the water pour over me, first freezing cold on my burning skin, then turning it up to the hottest I can stand, lathering soap in every part of me, including my hair. I want to drown the filth, the lies, the hurt, scour it away.

My throat and face are engorged and I don't recognize the sensation, don't realize that tears mix with the water streaming down my cheeks, not until I turn off the shower and the cascade continues. I sit on the toilet, clutching a towel around me, shivering in the warm room, unable to stop shaking, gasping for air between gut-wrenching sobs. At first, I wipe the tears away with a corner of the towel. Then, I give in to the torrent that I've held back for so many years, to the empty loneliness, to the twisted upside down misconceptions that had defined and distorted my life.

All that I did, the woman I have become, none of it has been rooted in reality. It was all based on a lie, one that I was all too willing to believe.

Gramma had been the Rock of Gibraltar in my life, the one person I was totally convinced I could depend upon. Now, to find out that she had been sucking away at me like a vampire, draining me of all that was mine and me.

I ache to hate her, to sear away any remnants of love and trust.

I will never forgive her.

Oh God! Why do I desperately want to talk to her, even now, after learning the truth? Especially now!

I catch a glimpse of myself in the mirror, a helpless, self-pitying creature sitting hunched over on a damned toilet seat. "*Merde!* Judith, get a hold of yourself!" I yell at my reflection. I stand, bending over briefly to wrap my hair in the towel. Then I straighten up, use another large towel to rub my body dry with brusque, sloughing strokes, and tie it around me.

Walking into the master bedroom, I realize that the room has changed somehow. Unlike the rest of the house, I haven't really finished ransacking it, haven't pulled down all the pictures and packed away every knickknack. In fact, Eddie closed the closet doors and took away all his boxes, except one that's less than half full, so that everything looks almost normal.

So why does the room feel so very different? Is it that I'm seeing Gramma and Grampa's bedroom anew?

It had been a room apart, a sanctuary of order and security. Now, I know the truth, that it had been a chamber of cold deceit and wretched manipulation.

No, there's nothing I want from her room, the lair where she destroyed Joe and me. I'm about to leave, to close the door on that room forever, when I see Grampa's college sweatshirt in the box Eddie left. Dropping the towel that's around my body, I put on the oversized sweatshirt. I then duck into the bathroom and grab my clothes. I'm relieved to know I will never again return to this bedroom where it all started.

I am done.

Bone tired, I climb the stairs to my room, hearing the creak on the step before the landing, but not looking back at their door, not wanting any of those memories.

I stuff my clothes in my suitcase, which I wisely hadn't unpacked, knowing I could never stay. But I keep the sweatshirt on as I get into my bed — the one that had once fit my body so perfectly — for the very last time. Everything is for the last time.

In a fog of exhaustion, I curl into a tight ball under the covers, and feel the tears leaking once more, silently, with no convulsions or will. I'm too exhausted to scream or gasp, too worn out for anything. I fall into a deadening sleep, praying only that I won't dream, that the nightmares of this day won't follow me where I can have no control over them.

MONDAY

I awake well before dawn, the darkness of the room
and of the world outside my window an eerie continuum of
a drugged-like sleep. A single looping nightmare gripped
me tightly through the night, trapping me in some small,
dark place, surrounded on all sides by Wayne. Not that I
could see him, but he was lurking nevertheless, taunting me,
pushing me, closing me in. Just as he was about to grab me,
I fought free and ran smack into Gramma, who held me so
tightly that I couldn't breathe. Suddenly, she wasn't there at
all, and the earth gave way under my feet. I was falling into
a bottomless pit. I struggled to fly upward, out of that place
of darkness, defying gravity by sheer force of will, though
my own weight kept dragging me down. Then, Gramma's
hand reached down and lifted me into wakefulness.

I jump out of bed, anxious to get going. Only a few
more hours, before I finally and permanently get away.
Whatever I have yet to accomplish on my To Do list will
either get done by the late afternoon when I leave to catch
my overnight flight from Kennedy, or it will just have to be
left undone.

I decide to not strip my bed and wash the sheets, as
I normally would. After all, the only important thing for
prospective buyers is that the room has to look good, with
an attractively made bed. No one will ever sleep in these
sheets again, not here, in this farmhouse. Nor am I concerned with doing a thorough cleaning, since I'll be hiring a
housekeeper to keep everything in tip-top shape until the
place is sold. Mostly, I must neaten up after myself, turn off
the heat and water, and make sure everything is closed up

against the elements.

Dawn is a red hint behind the trees by the time I have nearly everything done and take the kitchen garbage out to the dumpster. At first, when I step outside the back door, I feel naked and terribly vulnerable without Grampa's rifle. I had gotten used to carrying it around, the solidity of it in my hands. But I don't even know where the gun is; the police have probably taken it. Besides, Wayne and his friends are locked up. The terror of the past few days, the violence of last night — it's all over. If I continue to be fearful of being out in the open, then I'd be giving Wayne victory over me after all.

I take a deep breath of the cool morning air, square my shoulders and boldly walk to the dumpster. That's when I see the pieces of that shot-up misshapen chair, the one that Joe and I made our first year together. Something else to add to my long list of regrets: destroying that chair. I would have liked to have given it to Joe for his kids.

Joe. He didn't deserve what Gramma and I did to him. I have hated this village for its small-minded bigotry and ignorance. Now I must confess that I've proven myself to be a true daughter of Black Bear, just as hateful and prejudiced and judgmental as anyone in this village. How else could I have accepted her version of "truth," without question?

I have to see Joe, to apologize. Will he even let me talk to him, after the way I've been, all that I've done? I wouldn't if I were he, but I can't leave without trying my damnedest.

But I can't show up at his doorstep so early in the morning. It's not even 6:30 yet.

I suddenly have a wealth of time, and I know exactly where and how I want to spend it.

The woods surrounding the farm have always been a haven of loamy smells and fertile lushness, separate from everything and everywhere else. It's so very different from

Africa, where the soil leeches the spirit, even in the over-grown jungle where every root battles its neighbor. Nor is it anything like France, with its elegant, squared-off farmland that had been defined and civilized centuries ago. This still virgin forest is wild and gentle at the same time, essentially unchanged from the days before Europeans came to this continent.

I stroll through the familiar, comforting forest in an aimless manner, wandering where the paths pull my feet, until I stand on the protruding roots of the massive oak that holds our treehouse.

Grampa, Joe and I built the treehouse so long ago, that first year I lived here. Yet, it seems as good as new, with some of the planks looking as though they've been replaced recently. Joe's handiwork? Did he bring his kids here? Did he tell them about playing up there with me, when we were so very young and innocent? Does he think about that last time? Does he ever regret listening to Gramma, vowing to keep me "pure" despite my own clumsy efforts at seducing him?

I stand there for some time, looking up, remember-ing, both the fun and the sad times. Joe and I were a team, two halves of a coin. How it must have ripped him apart to break that. Did he wait all that year for me to pull him aside and tell him, "Okay, Joe, enough of this foolishness."

He was the protector, and I was the problem solver. But I didn't hold up my side of the bargain.

Did he cry himself to sleep at night as I did, until my body could produce no more tears?

I don't climb up to our treehouse, though my feet and hands recall the feel and placement of the planks so clearly that I probably could have done it blindfolded. However, I do something I've long wondered about, but never tried. This would be my last chance.

I walk to the other side of the tree, away from our nailed-in ladder of planks, press my full body and cheek to the bark and wrap my arms as far around the trunk as they will go. An enormous tree, I don't so much hug it as offer myself to it.

It isn't a sexual experience, as I imagined it would be, those many years ago, when Joe and I spied on Gramma in her private meditation. Instead, a deep peace seeps into me, like a reverberant hum, felt rather than heard, making me part of the tree, of the woods, if only for those few quiet moments.

On my way back to the house, I check the outbuildings, verifying all doors and shutters are firmly latched. Then I go into the barn and sit at Grampa's workbench, looking around me, drinking it in, searing it into my memory, as though I could ever forget this place and the times Grampa and I and, for a short while, Mom shared here.

I try to picture what it must have been like for Grampa after I left. Did he ever wonder why I didn't return, not even for a short visit? Did he believe the lies about how I had to find my own path, far away from the hate?

Yet, some of it weren't lies; I have to admit that much. Hate was part of my Black Bear experience from the beginning. But Joe's love made it bearable. Joe's and Grampa's and, yes, Gramma's, as distorted as that was.

"Didn't anyone show you kindness while you were here?" Rebecca's question echoes in my mind.

Of course, some were kind, but the mean-spirited bigots drowned them out. I had been a protected child with no defenses, never having needed them before. And I had been thrown to a pack of wolves who saw me and immediately knew that I didn't belong.

So, I learned about being hated and, eventually, how to hate — even sweet, innocent Joe. And now, Gramma.

Will the hate ever end? For much of my adult life, I've fought injustice, one woman at a time. But what of prejudice? Is that too ingrained a human trait to root out, too much a part of my own psyche?

Grampa didn't believe that was so. In his own quiet

way, moving forward day by day, he had as deep and stubborn convictions as Gramma. When given the chance, he trusted that people were basically good and kind. "Let them get to know you," he would say. "Give them time. You're different from anyone they've ever met, and that scares them a bit."

"It isn't fair, Grampa," I'd complain.

"No, it isn't fair, and I wish it weren't so. But you can do something about that, about the unfairness of it all, by just being your wonderful, beautiful self."

It was a lot to ask of a child. Gramma's way was easier for me.

I wish I could have been — could become — more like Grampa.

Finishing up in the house, I use a big black marking pen to label the boxes intended for the thrift shop "ANITA," so there'll be no mistaking them. Originally, I planned to simply leave the ones I want sent to me unmarked, except for the numbers that Jeff and the boys started, and I continued. However, I want no ambiguity that could result in the wrong boxes being sent to the wrong place, so I label each one, "PARIS," in large block letters.

It's a grueling job, tackling each stack of cartons, weaving my way to the next and the next, until I finally get to the end of them. I sit on the living room window seat, staring at the maze of boxes. What am I going to do with all this stuff? What did I think I was doing taking so much when I have no place to put it all?

The answer comes me so clearly, I wonder that I've been blind to it before. Determined to leave the farm forever — as Gramma intended I would — I was trying to pack up the entire house and take it with me. *Damn!* I've been allowing myself to be manipulated and controlled by her, even from the grave.

"No more!" I vow. "I will do what I want, what I believe is right, not what Gramma planned and schemed and

lied that I should do.

Only, I don't know what I want. This house was where Gramma carefully laid her traps for me and Joe, and where I felt so despondent that last year. But it's also where so much of who and what I am was formed, the place where my memories are most alive, of Mom and Grampa and Joe and me, and, yes, of Gramma, the Gramma I thought I knew.

I love this home, as much as I have long believed I hated Black Bear. Which one of those outweighs the other, I don't know. Until I figure it out, until I know for certain what it is that I really want, I can't sell this farm.

What amazes me is how calm I am in coming to this decision. It should be a shock that sends me in a tail-spin. But it feels right, good. The only thing in this whole mess that Gramma and I made that does feel right. Maybe, it's the beginning of fixing the muddle I've made of my life, of being finally free of Gramma.

Getting ready to go is now so very different from what I thought it would be, because I don't know if I am indeed leaving forever, or just for a while. I walk through the house, checking all the windows and doors, seeing clearly just how decimated it now looks with so much packed away. In my mind's eye, I can also see how it should be, how it would be, if I decide to unpack someday.

A flicker of light above the living room fireplace catches my attention. Gramma's *shiva* candle, still burning on the mantle. *Merde,* I almost forgot about that. Without a thought, I blow it out, knowing I can't leave an open flame in a closed, empty house. Just as my breath extinguishes it, I suddenly feel guilty, like a child who deliberately steps on sidewalk cracks, defying the powers that be to go ahead and break her mother's back. Not that I really believe a candle could light the way to heaven for Gramma. Still, is it wrong to blow out a *shiva* candle? Rabbi Cohen once told me, "The *shiva* candle is more a symbol of a personal connection to the beloved, than a religious obligation. It says, I'm thinking of you constantly, while this is lit." I doubt he was referring to the kind of dark thoughts of Gramma that presently haunt me.

In the kitchen, I'm about to turn off the lights when I spy a piece of green pottery under a corner of the counter — the lost fragment of my dragon mug. I take off my coat, get out the Elmer's and carefully glue it in place, sitting quietly with it for some time, to make sure the adhesive sets. Then I put it in the kitchen cabinet where it belongs.

I wander through the living room, Grampa's study, even their bedroom, taking one last look — perhaps forever, perhaps until I return. I put my coat back on, pick up my suitcases and purse and close the front door behind me, locking it. As I turn to leave, I touch the space on the door-post where Grampa nailed the *mezuzah* so many years ago. Someday, I might put it up again, in that same space, not because I'm religious, but because it belongs there, just as Gramps told me. "This is your home, too, Judith."

As I drive into the gas station, my mouth suddenly becomes dry. I can feel my heart racing. I don't know what I will say, or even if Joe will listen. Is it cowardly of me to be relieved when I see the sign on the locked door?

On an ambulance call, which usually takes about 2 hours. If you are paying by credit or debit card, the pumps are open. Sorry for any inconvenience.

It's an inkjet generated, plasticized sign with large black letters and cracked, yellowed edges. Much more formal and grammatically precise than anything I can imagine Joe writing. I wonder if a regular customer or someone in the ambulance corps created it for him.

But two hours starting when? Since I have no idea when the tones went off for the ambulance call, I can't know when he might be back. I check my watch: 9:40. Even if he left just before I arrived, I have enough time to wait for him and plenty of phone calls to make that will keep me busy for a while.

As I return to my car, I hear a young, high pitched voice yell, *"Martin!"* seconds before a large, black shaggy dog with white markings runs onto the lot from the sidewalk. A small blonde boy, about four or five years old, chases after the dog, frantically calling, *"Martin! Stop! Sit!"* Then, suddenly the dog leaps onto me, his front paws almost reaching my shoulders, his tail wagging a mile a minute. Despite his size and enthusiasm, nothing about him is menacing. I know immediately that this overly friendly creature has to be Gramma's Martin, the dog Joe gave her.

"Down!" the boy screams when he finally catches up with Martin. The dog obeys immediately, and the boy looks at me rather sheepishly. "Sorry, ma'am. I don't get it. He don't usually do that to strangers." Then, he smiles at me, and I have no doubt who he is. While he looks like Betty, with her chiseled features softened by his youth, the way his smile illuminates face, reshaping it to something much wider and open, and making his blue eyes sparkle so invitingly, that is entirely Joe.

"It's okay," I reassure him. "Maybe, Martin recognizes me. You know, sometimes a smart dog can tell when someone is from their family, even when they've never met." I offer him my hand. "I'm Judith, Martha Schmoyer's granddaughter."

"Oh, wow! You're her!" He stares at me for a moment, then takes my hand in his very small one, with all the dignity he can muster.

"And you're Henry, aren't you?"

"Yep. That's me." He squares his shoulders with pride.

I don't believe I've ever met a more self-confident child; I'm instantly charmed by him. "You know, I believe you're named after my grandfather."

"Yeah, I know. Granny Martha told me all about him."

Granny Martha?! Suddenly, I don't know what else to say to him, but Henry doesn't have a similar problem. Words pour out so quickly that I can barely keep up with him.

"Dad, too, he talks about Grampa Henry all the time. Not Mom, she didn't know him. You know... Granny Martha's with God and Grampa Henry now. Mom and Dad say I'm supposed to be happy for her, but they're sad when they say it. I miss her. I don't know why she had to go away. Mom and Dad went to a..." he screws up his face, as he struggles to remember the unfamiliar word. "... a funeral... to say goodbye to her. But they wouldn't let me go. Mom said it was for grownups only. Wish I could've said goodbye to Granny Martha."

Henry turns and looks behind him, as if he has just recalled something very important. I struggle to find the right words to comfort him. But he veers off in another direction before I have a chance. "I forgot! Mom's jumping mad right now. We walked all the way home, 'cause her car broke down again, and Dad's nowhere around, 'cause of the ambulance."

Just then, Betty rounds the corner onto the lot, carrying the baby in one arm and a bag of groceries in the other. She locks eyes with me. *"You!"* she sneers. She glances at her son and bites her lip, stopping herself from spilling whatever else she burns to say to me.

Walking toward us, she holds the bag out to Henry, who rushes to grab it, though it's almost half his size. I consider taking it from him, but Betty glares at me, as if daring me to give her a reason to let loose. She unlocks the door to the garage office, gently puts the baby in a playpen, then takes the bag from her son. The baby immediately curls up around a stuffed tiger and nods off to sleep.

It's a typical gas station office with the exception of the playpen and all the photographs of Betty, Joe and the kids at various stages of their lives. At first, the picture arrangement on the wall seems askew, until I realize that several are missing. I can see dark rectangles of paint where frames blocked the fading rays of the sun for some years.

"Henry, take Martin out back. He needs to do his business," Betty instructs him, her voice much more gentle than I have ever heard from her. Once the boy and dog disappear from sight and are presumably out of earshot, she turns on me, "What the fuck you doing here? You've done enough damage!"

Of course, she has every right to be angry. I struggle to remain outwardly calm and conciliatory. I take a deep breath to steel myself and say "I came to apologize. I was wrong, Betty, and I'm very, very sorry."

"Now?! Now, you apologize? You think that fixes things? D'you know Joe had no drink in eight years. Eight years! Not a single fuckin' drop! Then, you show up, the on-high woman herself, stirring up the old hurts, calling him a no-good money grubber, smearing his name, insulting him to his face, when all the crime he did was offer you a hand of friendship, and take damned good care of your gran' while he was at it. Shit! You're sorry all right. A sorry excuse for a human."

All my instincts tell me to deny and protest, but that's not why I'm here. "What can I say, Betty? You're right. I... I didn't understand." I hesitate, unsure what to say next. There's so much I hadn't understood. "The truth was kept from me until just now, so I couldn't know. But I should have seen it, should have known Joe couldn't do all the things I thought he did."

"Damned right, woman. Joe's better than any of us. Too damn good for his own good."

I sigh, feeling so very defeated and indefensible. "I know."

She stares at me. No, it's more of a decidedly unfriendly scrutiny. I can't recall anyone studying me with such open hostility since Cheikh, that bullheaded Senegalese shaman, read my spirit so he could decide whether to put a curse on me or help me establish my first *Les Femmes* upcountry outpost in his village. I wonder if Betty will find even a sliver of whatever it is within me that had convinced Cheikh to become my ally.

Neither meeting her gaze nor avoiding it, I look around the room, at the photos on the wall and on the steel desk showing joyous moments of marriage, birthdays, kids playing, parents laughing, including one of four of them on an ocean beach, from before the baby was born. A couple are of the kids with Gramma — in her garden and sitting in the kitchen at the farm. The awards for community service are mostly for Joe, though one is in Betty's name. On the computer monitor, the screen saver cycles through their wedding pictures.

Then I see the pile of frames behind the desk. The one on top is turned to the wall, mostly covering the rest, but I can see a corner of a framed cover of *Women Today*. I'm pretty sure it's the issue that has a picture of me in Accra on the front and the story about *Les Femmes* inside.

Betty sees what my eyes are focused on. "The only good thing in you coming back is I don't have to stare at those fucking magazine pictures every day. The perfect Jo. The dream girl do-gooder." Her words drip with venom and rage. "He finally let me take them down yesterday, but he won't let me throw them away, even after all you did to him."

"I am sorry, Betty." I repeat, not knowing what else to say.

"Yeah, well you apologized. Now, get the hell out of here." She turns her back on me and leans over the playpen, to tuck a blanket around her sleeping child, and idly arrange the toys.

"I have to see Joe," I insist. "When do you think he'll return?"

She doesn't turn around as she answers, "No telling. He's at a fire, and that can be hours and hours. Long as it burns, long as firemen are on scene, the ambulance has to stay. I'll tell him what you said."

"Betty, I can't leave without seeing him."

Straightening up, she turns and locks eyes with me again, "What the fuck do you want, woman? I won't have you messing with his head no more." Her eyes narrow. "If you think you're gonna just waltz in here and steal him away from me, you can fucking forget it. Joe's mine. That's a fight you ain't never gonna win. So, just get the hell out of here."

My heart skips a beat. What do I really want? What

is it that I think Joe will do when I explain and apologize? Does part of my subconscious hope I can turn back time? I look around me, at the pictures of the life he has made with Betty, and at the garage itself. I shake my head sadly. Despite all that was wrong in what Gramma did, in the end, she was right about one thing. I can't imagine myself belonging here with him, any more than Joe could be comfortable with me in Paris or Africa. Not now. Perhaps, if we had come out into the world together, discovered it and ourselves hand in hand, grown together, but it's far too late for us. We're very different people living such different lives.

"No, Betty. All I can hope for is Joe's forgiveness... and friendship. I know I don't deserve it. But I can try, if he lets me... if you let me. You have no reason to believe or trust me, but I swear, you have nothing to fear from me. Joe belongs with you; we both know that. The two of you have made a good life together... for you and for your children. Please Betty, forgive me for all the pain I've caused, and let me try to heal it. If not for me, for Joe's sake." My eyes burn, as I feel tears cascading down my cheeks.

Betty, who just a moment earlier was all coiled up and ready for a fight, simply looks at me and grins, a smug victory smile. She opens her mouth to respond, but her cell phone rings, before she can get a word out. Actually, it chimes the first few notes of *"I've Got You, Babe."* She pulls it from her jeans pocket and answers, "Yeah?" while still staring at me.

As she listens, her posture softens, though her eyes remain fixed on me, still trying to decide whether or not to believe me. She says into the phone, "No can do, babe. The car died at Buck's." I'm sure that Joe is on the other end.

"Don't know," she responds with a shrug he can't see. "Just wouldn't start."

Betty smiles at something he says. "Yeah, I know. Just as soon as ya get a chance."

She drops her gaze from me, and cups her hand around the phone, so I can't hear her every word, though I do catch her saying, "Me, too, babe." Then, looking up again and uncapping her hand, she says, "Don't worry. I think I can find someone to do the run. Bye." She slips the phone back into her pocket, and says to me, "If you want, you can do something useful and see Joe, too."

I know she's testing me, still weighing me to see what side of the balance I fall. But it doesn't matter. I must see Joe. "Yes, of course," I tell her. "What?"

"They need someone to go to Buck's, pick up drinks and sandwiches and take them to the fire at the old schoolhouse."

The abandoned school building that has haunted my nightmares for so many years? Poetic justice, I think. But it seems too providential, too coincidental, especially coming on the heels of the fire at the fairgrounds on the day of Gramma's funeral. There'd been talk at the *shiva* about an arsonist on the loose in Black Bear; is this his handiwork? I tell Betty, "I'll go."

"Good, but believe you me, Jo or Judith or whatever you call yourself these days, if you try anything with Joe, I'll get you, one way or another."

"I swear, Betty, all I want is to apologize and to try to right all the damage I've done. Thank you for giving me this chance." I start to leave, but turn, and ask, "Do you know anything about a phone call to Paris, a message that my grandmother needed me?"

"Are you really that dense?"

"Joe?" I ask, realizing that answer, too, had been staring me in the face.

"Who else? And look what it bought him."

How protective of Joe she is, not simply because he's her husband, but because he's Joe. If only I had taken as good care of him from the beginning. "I'm glad he found you," I tell her, and mean it.

Betty doesn't answer me, which I suppose is answer enough. She's already made quite clear that she would fight tooth and nail against any threat to her family. I'm grateful that her fierce loyalty and love includes securing a place in this world for Joe.

Doing a food/drink run for a fire is nothing new to me. Almost as soon as Joe learned to drive, Gramps would sometimes ask us to go to Buck's to pick up refreshments for the firefighters and ambulance crew, when they were on a fire that was going to take a long time to put out.

At Buck's, they've already prepared a large box of sandwiches and filled a couple of Styrofoam coolers with soft drinks and ice. A bag boy puts the stuff in my car, while I sign the firehouse account ledger. Immediately after I scrawl my signature, I realize that the firehouse will be charged for everything, albeit at a discounted rate. So, I scratch out my name and instead give the cashier my credit card and tell her to put $1,000 toward the firehouse account.

As I leave, I see the astounded cashier calling over the other cashiers and the manager. I assume it's the Black Bear grapevine churning, starting another rumor about me, but this time I don't mind.

Al Haas stands at the corner of Main Street and Evans Lane, diverting traffic away from the center of town where the fire rages. Too old to fight fires, Al still wears his fluorescent yellow uniform jacket and does what he can to safeguard the area. When he sees me, he walks over, and I open my window.

"Sorry, Judith. We've got a fire ahead. You'll have to go the long way round."

"I've got cold drinks and sandwiches for the guys," I tell him, pointing to the big cardboard box and coolers on the back seat. "Want something?"

"Not right now, but thanks, Judith."

He picks up one of the orange traffic cones and waves me through.

On scene, everything is the same kind of organized chaos I experienced at similar fires in my youth. Orange and red licks of flame and black smoke shoot high into the otherwise blue sky. The old wood cracks and pops and occasionally explodes. Fire trucks from a half dozen area companies encircle the old abandoned schoolhouse, their white and grey hoses snaking on the ground from a big inflatable pool filled with water. The fire must be a bad one for them to have called for additional trucks and volunteer reinforcements from nearby communities. Dozens of men and women, in yellow helmets, baggy canvas jackets, with yellow air tanks on their backs, and oversized pants tucked into huge wading boots, scurry here and there, shouting instructions to each other as they rush about their business.

Off to the side are three ambulances and one paramedic 4x4, far enough away to be safe, but close enough for the crews to be immediately available, should anyone be injured. Over a hundred gawkers mill about across the street, in front of Ehrhardt's Auto Supply and Grampa's store, and on the tarmac of the Ford dealership next door. It never fails; no matter how conscientiously the fire and ambulance folk try to secure a scene, people are drawn to fires, to the mighty terror of it all.

I pull up behind the Black Bear pump engine furthest from the fire. The smell hits me as soon as I open the car door — sharp and caustic — making my eyes tear. Yet, underlying it all is the homey, appealing flavor of a wood-burning stove. A couple of the guys help me unload the car. Immediately, several guzzle cold drinks; one firewoman scoops up some of the ice and wipes it over her sooty face.

I fill a brown paper bag with a couple of the sandwiches and drinks, and move my car out of the way to a spot near Black Bear's ambulance. Then, I just sit and watch. Joe is here, probably within yards of me. Now that I'm near him, I'm frozen with fear, shame and, yes, a small flutter of *joie du coeur*.

I don't know how long I sit there in the car, staring vacantly, not even seeing Jeff Smith approach. When he taps on the door, I lower the window.

"Hello, Judith," he says. "I didn't expect to find you here. Is everything okay?"

"Yes, of course." I don't know why I'm so self-conscious and unbalanced, especially given that it's Jeff. "How's Bobby?"

"He's O.K., nothing worse than a bad headache. The hospital called and said that he'll be released sometime this afternoon. Gene will pick him up, if I'm still here."

I sigh. "Thank God. I can't tell you how relieved I am to hear it. And Johnny, Tony?"

"Johnny's one lucky boy, no major injuries." Jeff shakes his head in amazement. "But he's going to have a whopper of a scar. We're hoping he'll be out tomorrow, Wednesday at the latest. Tony's with his family, which is probably the best thing for him right now."

"Jeff, believe me, I'm truly sorry they were hurt. It was foolhardy of them to jump in and try to rescue me. But I'd be lying if I didn't say how very grateful I am to them. To you and Rabbi David, too. I don't know what would have happened if you hadn't shown up when you did."

Jeff shrugs his shoulders and mumbles something about "damned fools." I'm not certain if he's talking about the boys, himself and David, or Wayne and his friends. He never did take compliments or gratitude well, being much more comfortable fading into the background.

I take the hint and change the subject. "I brought sandwiches and drinks. Do you want some?"

"I wouldn't mind a cold drink."

Getting out of the car, I grab the bag with the sodas and sandwiches and hand Jeff a Coke. I ask, as casually as I possibly can, "Is Joe around?"

"He's in the rig, handling a smoke inhalation case."

"Oh."

Jeff looks at me, in that gentle way that never probes or pries, but seems to read me so well. "If you want, I can take over and send him out."

My cheeks are suddenly warm. Good God, am I blushing? "Yes, please."

When I see Joe lumbering toward me, in his red and yellow ambulance jacket, I'm as nervous as a schoolgirl. He stops a few feet from me, but it feels like miles, years away.

"Hi... Judith."

"Hi Joe."

Then, we're silent, because we have too much to

say. We don't quite look at each other, not directly, but even with our eyes averted, we watch each other carefully. I know that I have to be the first to speak, but what can I say?

"Would you like a sandwich or drink, Joe?"

"No thanks."

"I've got a ham and cheese on rye, and a root beer." I hold them out; they used to be his favorite combination.

He looks at them in my hands, but then shakes his head no. I can't tell if he honestly doesn't want them, or if he just doesn't want anything I have to offer. Instead, he tells me, "About Saturday night... I'm sorry...I messed up. Then, last night...." Joe pauses, long enough that I wonder if he's become lost in his thoughts. When he starts again, I'm not even sure if he's aware of speaking aloud. "If I hadn't gotten drunk... if Wayne hadn't heard about it... he never would've dared to come anywhere near you." Joe pounds his fist against his thigh in rhythm to his words. "I'm a god-forsaken drunk! At least you're safe now, no thanks to me."

I hate seeing him so dejected. "It's my fault, Joe. I pushed you...."

"No. Getting drunk's something I did to myself."

I lean against the hood of the car, trying to close the chasm between us. "I know, but I'm sorry I made you feel that you had to." I pause, searching for the right words, then realize there will never be any right words for saying what I have to say. "Joe, I was wrong... about everything. I can't even begin to list all my failings. No, that isn't true, they're all so very clear now. I'll be replaying them for the rest of my life."

"Judith." He whispers so softly that I don't know if he's talking to me or just listening to the sound of my name.

"Did you know, Joe? Did you understand that I never knew about what Gramma got you to do? I mean, about your pushing me away that last year in high school."

"Yeah."

"I should have known, but I didn't."

"I didn't want you to."

"But why, Joe?"

He shrugs. "You had to leave, do the stuff you was meant to do. After I mangled my leg, I had nothing, no future to give you. I'd've held you back."

I hate hearing Gramma's poison coming out of his mouth, knowing he still believes it. "We could have been together all those years."

"It's done, Judith. Past. Could've beens don't matter. It's what happened. Over and done."

I realize that I'm hurting him all over again by insisting on talking about it. "Joe, are you happy?"

"Most the time. Betty's a good wife; we've got great kids. Yeah, I'm happy. And you, Judith? Are you?"

"I'm working on it. I think I need to get rid of a lot of demons from the past, then figure out who I am and what I really want in life. But I'm closer to being happy right now than I was a week ago."

"I was hoping you'd say, 'yes, I'm happy.' It's all I ever wanted for you, you know."

"I know, Joe."

"Can I help, Judith?"

"I think it would help, if you would call me Jo... if you would be my friend again."

"Did you really believe I ever stopped being your friend?" His lips tremble, and the words catch in his throat.

I shake my head and stifle a sob. "No, but I was too self-centered and angry and wrong-headed to be a friend to you. I hope I can fix that. I'm starting by calling off the lawyers. It's right that you should have Grampa's hunting lodge. I wish I could find some way to make amends for everything Gramma and I did to you. God! I can't believe I thought Gramma was your victim, when it was her all along... manipulating us, destroying all that we could have had together."

"Jo, you don't understand. Your Gramma loved you. In the end, I even think she might've loved me, too."

"God save us from that kind of love."

"No, Jo. God bless any kind of love. It mightn't be what you expect. Whose fault is that?" He steps toward me and puts his hand over mine, where it rests on the hood on the car. "Jo, you was always the answer finder, trying to make things work the way you wanted. But people make mistakes. We stumble around in the dark and give you what you want the least. Does that make their... our... love any less worthy?"

"Oh, Joe!" I lean over and press my face into his chest, wiping my tears on his jacket. He wraps his big arms around me. If Betty saw us, I'm sure she'd be worried. But she has nothing to fear. I'm safe here, in the warm, large softness that is Joe, safer and more at home than I've for a very long time. However, there's nothing sexual or romantic in it. I'm simply rediscovering a part of myself that I thought lost forever, the best part of myself that is Joe and me — Jo Joe — the being that exists beyond the two of us, because we love each other enough to not require anything else from each other.

Joe puts his hands on my shoulder, to hold me at arm's length, and looks at me. Though tears stream down his grizzled cheeks, his smile beams as wide and open as it used to before Gramma tore us apart. He then wipes my damp face with his rough, calloused palm, before letting go.

We sit side-by-side on the car hood, watching the fire, as that hellhole of a school burns. Amidst all that noise and chaos, I'm at peace. We don't talk, because no more words are necessary. Eventually, I tell him, "I'm leaving today, for Africa."

"Will I ever see you again, Jo?" His voice is low, quiet, almost as though he's afraid to hear himself speak.

Suddenly, one of the walls collapses, the rubble cascading into the grass, while sparks and dust shoot high into the air. If I were a superstitious person, I would take it as a sign that all that happened inside those walls was being scoured from the face of this earth, if not from my memories. But that's all they are... memories.

I look at Joe, and know that memories aren't enough. It's time for me to start living in the here and now... and for the future. That's when I realize that, yes, I will return to Black Bear. It's my home and where my best friend lives.

I squeeze Joe's hand. "Of course, you will. I intend to watch your children grow up until they're old enough to drive you crazy."

Jack, the EMT from last night, suddenly appears in front of us. "Joe! They've just pulled Steve out from under that wall. He's bad. Let's go!"

Joe hugs me briefly. "Wish we had more time."

"We will," I promise him.

The lights on the ambulance are already strobing, when Jack, Joe, Jeff and one of the firemen lift the gurney carrying Steve into the back of the rig, then jump in after it. I picture them strapping in their patient, starting the oxygen and doing a quick examination for critical injuries that must be taken care of immediately. Soon, the air horn blasts a "*whoop, whoop!*" to clear a path, and the ambulance races away to the hospital, siren screeching.

I don't leave immediately. Instead, I sit on the hood of my car while dozens of firemen and firewomen battle, then tame the fire. Among them are a handful of blacks, one, no, two Asians, and some Jews I recognize from the *shiva*. Yes, Black Bear remains a village filled with prejudice. What town anywhere isn't? But it's also a village of good will and good works, of everyday struggles and misunderstandings that sometimes overpower better instincts and of people who will work together, even if they don't always like each other.

I spot AH walking among the firemen who are taking momentary breaks, talking to a few. He sees me and heads in my direction, moving uncertainly on his two aluminum canes. I meet him halfway, walking almost as slowly as he.

"AH, thank you" I say, when we're still several feet away from each other, not willing to wait even a few steps to say it. I continue walking toward him, but I don't know what else to say. I lean in and kiss his soft, smooth cheek. He hooks his canes on his arms and hugs me with more power than I expect from one so old, putting all his passion for my family — our family — into his embrace, until I feel the bones of his body jutting into me.

I don't pull away fully until he regains his balance on his canes. "Judith," he says, in that quiet way he has of making one word mean so much.

"I know, AH," I reply to his unspoken heartache and love. "And I will remember. I promise you that."

"That's all I can ask. Goodbye, child. Be good to yourself."

"Not goodbye, AH," I tell him. "I'm not selling the farm, so I'll be coming back... whenever I can."

AH beams, as if he has just heard the best news possible. Maybe, he has. He kisses me on both my cheeks, French style, then walks away. I watch that dear old man as he crosses the street to his store. I will miss him. I hope that someday, I will see him again, but I know as much as he likes to pretend otherwise, he isn't indestructible. This may very well be the last time I will see him alive. Still, I will carry a part of him within me wherever I go, just as I will carry the other good parts of Black Bear.

Eventually, the old schoolhouse is reduced to a smoldering rubble. One by one, most of the trucks and cars leave, though the Black Bear tanker remains and continues to pour even more water onto the steaming pile of bricks and spars, until it's a sodden mess.

I can't believe the schoolhouse is really gone. The site of my worst nightmares, where I learned the over-whelming power of hate — mine as well as Wayne's. Hate, rage, bigotry, fear — mine, as well as Black Bear's. So much so that it distorted my other memories, of love and laughter and goodness.

As I drive away, I reflect back on the week, on the past seventeen years, on all I've been and done. And I realize that just as I'm part French and Pennsylvanian and African, Jewish and Moravian, life is a complicated mishmash that isn't easily delineated. I know now that it's time for me to slough off my childish need to categorize and define everything into easy-to-understand absolutes, into clear-cut blacks and whites. I feel empty, wide open, without the assumptions and scorn that held me together all these years. And I feel young and fresh as I face the world anew. Maybe, this time, I will get it right.

On the edge of town, I pass the new green and gold sign again, but on the outgoing side, it says, *"Come back soon to Black Bear."*

THE END

JO JOE STUDY GUIDE

A free *Jo Joe* Study Guide is available for Book Clubs, teachers, librarians and other discussion group leaders (at www.PixelHallPress.com/jo_joe.html).

To read Sally Wiener Grotta's essay about how memory becomes personal mythology, which is one of the themes of *Jo Joe*, please go to her August 18, 2012 blog entry *Malleable Memory* on www.grotta.net/blog.htm.

ABOUT BLACK BEAR, PENNSYLVANIA

Jo Joe is the second in a series of stories from Pixel Hall Press, set in Black Bear, Pennsylvania. The first was *Honor,* a novella by Daniel Grotta.

Black Bear, Pennsylvania is a fictional village in the Pocono Mountains created as a literary *folie a deux* by Daniel Grotta and Sally Wiener Grotta. Both Daniel and Sally are dipping into the same pool of invented locale and characters to write a series of separate stories and novels that will, eventually, paint a full picture of the diversity of life and relationships in a small mountain village.

ABOUT SALLY WIENER GROTTA

Sally Wiener Grotta is the consummate storyteller, reflecting her deep humanism and sense of the poignancy of life. As an award-winning journalist, she has authored many hundreds of articles, columns and reviews for scores of glossy magazines, newspapers and online publications, plus numerous non-fiction books. Sally's next novel will be *The Winter Boy* (which will be published by Pixel Hall Press in late 2013).

Sally Wiener Grotta is a frequent speaker at conferences and other events on storytelling and the business of writing, as well as on photography and the traditional tradespeople of her *American Hands* narrative portrait project. She welcomes invitations to participate in discussions with book clubs and other reading groups (occasionally in person, more often via Skype, phone or online chat), and to do occasional readings.

ACKNOWLEDGEMENTS

My heartfelt thanks go out to a number of individuals who gave me feedback and guidance on *Jo Joe*, especially Cynthia Dadson of Pixel Hall Press, for her support, edits and believing in *Jo Joe*. Thank you also to Diane Edwards, Bonnie Fladung, Nancy Foster, Arlene Gilbert, Rabbi Barbara Goldman-Wartell, Dr.Melvin Heller, Rabbi Peg Kershenbaum, Reverend Tammie Rinker, Anita Schneider, Roya Fahmy Swartz, Russell Wild, Lee Yeager and The Nameless Workshop. Amy W. Sosnov and Steven Sosnov gave me advice on Gramma's estate. Ef Deal and Deborah Gallen provided guidance on French cursing. As always, Daniel Grotta and Dr, Noel J. Wiener gave me much needed brainstorming, suggestions, morale boosting and unstinting edits. Of course, any errors of fact or judgment are mine alone.

Sally Wiener Grotta

ABOUT PIXEL HALL PRESS

Pixel Hall Press (www.PixelHallPress.com) is a relatively new, old-fashioned small publishing house that focuses on discovering literary gems and great stories that might have otherwise been overlooked. Our mission is to publish books that energize the imagination and intrigue the mind, and to be a conduit between readers and provocative, stimulating, talented authors.

Please go to the For Readers & Book Clubs section of the Pixel Hall Press website, to find out about various programs we offer readers, including free Study Guides for book discussion leaders, volume discounts on books, our Beta Reader program which offers access to free pre-publication eBooks, and the Author Connect Program which includes helping to set up book discussions with our authors for reading groups.

Join in on the discussion about books and publishing on Pixel Hall Press's Facebook page and on Twitter: @PixelHallPress.

Made in the USA
Lexington, KY
16 August 2014